RUM
FOR THE
PINEAPPLE
CUP

Also by Stephanie Siciarz

Left at the Mango Tree

Away with the Fishes

RUM FOR THE PINEAPPLE CUP

A Novel

STEPHANIE SICIARZ

PINK MOON PRESS
Rum for the Pineapple Cup
Stephanie Siciarz

Cover Art: Patti Schermerhorn
Cover Design: Andrew C Bly

Published in the United States by Pink Moon Press
ISBN: 0989686345
ISBN-13: 9780989686341

For Barry

CLOSING SALE

Pineapple Jewelry and Gems

SHUTTING OUR DOORS
AFTER 30 YEARS

EVERYTHING MUST GO!

30-40% OFF

Entire inventory of necklaces, rings, bracelets,
charms, pendants, earrings, cufflinks, brooches,
bric-a-brac, tie tacks, silver, gold, and gems.

Pineapple Jewelry and Gems
89 Bristol Street
Port-St. Luke
Tel. 30925

1

Head of Customs and Excise, Officer Raoul Orlean, was having a very bad day. Not the kind of bad day that came from spilled coffee on his trousers, or from the fact that some prompter patron had beat him to the newest book at the Pritchard T. Lullo Public Library. Not the kind that came from tough Customs cases, the ones with questions and clues that buzzed in his brain like nagging flies. Not even the kind of bad day that happened when Oh, the island he called his home, played the tricks that only Oh could play, bending the islanders' plans like braided palm leaves and drowning their good intentions in mocking rains.

Raoul's bad day was owing, in part, to a dilemma experienced by many a man before him, on Oh and elsewhere: he had forgotten his wife Ms. Lila's birthday. Ms. Lila was not the most demanding of spouses, but she *was* exacting on two distinct points. Her house must always look its best—both inside and out—and her birthday must never go un-remarked—nay, un-feted—by her husband.

To be precise, Raoul hadn't quite lost the birthday battle yet. He had remembered the occasion, if only in the nick of time. Though it was late in the afternoon, and though he had failed to wish Ms.

Lila "many happy returns" over breakfast, or to present her with a trinket before they went off to work, he could still surprise her with a night on the town. On Oh, at least Raoul's little bit of it, this usually meant a bite to eat in Port-St. Luke, at the Buddha's Belly Bar and Lounge, run by his good friend Cougar Zanne. But this year, the Belly (as it was more commonly known) might not be big enough to make up for Raoul's missed morning wishes. A fly in his head suggested he buy Ms. Lila a birthday gift, too, and an especially nice one at that.

Like all the forgetful men before him, Raoul knew the solution was a piece of jewelry, a bauble that sparkled or shined. And this is what determined the biggest part of his bad day. It wasn't the money, not that. Raoul wasn't rich, but he worked hard at his Customs job, as did his wife at hers, running the library, and together they managed quite well. The problem was that the jeweler Raoul preferred, Mr. Donald Finley of Finley's Fine Jewelers, was at a wedding on the nearby island of Esterina, and his shop was temporarily shut. Which meant that if Raoul hoped to buy his wife a bijou on her birthday, he had no choice but to do so at Pineapple Jewelry and Gems.

Which was, in turn, problematic because, well, unlike the rest of the islanders, who took bended plans and mocking rains for granted, Raoul Orlean believed only in the plainest of truths. Plain-as-noses-on-faces truths, is what he called them. He had no patience for island magic, for the chants of the meddling leaves or for the tricky light of the intrusive moon. If you asked *him*, mangoes no more spilled secrets than did storm clouds bully fishermen. The islanders were silly to think otherwise, and sillier still to think they might somehow, themselves, make use of the island magic that couldn't possibly be real in the first place. The mere idea of it made his truth-loving, fly-hatching head hurt.

Hence Raoul's very bad day: he was headed to Pineapple Jewelry and Gems, to buy an eleventh-hour birthday gift at half-past-five, from Cora Silverfish, proprietor. Proprietor, that is, and on-the-nose, magic-making, talisman-fashioning, island-worshipping witch.

2

It was no wonder that, with a name like Silverfish, Cora should grow up to work shiny metals, to heat them and cool them, to endow gold with shape and coax silver to life with her polishing mop. (True, it should have proven equally unremarkable had she set up a stall at the fishmarket, but her fate, it so happened, lay in karats not sparkling cod.) Cora's inclination for the metallurgic arts was not an easy one to navigate. Opportunities on Oh were few and far between, especially for a young lady broaching marrying age, who should have no more garish designs than a hard-working husband and a roof that didn't leak when it rained. A certificate from the clerical college, perhaps, if she were given to extravagance.

Typewriters held little allure for her, alas—except to imagine their stiff, lettered sticks simmered into slithery goo that could be pressed and poured and molded. Not into bangles or cufflinks. Cora hadn't found her eye for jewelry yet back then. For her, the sheen of steel or silver was much better suited to replicas of the glittering beauties of Oh, its pineapples and its palm fronds, whose perfect symmetry could be captured forever in lustrous paper-weights or on the handles of a tea tray. (Never mind that few of the islanders—who couldn't consume the *real* pineapples fast enough and who were content to carry their tea cups themselves—would have wasted their island tender on such trinkets.) That Cora even knew such creations were possible is the fault of Raoul's Ms. Lila, in fact, who, as then Junior Librarian, was navigating her own inclinations right about the same time. She had insisted on a Certificate in Library Arts, which her parents had reluctantly agreed to, and after a year on the island of Killig, the credentialed Lila Partridge was back and happily apprenticed to the Head Librarian on Oh.

When young Cora showed up at the library one day, hardly able to articulate what it was she sought, Ms. Lila produced an array of volumes documenting the use of metal from as early as ancient times. For breastplates and coins, for armor, swords, and ceremonial cups. For spoons and thimbles. In exchange, Cora showed Ms. Lila her sketches, the mangoes made of gold and the schools of snapper in weighty, etched silver. For weeks the two consulted and conspired, Partridge and Silverfish, armed with the full contents of the Pritchard T. Lullo card catalogue.

In the end, Ms. Lila's mastery of the library arts did not disappoint. Some pointed research on her part had uncovered not only the existence of a small and little-known museum on Esterina where Cora could learn the craft of metal-working, but also that of a little-known scholarship offered, if rarely, by Oh's Parliamentary Museum for the Preservation of Artistic and Historical Sciences. Thanks to Ms. Lila's digging and a smart volume on How To Get What You Want, Cora was able to convince the Museum's Curator that her departure was in their mutual best interest. She would spend a couple of years away from Oh at Oh's expense, she told him, then return home to set up shop. A souvenir shop to encourage tourism, or a gift shop to boost the economy. A cultural showroom, perhaps, with work by local youths whom Cora could mentor herself. Not to mention, Cora pointed out to him, the fact that no one had won the scholarship in over a dozen years, if brought to the attention of, say, the island newspaper, might cast doubt on the sincerity and the propriety of the Parliamentary Museum's preservation efforts.

The Curator didn't care about gift shops or mentored youths, but the Museum's reputation—and his own—were dear to his heart. He wouldn't allow either to be tarnished, and for this, he had been easy to sway.

Besides which, he was only too happy to ship Ms. Silverfish off.

———

Despite her passion for the potential of shiny metals, Cora departed for Esterina with a heavy heart. She was sad to trade her island for another, even if just for a little while. Unlike other young ladies one heard of from time to time, who sought refuge on snowy mountain tops or in the shade of foreign palms, Cora Silverfish had never desired to be anywhere but Oh.

This is very possibly why she returned to the island two years later even more eager to replicate its beauties. Only now, thanks to her training and apprenticeship, her creations were no longer limited to the heaviness of metal. Like ruddy branches that bore papayas radiant in variegated green, or the rugged sands that coddled blushing peach seashells, surely silver and gold must exist— Cora had come to believe—merely to hold and house a gemstone's lightness. On Esterina, she had become enamored, of tiger's eye and milky quartz, stones brilliant-cut or step-. She had discovered in this new family of minerals, a breath and changeability she had never witnessed in copper or steel. A mango made of gold was forever that, its shiny hardness a mockery to the imprisoned, paralyzed fruit. But a mango fashioned of citrine or peridot *moved*. It burst with yellow ripeness in the morning sun and by evening assumed an immature verdant density, as if it had somehow turned back the hands of time. How could Cora not find herself beguiled by this magic and waffling medium that mimicked the gypsy tides, or the moon's incessant, impermanent ebb?

Ms. Lila, bless her heart, had only scratched the surface with her ancient thimbles and her royal spoons. She had stopped short of introducing to Cora the gold that once dripped pearls from the ears of Egyptian queens or hung emeralds from the necks of the maharajas. Cora's clients on Oh would not be queens and maharajas, to be sure. They were fishmongers and bakers. Teachers and builders. Churchgoers. Still, she thought, a little sparkle would go a long way, and with even a dainty dose of amethyst or aquamarine, she could fashion (mostly) affordable Oh-inspired lures for the increasingly fashionable islanders. What's more, with the knowledge she had acquired of the incidental properties of precious gems (from a volume aptly titled *The Incidental Properties of Precious Gems*, by a Mr. Heinrich Kopt), she could, too, divine the perfect match of islander and gemstone. A steady clientele was guaranteed!

Only one problem remained. Even dainty doses of opals, quartzes, and jades required a substantial initial outlay. How would Cora afford amber and turquoise, and the tools she needed to turn them into works of island art? Where would she find the funds for files and drill bits, a torch, a kiln? For sterling silver, and gold in 14-karat? Desperate, Cora turned again to the public library, and to Ms. Lila, for help.

If pearls and emeralds had escaped the junior librarian the first time around, rainbow bills (Oh's paper money boasted every color in Nature's palette) and business loans were another matter altogether. Ms. Lila uncovered the existence—as little known as Esterina's museum or the Curator's scholarship—of government monies for which Cora qualified. There were loans for Small Businesses, for Women Starting Businesses, for Women Starting Small Businesses, and extra capital available for any citizen, male or female, opening A Branch of Business Not Yet Established On Oh. (Finley's Fine Jewelers hadn't yet opened its doors.) Before long—thanks again to Ms. Lila's digging and to the smart volume on How To Get What You Want (and thanks, too, to Mr. Kopt and a white-agate talisman Cora pocketed before presenting her case)—she had convinced the Ministerial Committee for Commerce to finance Pineapple Jewelry and Gems.

Ms. Silverfish was officially in business.

3

A grumbling and cursing Raoul, slapping his palm against his head in reprimand for the nearly botched birthday, trekked up the steep hill that led to Market Square. Pineapple Jewelry and Gems overlooked the market's farthest corner from the top floor of a two-storied building that below housed Incredible Ennis's Emporium of Shoes. The cement of the sturdy structure had seen many a pass of white paint and its clean, cool exterior struck Raoul as vulgar and boastful, towering above the dirt and industry of the vendors' stalls the way it did.

"Hmph!" he snorted, as it grew nearer with every step. When he was close enough to realize that the customers spilled from the jewelry store's showroom onto its abundant balcony, he stopped in his tracks and cursed some more.

Cora's closing sale had attracted quite a crowd, not only of purchasers of gems and gewgaws, but of islanders come to pay their respects. Her clientele had grown steadily over the course of the shop's thirty years, in step with Cora's reputation, and her regulars now couldn't imagine navigating Oh's ups and downs without her wares to guide them.

Though Cora would have balked at the whispers of witchcraft and spells, she took great pride in her ability to satisfy every customer. She could scarcely help it if, thanks to Mr. Kopt's volume and the incidental properties of gems therein, her finery managed to cure an ailment or straighten a peculiar bent. As for island magic, what the sun and moon and winds got up to once Cora's handiwork left her shop was little concern of hers. Though she wouldn't have balked at the whispers of Oh's bewitchery—on the contrary, she engaged in them with utmost enthusiasm—she would never think to take credit for the island's doings herself. At best, she liked to believe, whatever faculties her pieces possessed, whatever charm or strength, what *magic*, simply passed through her hands. Like droplets of tidewater that steamed their way heavenward to fall again with the rain. Droplets that could no more be claimed—by sea, air, or cloud—than could be fettered.

The islanders didn't know from droplets, but that didn't matter. They all agreed a piece of Cora's "pineapple jewelry" couldn't fail. And if it did, it looked so pretty that nobody cared. If she shut her doors forever, what would they do about birthday gifts and baptisms? Who would sell them a bauble to protect their unborn babies and stir the sleepy fish to bite? Surely not Donald Finley with his one-size-fits-all designs that looked nothing liked emerald mangoes or pearly moons? These, more or less, were the questions posed by the crowd on Cora's balcony as Ms. Lila's birthday teetered toward evening. Raoul took a last look up at the scene, then sighing to summon his courage, slowly climbed the outdoor steps to the jewelry store's pineappled door.

Inside, the commotion camouflaged his arrival, which didn't bother him one tick. Raoul waited well over an hour while the storm of consumers and questioners passed, using the time to size up the goods on display. He chose for his wife a pair of earrings resembling bunches of ripened damsel in miniature. From each earring, a handful of the ridged berries dangled in a pale, opaque yellow clump. They were modest little stones, which, Raoul decided, suited Ms. Lila better than the sparkling, light-lancing gems that made up much of Cora's inventory.

Yes, indeed! The dangling damsel would do quite nicely, Raoul told himself, pleased with his choice and feeling more hopeful about the turn the evening would take. He was equally pleased that his purchase would require no consultation with the infamous Ms. Silverfish. He would simply tell her to wrap up his earrings and he would be on his merry way, thank you very much.

He glanced around the shop. It was emptying at last, and miraculously no other patron had shown up after Raoul, which meant no witness to his folly. A man of his principles doing business with a reputed maker of magic, imagine! Raoul gave out an inadvertent and disdainful snort.

"I'll be with right with you," Cora addressed him in reply. Raoul nodded and directed an embarrassed half-smile at the young couple Cora was assisting. Prompted by his impatience, or so it seemed, they decided right then what they wanted, paid for their selection, and made a loud, joyful exit out the door and down the stairs.

"I'd like these, please," Raoul said, before Cora had even turned her attention to him. Standing over a display case across the shop from where Cora stood, he pointed through the glass at the earrings.

"Let's have a look," she replied, picking up her keys and joining him.

"These," Raoul repeated, pointing again for her benefit.

"Ah! The damsel. Lovely, aren't they?" She opened the case and handed them to Raoul.

"They *are* very lifelike," Raoul admitted, marveling both at the earrings and at his spontaneous exchange with Cora. "Of course," he added, collecting himself, "these are very tiny versions of the real thing."

"Oh, of course," Cora agreed. "But they look good enough to stew, don't they! Shall I wrap them for you?"

"Yes, please," Raoul said, following her back to the show-room's main jewelry case. "They're a birthday gift for my wife."

Cora smiled and ripped some gold paper from a roller attached to the wall behind her. Before she began wrapping, she tapped some keys on a calculator and handed Raoul a slip of paper. "Here you are."

Reaching for his wallet, Raoul eyed the bill. Twice.

"Excuse me," he said. "I think you've made a mistake."

"Have I? I *am* sorry," Cora replied, taking back the bill. She glanced at it and handed it to Raoul again. "No, no mistake."

"All *that* for some tiny bits of berry?!" he complained, holding the bill under her nose. "What about the shutting-your-doors sale?"

"Not to worry! You've been given a substantial discount. These 'bits of berry' as you call them happen to be the finest pebbles of yellow corundum, fashioned by hand into clumps of damsel."

Raoul looked at her blankly.

"Set in gold, to be sure," she added, as if that would erase whatever doubts he might still be harboring.

"I see. Well, in that case," he said, "all *that* for some pebbles of cardamom?!"

"*Corundum*, sir. Yellow sapphire. These are un-cut. Un-polished. Sapphires nonetheless."

Raoul's head buzzed suddenly with angry flies. "Now just a minute!" he protested.

Raoul didn't know much about fancy jewels, but he knew Donald Finley would never charge a fortune for some pebbles in want of a good polish. Did this Silverfish creature think she could con him into paying ridiculous prices?!

Before he could continue his rant, Cora spoke up. "Perhaps we could find something else. Something more suitable. I'm sure your wife has no need for these particular stones. Her liver is healthy, is it not?"

Raoul looked at her blankly again.

"Her liver is healthy?" Cora repeated.

Raoul gave his head a good thwack. Was he hearing correctly? Had this woman bewitched him while his back was turned? He wanted to accuse her of that very thing, but instead found himself answering her question, if indignantly.

"Her liver is as healthy as...as," he grappled for a fitting simile. "As healthy as yours or mine!"

"Good. I suspected as much. When exactly is her birthday? Is it today?"

"Yes, but I don't go in for that astrology-birthstone nonsense, if that's what you're suggesting."

"No, certainly. Too banal. You're absolutely right." She walked around the store slowly, rubbing her hands together and scrutinizing the display cases. She was used to dealing with islanders whose tastes were inconsistent with their pocketbooks (though in Raoul's case she rather suspected he was selling his pocketbook short).

"Hmm," she pondered aloud, surveying her stock. "I do have a lovely lizard cameo in chalcedony. Does your wife swim?"

"Y-y-yes," Raoul stammered, "but I don't see—"

"What about her name?" she asked him abruptly, halting her perambulations.

"What about it?" Raoul answered suspiciously. "Her name is Lila."

"Yes. L-I-L-A." Cora rushed back behind the main display case and stooped out of sight. Raoul heard her rattling trays and sliding small drawers until she raised herself to her full height again and motioned for him to come see what she had. She laid out a square of pale blue velvet on the counter and gently set upon it four stones, each the size of a small clove. The first was smooth, in indigo flecked with gold; the next, rough and purple; the third was mottled, light blue and milky white; and the last was a nearly-black dark blue, with threads of bright green dripping over its glassy surface.

"Here." Cora handed Raoul a jeweler's glass, so that he could take a better look.

He put it close to his eye and examined the four specimens. The stones were very beautiful, and they did look very nice lined up the way they were, but Raoul was confused. He could hardly give his wife a handful of colored (and tiny!) rocks for her birthday. "I don't understand," he said, when he had finished admiring their coordinated hues.

Cora picked up the flecked stone with a giant tweezer. "Lapis lazuli," she said, "for the top stone. From the caves of Afghanistan."

"The top of what?" Raoul asked, no less confused than a moment before.

"This." Cora reached into her pocket and pulled out a tiny vial made of glass that was capped at the top and bottom in etched gold. She set it on her palm and extended her hand toward Raoul.

"What's that?"

"A very old trick I picked up somewhere," Cora replied playfully.

"I beg your pardon?"

"Jewelry is not merely for decoration, Mr. Orlean." At the use of his name, the hairs at the back of Raoul's neck rose and prickled. It didn't surprise him that Cora knew who he was—Oh was small after all—but that she had kept her knowledge a secret until now unnerved him. So much so that he was unable to utter a word.

"Gemstones can be used for all sorts of things. To declare forbidden love, send a hidden message. To warn an unsuspecting friend or curse an unsuspecting enemy. One stone for each letter of a secret word," she explained. "LOVE. HOPE. EVIL. REVENGE."

Was it Raoul's imagination, or had the jeweler's voice become barely audible? He found himself leaned-in close to hear her and with a start he pulled away.

"Or in this case," she went on, "LILA. Lapis lazuli for the initial L, iolite for the I, lazulite for the second L, and finally, azurite." As she spoke, in turn she picked up each stone. "We fill the vial with the stones representing the letters of your wife's name, close it, and put it on a chain of 18-karat gold. To the naked eye, a beautiful pendant in strains of blue." Slowly she fed the stones into the vial. The azurite-for-A on the bottom, followed by the Lazulite-for-L, then the iolite-for-I.

"But behind the beauty, a secret." With these words she picked up the lapis lazuli again and held it to the light. "To ward off the spirits of darkness. Those that would dare consume Lila," she whispered, "from without or from within." Cora dropped the last stone into the vial. When she snapped it shut, Raoul jerked, startled.

"Shall I wrap it for you?" she asked cheerily, threading it onto a chain.

Raoul felt as if he had just been snapped out of an hypnotic trance. He pulled himself together and furrowed his brow. He didn't like the idea one iota, giving his wife a gift that smacked of magic. Circumstances greater than him were at play, alas (mainly, the passing hours and Ms. Lila's wrath), and so he acquiesced.

"Yes, please," he answered reluctantly. He pulled a wad of rainbow bills from his wallet, anxious to take himself far from Pineapple Jewelry and Gems and to get on with the night's festivities.

He bid the jeweler a tentative "thank you" and stepped outside. The warm Oh winds reanimated him and dispersed the strange aura that had engulfed him inside the jewelry store. Carefully he made his descent from Cora's establishment, the dainty berib-boned package clutched tightly in hand. He almost managed a smile at the thought of Ms. Lila's surprise. At the bottom of the steps, Raoul looked up at the darkening sky and turned happily toward home, his worries growing more distant with each early star.

Besides, he reassured himself as he walked, as far as *he* was concerned, his wife's gift *was* only a beautiful pendant in strains of blue. With little more behind it than a forgetful husband's fear.

4

"Ladies and gentlemen, a round of applause for a very special lady in the house tonight. Birthday girl Lila!" Bang hooted and cheered into the microphone, shaking a tambourine and egging on the crowd. Behind him on stage, the bass player plucked out a low, electric version of "Happy Birthday to You," which Bang took up at "happy birthday, dear Lila" and finished with the help of the Belly's patrons.

Luckily for the birthday girl, her no-longer-girlish complexion was camouflaged in part by the dimmed dinner lights, as was her embarrassment. Her smile, however, defeated even the darkness. Domestic bliss had been salvaged at the sight of Raoul's beribboned box, and Lila had happily accepted his invitation to a night out. She was just getting round to unwrapping her surprise, in fact, and grinned excitedly at the prospect, when Bang struck up his birthday chorus.

"Bloody fool!" Raoul snapped. Ms. Lila laughed.

"That's a fine way to talk about one of your very best friends!" she scolded him. She put an affectionate hand on Raoul's arm and waved to Bang with the other.

"He's just being Bang," she added, grinning still. "Aren't you used to him yet?"

Raoul grunted and sipped his beer. He was used to Bang, of course he was (their friendship was decades old), but Bang could be exasperating. That was part of his charm. Any islander could attest to it; they all knew him. Bang was an institution on Oh. By day, he hustled high-priced carvings to tourists at the airport (island bewitchery at its best!). At night he entertained at the Belly, on stage singing and playing marimba, or at the bar "giving talk"—if not to proprietor Cougar or taxi-man Nat, two other decades-old chums, then it was Raoul he was hassling. And having a damn good time of it. Bang was silly and endearing and ridiculous, his twenty-something self never scared off by the passing years or his graying locks.

On this particular night, Raoul had hoped to hover below Bang's radar, and with good reason. Like most of the islanders, Bang believed in magic. Not only did he believe in it, but once he got started, he droned on about it incessantly. If he got wind of Ms. Lila's birthday gift, it would be "Cora Silverfish-this" and "Cora Silverfish-that" until Cougar closed up for the night. In Raoul's making of the hasty birthday plans, Bang was a variable he had forgotten to factor in.

"Go ahead, open it!" Raoul prompted his wife. Maybe they could get it over and done with before Bang got off the stage.

Relishing her treat, Ms. Lila slowly untied the ribbon and gently removed the gold paper wrapping. When she saw the box with its distinctive raised-pineapple insignia, she stopped, disbelieving.

"Where is this from?" she asked Raoul.

"Pineapple Jewelry and Gems," he answered with nonchalance. "They're closing, you know," he added, as if this justified his custom.

"But you hate—"

"I know, I know. Just open it."

She opened the box and saw nestled in its soft, shiny, white satin, the vial of blue stones on its bright gold chain. She was stunned silent for a moment, then exclaimed, "Raoul! It's beautiful!"

"You like it?"

"It's exquisite! Help me put it on."

Good idea, Raoul thought to himself. Put it on and then get the wrapping out of sight. He fastened it around his wife's neck, where it fell in a perfect "V", its colors complimented by the lavender of her open blouse and the dark brown of her skin. He hated even to think it, but Cora Silverfish knew her stuff. It *was* exquisite.

"You know," Ms. Lila said, feeling the pendant with her fingers, "I take some credit for Ms. Silverfish's success."

"You?" Raoul was taken aback. "What are you talking about?"

She told Raoul the story of how at the library years before she had helped Cora find the museum on Esterina, the scholarship to study there, and the loans to open her shop when she returned.

"Why didn't you ever say anything?" he asked.

Ms. Lila shrugged. "I thought you hated the woman. Whenever her name comes up, you start ranting about magic and your truths-as-plain-as-noses-on-faces. I didn't want to upset you. Since when do you shop there, anyway?"

"I don't! I just wanted to get you something special for your birthday. Everyone's always going on about her jewelry. I thought you might like it."

"I do," she said, and kissed him. "I really, really do. I'm especially flattered that you compromised your noses for my benefit." She meant it. Ms. Lila knew what a sacrifice it must have been for her husband to cross Cora's threshold.

Silly Bang was not as sensitive to Raoul's gesture. As expected, when Bang's set was finished, he made a beeline for the bar, and then another for Raoul's table. He gave Ms. Lila a peck on the cheek and wished her well, all without noticing the wrapping and ribbon that might have forced Raoul to discuss his shopping trip. What Bang *did* notice was Ms. Lila's pretty pendant, and he complimented her on it.

"Isn't it lovely?" she said. "A birthday gift from my wonderful husband."

"You don't say!" Bang cried out, clapping Raoul firmly on the back. "Nice, my man."

"Thanks," Raoul muttered.

"Where'd you get it?" Bang wanted to know.

Ms. Lila tried to hide her amusement and replied on Raoul's behalf. "It's from Pineapple Jewelry and Gems."

"No wonder it's so pretty. That Cora Silverfish knows her way around a...a...what *are* those stones, Raoul?" he asked, peering in close at the pendant that lay on Ms. Lila's chest.

"Back off, will you?" Raoul pushed Bang away from his wife.

"Sorry, sorry," Bang chuckled. "So seriously, man, what are they?"

"She told me," Raoul answered, "but I can't remember now. It's four different blue ones."

"Well I can see that they're blue, but what do they do?" Bang asked.

"What do you mean, 'what do they do?'"

"Cora's things—her pendants, her bracelets, her tea trays—they all *do* something. Boost your crops or curse your neighbor. Settle your stomach. What does this one do?"

"Nothing!" Raoul protested. "It's a beautiful blue pendant. Nothing more."

"Well, did you ask her?" Bang insisted.

"Ask her what?" Raoul was losing his patience.

"Did you ask Cora Silverfish what the pendant does? Maybe she just forgot to tell you. You should go back," Bang suggested.

"That won't be necessary," Ms. Lila interjected to spare her husband any further discomfiture. "You know Raoul, Bang. I'm sure Cora saw him coming and gave him a piece from her non-magical line. Just leave him be now."

"Suit yourself," Bang told her. "But if I were *you*, I'd want to know what sort of magic it was I had noosed around my neck."

With that, Bang picked up his drink, tipped his cap, and left.

"Bloody fool!" Raoul said again. Only this time Ms. Lila didn't laugh. She didn't scold him, didn't put an affectionate hand on his arm.

She did put her hand to the beautiful blue pendant, did—with nervous effort—swallow. Did want to tell her husband, 'now, now, dear, he's just being Bang,' but her throat shut up tight—funny, that—and so she didn't.

5

L ila never was the superstitious sort. Which perhaps explains her tolerance for Raoul's antics in the service of battling magic (he had been known to bivouac alone on suspect beaches and parade barefoot around town with binoculars bouncing on his chest) and the fact that the morning after her birthday, she promptly pushed Bang's words straight out of her head—or tried to. Her necklace was a thoughtful, lovely gift, and that's all there was to it. If it really did have magic powers, good or bad, she wasn't certain she believed in their efficacy. To be sure, for a few brief seconds the night before, she had contemplated a trip to Cora's just to be safe—who wouldn't?—but then her reason got the better of her. By the time she awoke, the stark light of day had blotted out any hint of doubt that remained.

Raoul, on the other hand, jumped out of bed with no doubts in need of blotting. For years now, Bang's theories had been rel-egated to a corner of Raoul's brain that, like a file in a cabinet, was simply labeled "Folly." Not even his flies bothered with it. Besides which, Raoul was as pleased as rum punch with himself for saving the birthday the way he did. He had forgotten how enthusiastically Ms. Lila could show her gratitude when circumstances warranted. With a satisfied smile he surveyed the twisted bedsheets and for a few brief seconds was almost glad he had gone to see Cora.

"Good morning, sleepyhead." Ms. Lila flitted into the bedroom and set about stripping the bed. She was one of few women on Oh who boasted a top-of-the-line washing machine (one of few who boasted *any* washing machine for that matter), and she wanted to give the linens a spin before she went to work.

"You look especially lovely this morning, my dear," Raoul told her sheepishly. She did. She was wearing a pale blue blouse and her hair was perfectly plaited. "Where's your necklace?" Raoul exclaimed, noticing her bare cleavage. She hadn't managed to lose it already, had she?

"My necklace?" Ms. Lila repeated, surprised. "Since when do you take note of such things?"

"Since I had to walk right into a witch's den to get it, that's when. Don't you like it? You said you liked it." Raoul found himself spitting out all his sentences at once.

"Well, of course, I do. I just...well, I suppose I just didn't think to put it on this morning," she replied, balling up the sheets and stuffing them into a basket. "I thought I'd save it for special occasions," she added over her shoulder as she walked from the bedroom to the bathroom, where her washing machine was located.

"Nonsense!" Raoul hollered after her. "It's too pretty for that. You should wear it every day." He rifled through the things in her topmost dresser drawer and found the box from Cora's shop, the pendant neatly arranged inside it. With a yank he pulled it out and chased after his wife.

"Let me fasten it for you," he insisted, wrapping it a bit too enthusiastically around her neck from behind as she bent to load the washer.

"Wait just a minute!" she protested. "You'll choke me!"

Clutching the pendant flat against her chest to keep both the chain and her neck from snapping, Ms. Lila shut the front of the washing machine and maneuvered herself upright. "There," she huffed. "Go ahead."

Raoul fastened the clasp, then turned his wife around to have a look at her. "Perfect," he said, and went to bathe.

While her linens and her husband lathered up, Ms. Lila put on the kettle for breakfast. Warm oats with fresh plum. As she poured and stirred and sliced, she caught herself humming—a very good sign, this. Her librarian's logic told her that if the vial around her neck were indeed filled with bits of malevolent gems, then light-hearted humming couldn't possibly be possible.

"That's *that* settled," she decided, pouring two cups of lemongrass and drowning the last of her doubts. "Raoul," she called. "Hurry up! Your tea will get cold."

Raoul joined her in the kitchen, after first popping out to the verandah to scoop up his copy of the *Morning Crier*. Home delivery (available for a fee) was not the fashion on Oh, but Raoul was among the island newspaper's few subscribers, his duties as Head of Customs and Excise requiring that he keep abreast of the island news the paper fashioned. Compared to most other waking islanders, who got their morning news from the local radio and purchased the *Crier* later in the day, Raoul felt Continental sipping his tea with fresh, folded morning edition in hand (a feeling he kept to himself, however, not entirely sure of the Continent to which it referred).

"Anything going on?" his wife asked, as he sat down.

Raoul had a quick look at the front page. "Nothing out of the ordinary," he said. "Taxes are up. The sea level's down. At least Bruce has stopped putting sunsets on Page One."

Ms. Lila laughed. She set their breakfast bowls on the table and took her seat across from Raoul.

"Smells good," he said. He flipped through the *Crier*, looking for an article to read while he ate, and chose a Page Six exposé on impure nutmeg oil produced at Luckmont Point. Tsk-ing and shaking his head, he folded his paper and raised it to eye level, leaving Ms. Lila face-to-face with a full-page Page Seven ad: the closing sale continued at Pineapple Jewelry and Gems.

Ms. Lila studied the ad and sighed. If only she could swallow her doubts with her morning plum! Then she had an idea.

"I was thinking, Raoul," she started.

"Mmm?" Raoul replied from behind his paper.

"Well, seeing as how beautiful this pendant is," she said, fondling the vial around her neck, "and what with the closing sale and all..."

"Mmm," he said again, his head full of nutmeg oil.

"It's just that, I mean, you know I never bother with extravagances, but with prices at forty percent off, I thought I might go have a look. Maybe find some earrings or a bracelet to match my birthday gift."

"Mmm."

"Then you don't mind?"

"No, no, of course I don't."

That was easier than she thought! Ms. Lila smiled, pleased with herself, and calculated whether she could get to Pineapple Jewelry and Gems before she opened up the library. There were still the sheets to collect from the washer and hang in the sun. What time did Cora open up her shop?

"Wait!" Raoul said, peering around his morning news. "Mind what?"

"Mind if I buy some earrings or a bracelet to match my birthday pendant," Ms. Lila said quickly and casually.

"Oh, no. Right. I suppose Finley will be back before long. His shop's bound to have something nice."

"Finley? I thought I'd go see Cora. What with the sale and all. Weren't you listening to me?"

Ah ah. Tricky territory.

"I always listen to you, dear," he answered. "But what's wrong with Finley's Fine Jewelers?"

"The prices, for one! For another, the stones won't be perfectly matched," she argued. Then she added in honeyed tones, "I thought you picked *these* stones especially for me, because you knew how much I'd like them."

More tricky territory, but Raoul had no intention of losing his footing to Cora Silverfish.

"That's true, dear, but with the sale, Cora's just about sold out her stock," he improvised. "Don't waste your time. We'll get Donald to match something up—whatever the cost. I promise." He patted her on the hand.

Ms. Lila shrugged. Not much of an argument, but better to let Raoul think he had won. "I guess if you insist," she officially capitulated.

"I do," he said firmly. "I do insist." Raoul went back to his exposé, while Ms. Lila stared at Page Seven. She was trying to recall *when* in her married life, if ever, Raoul had insisted she *not* do something. He hadn't complained when she bought her washing machine. He didn't mind if she stayed late at work. Whether she spent her Saturday afternoons at the Staircase to Beauty Salon or sweeping the church made no difference to him.

She glared at the newspaper that covered his face, as if she might by force of concentration see straight through it and into his brain, spot the fly that buzzed in there, warning him to keep her away from Cora. He had come out of Pineapple Jewelry and Gems unscathed, hadn't he? Why couldn't she pay a Pineapple visit, too?

The answer came by way of a fly that suddenly swooshed past her nose and landed smack dab in her oatmeal. It stared at her defiantly, a reminder of her husband's position on the matter of the matching earrings. Ms. Lila watched it for a moment, deciding her course of action. She knew what she had to do. In one gracefully violent movement, she swung the dishtowel that lay thrown on her shoulder straight into the bowl of oatmeal, which wobbled with a clatter, spraying oats every which way. The towel knocked into Raoul's paper, too, pushing it up against his nose and upsetting the cup of tea he held in his other hand.

"Bloody hell!" Raoul jumped up, startled and doused in hot tea. His chair crashed to the floor behind him. "What happened?" he cried.

"I'm so sorry, dear!" Ms. Lila said, stifling a smirk. "There was a fly buzzing around my breakfast a bit too insistently." She stood up and began to wipe the table.

"See?" She righted her bowl and pointed inside it, to where an insect corpse slid on a tiny wave of oatmeal. Raoul leaned in to have a peek, then looked up at his wife again. He furrowed his brow, disbelieving she had soiled his trousers, crumpled his paper, and toppled his tea cup for the sake of an insistent fly.

"What?" she objected, noting his bewilderment. "I got it. It's dead."

6

The rains of Oh have been known to send an innocent man to jail. They've also kept some guilty ones free, by washing away the signs of crimes committed. The rains trigger rainbows and urge up corn and peas. Sometimes they make themselves scarce just for the sport of it. When that happens, when the drizzle isn't there to frizz your hair or the downpours to dampen your plans, rest assured. Oh will never leave you high and dry. If the rain clouds can't get you, your top-of-the-line, Spin-O-Matic washing machine will. Just ask Ms. Lila Orlean.

Despite the demise of the fly who bothered her breakfast on the morning after her birthday, and the implication that she might find a way to triumph over Raoul and his fine Finley jewelry, Ms. Lila was having a very bad day. Not the kind of bad day that came from a tear in her stocking, or from the fact that some less-than-prompt patron had kept the newest library book too long. Not the kind that came from a tiff with her husband, whose obsessions buzzed in his brain like busy bluebottles. Ms. Lila's bad day was the kind that happened when Oh, the island where she had her tidy home, played the tricks that only Oh could play, tripping her up in an inch of water and drowning her intentions in soapy suds.

When she had cleaned up the mess in the kitchen (broken cup, spilled tea, splattered oatmeal, dead bug) and calmed down a dripping Raoul, Ms. Lila surveyed the damage: three dirty dishtowels, a spotted tablecloth, and an unwearable workshirt stained with lemongrass (she had managed to wipe Raoul's trousers clean). She cleared away what remained of the dishes and took the towels, shirt, and tablecloth to pop into the machine, where, she assumed, the bed linens had finished their spinning. She left a bare-chested Raoul at the bare wooden table, with a fresh cup of tea and a *Crier* slightly worse for the wear.

"I'll just hang the sheets on the line and we can go," Ms. Lila's muffled voice called to him as it neared the bathroom.

Raoul's cottage, for its ample veranda and clean, painted walls, was cursed with rooms of mismatched flooring. The lounge and the kitchen and the verandah were perfectly even. The two bedrooms, however, a small one and a bigger one where Raoul and Lila slept, were raised up comparatively by about one inch—which gave the adjacent bathroom the impression of being lower by an inch and a half, though in truth it sank only a half-inch below the bulk of the house. Perilous to the odd guest, the ups and downs of the happy home were familiar obstacles to the Orleans, who knew where to step without looking. Thus, when Ms. Lila reached her sunken-in bathroom, her arms full of things to launder, she confidently dropped her foot through the doorway, without bothering to see what was what. Or that her Spin-O-Matic had sprung a leak.

The bathroom was a quickly filling pool that before long would storm the threshold of the bedroom. But not even that was the reason Ms. Lila's day was so very bad—any islander could weather a little storm. The real problem lay with her dropped foot, which found the altitude (or lack thereof) that it expected, but a humidity for which it was entirely unprepared. Her vision blocked by the bundle in her arms, her brain tried to connect the slimy sensation underfoot with what she knew to be her hard bathroom tiles. For a full second—the time it took her to fall over backwards, break her ankle, and knock her head on the bedroom floor—she wondered if she had somehow managed to forget an egg in her apron pocket, one that might have bounced out and broke underfoot.

It took only a second more, once she landed, to realize that she hadn't walked on egg whites but was the victim of a loose, gurgling hose and bubbly detergent.

"Raoul!" she cried out, laying on the ground and assessing the pains in her head and her ankle. "Raoul, help!"

He was there in a flash. "What are you doing?" he yelled, seeing her stretched out between the bedroom and the bath.

"What do mean, 'what am I doing?' you silly fool!" Lila would have called out, had she not been stunned into silence by the stars that burst in front of her eyes. Instead, she simply lifted her hand into the air, grabbing for Raoul's.

He came closer and met her hand with his.

"Lordy! Are you alright?"

Ms. Lila closed her eyes and gently nodded her chin up and down. The stars were subsiding and she pointed her arm in the direction of the hose. Raoul rushed to turn the handle that shut off the water supply.

Kneeling at her side then, one knee in each room, he asked her, "Did you hurt your head?"

"I don't think so," she answered reluctantly, trying to decide if it were true.

"Let's get you up," he said. "You're all wet."

She sat up, positioning herself so that Raoul could help her stand, and winced.

"My ankle!" she complained.

She looked at it and saw that it was bent in a slightly unusual fashion. Her instinct was to reach out and twist it back into place, but of course that wasn't much help. "I think it's broken," she said, looking worriedly at Raoul.

"Now, now, don't worry. Main thing is your head's okay. I'll call Nat."

Nat Gentle was a longtime friend of Raoul's who drove a taxi. Nat had spent much of their thirty-year friendship using up old cars and looking for a wife, and had only six months before purchased a brand new vehicle of his own. Shortly after, in his champagne-colored minivan taxi, he picked up a lady who soon became his bride. Bang and Cougar liked to tease him that the two events were related—the purchase and the wedding that followed—but Raoul didn't have the heart.

In the kitchen he dialed Nat's number.

"Nat! Is that you?" he gushed, when Nat picked up the receiver at the other end.

"Raoul?" Nat answered. Odd to have a call from Raoul at an hour like this. "I'm just leaving the house. What's up?"

"Lila fell and hurt her ankle. We have to get her to the hospital."

"You're at home?"

"Yeah."

"I'm coming now."

Even on Oh, where timing is approximate at best, "now" means "now" when a bona-fide friend (or his wife) is in need, and Raoul and Nat were as bona-fide as you could find. Nat kissed his new wife goodbye and jumped in his taxi. It took him less than fifteen minutes to reach Raoul's house, during which time Raoul was able to drag Lila well into the bedroom and prop her against the foot of the bed. While they waited for Nat to arrive, she gave Raoul instructions: for packing her a change of clothes (she didn't expect to remain long at the hospital, and once mobile, she would have to put on something dry); for mopping up the soap and water in the bathroom (he may as well use the soiled tablecloth and dishtowels, which had fallen onto the floor, and chuck the lot of it into the bathtub for now); and for helping her to make a neat and official sign that they would stop and post on the library door ("Due to unforeseen circumstances, the Pritchard T. Lullo Public Library will not open today. Our deepest apologies. We look forward to assisting you tomorrow."). Raoul quibbled about the last part, not wanting his injured wife to go to work the next day, but it was Ms. Lila's turn to insist.

Finally, she instructed him to put on a clean shirt. In all the fuss, Raoul had forgotten his own half-nakedness.

When Nat showed up, together he and Raoul carried Ms. Lila to the van, where they slid her across one of the back seats, her injured leg propped up in front of her. At the hospital, as Raoul helped her hobble inside, Nat offered to wait outside and drive them home again, but Raoul told him there was no need. They were certain to be there for hours, Raoul's Head-of-Customs clout notwithstanding.

In the waiting area, Ms. Lila began to get scared. Her ankle was swelling up and the reality of what had happened was setting in. Would they have to operate? Would she have to stay in the hospital? Who would take care of Raoul? What about the library? Who would see to that?

Raoul saw the worry on her face and tried to calm her down.

"Don't trouble yourself, dear," he said, squeezing her hand a bit too hard. "The library and that busted washer are simple things. We'll sort them out."

Ms. Lila had for years resisted pressure by Raoul and the Ministry of Education and Talent to train a suitable replacement for herself. It wasn't jealousy with regard to her post. It just never seemed necessary. She and Raoul never traveled, and she had never been sick a day in her life. Grooming a replacement seemed a waste of both her time and public resources.

"I've told you for years to get yourself some help there, haven't I?" Raoul preached. He had gone from trying to calm his wife to trying to stay calm himself. He hated to wait, and a very long hour had passed since he pushed Ms. Lila's completed Medical History form through the window that said Admittance (ironically so, he thought, seeing as how the room that lay beyond it was as inaccessible as the bottom of Crater Lake).

"Lila Orlean." A nurse appeared from a just-opened door and called out Lila's name.

"Over here," Raoul answered, standing up and waving a hand. He looked down at his wife's puffy ankle. "She can't walk like this."

The nurse nodded and returned a minute later with a wheelchair. She helped Raoul hoist Ms. Lila into it, and Raoul followed the nurse deep into the hospital, pushing the chair behind her.

"She'll need an X-ray," the nurse declared, steering them into an examination room. "See if you can get her into this." She handed Raoul a neatly folded, but decidedly faded cotton gown.

In the island heat, Ms. Lila's wet clothes had long since dried, but the soft, clean gown was welcome. She undressed herself from the waist up, then let Raoul support her as she bounced on one foot and struggled to free her bottom half of its skirt. By the time she was changed and back in the wheelchair, the nurse returned to roll her away, instructing Raoul to wait in the exam room while the doctors took care of his wife.

More waiting! He huffed at the empty room. There was a phone in it and he took the liberty of calling his office (he was Head of Customs after all) to inform them of his whereabouts. After that he paced back and forth, studying the details of the space to kill time: the scuffed tiles, the strange implements, drawers that hid heaven-knew-what. He tried to recall the series of events that had taken place that day and could scarcely make the jump from his warm oatmeal to the hot, cramped hospital room in which he found himself. He knew one thing, for sure. He planned to give them a piece of his mind at Higgins Hardware, Home and Garden for the faulty installation of the washing machine! His poor wife could have cracked open her skull when she fell. He was half-tempted to find a lawyer, only island law never added up to much. Raoul knew that firsthand. Still. He might have lost his precious Lila and, truly, then where would he be?

"Mr. Orlean?" A nurse stuck her head in the room, interrupting his nightmarish daydream of a Lila-less life. "We had to remove this, sir." She extended a closed hand in his direction. "From your wife."

"Remove?" He stumbled backward, horrified. Good god, had they taken off a toe? Why were they giving it to *him*?

"Sir, please," she snapped. "We're very busy." She grabbed him by the wrist and carefully dropped onto his palm Ms. Lila's birthday pendant. "It might humbug the X-ray machine, and we didn't want it to get lost."

"Thank you," Raoul whispered, composing himself. Good grief!

Alone again, waiting for his racing heart to slow, he studied the weight of the pendant in his hand, moved it around in his palm. It really was pretty. He held it up and looked at the stones one by one. He couldn't remember what they were called, but he would never forget Cora's bone-chilling explanation of what they were for: to ward off the spirits of darkness that would dare consume Lila.

Wait just a minute! Could the pendant have saved his wife's life? But for its stones in strains of blue would Ms. Lila be dead or concussed? Under normal circumstances, Raoul would never entertain such a notion, but in the quiet of the strange empty hospital room, the stress got the better of him. He broke down and he sobbed, grateful to the core that he hadn't lost his wife. He even decided a proper "thank you" might be in order. Yes. He would swallow his pride and his plain-as-noses-on-faces philosophy— "Just this once, let that be plainly clear," he announced to no one at all—and go see Cora to express his gratitude.

Back where she lay in the X-Ray department, Ms. Lila was thinking the very same thing. Or almost. She too had pondered the pendant, only to a much less happy end. A visit was in order alright! Ms. Lila might not get to Cora's today after all, but she would go see her the minute her crutches allowed. She would demand to know what evil spell the woman had cast on her and why. Would tell her how she had nearly broken her neck while the wicked pendant was strapped around it! It was only by the grace of the angels in heaven that she had escaped with little worse than a fractured foot (strictly speaking, her ankle was fractured, not her foot, and severely so, but in island parlance anatomy was fluid). She crossed herself at the thought of what might have been. "Just let Raoul try and wrap that chain around my neck again," she announced, though no one was around. Huh!

While Raoul and Ms. Lila made their respective plans and sorted aloud through their raging emotions, high above the market square in her top-story shop, Cora Silverfish's ears were burning. They *must* have done, for besides the Orleans, yet a third raging someone was right then planning a visit to Pineapple Jewelry and Gems. A someone with concerns far greater than a magic pendant and a deadly bathroom floor. And that someone would see to Cora Silverfish before anyone else had the chance.

7

Seafus Hobb was as proud an islander as Oh had ever seen. He was both haughty-proud of himself and house-proud of his island, and the combination, though sweet in his youth, had soured into a mean and ugly thing as he aged.

In his boy days, young Seafus reveled in his island life. He hiked hills, planted peas, and fished fish. He made friends with noisy birds and slithering lizards, played with cats and dogs and goats and rabbits, and picked flowers for his aunties and his grandma. He built himself a tree house (he called it a tree house; it was more a platform in a tree) with some planks and nails he scrounged, and climbed up into it to do his homework. From his tree house, Seafus overlooked a village scattered on the side of a hill. Between grammar and history, he studied treetops (papaya, cashew, mango, almond) and rooftops (sheets of corrugated plastic or of galvanized steel, tarpaulins, rotting pieces of board). The poverty, his and his neighbors', clashed with the richness of the foliage and the fruits, and planted a seed of its own in Seafus's unknowing heart.

As he grew, Seafus Hobb wanted nothing more than to become a famous cricketer. Not only for the money and the women, nice as both would be, but for the chance to take Oh's national team to the Cricket World Cup. He wanted fame, but for Oh and himself equally; wanted to draw worldwide attention to his small island home, attract tourists and investors. Seafus dreamed of bringing fortune—massive amounts of it, in the form of legal tender— to his country. When he was too old to play cricket, he thought perhaps he'd run for Parliament, help steer and protect his now fortunate country. He would call his party the Wicket Coalition, because Nothing Would Get Past It.

It was an admirable dream and, for a while, not out of his reach. Seafus was a batsman born; islanders took buses on Sunday afternoons to see him play on the pitch at Loucy. He took his village team to the championship at Port-St. Luke, the Port-St. Luke team to the Island Cup, and Oh's amateur team to Killig for the Inter-Island Amateur Finals. Then, on a windy Sunday that Seafus would never forget, Oh's top-most coach approached him and invited him to join the national team.

At last!

Seafus's dream was right on track.

Cora couldn't remember the last time she'd seen Seafus Hobb, not that she cared to. If one had been incidental to the other's dreams, it was a million years before. What either had managed to do (or not) in the meantime was...what? Merit? Magic? A shift in the island wind? They had both long said what needed saying, and they hadn't exchanged a word since. Cora rather preferred it that way. That she should now climb the stairs to open her shop and find him waiting, stuck to her doorstep like a slip of an insect in age-old amber, made her drop her keys in shock.

As she bent to collect them, she collected herself, and stood up determined to keep the upper hand.

"Cora, how nice to see you," he said, his tone inconsonant with his words.

"Come to do some shopping?" she replied indifferently, forcing him off the doorstep and out of her way as she put the key in the lock.

"I did read about your sale in the paper. I have to say I was surprised."

They entered the shop and Cora turned her gaze squarely on his. "What business of yours would my sale be?" she asked.

"None at all," he gushed, and he raised his hands in defense.

"Good. Now what can I show you?" she asked as she disappeared into the back where her stock was locked in a safe. Her muffled and disembodied voice added, "You aren't ill by chance, are you? I have some bloodstone for hemorrhaging, if you like." She didn't specify whether the gem would check or induce his bleeding, a detail not lost on Mr. Hobb.

"No, no," he called out good-naturedly. "That's not why I'm here."

"Pity," Cora answered, as she came back and set a pile of jewelry trays on the empty counter. "The prices being so good just now and all."

She stooped to arrange the trays on the shelves inside the empty glass showcase, readying the shop for the day's custom. She worked as if Seafus weren't there. Cora knew he wanted something—didn't he always?—and she wasn't about to invite his request. When the case was full, she locked it up and returned to the back for more baubles to display.

With Cora out of sight, Seafus mustered his courage. "As I said," he yelled out, "your discounts are no concern of mine, but I was wondering about your shop closing."

Cora appeared again, her hands full of shiny silver bric-a-brac, lifelike mini pineapples and a heavy, mocking half-moon paperweight, which she held up and polished in front of him. "What exactly about my shop's closing bothers you?"

"Is it wise?"

"Wise?" she repeated, setting down the moon. "You're looking out for me. How thoughtful."

"Well, you're not young and you're not married. How do you plan to support yourself?"

"So this is a financial call then? Are you a banker now, too? I know you have your...fingers in a number of pies, shall we say. I didn't realize savings and loans was one of them."

"I can't help but feel somewhat responsible for all of this," he said, shrugging his shoulders and turning his head to admire the interior of Pineapple Jewelry and Gems.

"A debt long repaid!" she snapped. "With more interest than I care to count!"

"I just think that closing the shop is not the...healthiest of options. That's all. What if something happened to you?"

"You're not threatening me, Seafus?" she chuckled.

"Not at all, my dear!" he cried. "I was merely referring to the health of your bank account. I worry about your needing money." As he said it he picked up the heavy, mocking silvery moon and weighed it in his hand, as if calculating how hard and how fast he could throw it, and the damage it would do if he did. Watching

Cora watch him, he set it back down on the top of the showcase with a bit too much force. They heard it smack against the glass and listened as its curved underside shook itself still.

"Just think about what I said, hmm? I think closing right now would be the wrong thing to do." With that, he knocked his knuckles jovially on the case and left.

Cora looked at the quiet and abandoned crescent moon, smudged and dirtied from Seafus's hands, and rushed to follow him. He was halfway down the steps to the street below, when she stuck her head out the door.

"Wait!" Cora yelled.

Seafus stopped and looked back at her with a satisfied grin. He hadn't expected to talk her round so easily.

"What about a bit of sardonyx?" she offered sweetly. "I'll let you have it for fifty off."

Seafus, unamused, gave his head a nearly imperceptible shake and continued on his way.

"Come back, Mr. Hobb," a smirking Cora taunted his descending silhouette.

Her smirk gave way to a cackle as Seafus reached the bottom of the steps and walked off into the sunlight. "I promise," she hollered after him in a derisive sing-song, "it will make all your dreams come true!"

8

It appeared as though the string of very, very bad days that had entangled Raoul and his wife in turn, was, on the morning of Ms. Lila's mishap, twisting itself around Cora Silverfish and Seafus Hobb, too, stretching itself from the hospital to the jewelry shop to the Parliamentary Museum on the other side of town.

If Cora suspected a bad day as she watched Mr. Hobb walk away, just how very *very* bad her day was meant to be turned crystal clear when Raoul Orlean showed up in his wake.

"Lord have mercy!" Cora said to herself. Had the whole island gone mad? First a visit from Seafus Hobb and now Raoul Orlean was coming right toward her, for the second time in two days! She held her breath, hoping he was headed for Incredible Ennis and a new pair of shoes, but alas, no. Raoul saw her at the top of her stairs and gave her an embarrassed wave, then embarked on the climb to the shop. She raised her hand and nodded to him, and went inside to wait. Raoul was hardly one of her loyal customers. If he was back so soon, it was because he had a complaint.

"He better not get my dander up today!" she huffed. (Her dander was in fact already good and up, thanks to Seafus.)

After Raoul and Ms. Lila had finished at the hospital a short time before, Raoul sent his wife home with Nat, who had come back to the hospital to check on them just as Ms. Lila was discharged. Since she couldn't abide her husband's company right then and there, she sent him off to work, insisting that Nat would be more than capable of getting her and her shiny new crutches into the house. ("Are you absolutely sure, dear?" Raoul had asked her, and she had answered, "Oh, very much so.")

Before going to his office, Raoul, who was a man of his word (even a private word announced to no one at all), had other business to take care of. He owed Cora Silverfish a thank you for sparing his beloved Lila. Raoul walked all the way to Pineapple Jewelry and Gems from the hospital, and as he did, the fresh morning air cleared his head, and bolstered both his pride and his plain-as-noses-on-faces philosophical views. So much so that by the time he reached Cora's staircase, he had decided to abandon his plan. Island magic never saved a man's soul as far as Raoul was concerned, nor certainly that of a woman! Lila's fall was a fluke, and pretty, strained pendants, blue or otherwise, had nothing to do with a poorly installed Spin-O-Matic.

But because the string of bad days had already wrapped itself tightly around Cora's waist, as Raoul approached the building that housed her shop, he had spotted Cora, and she him, and so there was no turning back. As he climbed the stairs, he hadn't the foggiest notion of what he would say to her, a "thank you" now out of the question.

"Good morning," Cora sighed at him when he pushed open the door.

"Hello," Raoul replied hesitantly. He still had Ms. Lila's pendant in his pocket, and for lack of something better to say or do, he pulled it out and laid it on the glass counter.

48

Cora looked at it, then looked at him, and waited.

"I bought this yesterday," Raoul said rather unnecessarily. "For my wife's birthday."

"Yes, I know."

Again she waited. The silence was awkward and Raoul wasn't sure how to break it. For a split second, he thought of grabbing the pendant and disappearing out the door and down the steps, and never looking back.

Instead, he told Cora what had happened that morning. That his wife had fallen and fractured her ankle and nearly cracked her skull on their flooded and mismatched flooring. For the second time that day (and it was hardly ten o'clock!) Cora found herself faced with a man whose business had nothing to do with hers.

"Come to do some shopping?" she tried for the second time, ignoring the story of Ms. Lila.

"No," Raoul said. "That's not why I'm here."

Cora watched him blankly. She hadn't invited Seafus's request and she would certainly not invite Raoul's.

Truth of the matter was that Raoul didn't know himself why he was there, what with his change of philosophical heart. Then he got an idea. He stood up taller, puffed his chest, furrowed his brow and, pointing at the necklace, he said, "You told me that thing would protect my wife!"

Cora smiled. Well, well.

"Well?" he demanded.

"Is it a refund you want? Because this was a closing-sale item." She pointed to a small sign on the counter by the cash register. It read ALL REDUCED SALES FINAL.

"No, that's not why I'm here," Raoul said again. How would he explain it to his wife if he went home without her necklace?

The hospital nurse must have told her that Raoul was the one who had it.

Cora raised her eyebrows at him expectantly, as if to say, "Then why *are* you here?"

"As I said," Raoul stammered, "you said, I mean, when I bought it you told me..."

Cora couldn't cope with him anymore. "Are you saying," she interrupted, "that you don't think it works? That it didn't protect her as I said it would?"

"Uh, yes. Yes, I'm saying that," Raoul said with less conviction than he would have liked.

"Tell me, Mr. Orlean, what else do you think? Do you believe in the properties of this pendant? Because my guess is that you don't."

Raoul hadn't seen *this* coming! How had a near "thank you" turned into a debate with an island witch? "As a matter of fact, no, I don't," he said. "Now that you mention it."

"Then the pendant met your expectations?"

"Well, yes, I suppose, but that's not..."

"That's not what? You scoff at my products and then dare to complain when they do exactly what you expected them to?"

"But you said..."

"I know what I said!" she yelled and pounded her fist. "I said it would protect your wife from the spirits of darkness, and that it shall, Mr. Orlean, whether you believe it or not. I did *not* say it would protect her from faulty bathroom hoses or crooked floors!"

It was Raoul's turn to stare in silence.

"I am a jeweler," she added, wagging her finger at him. "Not a plumber."

Raoul couldn't exactly argue with that. He wished he had never come to see Cora, and had resorted to his earlier plan of escape.

He picked up the pendant and disappeared out the door and down the steps, never looking back. He might have muttered a "good day" as he walked out, and Cora might have answered in kind, but Raoul wasn't entirely sure, such was his hurry to get away. From the landing outside her door, Cora watched him descend, his silhouette, like Seafus's, growing tiny and insignificant as it was swallowed by the mid-morning sun. Like a slip of an insect in age-old amber.

———

On the other side of town, at the Parliamentary Museum for the Preservation of Artistic and Historical Sciences, Seafus Hobb's very, very bad day had Cora's name written all over it. Her remark about his dreams had cut to the quick. He sat in his office, fuming, and cursing her name. So he wasn't the far-famed sportsman he had hoped to become. What of it? His pride hadn't suffered for a little change in plans! On the contrary, with every failure it reared up and took over just a bit more of his heart, narrowed his perspective, and drove him to succeed whatever the cost.

In the end, Seafus Hobb had carved himself a more-than-respectable place on the island, all things considered. He had stature. He commanded respect. The Prime Minister himself knew Seafus's name. In his capacity as Curator, Seafus had single-handedly elevated Oh's Parliamentary Museum to the level of international archive. If no one beyond Oh's shores had noticed it, well, that was hardly Seafus's fault. His dream may have got derailed, but his pursuits in the interest of fortune and Oh had never been marked with such single-minded vehemence.

Hence his visit to Cora Silverfish and the start to his bad day. It was true, like she said, that Seafus had his fingers in a number of pies, and Pineapple Jewelry and Gems was one of them. He couldn't let her close up shop. He *wouldn't*. In his pursuit of Cora, too, he would be as vehement as he knew how, and he would succeed whatever the cost. He had learned long before how to keep an island witch under his thumb. The question of Cora Silverfish, then, wasn't really what determined the very-very-ness of the bad day at hand. It was another question altogether, one that made Seafus's blood surge with fury and resentment. A question he struggled not to think about, but had been forced by Cora to recall.

How had he, Seafus Hobb—a top-drawer, first-string, blue-chip cricketer with world-class designs—turned Curator in a two-room, bush-league, back-stair museum on an island that no one in the world thought twice of?

9

Ms. Lila was sad. She lounged on her sofa—if propping a plastered foot constituted "lounging"—and stared out the window. The island had cooked up one of its extra-special days, the kind when the sky was so blue and clear that even the moon turned up to admire it. If she tilted her head just so, Ms. Lila could see its faint powdery crescent hanging amidst the glowing fronds of a tall and distant palm. The birds hummed and tweeted. Every flower stood at attention, each red yellow orange fuchsia face turned up to the sun that dripped and melted over the scene, as if sealing its beauty, like a glaze on a painting in a museum. It was the kind of day on Oh that local singers wrote songs about, a day for falling into luck or into love, not into a puddle of water on a bathroom floor. A day that made a good mood *de rigueur* and every gloomy Gus doubly disconsolate, once for being sad in the first place and again for breaking the rules.

For her part, Ms. Lila was sad three or even four times over. Besides her gloomy mood and the island's scornful cheer, there were the problems of her fractured foot and, worse, her blue birthday pendant. Although getting herself home and away from the hospital had settled her mind somewhat, Ms. Lila couldn't shake the thought that the pendant was what had tripped her up earlier that day. Bang's words played over and over in her head. So too did Raoul's impatience to fasten the pendant around her neck, and his insistence that she stay away from Cora. It was this last thing that made her woman's intuition stand up and take note. It implied that if Cora were up to something, some evil spell dressed-up in shades of blue, Raoul knew all about it. And if he knew all about it, why on earth would he play along? Why would plain-as-noses-on-faces Raoul protect an island witch? Why indeed shop at her store to start? There was only one answer that Ms. Lila could come up with and she didn't like it one bit. Something was going on between her husband and Cora Silverfish. Was he smitten with her? Had she cast a love spell on him? Preposterous theories, Ms. Lila decided, but island men were known to stray. Had she fooled herself all these years into thinking Raoul was any different from the rest?

Poor Lila! Her broken foot and her breaking heart were sending her into flights of fancy that under normal circumstances she would never have entertained. Alas, the seed of suspicion, once planted, sprouted viciously inside her head, like a fat and thorny cactus that poked and pricked her every thought. Her head began to ache even worse than her ankle, her thoughts knocking about her skull like peckers on wood. She had to calm down, she told herself. She was getting into a panic. Only the knocking wouldn't stop. It grew louder and more forceful. Ms. Lila got scared. Was she going mad? Instinctively she called out for her husband. "Raoul! Raoul!"

"No, no, it's just me," a voice answered. "Bruce." Ah. Bruce Kandele. Editor-in-chief, copyeditor, reporter, and special correspondent of the island's *Morning Crier*, and always on the hunt for its next front page.

"I've been knocking for five minutes. Can I come in?" he shouted from the verandah.

"Yes, yes, come in," Ms. Lila shouted back to him. "I can't get up to open the door."

"Don't I know it!" Bruce exclaimed, letting himself in, and falling into Raoul's favorite armchair. "I saw your husband and he told me what happened. That's why I'm here."

"I don't understand," Ms. Lila said, raising herself up taller on the sofa. "Raoul sent you?"

"Raoul? Heavens, no! You know how he is about this sort of thing. But it's been going on for too long and people have a right to be informed. I've stopped the presses on tomorrow's edition, you know. I had to come see you as soon as I heard, and get your side of the story."

"Oh, I don't know about that," she said, shaking her head hesitantly.

"My dear Ms. Lila, we cannot allow one person—however pleasant she or he may seem—to continue jeopardizing the lives of our citizens. I come in my official capacity, and it's your civic duty to give me an interview."

Ms. Lila's eyes grew wide. "Then you honestly believe my injury was a result of intentional malice?" Dare they accuse Cora Silverfish in black and white?

"Perhaps not directly speaking. I don't think anyone foresaw your mashed-up foot—*per se*—as they say. But the malicious intent was there sure as the sky comes in shades of blue."

Ms. Lila couldn't believe what Bruce was telling her. Why on earth would Cora Silverfish wish any evil upon her? They had spoken at length only twice in thirty-some years, and Ms. Lila prided herself on having been rather helpful to Cora both times, or so she thought. No. Bruce must have it wrong.

"But why me?" she argued. "I've never done anything to justify this sort of ill will. I think we may be jumping to conclusions."

"It has nothing to do with *your* behavior," he explained, reaching out and gently putting his hand on hers. "I'm afraid," he sighed, "it has everything to do with your husband's."

"My husband's?" The hairs on the back of Ms. Lila's neck, had she had any, would have stood straight up. "What are you saying, Bruce?"

"I don't want to cause you any undue stress in your condition, my dear, and if it weren't for my journalistic duties, I'd keep my mouth shut, you know. But since you ask, let's just say that Raoul has...well, gotten himself in over his head. When you try to eat your cake and have it too, one of the bakers is bound to get jealous and cause trouble for the other."

Ms. Lila's throat burned and tears began to form in her eyes. "So my ankle is hurt because—"

"Your ankle is the 'trouble,'" Bruce interrupted.

"Which means Raoul is..." She couldn't say it out loud, couldn't believe that her husband was having his cake with Cora Silverfish when everyone knew that Ms. Lila's baking was beyond reproach.

"Now, now, dear." Bruce patted her hand. "I have no intention of mentioning Raoul's name. It's not my business what he gets up to. I do, however, have to report on criminal activity. When one islander ends up on crutches on account of another, it constitutes a crime in my book."

Ms. Lila's head was spinning. Her husband was cheating on her, Bruce had all but confirmed Raoul's mistress's hand in her injury, and now Bruce wanted to put it all on the front page? Her broken-heartedness turned to fear and back. And back again.

"Bruce, even if what you say is true, couldn't we handle it privately? I'm not sure it's wise to expose this...this...magic or whatever it is in such a public way. Think of what could happen to us! I've already got one fractured foot!"

"Oh this is no run-of-the-mill 'island magic' story, Lila. This is willful endangerment of a fellow citizen, driven by very base and human emotions. You have nothing to be afraid of. I suppose you've seen the worst of it anyway. Your guard is up now. You know what to watch out for."

Ms. Lila felt utterly and wretchedly alone. Should she give Bruce his interview and expose Cora's magic and malice for what they were? Normally she would ask her husband what to do when she was confused. She didn't dare turn to Raoul this time, not least of all because she feared he might just take Cora's side over hers.

This last suspicion is what finally sent her—in a flush of female pride—over to Bruce's side. If he wanted his exposé, then he would have it, Cora Silverfish be damned! She would tell him everything. From her birthday dinner and her pendant in blue, to Bang's theories and Raoul's fishy insistence that she keep away from Cora and keep the stones around her neck at all times. She would tell him about her flooded floor and her fall, about how she spent the better part of the morning in hospital and now found herself a prisoner in her very own home, all while the Pritchard T. Lullo Public Library remained shuttered-up. She only wished she still had the pendant in hand so that Bruce could photograph it for his front-page spread.

Soapsuds Sabotage
Wife of Prominent Official Falls Victim to Faultily Installed Spin-O-Matic

Early yesterday morning, Ms. Lila Orlean of Port-St. Luke suffered a serious injury when the hose connecting her recently purchased automatic washing machine to the water supply in her home detached itself, flooding her bathroom with slippery bubbles. As she stepped into the room unawares, to empty the machine of freshly-spun linens, she fell to the floor, bumped her head, and had to be rushed to hospital, where she was diagnosed with a fractured ankle. Readers of this newspaper will agree that, but for the grace of God, Ms. Orlean may well have cracked her skull and died. She acquired her Spin-O-Matic at Higgins Hardware, Home and Garden, owned and operated by Mr. Howlander Higgins, who is currently embattled in a turf war with Alexander Ashbee of Ashbee's Appliances, Tackle and Tools, who also sells the famed machines. This reporter has reason to believe that, driven by greed and in an attempt to damage the reputable Higgins name, someone from the Ashbee establishment bribed a Higgins staff member to install the washer incorrectly, resulting in Ms. Orlean's injury. It is no coincidence that the mishap occurred in, of all homes, that of Ms. Orlean, whose husband, in his capacity as Head of Customs, is responsible for regulating the number of machines entering the island marketplace. It is known that the Customs Head, in an effort to fulfill his duties while still keeping both merchants happy, equally divided the allowed number of machines between the two, resulting in the general dissatisfaction of all parties involved. In her fall, Ms. Orlean risked damaging irreparably a valuable piece of jewelry given to her by her husband as a birthday gift the very night prior to her ordeal. A "beautiful pendant in strains of blue," as Ms. Orlean describes it, it is obviously of significant sentimental value to her, as she mentioned it repeatedly throughout our interview. She also stated that the pendant was purchased at Pineapple Jewelry and Gems (Cora Silverfish, proprietor)—where, as it happens, closing-sale discounts of 30-40 percent are currently to be had, as first advertised in this newspaper two days ago.

10

"Bloody bloody fool!" Raoul cursed, slamming his folded-up copy of the *Crier* on the breakfast table, as if killing over and over an especially despicable fly.

"You're making an awful lot of noise. Have you seen it, then?" Raoul heard Ms. Lila's words before he saw her, her trek from the bedroom slow-going on crutches, though he had no idea what she meant. When she finally reached the kitchen and maneuvered herself onto a chair, she found a still-noisy Raoul seated across from her, cursing and fuming.

"Why the hell does that man feel the need to put my business on the front page of his silly paper all the time? Am I the only source of amusement on this God-forsaken island?"

"I hardly think that kind of talk is proper," Ms. Lila coolly scolded him. "You can't blame God—or Bruce—if you've gotten yourself into trouble. Let me see it," she barked, snatching the paper out of his hand. (In Bruce's defense, this business-in-the-paper business was a trend begun by Raoul himself some twenty years before, when he placed a very peculiar and personal ad to help determine his granddaughter's paternity.)

Raoul watched Ms. Lila, puzzled. What had gotten into her? She had given him the cold shoulder since the night before, mumbling to him only the strangest of claims ("My guard is up. I know what to watch out for now, you know.") and admonitions ("Just you wait till morning!"), and now she was barking and snatching in a way he had never before seen. Had the hospital underestimated her bump to the head? As she read the article about the Spin-O-Matic, Raoul saw her face go blank and her shoulders visibly shrink. Was she alright?

"Bloody, bloody fool," she hissed, setting the paper on the table defeatedly.

"Well that's what I said," he announced, vindicated and suddenly re-preoccupied with his own affairs. He picked up the paper and read the article again. "Not only has Bruce revealed sensitive and confidential economic information, but he's told the whole bloody place that I shop at Cora's!"

"Cora's?" Lila repeated. Had her husband always referred to Ms. Silverfish with such familiarity?

"Oh! That reminds me," he went on. "Here." He set her birthday pendant and balled-up chain on the table and slid it toward her. "They gave it to me yesterday at the hospital. I forgot to give it to you."

She looked at it, as if she didn't know what it was or what she should do with it.

"Do you want me to put it on for you?" he asked offhandedly.

Or did he? Was his offhandedness too offhanded? Of the sort that denotes anything but? Lila's guard was up, it was!

"Do you *want* to put it on me?" she asked him, screwing up her forehead and scrutinizing his gaze.

"Well, I will if you want to wear it," he said.

"You think I should wear it," she said.

"You did say it was exquisite," he said.

"Suitable for special occasions," she said. "Not for every day."

"Nonsense." He got up and walked around the table, gave her a peck on the cheek, and hooked the pendant around her neck. He doubted it would protect her from anything, but he felt more certain than ever that his wife was unwell, and if island magic couldn't help her, it certainly couldn't hurt. "You look beautiful," he told her. "You should never take it off."

Wait a minute. She did look very beautiful. Her hair was done up and her blouse was stiff and neat. "Why are you all dressed-up?" he asked her.

"I'm not 'dressed-up,' I'm dressed for work," she said.

"You can't go to work in your condition!" he said.

"I most certainly can," she said.

"I think you should stay in," he said. "This article of Bruce's will have the whole town talking. You won't have a moment's peace."

"I'm not going to hobble about town. I'm going to sit behind my desk at the library. I can't think of a more peaceful place than that, and I can't bear to keep it closed another day."

Raoul shrugged. He was loath to argue with any woman, especially one who was injured and cranky and not quite herself. "You don't expect to *walk* to work, do you? I'll call Nat."

"I already did," she informed him. "He'll be here at eight o'clock."

"Then I better make you some breakfast," he offered. "What would you like?"

Ms. Lila looked at Raoul. His expectant and out-of-place presence at the helm of her stovetop melted her heart. Raoul was a good man, wasn't he? Hadn't he always been? Had she let her imagination carry her away? She practically told Bruce that Cora tried to kill her with a magic pendant, and Bruce, a veteran newspaperman, hadn't thought twice of her story. Hadn't thought it was the story at all. Perhaps she was getting worked-up over nothing. She sighed and looked up at Raoul, about to say "Just a slice of toast, please," when she caught him staring at the pendant in her cleavage with a funny glint in his eye.

She changed her mind about the toast and jumped up, wincing as she put weight on the ankle she forgot was fractured. "I'll just start heading out and wait for Nat in the yard," she said, leaning on her crutches.

"Suit yourself," he smiled at her. Typically, seeing as how it was Tuesday, Raoul's day off, he would have met up with his wife at the library and spent the day there, reading through the new books she had to show him. Thanks to Bruce, that wouldn't be the case today.

"You won't see me at the library later," he told her. "I have some business to take care of."

"Okay," she said, moving to go. He gave her another peck and watched her plunk purposefully across the kitchen and out the door, like a burdened and lopsided bird. To Raoul it seemed she couldn't get away from him, and into Nat's company, fast enough.

Hmm.

Odd, that.

II

So how *had* a top-drawer, first-string, blue-chip cricketer with world-class designs gone from test matches and cheering crowds to fossils and pottery and tours for school-aged kiddies? How had the dreams of Seafus Hobb gone so far astray?

Seafus himself—dare he speak of it—would tell you that he was tricked: seduced, bamboozled. Bushwhacked by a girl with eyes that twinkled silver and gold. He was a victim of sorts, it was true, just not the sort he would have you believe. His pride— not a woman—was his undoing. And as it undid him, the well-intentioned boy of the treehouse above the papayas became a man with a spirit as dark and as bitter as a cocoa ball.

What exactly he did to turn the wheel of island fortune so drastically in his disfavor, almost none of the islanders knew. There were whispers, of course—there always are on Oh—but who could ever be certain that it wasn't just the wind playing tricks? All anyone really remembered was that one day Seafus was no longer himself. The whispers, real or play, had gotten under his skin. Suddenly his bowling and his batting went bad, his fielding turned funny, and he couldn't wicket-keep to save his soul. The islanders will tolerate a poor showing in many places—government ministries, soca contests, and even in church—but rarely do they forgive it on the cricket field. Before long, Seafus's dreams of world-cup renown (for both himself and for Oh) were gone, and he had no idea where to look for them, so wide and so far had they been scattered by the island winds. Seafus Hobb was stumped.

Soontime, though, those same island winds, for better or for worse, blew him straight onto the path that was to be his destiny. As his cricketing fame fizzled, he acquired a certain celebrity among Oh's shadier dealers, the girls from the seedy port bar and their clientele, men who—like Seafus—were bitter about their scattered dreams and formed a quiet alliance to further their respective causes, at any cost. Indeed, Seafus found himself surrounded by future statesmen, captains of industry, and holders of public posts. Like a row of toppling dominoes, each would help the next get to where he was headed.

When it was Seafus's turn to topple, he landed at the museum. Though "Curator" was very good as far as museums go, it had nowhere near the ring of "world-cup champion." To bridge the gap between the two, Seafus decided, he would have to turn Oh's Parliamentary Museum for the Preservation of Artistic and Historical Sciences into one unlike any other. Perhaps he was still in time to claim the fame and fortune he and his fatherland deserved. As Curator (one planted by the seedy port alliance, no less), he might just as easily have spent his days reading newspapers in the comfort of his office and his nights attending dinner parties at the prime minister's home, then retired to a government-funded beach house complete with fat pension and slim housekeeper. But Seafus's ego, inflated by years of adulation in the stadiums of all the islands around, and bruised into bitterness by his fall from athletic grace, would now not settle for so little. The Museum was Seafus's new cricket pitch and there he planned to shine.

With the help of his fellow dominoes, he secured easy loans and easier grants and had the museum renovated. He turned one small-ish room into two large-ish ones, added yet another (with a stage) in which to host cultural discussions and proper soirees, and had toilets installed for visitors. Above all this, he built a library for himself (that he might keep abreast of acquisitions) and an office in dark, polished wood. The above and the below were connected by a chic and hidden spiral staircase, equally dark, and suggestive of private and elite goings-on overhead.

At first, Seafus's intentions were good. The personal library and secretive stair were perhaps a bit much, but an indulgence easily permitted to a man so intent on furthering the islanders' knowledge, for this is what was generally understood to be his aim. Little did the renovators, loan-makers, and granters of grants imagine that Seafus had no more interest in furthering island knowledge than they. What Seafus wanted was renown, not *on* Oh as much as off of it. Only in this way, he had convinced himself, could he really help his homeland. By putting Oh on the map—or making its dot on the map a bit bigger—he could increase its importance and its appeal and before long, surely, the dollars and pounds and pesos would start pouring in. Then, with their bellies full, they could all worry about things like knowledge. Alas, Seafus's pride did not connect the dots from museums to maps to money. It merely told him to stuff his museum to the brim, with any artifact and ancient vase he could get his hands on.

In this, he was not unsuccessful. The museum, under his early tenure, had got hold of everything from an authentic (if small-sized) Renaissance painting to a Chinese sword and the tooth of a tyrannosaurus rex. In fact, each glass case boasted a more valuable and random array than the next. The effect, sadly, was not of a world-class collection but of a crazy cache, a hodgepodge amassed by some wealthy and indiscriminate hoarder who stacked cracked Aztec pots on top of faded French manuscripts and hung centuries-old batiks from Malawi next to early-American wagon wheels. The islanders, who had never seen a museum of such caliber, had no idea what a glorious mishmash it was; and Seafus, concerned only with adding to it, grew more and more frustrated when island tourists alternately oohed-and-ahhed and chuckled as they pointed at and perused the museum's holdings.

Laugh at him, would they? Seafus snorted to himself. He couldn't believe that, with all its collection, Oh's museum was still not up to snuff. But clearly it must not be, for no one beyond Oh's shores was talking much about it (nor within them, truth be told), and the pounds sterling had yet to trickle in. Well, if they thought he could do no better, Seafus gloated, they were wrong. There was just one little obstacle to Seafus's surely still-imminent fame, and that was funding. It took massive amounts of money to buy bits of Ming vases and purses of penguin pelt, and no amount of dominoes could get him the cash he needed to keep up his purchases.

And then Seafus hatched a plan.

He ran from his darkly-wooded office to his private library next door. Scattered on the floor were some enormous scraps of wrapping from an Eskimo painting he'd recently acquired. Seafus picked them up and smoothed them out across the vast table that filled the library's center, and with a pencil he furiously mapped out the island, all of Oh spread out before him. He scribbled and scratched out, then scribbled and scratched again, stopping now to tap his chin, now to smile with wicked satisfaction. By the time he was finished, the map was crisscrossed with arrows, and a ring of X's marked the spots where his plot would play out, a ring topped with a new and shiny gem.

———

Seafus, sitting in his office and waiting for his very, very bad day to end, couldn't help but smile at the memory of that other day so many years before when he had gone into his library and taken his future in hand. True, he still wasn't famous, not yet, and neither was Oh, but who knew better than he how quickly island fortunes and futures could change? How one day from the anonymity of stiff, leafy darkness the sun coaxed the round and puckered pineapple, then turned it into glittering gold. It was only a matter of time before someone realized what he had accomplished. Only a matter of one great mind, on a very good day, sticking his nose into the museum and sniffing out the truth.

12

Raoul Orlean spent the day after the day after his wife's birthday trying to forget about her birthday altogether. It had all gone sour this year, his initial forgetting, his reluctant visit to Cora, Ms. Lila's fractured foot. He couldn't wait until the whole silly to-do was but a memory, though he suspected the crutches would be a reminder for at least six weeks to come—and the pendant, for heaven-knew-how-long after that. Still, he had to admit, the pendant was a stunning selection, and it suited his wife perfectly. So perfectly, he thought, that it had been worth even the trip to Cora's shop, a trip he did not, however, wish publicized more than need be. Which is why, on the day after the day after, instead of spending his Tuesday off at the library, Raoul planned a visit to the grimy-windowed offices of the *Morning Crier* and a tongue-lashing for Bruce.

Bruce wouldn't be fazed in the slightest, for tongue-lashings were a fixture of Raoul and Bruce's relationship. The two had cause to collaborate from time to time, both of them being investigators of island matters, and often Raoul failed to appreciate the finer points of Bruce's journalism, a shortcoming Bruce encountered in so many of the islanders that he had learned not to take it to heart. In the case of Raoul, especially, he knew it was only a matter of time before the lashes turned into appeals. Raoul knew it, too, though he hated to acknowledge Bruce's usefulness, and, as a matter of professional principle, held it his duty to call Bruce to task every now and again.

"Bruce!" Raoul called out as he reached the newspaper offices and burst through the door. "I have a bone to pick with you!"

Bruce, who sat tapping his desk with a pencil and thinking about the next day's front page story (or lack thereof), sighed resignedly, as if dealing with a small child unable to understand grown-up business and said, "I know, I know. You're vexed about the Spin-O-Matics." Thank heavens he did, because Raoul suddenly realized that Customs, and not Cora, was a far more professional leg on which to stand.

"That's right! Never mind that you make groundless accusations," he shouted, "but you make me look like I'm somehow to blame! Like I can't do my job properly! No one on this island takes his position more seriously than I do, you know that."

"Oho!" Bruce chortled. "I know all about your seriousness. We all do. But you fail ever to consider mine. I have a paper to fill, you know."

"That I do! You're always filling it with my business!"

"Not *your* business, Raoul, *island* business. Is it my fault you have your nose in whatever's newsworthy around here?"

Raoul couldn't immediately think of a good quibble for this claim, though he was sure there must be one, and was forced to fall back on Cora: "Then it's newsworthy, I suppose, where I choose to do my shopping?"

Bruce laughed and shook his head, as if with compassion for poor Raoul's stupidity. "Well of course it isn't," he said. "The part about the pendant is what we in the media call 'the human touch.' Makes all the clap-trap about Customs and washers tug at the heart. Hard-working husband buys the loyal little woman a sentimental bauble that's nearly crushed to bits, and all because of some greedy scheme by the Establishment. Honestly, Raoul. It's textbook!"

Raoul felt the muscles in his neck tense in frustration. Sometimes he couldn't believe that Bruce said the things that he did. "What bloody scheme would that be? A faulty hose? It was nothing more than an accident! And if by 'Establishment' you mean Howlander Higgins, then heaven help us all! With his half-priced manure and his Discount Thursdays, no telling what he could get up to. Or am *I* supposed to be your Establishment, hmm? Single-handedly maneuvering the government, am I?"

"I don't expect you to understand, Raoul. Nobody understands. It's a cross I've learned to bear," he stated plainly, and shrugged his shoulders.

"Just tell me who it was at Customs who told you about the arrangement I established—I mean, arranged—I mean—who did you bloody talk to?"

Before Bruce could refuse to answer, Raoul already knew what was coming. They had had this discussion before. In fact, Bruce had it with pretty much anyone who had ever been mentioned in one of his news stories.

"Raoul, no disrespect to you or your office, but you know that to me my sources are as sacred as the little Anglican church." (The little Anglican church, in Thyme, so-called so as not to be confused with the bigger Anglican church, in "town," or Port-St. Luke, was, by virtue of its survival after a hurricane that once blew the tops off every other church on Oh, considered sacred ever since, by Anglicans and otherwise.)

"Sacred? I find it hard to believe that any source of yours has a sacred bone in his body," Raoul objected. "And if that sounded disrespectful, I fully intended it to!" Raoul turned and stormed out, leaving an amused Bruce to take up his tapping again, still no closer to a front-page spread.

If Bruce's article had inadvertently ruffled Raoul's feathers, it had just as accidentally fanned and fluffed up jeweler Cora's. Since the initial rush of customers after her announcement that she was going out of business, closing-sale clientele had dropped off. Now, thanks to the *Morning Crier*, the entire island knew Raoul Orlean was a Pineapple patron, and if *that* wasn't an endorsement as plain as a nose on a face, then nothing was! Cora laughed as she set the newspaper aside and imagined Raoul's chagrin.

Glancing about the store, Cora felt a sense of satisfaction, coupled with cautious optimism. It was half past nine, the display counters already filled and shiny. She decided to open up shop. A bit early, but with Bruce's new publicity, perhaps a few more souls would cross her threshold. While she waited, Cora would work on a gemstone brooch that looked like the island moon—an almost full moon. She had made it the day before out of an unusually pale piece of larimar, more white than blue, but with just enough celestial pallor to perfectly mimic a thin cloud at dusk. It was a flat moon, dull and veiled; but even from behind its larimar cloud, power unimagined could be deduced.

As Cora labored at the nicks and bumps that would give her moon its texture, she heard footsteps on the stairs outside the door. Aha! Bruce's news was paying off already. She rose from her worktable, tucked just inside the doorway that led from shop to stockroom, and brushed the larimar dust from her blouse. As she entered the shop proper, she noticed that the footsteps were accompanied by voices, agitated whispers, rather, as a man and woman bargained over Cora knew not what. A husband and wife, she assumed, trying to decide how much money they would let themselves spend.

A husband and a wife it was indeed, though with no legal connection between them. The husband was taxi-driver Nat; the wife, Raoul's Ms. Lila. En route to the library, she had coaxed Nat into carrying her—literally—to Cora's shop. She told him that Raoul had given her permission, nay, encouraged her, to invest in some earrings to match her pendant, and she simply couldn't wait. She failed to mention that Raoul had adamantly recommended Finley's Fine Jewelry for the purchase, though her swearing Nat to secrecy soon told him something wasn't right. As she clutched her crutches, Nat awkwardly carried her up Cora's steps, whispering at her doubtfully: "I still don't understand why I can't tell Raoul."

"Shh!" she whispered back. "Don't worry. Just put me down on the landing and come back in ten minutes to collect me. I want to surprise Raoul, is all. Promise me," she insisted, "not a word!"

Nat didn't like keeping secrets from Raoul, a lesson he had learned long before, and firsthand, beneath a moonlit mango tree (but that's another story). In the end, though, Ms. Lila's persistence (and Nat's pity) won the day. She looked pathetic to him, bent over her crutches, begging him to let her do her shopping. Nat decided it was best to let Raoul and Lila sort out their marital finances themselves. If Ms. Lila wanted to splurge on fancy earrings behind her husband's back, well, it was certainly not Nat's place to break the news to Raoul. He would notice it soon enough anyway, Raoul would, either dangling from Lila's ears or seeping from his bank account, which he checked on at the Savings Bank at least once a week.

Thus Nat justified his participation in the affair.

Left to her own devices, Ms. Lila thumped and scraped her way into the shop and up to the display case behind which Cora stood. "Good morning," Lila said.

"Good morning, my dear," Cora warmly greeted her. "It's been a while, hasn't it?"

"Yes...yes it has," Ms. Lila hesitated, surprised by Cora's gracious welcome and struggling to recall the last time she and Cora had crossed paths at the market in town.

"I've just been reading about your accident in the paper," Cora announced, looking in the direction of Lila's leg. "Would you like me to get you a chair?"

"No, thank you. I won't be long."

"You came to see the closing sale for yourself, did you? I have some very pretty things left."

"As a matter of fact, I came to talk to you about *this*," Ms. Lila replied, pulling the bunched-up chain and blue pendant from her pocket and setting it on top of Cora's glass counter.

"I see." (Truly Cora did, though she pretended not to.) "Is the chain the wrong length? Do you need me to shorten it?"

"The chain is fine. It's just that, well, you see..." Lila tried to make her point, gave up, and tried again, raising herself as tall as she could while still keeping hold of her crutches. "In truth, Cora, it's about the accident—"

"Of course it is!" Cora interrupted. "How silly of me! I read that your pendant was nearly damaged when you fell. I suppose you want me to have a look at it to make sure nothing's come loose? Just give me a minute." With that, Cora swept up Lila's pendant and ducked through the doorway to her table in the back.

Which was not so far in the back of the tiny shop that Lila couldn't see Cora at work, tapping, twisting, and pulling at the vial of blue stones. "It seems fine to me," Cora called out to her.

Ms. Lila watched her, trying all the while to muster the courage to mention the real reason she had come: to find out what magic Cora had foisted on her. Before she could do so, she was distracted by a whitish disc on Cora's worktable.

"What's that?" Ms. Lila asked, pointing to it with the tip of her nose, her fingers firmly embroiled in her crutches.

Cora rose from her table and returned to the counter where Ms. Lila waited. She laid out a soft velvet mat of deep crimson, and deposited thereon the pendant in strains of blue and the unfinished moon. "I'm still working on this one," she explained.

"May I?" Ms. Lila asked. She had abandoned one crutch and pressed her weight on her elbow, which in turn pressed on the sturdy countertop, leaving her hand free to pick up the larimar moon.

"Help yourself."

Ms. Lila held the moon in her hand, her eyes drawn to it as if by hypnosis. She didn't know how long it held her captivated, perhaps only the most fleeting of instants, though when of a sudden she felt herself come to, she couldn't say for sure. With a shudder,

75

Lila let the sculpted moon fall on the soft plush velvet, whose color now seemed that of blood.

"A strong piece, eh?" Cora beamed.

"You mean it has powers?" Lila asked, her reluctance having been shuddered right out of her.

"Oh, very much so. That's larimar. A hard stone, but one that softens the wearer, gives him—or her," she specified, with an eye to making a sale, "a new perspective on an old problem. It brings wisdom. Do you feel it?"

"So it's magic?" Lila asked tentatively, ignoring Cora's question.

"I didn't say that."

"Aren't all your pieces magic?"

"So people say," she smiled. "I just shape and polish pretty rocks."

As she said it, Cora's eyes didn't meet Ms. Lila's. They drifted out the door at the opposite end of her shop (the door that led to a narrow balcony), and landed on the street—or more precisely, on Seafus Hobb, who stood in the street, hugging a small parcel to his chest and staring up at Pineapple Jewelry and Gems.

Twice in two days? Cora wondered, watching him. What the devil was he up to now?

She sighed and turned her attention back to Ms. Lila. "If you're interested in the moon, I can finish it up for you today. You could come back."

Lila's eyes had followed Cora's out the door and onto the balcony, but had stopped there, uncertain of what they were seeking.

"Thank you. That's very kind, but really I came about the pendant."

"Well, if you're sure," Cora replied unconvinced. "Feel free to have a look." She motioned with her hand in the direction of the various glass cases that filled the shop, including the one the pair of them were bent over, but even as she spoke, her eyes again drifted away from Lila, out the door, and into the street. Seafus Hobb had lit a cigar and stood smoking it in the morning sun.

Lila's eyes again, too, followed Cora's, and once more found themselves stuck alone on the balcony that hugged the second floor. Why was Cora ignoring her and staring into thin air? Had Lila done something to offend? Driven Cora to distraction with her questions, or irked her by not buying up the moon? Never mind, one last query and Lila would be on her way. She would demand to know if the pendant Raoul had purchased, with all its pretty rocks, had any powers of its own, and what exactly those powers might be.

She turned away from the balcony, hoping that Cora would do the same, and braced herself to say her piece. Cora, however, continued to ignore her, so Ms. Lila cleared her throat, and was about to insist, when she caught sight of the moon on its velvet bed. There seemed to be a face in it now that Lila hadn't noticed before. She cocked her head and tried to be sure, but the dents and contours moved as the sunlight and shadow played off of them. She tilted her head the other way, but each change of perspective only revealed another of the moon's *many* faces—all of which seemed to be gazing up at Cora, who was gazing out past the balcony.

Lila looked from the moon to Cora and back, sure there was a thread between the two that she was supposed to see and grab hold of. A silvery wisp of a notion that twisted and shimmered between the balcony's sunlight and the larimar moon. Lila's mind had almost caught a glimpse of it, almost sensed its tension, when she heard Nat coming up the stairs to collect her.

Trampling it, with each step, into a knotty and elusive web.

13

Tongue-lashings and secret outings were not the only indelicacies served up the day Ms. Lila spied on Cora, and Raoul called Bruce to task. The ones dished out at Customs and Excise were equally as rich.

The Office of Customs and Excise, of which Raoul was Head, was located in the heart of Port-St. Luke in a two-story building of cement, painted pale green and interrupted by pairs of tall white shutters. The actual Customs work, however, took place elsewhere. Headquarters merely collected and archived the forms and reports filled out and compiled at the airport or at one of the island's seaports.

If, for example, a shipment of two dozen Spin-O-Matics arrived by freighter at the commercial port on the outskirts of town, it would be unloaded, stored, inventoried, protocolled, and, in this particular case, split into two monstrous piles, one for Higgins Hardware, Home and Garden and the other for Ashbee's Appliances, Tackle and Tools, as per order of Raoul Orlean. To Howlander Higgins and Alexander Ashbee, then, notices would be dispatched—and copies forwarded to the Customs Head—summoning them to collect their property within thirty days or renounce their claims to it. "Collecting property" meant turning up with both pockets stuffed, one with rainbow banknotes for the official duty to be paid and the other with bills to pay off the dockhands, who if not properly compensated might regret to inform you that your washing machines had tumbled accidentally into the sea. Whether such blackmail was a function of the workers' dishonesty or of a State Budget perpetually in the red is a distinction better left to the likes of Bruce. Fact of the matter was that the dockmen were hungry, and someone had to pay for the dumplings and fish.

Which is why Raoul figured that the docks was a good place to start his search for the person who might have, for a fee, tipped off Bruce to the washing machine scheme. Systematically he questioned all the dockside employees, reminding them of their civic duty and of their pledged loyalty to his rank, but as his rank didn't butter their day-old loaves of bread, he found their recollections wanting. Quite likely—he convinced himself—Bruce hadn't bothered with the blue-collars after all, and had made an indoor appeal instead, white-collar to white-.

More at home among the clerical staff than amidst the brawn of the portsmen, Raoul meandered comfortably among the offices housed in a section of the Customs warehouse, as well as through the adjacent storerooms designated for the Island Post. Here, under the watchful Customs eye, letters were bagged and parcels sorted, by means of a system not unlike the one for the Spin-O-Matics. In office and storeroom alike, alas, despite Raoul's threats and accusations, the staffers denied having spoken with Bruce. Not a single one of them had even seen Bruce nosing about, which for Raoul only confirmed how sneaky the newspaperman could be when he put his mind to it.

Never mind. Raoul could be sneaky himself, if he tried, and he knew how to collect his clues, how to line up the variables in an equation that would add right up to Bruce. So as to first give the Customs Officers the impression that he had bought into their denials part and parcel, Raoul decided to kill some time in the postal storerooms. He would perform an impromptu inspection, while cooking up a sneakier means by which to resume his investigation.

Raoul didn't bother with the flat envelopes, since Customs usually had little to do with those. The small parcels were somewhat more intriguing. Far too little to be housed with the barrels and shipment containers, with the washing machines and motorcars, small parcels officially consisted of any package, box, carton, or lopsided envelope that could be lifted and carried by a man of average strength and stature for a distance of fifty meters with ease. Since most of the small parcels were very small indeed, they were sorted and stuffed into large wooden cubbyholes, each marked with the name of the locality to which collection notices had been sent. There was Easterville and Tempperdu, Chanterelle and Glutton Hill, Mt. Tulip, Thyme, and Port-St. Anne.

"What about the parcels for town?" Raoul asked. "Where are they?"

"Too many for the cubbies," curtly replied a man who didn't fancy the Head of Customs over his shoulder as he tried to sort and stamp. "Over there." With his head he motioned Raoul away from him.

Indeed, at the opposite end of the storeroom Raoul found the parcels waiting to be collected by the addressees of Port-St. Luke. They were piled onto three large wheelbarrows, divided alphabetically (A-J, K-Q, and R-Z). Raoul saw a young man in shirtsleeves and tie adding parcels to the three wheelbarrowed heaps and asked (more authoritatively, this time), "The status of these, Officer?"

"Inventoried and protocolled, sir."

"Inspected?"

"No, sir. We wait and open each parcel for inspection in front of the addressee."

"Of course you do," Raoul agreed. He appreciated the young man's exactness. "As you were, Officer. I'll just have a look around."

The young man, named Garvin Charles, nodded at him deferentially.

Raoul sniffed around the wheelbarrows, picking up packages at random. So many! What was everyone getting from all over anyway? Who needed anything more than what they could get right here on Oh? The sun to warm your head, the sea to cool your feet, more pineapples and swordfish than any heart (and belly) could hope for. For his part, Raoul tried never to set foot off the island. A short trip to next-door Killig or Esterina, maybe, but farther than that and you were asking for trouble. The one time Raoul took a distant trip—the *one* time—he had lost his most prized possession (his first wife, Emma Patrice). He hadn't taken a vacation since.

Shaking his head, Raoul walked away from the wheelbarrows to where Garvin was inventorying and protocolling the still-unprocessed parcels scattered on a long wooden table. Here, too, Raoul picked up packages at random. He spotted one from a place he couldn't even pronounce. Hmph, he snorted to himself, considering it a personal affront that his tiny island nation should have to endure such assaults as lopsided envelopes with peculiar postage stamps, cancelled in other than the Queen's own English. The cheek!

Raoul was about to put the parcel back where he found it, when the address (and addressee) caught his attention. Cora Silverfish, Pineapple Jewelry and Gems, Port-St. Luke, Oh (it said). Raoul snorted again. "Well, doesn't that just figure."

"Sorry, sir?" Garvin inquired. "Can I help?"

"No need. I'm going to conduct a random inspection of this parcel."

"We're not really supposed to do that, sir."

"I beg your pardon?" Raoul snapped.

"The parcels, sir, they're not supposed to be opened until the addressee is present. Otherwise they accuse us of stealing the contents."

"What did you say your name was?" Raoul asked, craning his neck to read the young man's badge.

"I didn't, sir. It's Charles. Garvin Charles. If I might say so, sir, it's an honor." With that Garvin's face broke into a twinkling, big-toothed smile, and his hand extended toward Raoul.

"Thank you, Mr. Charles. Likewise," Raoul replied, shaking the boy's hand. Suddenly the twinkling and punctilious young officer reminded Raoul of himself thirty years before, stamping passports at the airport with the same gravitas that characterized Garvin's safeguarding of his small parcels. "You are no doubt aware, however, that should any parcel be deemed suspect, the Office of Customs and Excise has every right to inspect it even in the absence of the presence of the addressee."

"You deem this parcel suspect? May I ask why, sir?"

"No, Mr. Charles, you may not, but your efforts to comply with Customs procedures and regulations are duly noted. Now hand me that knife."

Raoul cut open the lumpy, padded envelope. He had little genuine reason to suspect that he would find anything of interest inside, but couldn't let Officer Charles see him shirk from his original intent. With effort he wrenched his hand inside the stuffing and pulled out a wrapped rectangular object that, unwrapped, proved to be a glass and wood frame—a glass and wood frame with a big insect inside it.

"It's a dead butterfly," Garvin announced disappointedly. He didn't know what he was expecting, but certainly something more salacious than that.

"It's not a 'dead butterfly,'" Raoul slowly corrected him. "It's a Black Diamond." In an astonished whisper, he added, "A perfectly-preserved Black Diamond." It couldn't be!

"What's a Black Diamond?" Garvin asked.

Now not every Head of Customs of every tiny island nation floating in the seas could answer such a question, but Raoul Orlean could and did. A Black Diamond was a very rare butterfly spotted less than a handful of times in a handful of decades, and indigenous only to Micronesia. (Well, that explained the provenance Raoul couldn't pronounce.) It was black as darkest night and speckled with crystalline flecks that resembled tiny diamonds (or the stars, some said). So rare was the Black Diamond butterfly that many said it didn't exist. That Raoul should even know of it was due to the simple fact that he devoted every Tuesday, his day off, to the newest acquisitions of the Pritchard T. Lullo Public Library and that, not two months before, Ms. Lila had proudly presented him *The Wingèd Wonders of the World*, amongst which the Black Diamond sat prominently (though not in photo, but in artist's rendition).

"How on earth did she get her hands on such a specimen?" Raoul wondered aloud. "And why?"

"Shall I seal it back up, sir?" Garvin offered, unappreciative of the dead butterfly's worth despite Raoul's description.

"No. Thank you. I'll deliver this to Ms. Silverfish and see to the duty myself."

"Ms. Silverfish doesn't pay duty, sir," Garvin stated. "She benefits from concessions."

"What are you talking about? What concessions?"

"For A Branch of Business Not Yet Established on Oh."

"What the hell does that mean?" Raoul hollered. "She's been in business thirty years!"

"Yes, but when she opened up her shop, there were no jewelry stores on the island. At the time, one of the government incentives to open A Branch of Business Not Yet Established on Oh was customs concessions *ad vitam.*"

"Ad vitam?"

"It means 'forever.'"

"I know what it means! How many other businesses still benefit from these concessions?"

"A few, I suppose, but they don't really import much. Cora's is the only one I ever see. She gets parcels all the time. They go straight to Dwight. I gave him one for her this morning already."

"Who's Dwight?" Raoul demanded.

"Customs Officer Dwight Williams. He sits right over there, but he had to leave for a while."

"Why do all of Cora's parcels go to this Dwight Williams?"

"Couldn't say," Garvin shrugged. "Been that way since I started two years ago. I figured because Cora must import valuable things, you know, stones, gold. I guess they trust Dwight."

Raoul went to Dwight's desk to examine the other parcel Cora had received that day, but it was nowhere to be found. Not on top of the desk, not underneath it, not in any of the drawers.

"Where is the other parcel for Cora?" Raoul asked Garvin. "She collected it already?"

"Nah. Maybe Dwight locked it somewhere safe."

"Where did you say he went?"

"I didn't," Garvin answered. "Dwight just left. He didn't say where to."

Raoul was appalled. He couldn't decide what was worse: customs officers leaving their posts or decades old concessions on precious gemstones and priceless butterflies. For good measure, he was appalled, too, that Cora was dealing in Black Diamonds in the first place! With her parcel in hand, he gave Garvin a nod and left, forgetting all about Bruce and the loose-lipped dockhands.

Raoul was known to get flies, fixations that flitted inside his head for days or weeks at a time, but never before had a butterfly rattled his brain. What was Cora Silverfish doing with a butterfly at all, let alone one of such tremendous value? It wasn't lost on Raoul that Cora dabbled in diamonds (of the non-wingèd sort) for a living. Did she cook them up with butterflies and magic?

With the palm of his hand, Raoul gave his head a good swat. He didn't believe in magic! Magic didn't exist. Damn butterfly was making him dizzy!

Raoul could think of only one way to rid himself of the butterfly in his brain, and that was to confront Cora Silverfish with the one tucked under his arm. He sighed. Three visits to Pineapple Jewelry and Gems in three days. What was his world coming to?

He shook his head in self-pity and headed back into town. Raoul decided he would never forget Ms. Lila's birthday again. Ever.

———

Headed away from town at the very same time that Raoul made his way to Cora, was none other than Officer Dwight Williams, who, had he not ducked into a rum shop for a celebratory swig of under-the-counter (moonshine whose magic put Cora's moon-shaped brooch to shame), would have caught Raoul's eye for certain. Uniformed Customs officers didn't, as a rule, go walkabout mid-morning. But Officer Dwight's pocket was newly lined (and lightened one small parcel), and a tipple was in order. Just as well. He knew nothing of butterflies, living or dead, and wouldn't have told Raoul if he did.

He would, however, have delayed Raoul's arrival in town, delayed it long enough that Ms. Lila, upon reaching the street at the bottom of the jewelry-store stairs, wouldn't have mistaken her husband (who reluctantly lingered thereabout) for the distraction that had drawn Cora's eyes past the balcony again and again (the real distraction, in the meantime, having snuffed out his cigar and with a wave of his parcel bidden Cora farewell).

Long enough, too, that Raoul wouldn't have caught sight of his wife with Nat. Wouldn't have watched him carry her tenderly down the steps and situate her inside his minivan taxi, tuck her skirt inside the door. Wouldn't have discovered that the two had been joining fortunes behind his back, in the den of an island witch. Or have put together the variables that added up to what they added up to, and left him nearly unable to breathe. Raoul wouldn't have realized, re-doing his maths, what in that moment was maybe the worst affront of all: that the public library must have stayed shuttered up, if Ms. Lila was out and about.

As Raoul stood across the street from Cora's store, not having been delayed by walkabout Officer Williams, and having seen what he saw and discovered what he did, the only thing he could think of was his very favorite book. *All* his favorite books, in fact, which were part of his heart and his soul. If Ms. Lila began making magic, Raoul worried, what would happen to them then? Without the librarian's touch and her loving care, how ever would his hardbacks get on?

Surely the World's Wingèd Wonders could never survive, day after day in the dark. With no light, and no love. With no air.

14

When the islanders didn't know what to do, they did nothing. Sooner or later, if they were patient, the next step became clear. The rain washed it clean, the sun dried it. If it was night-time, the moon lit it up. Raoul Orlean was the exception. When *he* didn't know what to do, he didn't stand around and wait for the wind to whisper the solution in his ear. Rather, Raoul did one of two things: he went to the Belly for a beer with his mates or he pulled out his magnifying glass (metaphorical sometimes, some-times not) and looked around (and underfoot) for clues. Because if one looked long enough and hard enough on Oh, sooner or later he (or she) would stumble onto, or into, something.

On the mid-morning that Raoul spied his Lila with Nat, a beer at the Belly didn't sound as soothing as usual. For one thing, Cougar's hospitality was doubtful before noon; for another, the mates Raoul usually drank with were Cougar, Bang, and Nat him-self. No, this time not beer but clues it would have to be, to soothe the shock of what he'd witnessed. Not even clues about Nat and Ms. Lila, not exactly. Raoul was still too confused for that. He was at Cora's on official business and official business it would be. He pulled back his shoulders, smoothed his shirt, and headed up her stairs, the dead Black Diamond in the palm of his hand.

From inside the shop, Cora watched him collect himself, parcel in hand, and convince himself to come up. She couldn't help but wonder why men with small packages were dawdling outside her building on that otherwise perfectly ordinary island day, though between Seafus and Raoul, the latter was far less of a bother. At least he bought something once in a blue moon.

"Mr. Orlean, is that you?" she called out, when she finally heard his steps on the landing.

Raoul peered inside, his bravado a bit blunted by the flat surprise attack.

"It's *Officer* Orlean today, and how did you know it was me?" (Raoul had been conducting his surveillance of her shop camouflaged amidst the branches and the plumage of a frangipani. Surely she hadn't spotted him from so far away.)

"Just a hunch," she smiled at him. (Or was she making fun?) "Is this an official call, then?"

"Yes, as a matter of fact."

"Because I thought that maybe," Cora continued, as if Raoul hadn't said a word, "you were here to pick up something else for your wife. She quite admired this brooch shaped like the moon just now."

"She was here?" Raoul tried to ask offhandedly.

"She only left a few minutes ago. Odd that you didn't cross paths."

"She came to look at...at *that*?" Raoul asked, pointing at the moon.

"To tell the truth, I think she came to ask me if my pendant made her fall. But she saw that and got distracted."

"Did it?" (Make her fall, he meant, the pendant.)

90

"It is a strong piece." (The moon, she meant.) "Here. Look at it. It should give you new perspective." She handed him the moon and Raoul was too stunned to refuse it. Was he really discussing magic with Cora Silverfish, when his wife had just...well, just done whatever it was she had done, and the world's rarest butterfly warmed in his sweaty palm? Because that was already more perspective than he could manage. He didn't need some jewelry moon looking down its nose at him and making him feel a fool, which is exactly what the larimar moon was doing. Raoul set it down, anxious to be rid of it.

"It's not finished, as you can see," Cora said, "but I told your wife I could have it ready for her by the end of the day, if she'd only come back."

Raoul had stopped listening to her. Shaking off the moon's stares, he heard only the gentle batting of butterfly wings inside his head. Before he could lose his focus again he blurted out, "I came about this," and put the parcel on Cora's counter.

"Aren't you too high-rank to be delivering parcels?" she asked, making fun for certain.

"Open it."

In fact, it already was open, as all of Cora's parcels always were when she got her hands on them. She pulled out the butterfly and waited for Raoul to explain his official business.

"Well?" he prompted, waiting for an explanation of his own.

"It's a butterfly. A very pretty one, too," was all she said. "Is it illegal to import them?"

"Generally speaking, no. But it *is* illegal to sneak in priceless Items Unrelated To Your Business using concessions for A Branch of Business Not Yet Established on Oh. The last time I checked, you did not sell butterflies, Ms. Silverfish."

"That's not entirely true," Cora replied. She walked across the shop, opened up a tall glass curio with a key she pulled from her pocket and gently removed a gold bracelet. Dangling from it were half a dozen golden butterflies with enameled wings. "What do you call these, Officer Orlean?" She shook the bracelet at him with her outstretched arm.

"Those aren't real!" he objected.

"Don't they look real? Where do you think I get my inspiration?"

Raoul wasn't buying it. She was up to something, he could smell it.

"If that's the case," he said sarcastically, "then we're all lucky you didn't import the moon as well, aren't we? I'm sure you could afford it, if you can afford a butterfly so rare it barely exists."

"I must admit that the moon is a favorite muse of mine," she chuckled. "But as to the butterfly, it just so happens that this one is a gift," she explained. "From a business associate. I have no idea of its cost or how it was paid for, and I wouldn't dream of asking." (Though of course she did, and would.)

"You import a lot of 'gifts,' do you?"

"This is the first," she beamed. "Not a bad start, eh?"

Cora had in the meantime walked back to the main counter, where the moon-shaped brooch lay staring up at Raoul. He couldn't quite think straight while it watched him, though he wouldn't have gone so far as to call it "strong" the way Cora did. He was entitled to some befuddlement, after what he'd been through that morning, but he wouldn't let Cora Silverfish see it. A couple more questions for the sake of appearances, and then maybe he would check Cougar for that beer after all.

"Just a couple more questions," he told her, trying to sound as official as he could. He wished he had thought to bring his notepad. Nothing looked more official than when he took notes on his pad. "How often do you receive parcels?" he pressed on.

"I couldn't say. Couple a week maybe."

"You collect them at Customs, at the main port?"

"If they aren't delivered."

"Delivered? By whom?"

"By Dwight Williams for as long as I can remember. I suppose they don't like to keep the valuable items laying around the offices."

"Yes, I suppose that's why," Raoul agreed.

With that he pronounced hasty thanks and a perfunctory goodbye and hightailed it out of Cora's shop. He felt as though he might faint before he could get himself away, the collar of his shirt squeezing his neck tighter and tighter, the pale bluish moon making him feel confused and foolish.

Once outside, he slumped against the frangipani tree and tried to clear his head. He shook it (his head) from side to side to erase the image of the brooch peering up at him from Cora's counter. He took deep breaths. Slowly, the image faded and he regained his senses.

First things first. There were some Customs procedures that needed looking into. Valuable items or not, this Dwight Williams shouldn't be taking such liberties, leaving his desk in the middle of the day and making personal deliveries. Then there was Cora. Her items needed scrutinized more carefully. Concessions only counted for business imports not for wingèd wonders.

From the door of her balcony, Cora watched Raoul leaning and shaking and breathing, and making sense from nonsense. She tried to recall his image a few minutes earlier, clutching the small parcel with the butterfly under his arm, and the image of Seafus

Hobb before that, clutching a parcel of his own. Was it one and the same? Had Raoul somehow gotten hold of it? What did he know? She looked down at the butterfly in her hands and shook her head in disgust.

Seafus twice in two days and Raoul three times in three. Was there a connection she hadn't seen before? Because if so, Cora Silverfish was going to have to choose a side. Raoul was a bit of a bumbler; everyone on Oh knew that. Usually, though, he got the job done, more or less—everyone knew that, too—and he was trustworthy and fair. Maybe too much so, she thought. He might be too soft.

Still. If her larimar moon had failed to entice *one* Orlean, perhaps it might entice the other.

Cora smiled at the butterfly that twinkled as if it had diamonds in its wings and decided she had perhaps been given two gifts that day, not one.

"Not a bad start, indeed," she said aloud, and, cackling happily, went back to work.

———

Outside, as Raoul collected his thoughts, one last one fell in line. It suddenly seemed to him that he had heard Cora say she was finishing the moon brooch for Lila. Could that be? His Lila had never bothered with such baubles before. Then again, she didn't lie to him or buy into magic. Or did she? Raoul felt as though since breakfast he had lost her and found someone else in her place. She wasn't normally a vain woman, Ms. Lila. If she wanted that brooch it could only be because she knew of the effect it would have on him. She would pin it to her collar and it would watch him all the time, belittling him. No! he stomped. There were some things a man couldn't stand for in his very own home. Just let her try and turn up with it! As for Cora Silverfish, well, she had better watch her step, too.

"Selling butterflies, my foot!" he shouted in the direction of her store.

"Raoul! Hey, man, what are you going on about in the middle of the street? Can I give you a lift?" It was Nat, in his champagne van, acting as if Raoul should have no reason to refuse him. "Hop in."

Face to face with Nat, Raoul couldn't muster the fisticuffs he'd pictured in his head at some point that morning. All he could do was decline Nat's offer, and fairly politely at that. "No thanks," he told him, and set off on foot—a walking fool is better than a sitting fool, the islanders say—grumbling under his breath about butterflies and magic and the library and beer. And cursing the man in the moon.

15

Cougar Zanne, proprietor of the Buddha's Belly Bar and Lounge, liked a good lime (the kind that meant "to party," not the kind for making juice). He organized three big limes each year in fact. There was the Annual Marimba Festival (won yearly by Bang), the party for Old Year's night (to welcome in the New), and the Pineapple Lime, which capped off the Annual Harvest Football Tournament (more commonly known as the Pineapple Cup). Pineapples were harvested in every month on Oh (the persistent plants never stopped bearing fruit), but July was more bountiful than most, and so to give thanks for the juicy fruits—and to get them off their hands—the islanders had devised the tournament. At the thrice weekly (or so) football matches, they set up stands and sold ice cream, cakes, juice, and fritters, naturally all pineapple-based. Then when the tournament was done, Cougar, who himself had bought up a good portion of the pineapples harvested (and plenty of rum), served at the Lime rum-and-pineapple punch, piña coladas, and pineapple wine fermented precisely twenty-one days.

The month-long tournament welcomed a dozen teams from all over the island, and if the Pineapple Lime was its crowning glory, the March Past got things started in style. One by one, the uniformed teams were introduced, each marching in step around the perimeter of the pasture that served as playing field in Port-St. Luke, then taking position center-field to march some more (in place and in formation), until every team was lined up and present. Finally, all the players stomped their feet in unison, in an impressive display of rhythm, resolve, and muscle.

Higgins Hardware, Home and Garden sponsored a team, as did Ashbee's Appliances, Tackle and Tools. Garrison's Auto Mart always entered the competition, and the Police, the Island Post, the Savings Bank, and Seafus Hobb's Parliamentary Museum all had teams, too. This year, Customs and Excise was getting in on the affair, along with some other newcomers: Trevor's Bakery, Belmont Stationery, and Campbell's Drug & Sundry from town, and Piper's All-Stars from Tempperdu (a rag-tag crew of unemployed young men, sponsored and uniformed by their local parliamentarian, Gerald Piper).

Before fixtures were even fixed or matches played and scored, rivalries thrived among the different teams, some historical, some newly-minted: the Police were the defending champs and so hated by all the teams, Garrison's Auto Mart more than any, since Garrison's gave up the title to the police the year before; Higgins Hardware and Ashbee's Appliances were, thanks to Bruce, both hotter than usual; Belmont and Campbell's were at odds, as the goalkeeper of the one team had stolen the girl of the goalkeeper of the other; Piper hoped his All-Stars would win, to make a parliamentary point; Trevor would be happy as long as his team wasn't the first knocked out; and Customs and Excise just hoped to make a decent showing. The Museum team was notoriously mean, and Seafus was determined this year—come what may—to take the trophy home. The trophy, a two-foot-tall variation on the pineapple theme, owed its design and production each year to none other than Cora Silverfish; its unveiling inspired as much anticipation as the tournament's final match-up.

On the day of the March Past, the whole island was in attendance, everyone connected in some way or other to a team, a player, or a peddler of pineapple snacks. Raoul, Ms. Lila, and Cougar, Bang, and Nat were all there together, and not as awkwardly as you might expect. In the week since the fateful day after the day after Lila's birthday, Raoul's head had cooled. Still not knowing exactly what to do, however, he employed his two usual methods: by day he kept quiet and searched for clues, and by night he drank beer at the Belly. Ms. Lila, who was broken-hearted and frightened for her life, likewise didn't know what to think or to do, and so in true island fashion she did nothing—except to spend as much time as she could in the safety of the library, which went far in convincing Raoul that all hope was not lost. He even let Nat continue to drive her to work, since he couldn't bring himself to speak aloud a reason why he shouldn't. Nat, for his part, was a very cool customer, drinking and joshing with Raoul at the bar, acting as if nothing unusual had taken place. An easy stance to assume, since on that fateful day in question, Nat's arms were too full of Ms. Lila to have noticed either Raoul catching sight of his wife, or vice versa. As far as Nat was concerned, his conscience was clear, since Lila had left Cora's shop without spending a dime.

In short, and considering their pickle, they all did a bang-up job of pretending to get along—until Bang up and stirred the brine.

The five of them, Raoul, his wife, and his three best mates, upon reaching the playing field, had commandeered a front-row piece of bleacher, so Ms. Lila could rest her foot while they watched the March Past more or less together. More or less, because when the team from Trevor's Bakery was called to march, Bang (who had agreed to do Trevor a favor and play) had to go take his place in line. Nat, meanwhile, was back and forth, shuttling business-doing ladies with coolers of cold juice. Cougar, every time the Minister of Sports and Culture mentioned the upcoming Pineapple Lime, jumped from his seat and strolled the length of the field, waving and playing to the crowd. At last, though, the March Past was done, their group reconstituted, and cold Oh's Gold beer passed around. Even Ms. Lila indulged, on so hot and so festive a day.

Decked out in his blue and green bakery uniform, Bang was feeling even more festive than the others. "So," he said, relishing the icy drink in his hand, "who do you fancy will take the pineapple this year? Raoul, you think your Customs guys can do it? You ought to be playing on the team yourself, you know."

"Ahh!" Raoul complained. "I'm too old for that."

"Coaching, then," Bang said. "Anyway, you're practically the same age as me! Trevor thinks we over-40s can win, but I doubt it."

"I'll say," Cougar agreed, with a hearty laugh, "since most of you are over-50s at the least." Which made the rest of them laugh heartily, too.

"Okay, okay." Bang took his ribbing good-naturedly. "You'll cheer for me, won't you, Lila?" he asked her, batting his eyelashes in a plea for her favor.

"In the state I'm in, I suppose I'll cheer for whoever gets me to the match and finds me a seat where I won't be trod on," Ms. Lila replied.

"My dear Lila," Nat said, "I will happily drive you anywhere you want to go. You can count on me."

Raoul raised an eyebrow.

"Just don't wear that bad-luck birthday necklace to any of my matches," Bang said.

Raoul raised his other eyebrow. "What are you talking about?" he barked at Bang. "That's a perfectly fine piece of jewelry."

"You don't have to tell me," Bang smirked. "I read all about it in the paper."

"The paper said my pendant made me fall?" Lila asked, excitedly.

"He's talking about the washing machine story," Nat answered her. "Bang likes to put two and two together. You fell, you were wearing the pendant from Cora, so that means the pendant made you fall."

"It's not me alone who says so," Bang corrected. "Raoul, you can't go around your whole life trash-talking magic and then expect Cora to sell you a piece of jewelry that won't kill you." Bang shook his head, amused.

"Leave him be," Nat told Bang.

"You stay out of this," Raoul snapped at Nat. "I don't need the likes of you defending me."

"Likes of *me*? What do you mean by *that*?"

"Raoul, apologize to Nat," Mrs. Lila ordered. "That wasn't nice."

"Well, I'd expect you'd take his side, wouldn't you?" Raoul snorted. He gulped down his Oh's Gold and got up. "I think I'll walk home," he said.

"Raoul, wait! Come back!" Cougar shouted. "They were only kicksing."

But Raoul just waved his hand at them, without even turning around, and left the pasture.

"Well, that's odd, even for Raoul," Cougar said. "He's been acting funny all week. Lila, you have any idea why? Is he still vexed at Bruce? He have some new case or something?"

"I don't think it's Bruce," she said sadly. "He's been funny at home, too. I think it's that woman."

The way she said it—"that woman"—made Cougar, Bang, and Nat sneak a knowing glance. Raoul was always odd where island magic was concerned, and Cora was about as much magic as you could ask for. They gave each other a shrug, as if to say, "Ah, well, is that all? This too shall pass, as Raoul's flies eventually do."

"I wouldn't worry, Lila," Nat told her, patting her on the shoulder. "Raoul will be fine."

"Sure!" Bang added, taking her hand. "But to be safe, don't wear that necklace."

"Bang!" Cougar and Nat shouted in unison.

"What?!"

"Ignore him, Lila. Let Nat take you home," Cougar suggested. "Let's help her up."

Together they got her up and onto her crutches, and kicked aside the empty beer bottles that had gathered on the ground at their feet.

"Don't worry yourself too much," Bang and Cougar both called after her, while Nat escorted her away. Nat could see in her face that she *was* worried, though, and afraid. She was afraid there was more to Raoul's mood this time than his usual fuming about magic, and afraid that her husband would *not* be fine, and afraid that she had every reason to worry herself silly, despite what anybody said.

Yes, Ms. Lila was undeniably worried and afraid. Nat could see it, and—funny, that—now, so it seemed, was he.

———

Also present at the March Past that day were Cora Silverfish and Seafus Hobb, Cora drumming up business and talking about the trophy to come, and Seafus with his team. The two were hardly there together—they kept a football field between them most of the time—yet each considered the other's presence most awkward, for both were as worried and afraid as Nat or Lila. The Curator's worries ran the gamut from the fate of his team (his strikers were unruly, his goalkeeper full of conceit) and his museum (his reputation was at stake, and that of Oh!) to Cora's closing her shop (how to stop her?) and one pricey Black Diamond gone AWOL (where could it be?). Cora, on the other hand, feared just one thing: that for all of his looking and for all of his clues, Raoul might not put two and two together in time to save Pineapple Jewelry and Gems.

Like two bothered bees, Cora Silverfish and Seafus Hobb hovered, one at each end of the playing field, hot and bothered but reluctant, just yet, to sting, their angry buzzing lost, for the moment, to the players' stomping chorus and the pomp of the pineappled day.

16

Secrets were a funny thing on Oh. Sometimes you nearly tripped over them as you walked into town, and other times they were buried more deeply than the roots of a mango. Between these two extremes, the tripping and the mango roots, were categories of concealment ranging from clever to comical to cruel. The very worst kind of secret was the kind that wasn't a secret at all, the kind that everyone whispered about, pretended not to know, seemingly to spare another's suffering but in practice merely prolonging it. When the sufferer knew the secret as well, but believed it to be his own, the discovery that his pains had been whispered of all along was completely and utterly devastating. Enough to drive him from his whispering friends in a huff and a hurry, before he vomited his Oh's Gold beer into a bush.

Now, Raoul was not in fact one of those horned husbands who discovered that his friends knew his painful secret, but at the March Past that day he had convinced himself that he was. The way Nat played chivalrous with Lila, Bang's jokes about the birthday pendant, and Cougar condoning their carrying on. To Raoul, the discovery was crystal clear: Nat and Ms. Lila were sleeping together, and Bang and Cougar were in on the affair. Who else on the island, he wondered, was whispering about him behind his back? Pitying him, or laughing at him? Taking him for a fool?

If these were the flies that crossed and double-crossed Raoul's brain as he knelt sick and choking over a crocus not far from the pasture, his fuzzy judgment was to be pardoned, as was his paranoia. You see, a week had gone by since he had spotted Ms. Lila and Nat, and for all his beers at the Belly and all his searching for clues, he had yet to turn up any proof of what they were up to. He had baited Nat at the bar, tried to get him drunk and bragging of his conquest, had even hired a taxi to follow Nat's own about town. All to no avail. At home, Raoul paid close attention to Ms. Lila, to her words and her manners, and although she was certainly nervous and definitely not quite herself, she offered Raoul no more proof of her straying than Nat did of his. The only distinct clue he could put his finger on was her reluctance to wear her birthday pendant, which Raoul suspected was to keep her lover's jealousy at bay—hurtful, yes, but hardly evidence enough to confront them.

Any other horned husband on Oh might have, at this point, asked himself how horned he really was. He might have asked his wife for an explanation of the clandestine visit to Cora's or engaged her in a shouty row until the whole truth (or lack of it) had come out. But Raoul Orlean was like no other island husband, horned or otherwise.

Years before at the Public Library, Raoul had happened upon one Mr. Stan Kalpi, and in times of trouble, he liked to ask himself what Mr. Stan would do. Stan Kalpi wasn't a library patron, or an islander known for his wisdom; he was the protagonist of what had become Raoul's favorite book. The book's jacket was white, with a black silhouette of Mr. Stan, and had, from the very first, appealed to Raoul's black-and-white, truths-as-plain-as-noses-on-faces propensities. Like Raoul, Mr. Stan, too, was a man of truths, mathematical truths, and to arrive at them, he collected, lined up, and added his variables—variables he plucked off the breeze, if need be, or wedged out of the mud with naked toes. (Raoul over the years had found variables on the beach, at the library, even painted on the side of his house.)

If Stan Kalpi suspected *his* wife were cheating on him, he would sniff at the wind and listen to the leaves, leave literally no stone unturned in his search to solve the equation—which is why Raoul smelled suspicion on Nat's beer-y breath and heard guilt in Bang's and Cougar's quips. Still, Raoul reasoned, as his head began to clear and he stood himself up and straightened his shirt: sounds and smells, while progress, were not enough to tell the whole mathematical Stan Kalpi truth.

He started his walk home via a wooded shortcut, head a-buzz and trying to figure out what next he should do. The afternoon was winding down and though the sun had yet to set, the moon was already a chunky white wisp in the blue island sky overhead. With the moon looking on, Raoul kicked a stone all the way to his pink cottage door, mulling his missing variables on the way. If Nat + Lila wasn't yielding the proof he needed, then there was another x he needed to define. But what? Where? Raoul sat down in his favorite chair on the veranda, leaned back his head, and closed his eyes. The gardenias' lusty perfume filled his nose, while the happy shriek of the treefrogs filled the night air. He sighed and let his troubled heart lighten, if just for a minute. In the palm of his hand he bounced the rock he'd kicked home, feeling the stone's coolness, admiring the way it was sharp and flat at the same time. How it managed to be so, he must have dozed off wondering.

"Ahh!" he spat, when he finally jolted awake, remembering the March Past and his pain. He jumped up from his chair and flung the stone into the grass, fished in his pocket for the front-door key. Lila would be reaching home before long and Raoul still had to decide what to say to her when she did. He wriggled the key into the lock, slowed by the darkening dusk, as a glint on the ground caught his eye. He turned and saw twinkling at him the stone he had just discarded. He squinted and from afar studied it, the vertex in a perfect angle formed by himself and the moon. Surely it wasn't the dull rock he'd kicked home that now shined in the moonlight like some kind of precious gem? He blinked and leaned and squinted some more, adjusted his perspective until the shiny gem turned back into the simple stone he thought.

"That's better," he grumbled. He could see it clearly now. Just a stone, it was. A stone + starlight was all it had been. Or maybe a stone + the silver moon. Little difference, Raoul shrugged.

He twisted the key with a click and pushed in the squeaky door, then took one last look outside, just to make sure. His eyes revisited the angle he had noticed before, darted from simple stone to silver moon to simple stone, to the tips of the shoes on his feet.

Then the dull rock winked and glittered again, once more a gem in the grass. So Raoul's eyes set off again, too.

Gemstone, silver moon, gemstone, silver moon, they went, and stopped at the pocket from which he had earlier fished his key. And there it was. His x.

He could see it very clearly.

Gemstone. Silver. Fish.

By the time Ms. Lila got home, Raoul had showered off the March Past and was feeling cool and almost chipper. He had figured out what his next step would be and despite the deception he was aiming to prove, the fact that he knew what to do in the morning went a long way in soothing his mood. He sat sipping bush tea and listening to a soca tune on the radio, tapping his fingers in time on the table's edge.

When he heard his wife struggling across the threshold with her crutches, he jumped up to help her. "Good night, dear," he welcomed her, and stood near enough that she could lean on him if she chose.

She didn't.

"Good night?!" she snapped. "You're in a fine mood after that display at the playing field! What came over you, talking to your best friends so rudely?"

"Sorry for that," he said. "Sorry." And he *was* sorry, but not for the reasons that Ms. Lila imagined. He was sorry he had tipped his hand, sorry he had let Nat and the others see how upset he was when he should have been keeping his cool.

"Honestly, Raoul, what is the matter with you? You haven't been yourself lately at all."

"Haven't I?" he asked. "Are you sure you aren't the one who isn't herself?"

"Of course I'm not myself!" she hollered. "You try dragging these things around all day and see how you like it. I can hardly shelve a book at the library, balanced on one foot and clutching a crutch for dear life."

For the tiniest of moments, Raoul wondered if she wasn't telling the truth. Was it possible that he had found no clues because no clues were to be found? Was Lila acting funny lately merely because of her foot? Perfectly natural doubts, these, ones any ordinary man would entertain. But Raoul was not your ordinary island man who believed the trees made magic and the raindrops had their say. Besides which, hadn't Lila been visiting Cora for no good reason, and doing so wrapped in Nat's arms?

An ordinary island man might have posed this question to his wife directly. If Raoul didn't, it wasn't because he wasn't ordinary (though of course he wasn't). It was because Ms. Lila was his world and because, despite all his posturing and his variables and his clues, he didn't dare mention the secret between them. For once it was spoken, once it hovered in the air, it would belong to the island wind. Which would bend it, and puff it up, blow it about. But not truly relinquish it, ever. Not even to Mr. Stan Kalpi himself.

17

It's a pity Raoul didn't stay longer at the pasture, for the shiny moon was busy there too, shedding light on more than rocks and pockets.

While Raoul and Ms. Lila retired to bed, and Bang, Cougar, and Nat retired to the Belly, the post-March Past festivities wound down, each bare-chested team re-closing its ranks, recognizable now only by the rumpled jerseys that hung around the players' necks or from the waistbands of their short pants. As transport home was negotiated (there were island buses, taxis real and make-shift, and a handful of marchers with cars of their own) and home-turf party plans arranged (the night was still young, the island's rum shops just hitting their strides), the pineapple peddlers packed up and shoved off, and Cora, who had waited for the sun's departure before making her own, set off to see a man about a butterfly.

Seafus Hobb had had his eye on Cora for the better part of the day, but a conversation with her was more than he had hoped for. When he sent his Museum team home in the two vans he had purchased for football team purposes, and took one more look in her direction before heading toward his own oversized black jeep and a night at the seedy port bar, he couldn't have been more pleased to see Cora coming his way. Had she come to her senses all on her own? Good girl, he thought.

"Good night," he greeted her cheerfully.

"Good night," Cora answered him, with equal cheer (which Seafus found just a hint disconcerting).

"You thought about what I said?" he asked her.

"What was that?" she asked him.

"About closing your shop—or *not* closing it, that is. About how wise it would be."

"Oh, that. No, I haven't thought much about that," Cora lied. "I came to tell you about a Customs delivery I received a few days ago."

Seafus's eyebrows arched. "Oh? Dwight was by?"

"No, nothing like that," she told him smugly. "This one was delivered by the Head of Customs himself."

"Oh?"

"You sound surprised. Seems it was quite valuable and, as it didn't exactly fall under the category of articles for jewelry concessions, Head Officer Orlean felt inclined to investigate."

"What did you tell him?" Conscious of the few stragglers still lingering in the playing field, Seafus Hobb plastered a smile on his face, but his voice betrayed his plaster cheer.

"I said it was a gift," Cora explained.

"He believed you?"

"No, I don't suppose he did. I wouldn't be surprised if he dug a bit deeper into the matter." Cora seemed to be enjoying herself.

"Careful, Cora," the Curator warned. "The clues he finds might point in all the wrong directions."

"I know," she answered him. "I've known it for years and that's long enough. Everything has its time, you know, Seafus." She waited for him to say something, but he didn't, so she began to walk away. "Good night, Curator," she called to him over her shoulder.

"Wait!" he called out, displaying more excitement than he'd have preferred and hurrying to her side. "You never told me what it was that Officer Orlean delivered to you."

"Didn't I?" Cora smiled. "It was nothing. A butterfly of some sort."

"Give it back to me, you witch!" he hissed in her ear as he grabbed hold of her arm. "It's worth a fortune."

"I'm afraid I can't do that. I told Raoul Orlean that it was a model for one of my pieces. How would it look if he stopped back in and it was gone? He's a regular customer, you know. You must have seen it in the paper. His wife, too."

"Don't you—" Seafus began, but Cora cut him off.

"You should keep better hold of your parcels next time."

Seafus looked at her strangely and loosened his grip on her arm. "I don't know what scheme you're cooking up with Raoul Orlean," he whispered, "but I've told you before that if you get in my way, I'll send you straight to Paradise!"

"I doubt you could find the way," Cora snapped back at him.

The Curator chuckled and backed away.

"Good night, Ms. Silverfish," he simply replied, with a new and eerie calm about him. Then he strolled off, whistling into the dark.

When Seafus Hobb threatened to send Cora Silverfish to Paradise, he didn't mean a cushy cloud on St. Peter's right hand side, not exactly. He meant Paradise Cemetery, Oh's most lush and flowery—which of course amounted to the very same thing. The islanders didn't like to mention death by name, not in surroundings so ripe and so alive, and certainly not when life was the only richness many of them possessed. A dying islander was said to be "on his way to Paradise," the earthly one, the celestial a matter between himself (or herself) and God. So Seafus's was a (repeated) threat of murder, pure and simple.

Though over the years Cora had watched Seafus wane, from haughty youth into desperate middle age, she knew what he had once been capable of and didn't doubt that the bitterness in his heart had waxed and bloated even as his chest had shriveled and caved. She knew, too, that everything really did have its time, and that it was time for her to stop protecting Seafus Hobb. Hadn't the island itself given her any number of signs? The last islander she would ever have dreamed to cross her threshold, Raoul Orlean, had turned up not once but three times. He had even made a purchase, one to ward off evil, no less, whether he believed in it or not. In the space of a week—not even—hadn't Raoul, of all the parcels that had made it past Customs over the years, gotten his hands on one of Seafus's? And what a one it was! A priceless butterfly that sparkled like diamonds.

Wasn't the island telling her to—finally!—make her move? Cora thought so but she wasn't completely sure. Exactly what move was it that she was supposed to make? She had already confronted Seafus. All that was left was to talk to Raoul. Was she supposed to seek him out? Convince him to investigate the Curator? She couldn't exactly stroll into Raoul's office at Customs and Excise as if she were paying him a friendly call; he would likely not believe a word she told him. No, Cora had to act more cautiously, so that Raoul didn't realize what she was dragging him into.

She paced around the pasture for a while, nearly alone in the darkening night, bathed in the light of the silver moon and the crystalline stars. She wondered if the island might help her further, send her yet another sign, when she heard squeals from the few pineapple revelers who still hadn't gone home or to party somewhere else. They were pointing to the sky behind her. She turned to see what they were fussing about and there, opposite the moon, was the longest, brightest moonbow she had ever seen. Not that she had seen many, for moonbows were rare even on Oh. Cora turned her palms to the sky to feel for the drizzle she hadn't noticed before, but there was none. Odd that, a moonbow with no rain.

Cora studied the prism splashed across the sky before her. She could pick out the ruby red, the orangy amber, and a yellow as fiery as a fire opal. Next came a strip that shined as bright as green garnet (which Mr. Kopt's *Incidental Properties of Precious Gems* would denote as "uvarovite"), and then a deep lapis lazuli that was neither blue nor purple but something heavenly and in between. It nearly took Cora's breath away to see the gemstones she adored reproduced by the moon, made from an island wonder. In her line of work, it was usually the other way round, almond leaves made of uvarovite, mangoes of fire opal.

Over and over she let her eyes take in the palette, ruby, amber, fire opal, uvarovite, lapis lazuli. Ruby, amber, opal, uvarovite, lapis lazuli.

Rubyamberopaluvarovitelapislazuli.

RubyAmberOpalUvaroviteLapislazuli.

R(uby)A(mber)O(pal)U(varovite)L(apislazuli).

There it was. She saw it very clearly!

Oh was talking to her, and Cora understood. She need no more seek out Raoul to make him help her, than the island need seek out rain to make a rainbow.

Cora need only wait, for Oh to march Raoul past her.

STEPHANIE SICIARZ

March Past Moonbow
Harvest Football Tournament
Opens to Celestial Phenomenon

Late yesterday evening as crowds dispersed from the playing field in Port-St. Luke, at the conclusion of the March Past launching the Annual Harvest Football Tournament, a moonbow is reported to have been sighted overhead. Witnesses in the pasture describe a rainbow-like event in the sky opposite the ascending moon, despite the fact that it was not raining at the time. A rare atmospheric occurrence, moonbows in fact typically require precipitation in order to form, and a very full moon in a dark, starless sky in order to be seen. The moon, though substantial, was only almost-full, however, and the stars were out in full force. When asked to explain the unusual phenomenon, Col. Bryden Hayes of the Meteorological Branch of the Island Military suggested three possible explanations: a high-altitude rain shower imperceptible to observers below; an optical illusion resulting from a high concentration of vehicle headlamps and/or streetlamps in the area; or island magic. Supporting Col. Hayes's optical illusion theory is the fact that there were no reports of moonbow sightings from any other points on the island. Propping up his invisible rain and his magic is the fact that well over two dozen individuals across the pasture claim to have shared in the singular illusion, all giving independent but similar accounts of what they saw. Among these were the Rev. John Johnson of the Baptist Church in Beaureveille and Dr. Branson Bowles, instructor at the Boys' Secondary School in town, both considered particularly reliable witnesses. The last reported sighting of a moonbow on Oh was nearly two decades ago, some weeks prior to the collapse of the government luncheon pavilion, located in Parliament Park and designated for use by MPs and other government employees. This reporter is prompted to wonder what significance the latest moonbow might bear for the so-called Pineapple Cup, appearing on the site and date of the March Past as it allegedly did, though officials are quick to dismiss any relevance. According to a Tournament organizer from the Ministry of Sports and Culture, "A pineapple is a pineapple and a moon is a moon. What could the one ever have to do with the other?"

117

18

"Looks like we missed quite a spectacle last night," Raoul told Ms. Lila, as he looked at the *Morning Crier*'s front page. They were in the kitchen, ready for breakfast, both pretending Raoul's outburst from the day before had never taken place. It was a beautiful morning, one of Oh's best. The sun was bright but not blistering, birds chirped merrily; their song carried through the kitchen window on a gentle, cooling breeze. So fine was the island's mood that it cheered even the interior of the Orleans's cottage. Ms. Lila, who had become more efficient on her crutches, scraped almost briskly to and fro, toasting bread and making tea, humming all the while.

"What spectacle would that be?" she asked distractedly. She had balanced her weight against the countertop and with two free hands was twisting open a jar of her homemade guava jelly.

"A moonbow. 'Course Bruce is trying to make it sound magical, like it might mean something for the tournament."

"He always gets the wrong end of the stick, doesn't he?" she commented, shaking her humming head.

Luckily the kitchen in the Orlean cottage was small, as most of the rooms were, and so Lila turned herself around and easily reached the table, where she placed the jellied toast. One by one she added two cups of tea as well. Finally, she sat down, ever-so-slightly out of breath.

"I wish you'd let me help you," Raoul scolded her.

"I told you, I don't need any help. I can take care of myself." Before the cheerful morning could turn dour, she quickly added, "So is there a picture of the moonbow?"

"Nah. They aren't even one-hundred percent sure it really took place. It might have been an optical illusion. Probably just some streetlamps and headlamps and too much pineapple wine. You know how it is around here. People see all kinds of nonsense if they look for it hard enough."

"Do they?" Ms. Lila asked, wondering if she was guilty of that herself. Since the day she'd spotted Raoul outside of Cora's, he'd given her no further reason to suspect anything was amiss. When she called him at the office, he was always there, and when he went out at night, he only ever went to see his mates at the Belly. Nat had assured her of that. Was it just coincidence that Raoul was outside Cora's when Cora's eyes were drawn outside?

Maybe it was the morning's finery, but for whatever reason, Ms. Lila decided a show of faith was in order and abruptly she stood up.

"What's wrong?" Raoul barked.

"Nothing! Finish your breakfast. Nat will be here soon to take me to the library and I want to finish dressing."

"You are dressed."

"I thought I'd wear my birthday pendant today. It matches my blouse."

"Really?" Raoul was so delighted—a bit too much so, if you asked Ms. Lila, who almost had second thoughts about putting the pendant back on—that he grinned from ear to ear. So she wasn't keeping his gift out of Nat's sight after all. A fine morning, indeed!

Still...there was one little fly that flitted about his brain, one that the blue birthday pendant couldn't quash, and that was the sight of Ms. Lila in Nat's dark brown arms, her own arms wrapped around his neck. And not in front of the library, mind you, or in front of the Island Post, but in front of Pineapple Jewelry and Gems, of all places!

No, there still was something that wasn't quite right, and as the moon had pointed out the night before, Cora Silverfish was the key. Raoul, however, couldn't just barge into the jewelry store demanding she tell him what she knew of his wife's dalliances. He wasn't nearly so clumsy as that! He had to act more cautiously, so that Cora didn't realize what he was dragging her into. He needed a ruse to confront her, but what?

His musings were interrupted by the sound of Nat's car outside. "Lila," he called. "Nat's here."

"Tell him I'm coming just now," she hollered, making her way from the bedroom.

Raoul stuck his head out the door and did just that, giving Nat a wave at the same time.

"You good, Raoul?" Nat called through the window of the vehicle, wondering if the previous afternoon's storm had blown over.

"Yeah," Raoul answered him. "I'm good." Which he mostly was, but for that one stubborn fly.

Raoul watched Lila situate herself and her plaster-cast ankle in Nat's taxi, and then watched the taxi drive off. Lila looked especially pretty, in her pale blue blouse, with the blue birthday pendant hanging between her breasts. Raoul couldn't decide what complimented what, but the combination of cotton, cleavage, and Cora's handiwork was so appealing that he had been reluctant to let Lila leave him for even a minute.

He sighed and decided to head to work. The walk into town might give him some ideas about Cora, for it was very clear to him indeed that his heart would be troubled, where Lila was concerned, until he put his fly to rest. He had to admit, though, that it was hard to have a heavy heart on a day as bright as this one. Maybe Colonel Whatever-His-Name-Was was right, and a high-altitude shower the night before had taken the edge off the heat. The wind was gentle and soothing as Raoul made his way without breaking a sweat. The sky looked about as blue as it ever got, without a single cloud in sight. Even the trees seemed to stand taller, he noticed, hoping to get as close to it as they could. He spotted hummingbirds and butterflies, smelled allamanda and frangipani, heard bananaquits and mockingbirds.

"Hold up!" he told himself, stopping in his tracks and back-tracking in his head. Mockingbirds, bananaquits, frangipani, alla-manda, and...butterflies! The Black Diamond had gotten him into Cora's once. Perhaps another package could get him in again. Raoul had only just passed the main commercial port at the edge of town. Quickly he turned himself around, anxious to see what other butterflies he might find there to shush the fly in his head.

It took him just a few minutes to walk the length of the docks and reach the postal storerooms, where he was greeted by Customs Officer Garvin Charles.

"Mr. Orlean. Good morning, sir." Garvin rushed to shake his hand. "Nice to see you again so soon, sir. Can I help?"

"Thank you, Mr. Charles. Yes, you can help. I'm here regarding the matter of the Customs concessions for Cora Silverfish."

"Is there a problem, sir?"

"No, no, nothing like that. Just a routine looking-into," Raoul assured him. "You have anything for her?"

"I think I did see a small parcel for her. I haven't inventoried or protocolled these yet," he explained, walking over to the wheelbarrow designated R-Z and rifling through the packages. "Otherwise I'd have passed it along to Dwight Williams already."

"Because this Dwight processes all the parcels for Silverfish," Raoul clarified.

"Yes sir," he said, rifling some more. "Ah! Here it is!" Garvin handed Raoul a small but heavy parcel.

"From Australia," Raoul said, reading the postal stamp.

"Would you like my knife, sir?" Garvin asked him, hoping an inspection was in order. Surely such weighty contents would prove more exciting than a dead butterfly.

Raoul hesitated, put off that Garvin Charles had guessed his next move, then finally said, "Yes, thank you."

Whether Raoul or Garvin was more interested in the contents of Ms. Silverfish's package on that fine Oh morning, it was hard to say. Raoul was in search of a much-desired ruse, and Garvin got a thrill at the thought of peeking into Cora's private contents. She was famous on Oh, after all, or infamous. Garvin felt important, too, inspecting packages alongside the Head of Customs and Excise himself, also rather famous, or infamous, on Oh.

Raoul cut the string and pulled away the brown paper, while Garvin, with difficulty, feigned indifference. Inside the paper was a lopsided sphere of plastic and tape. Raoul sliced at it, peeling away layer after layer until he reached its core. Garvin stole a glance over Raoul's shoulder.

"Rocks," he said. Pretty rocks, but even so. They weren't much better than the dead butterfly, as far as Garvin was concerned.

"Must be some kind of gemstone," Raoul replied, fingering the five rough-edged pieces inside the package. They were mostly a purplish red, pinker in some spots and deeper burgundy in others. He held one up to the light and its redness brightened. Though all five fit more or less in the palm of his hand, even Raoul could tell that whatever it was, it was enough to make an awful lot of baubles. What was Cora doing importing such quantities—and so costly, or at least Raoul imagined the rocks to be costly—when she was about to close up shop?

Odd, that.

"Wrap this back up, will you?" Raoul ordered Garvin. "I'll take them to Ms. Silverfish myself, but first I'd like to have a word with Dwight Williams. Where is he?"

"Here I am," answered Dwight, who had just walked in. "What's the meaning of this?" he demanded, as he realized what was going on. "Garvin, you know all the Silverfish packages are supposed to come straight to me!"

Garvin looked at Dwight wide-eyed. Didn't he realize who he was talking to?

Raoul, who had had his back to the doorway, turned and looked at Dwight wide-eyed, too. "Officer Williams," he said. "My name is Raoul Orlean, and I think we need to have a chat."

"Mr. Orlean. Of course. My apologies, sir. I didn't recognize you from behind. How can I help?"

Officer Williams had something about him that Raoul instantly took a disliking to. His manner was too pompous, too slick. The way his tie hung loosened and the too-garish buckle on his belt told Raoul that Dwight Williams lacked the proper respect for his own position and for Raoul's. For the entire Customs branch of government, in fact, Raoul suspected—which might explain why at nearly Raoul's age this officer Williams had never risen higher in the Customs and Excise ranks than the dockside postal storerooms.

"Officer Williams, twice I have come to this office and twice I have found your post empty. How do you explain this?"

"My apologies, sir. I was in the bathroom. Maybe that's where I was last time, too, or I might have been on my mid-morning break."

Raoul didn't buy it, but he had bigger fish to fry just then. "Tell me about your arrangement with Ms. Silverfish," he ordered.

"My arrangement, sir?"

"Officer Charles here tells me that all parcels for Cora Silverfish have always gone, and still go, directly to you for processing. As you just said yourself."

"Yes sir. Been that way for as long as I can remember, sir. Truly I can't remember how it came to be so," Dwight explained.

Flimsy, but Raoul was inclined to believe the man. Raoul himself had witnessed over the years the way government procedures endured by force of inertia, long past their usefulness, assuming they had been useful to start.

"You have some special connection to Ms. Silverfish?" Raoul asked.

"No, no...no sir," Dwight stammered. "Maybe she likes me," he winked, trying to lighten the tone of their interview. "She's a single lady, you know, sir, and I help her out, maybe deliver her a package once in a while."

"Yes, she mentioned that," Raoul said. "Under whose authority do you deliver these packages?"

"Don't know, sir," Dwight replied. "I've always just done it from time to time. Maybe it was by request of Ms. Silverfish herself. She certainly doesn't seem to mind," Dwight sniggered, "if you understand what I mean, sir."

Raoul looked at Dwight and shook his head in disgust, though whether disgust at Cora or Dwight—or both—he wasn't yet sure. "Very well," he said. "Carry on."

Then directing his gaze at Garvin, he added, "Officer Charles, please show me the rest of this facility."

"Yes sir," Garvin answered, showing Dwight a quick shoulder shrug before grabbing the re-packaged rocks and following Raoul out the door.

But Raoul didn't stop walking until he had reached the end of the docks, giving Garvin no opportunity whatsoever to show him the facility or how it was organized. It was all Garvin could do to keep up with Raoul's brisk step.

"Mr. Orlean," he objected, huffing and rushing, "we're bypassing the main areas of the port, sir."

"Hush, Garvin!" Raoul told him. They had reached the road that led to town and Raoul turned to face him. "Officer, I'm not interested in any tour. I need you to take on a very important and top-secret assignment."

"Yes, sir! At your command, sir."

"I want you to keep a log of all the packages that arrive for Cora Silverfish. Date, size, weight, provenance."

"Should I hide them from Dwight?"

126

"No! Dwight must not get any ideas that you're doing anything different from what's always been done. Do you understand?"

"Yes, sir."

"Try to keep an eye on what he does with Cora's parcels— Where does he store them? Does he open them? When does he deliver them? That sort of thing—and if you ever get a look at what's inside one, inform me immediately."

"Yes, sir. Is Dwight in trouble, sir?"

"I don't know yet, Officer," Raoul said, pensive and annoyed at once. "I don't know."

And he didn't. Raoul had found his ruse alright, but he had picked up a few new flies in the bargain. Why was Cora importing costly gemstones if she was closing down her shop? And what was a slacker like Dwight Williams doing, going out of his way to deliver her goods to her door? Something didn't add up, which is why Raoul was pensive, and it bothered him that he should turn his attention just now to any other fly than Ms. Lila's, which is why he was also annoyed.

"See what you can find out," Raoul reiterated. "I'll be in touch."

Garvin nodded in compliance and handed Raoul the package with Cora's red gems.

Raoul took it and turned back toward town, headed for Pineapple Jewelry and Gems instead of his office at Customs Headquarters. He walked with his head down, by-passing the fine frangipani and the hummingbirds, and looking right through the bright allamanda, while the cloudless sky pressed down on him, bluer than blue.

19

Ms. Lila was not the only one to start her day with hum and gem. At the jewelry shop to which Raoul was headed, Cora Silverfish, too, had noticed the prime island morn and as she worked, she hummed a jaunty carnival song about a cricket match that had been notoriously fixed.

Inspired by the beauty of the butterfly that had fallen into her lap a week before, and by a local diver's timely find, Cora had carved the butterfly's likeness out of black coral from Oh's own coastline. She was in the process of polishing its wings, which she then planned to speckle with in-laid crystals. She had tacked fine-grit sandpaper to her worktable and, goggled and gloved, was rubbing the butterfly back and forth across it at different angles. Most of the stones Cora shaped and faceted were too hard for hand-polishing and had to be worked with a mechanical lathe, but not coral. Coral was soft enough that she could work it by hand from start to finish, and even with gloves on, she relished the feel of its dainty heft underneath her fingers—all the more so because this particular coral truly belonged to Oh. She was almost disappointed when she heard the tread of a customer on the staircase, forcing her to stop what she was doing.

She got up and positioned herself behind the display case and was stunned to see through the glass of the door none other than Raoul Orlean. My, my, didn't the island work fast when it wanted!

"Good morning," she greeted him, smiling. "Back again?"

Raoul gave her a funny look, and Cora remembered she was still wearing the goggles that shielded her eyes from the coral dust stirred by her polishing.

"Sorry for that," she giggled, removing them.

"Am I interrupting something?" Raoul asked tentatively. He had never imagined that Cora's occupation required such stern accoutrements.

"Yes, but that's alright. Customers first. As a matter of fact, you might be very interested in what I was working on." She ducked into the back and returned with the black coral butterfly in the palm of her dirty-white glove.

Even rough and unfinished, Raoul recognized it. "The Black Diamond!" he cried out.

"The what?"

"The butterfly from the other day, the Black Diamond. That's it!" he said, nearing his nose to her palm to take a better look.

"Is that what it's called?" she asked him. "I had no idea. Suitable though."

Raoul noticed tiny holes in the butterflies wings. "Will you put diamonds in there?" he asked.

"Heavens, no, not for my clientele. Just crystals. But they're very shiny. The effect will be the same. And the coral is local, so that keeps the cost down, too."

"Local?" Raoul had never seen anything like the black stone before him on Oh.

"It's black coral, from Sinner's Cove," Cora explained.

"Sinner's Cove?" Raoul was stunned at the mention of it. Years before, a Customs sting he had orchestrated went terribly wrong there and a man had died (sent to Paradise while protecting Raoul). He hadn't thought about the place in years.

"You know Donald Fitzgerald? The one who does fancy dives for the tourists, right in town?" (Port-St. Luke was shaped like a crescent moon, the inner crescent situated entirely on the water.) "He found it at the Cove last week. Have you come looking for another gift for your wife?"

"No," Raoul muttered, his head still recovering from the painful memory of Sinner's Cove. It was the first time he had ever watched a man die.

"Because if you are," Cora continued from her workroom, where she had momentarily retreated to set down her butterfly, "coral is a great protector...from jealousy...and negativity. Above all," she told him, now back at the display case and looking him straight in the eyes, "it strengthens love."

"No, thank you," he replied instinctively, before wondering a second or two if some black coral might not be in order for Lila, to strengthen her love for him. "No," he decided, "I'm here on official business."

"I see," Cora said, expectantly. "Go on."

"I've come to discuss your Customs arrangements."

"Oh, dear. Have I received another illicit insect?"

"This isn't about the content of your parcels, not this time. I'm here about your arrangement with Dwight Williams."

"Dwight Williams?" she repeated. Just how much did Raoul already know?

"Yes. Customs officials are not your personal errand-boys—I mean...men. Last time I was here you failed to mention that it was you yourself who arranged for Dwight to make occasional deliveries to you, for no better reason than that you fancy him!"

Cora burst with laughter, a reaction that Raoul, when interrogating a suspect, rarely found promising.

"Me? Fancy Dwight Williams?" She was laughing so hard she could barely talk. "Are you mad?"

"You're saying you never asked him to deliver any packages?"

"That drunk old fool—who was a drunk *young* fool before that? Never," Cora answered him, calming down and wiping tears of mirth from her eyes.

"Then I must inform you that I plan to look deeper into this matter," Raoul announced.

"As well you should," Cora agreed.

"I should warn you that I may need to come back here to ask you some more questions," he said.

"Yes, of course. By all means. You must do your job," she insisted. "Then I suppose I will see you soon. Is there anything else I can help you with today?"

Raoul had almost forgotten the gemstones he held in his hands. "Ah! Yes. I brought a parcel for you."

"How very kind," Cora smiled, "since Customs officials aren't my errand-men."

Raoul let out a bothered snort and Cora cut into her parcel. When she caught sight of the contents, her smile turned into a wicked grin. "Well, well," she said, "imagine you of all people delivering these stones to me."

"What do I have to do with anything?" Raoul snapped, sensing that Cora was having fun at his expense. "What are they?"

"Almandine, they're called. See how bright the redness becomes in the light?" she showed him, holding up a stone to catch the sunlight from the balcony.

"Almondine," Raoul whispered. First Sinner's Cove and now Almondine? The woman really *was* a witch! Almondine was the name of Raoul's only granddaughter, known by all the islanders for her white, white skin and her bright red eyes—eyes very much like those of the man who died that faraway night on Sinner's Cove.

"*This* almandine is said to lighten black souls," Cora told him, still gazing at the sun-lit crystal. "What about yours?" she asked, turning her attention back to Raoul. "How is your granddaughter? She's still away?"

"Yes, but she's happy where she is." Why was tight-lipped Raoul telling this woman his personal business? "She comes to visit now and then, you know." It was as if Cora looked inside him and saw what he was thinking, and so he couldn't help but say it aloud to confirm for her what she'd seen.

Raoul's flies were darting fast and furious now. He needed Cora to find out about Lila and Nat, and Dwight Williams—a fly in his own right—was proving to be just the pretense Raoul needed to keep Cora close. Along with the flies, though, there was fear in his head as he gazed at Cora across her glass showcase, and an old island adage that buzzed insistent between his ears: What's sweet for the mouth, it said, might be bitter for the belly.

Hastily Raoul said goodbye and took his leave of Cora, of her almandine and her black sinner's coral, and, once outside, eagerly drank in the mid-morning air and the not-too-hot sun. He turned toward his office and started to walk, not resisting the urge to look over his shoulder at Cora's shop at the top of the stairs. What was he doing? Raoul asked himself, as he worked out the bugs in his skull. Was he headed for a bellyache, joining forces with a magic-making jeweler who could look inside his soul?

In the end, it was his heart that took the day. Ms. Lila was all that mattered, it told him, and if it took Cora Silverfish to get to the truth, then Cora Silverfish it would be. Of course the bugs, they knew better; but Raoul wouldn't listen when they tried to warn him of the sticky dangers in store. They knew about Stan Kalpi and about Sinner's Cove, and they knew that Raoul's tricky doings—his cunning with Cora to discover what Lila was up to, and who she really loved—would end bittersweetly, with a thundering toothache and a kick in the gut.

20

Seafus sat thinking in his office at the Parliamentary Museum. His chair was turned away from the desk and he looked out the tall windows (doors they were really) that opened to a ledge too narrow to be called a balcony, overlooking Finton's Furniture across the way and the junction of Market and George Streets below. A gentle breeze swayed the thin white curtains that hung pale and loose against the dark stain of the wooden window-doors, and the noise of the morning rush wafted in. Hovering just one story away from the ground, the ledge allowed in crystal-clear snippets of neighborly chatter and the "good mornings" of the islanders passing each other as they walked to work or walked their children to school. When the stoplight at the junction turned red, Seafus could even hear the "old talk" that bounced around the inside of the buses, about the first match of the Pineapple Cup (Ashbee's Appliances v. Garrison's Auto Mart, scheduled for later that week) and the high prices of milk and gasoline. When the light turned green, the buses carried the old talk away, leaving exhaust smells behind to get tied up with those of fried bakes and fishcakes, breakfast sizzling at the nearby Serve-Ur-Self Café.

While the fishcakes fried and Garrison's supporters bashed the team from Ashbee's (and the price of milk got no lower), what Seafus Hobb thought about on that fine Oh day sent his blood pressure soaring.

Cora Silverfish, it seemed, was setting him up—or at least not keeping his cover as tightly as she should. She seemed pleased in the playing field when she told him Raoul Orlean might not stop at the butterfly, that he might dig deeper. And she didn't seem bothered by what Raoul might find, now why was that?

But never mind Cora. What about this Mr. Orlean? Seafus had never worried about the Customs Head before and he searched his mind like a Rolodex to recall what he'd ever heard about Raoul. Most recently Raoul had been involved in the washing machine scheme, the one in the paper, with the hardware stores in town, and before that his reputation was mixed. A few well-known coups in his tenure at Customs, but a bit of a nutter, too, if Seafus remembered right. Always digging for clues in the dirt or the sand or some such nonsense. Married to that pretty little librarian, wasn't he?

Seafus Hobb was no stranger to the Pritchard T. Lullo Public Library. Before his own private one at the Museum had been stocked with all the books that he needed, he spent many an hour at the island library studying up on artifacts and curios, on pottery and paintings, footstools and furnishings, manuscripts, mummies, and more. Anything he might procure—for money was no object—to make his museum famed on a worldwide scale. Ms. Lila, he recollected, had been helpful and kind, supplying all the almanacs, indices, and encyclopedias a man could ask for. Raoul Orlean was a lucky bugger.

Before Seafus could decide how much of a threat Raoul posed, if any, his thoughts were disrupted by footsteps on the spiral stair that led to the museum's upper level. He immediately swiveled his chair to face the landing, for nobody was permitted ascension unannounced. Even Seafus's assistant, Joanie Daniel, had to phone above from below before climbing up to see him. As with the best of rules, however, this one too had its exception, and it called itself Williams. Dwight.

Seafus waited for Dwight to appear, trying silently to focus on his predicament: Cora, Raoul, the jewelry shop, Customs.

When Dwight finally arrived, Seafus simply said, "Well? What have you got?"

"Nothing today, sir. It's nothing like that."

"You shouldn't be seen here any more than you have to," Seafus fired back. "If you aren't delivering, why have you come?"

"Something happened," Dwight explained, "and I thought you should know."

"Oh?"

"The Head of Customs, Raoul Orlean?"

"Go on," Seafus said, sensing his blood pressure creep even higher.

"He came to the docks today and he was asking about Cora."

Seafus stood up, to speak with Dwight at eye level. "Asking what? Tell me everything he said."

"He didn't stay long. He wanted to know why I wasn't at my desk when he came before and—"

"He came before?" Seafus interrupted.

"I guess so."

"When?" Seafus snapped.

"I don't know. I said I was in the bathroom or on my break maybe. Then he asked about Cora. He wanted to know who gave me authority to deliver to her."

"What did you tell him?"

"I said it's been going on for so long, I couldn't remember how things came to be that way. I said sometimes I deliver to her, is all, and it must be Cora who arranged for it."

"Did you tell him anything else?" Seafus asked.

A slick smile slid across Dwight's face. "I said Cora liked it when I delivered to her," he drawled, proud of himself. "You know, like she fancies me."

Idiot! he thought. Then Seafus reminded himself it was precisely Dwight's lack of intellectual curiosity that had spurred Seafus to recruit him so many years before.

"Is that all you said?" Seafus asked again, bracing himself for Dwight's reply.

"That's all."

"And what did Raoul say?"

"He said, 'Carry on,' and he went."

Seafus stared at Dwight. It appeared there was nothing more to learn or to say. He pulled a fat wad of rainbow-colored banknotes out of his pocket and separated two of them for Dwight. "Here," he said, handing them over. "Good work. Keep your eyes open."

"Yes, sir," Dwight assured him, grabbing the bills with glee. "Thanks." Then Dwight left the office and descended the spiral stair.

Seafus turned himself toward the window again, letting the cool breeze relax and refresh him as he pondered the news that Dwight had brought.

So Raoul Orlean had been sniffing around, asking questions about Cora's parcels. Didn't seem like much of an investigation to hear Dwight tell of it. Could it be a simple coincidence? Was Seafus getting paranoid for nothing? Because one little butterfly had slipped through the net? Surely no one but Seafus himself even had any idea how much it was worth.

"Yes, that's all it is," he calmed himself. Raoul had happened upon the butterfly at Customs and become curious. In the end he gave it back to Cora. He didn't confiscate it, didn't make a big fuss. It was Cora blowing things out of proportion, trying to scare him because he told her not to close her shop.

Seafus sighed and rubbed his temples. As he had done countless times over the years, he cursed the island skies for the cloud that Cora Silverfish had been since the day he met her.

He leaned back in his chair. His eyes were closed and he took in the sounds and the smells of Port-St. Luke. There was a sharp scent of pineapple that was unusual, just there below his window in the center of town. He heard the voice of a policeman and realized that someone had set up shop on the corner, selling the fresh fruit to passers-by. Probably one of the vendors from the March Past, with leftover pineapple to get rid of.

Seafus was amused as he listened to the two men reason, wondering which would have his way in the end. The officer insisted the man needed a permit to peddle his wares at such a busy junction. Why not take his business to Market Square? The man with the pineapples protested: his burlap sack of produce was too heavy, and had a big hole; Market Square was up Market Square Hill.

Realizing they were at an impasse, the officer finally asked, "You have juice, too?"

"Yes, sir!" the man replied, and he pulled from his holy sack a bottle wrapped in tin foil, which was then wrapped in a series of plastic bags, and sealed with a rubber band. He freed the bottle from all of its wrappings, which had kept it nice and cold despite the heat (even a fine, breezy morning on Oh was still tropical warm), and handed it to the officer, clearly expecting no coins in return.

The officer tasted the cold juice and nodded his head in approval. He took a furtive glance round then told the man to 'Carry on' and went.

Seafus smiled. Every man had his price, and it was rarely just one bottle.

"Carry on!" he mocked. "Huh!"

Then the Curator opened his eyes and sat straight up in his chair.

Carry on.

Raoul had told Dwight to do the very same thing, hadn't he? Despite questioning the very things that Dwight was doing. What sense in that?

Unless...

If Dwight carried on, then Raoul could keep watch. Survey the crime in the making and have his cold juice at the ready.

Raoul wasn't the nutter that Seafus believed. "Well, well," he said out loud and rubbing his palms together. "How about that?"

A man less seasoned than Seafus might have been worried to learn that the Head of Customs was digging very near where his secrets were buried. Not Seafus Hobb. Unknowns bothered Seafus, veiled threats, or a nobody (a woman no less) like Cora Silverfish putting his power in question. A known adversary was a fish of a different color. In Seafus's heart, with the dark and the bitter,

140

there lingered the shadow of the champion that once was. He was an athlete born, never mind that the island fates had changed their minds about his future. Competition—and winning—was in his blood and in his bones, and a fine day on Oh it was indeed, when Seafus found a rival worth beating.

21

Over the course of the week that followed, it was business as usual on Oh. Customs and Excise functioned with Raoul at its head, Cora carved coral and continued her closing-doors sale, and Ms. Lila managed the books at the public library, her still-fractured foot notwithstanding. The Pineapple Cup, too, was well under way. Ashbee's Appliances knocked out Garrison's Auto Mart, Higgins Hardware knocked out the Island Post, and the Customs team, the last of the week's casualties, was trounced by Trevor's Bakery, six-nil.

Business as usual, that is, unless one looked more closely.

Like with one of Cora's gemstones, a little shift in the light revealed any number of facets to the usual goings-on. Take the tournament, for example. Trevor's star player had been none other than Bang himself; the whole week long he taunted Raoul for the Customs defeat, from the moment Raoul entered the Belly to the moment he left. As for Ashbee and Higgins, their respective wins sent them both to the Second Round, where they would play each other, thus continuing their washer war on the football field. Ms. Lila, she not only managed her cast, her crutches, and her books, but her birthday pendant besides; since her show of faith, and the elation it provoked in her husband, she hadn't removed the pendant but to sleep. With each disaster-free day that passed, her jaw unclenched and her shoulders untensed, and she nearly convinced herself there was nothing to fear but her silliness. Cora, on the other hand, feared only that she had overestimated Raoul; a week gone by and not a word or a single return visit. Why was the island making her wait? she asked it, as she sanded butterflies and shaped almandine. And Raoul, well, he was the most multi-faceted of all. While Customs and Excise functioned with himself at the head, he had quite a few flies in his bonnet: at the docks Garvin busily spied and logged Cora's packages, reporting to Raoul every day; at the Belly, Bang's incessant ribbing sent Raoul home early every night, wondering if Bang wasn't in cahoots with Nat (never mind that at home Raoul found his wife alone and waiting for him); and in town—as Raoul walked the streets or waited at the Savings Bank or bought mauby juice at Delicious Delicia's—he had the distinct sensation he was being followed. There were eyes on him surely as he sipped from his icy cup, watchers lurking as he checked on his accounts. When he tried to identify them, the watchers and the lurkers with their furtive eyes, he couldn't. Not when he looked about slowly and carefully for clues, and not when he turned like a shot, hoping to shock his stalker.

No proof positive, then, no doggers caught in the act, but they were there. Raoul could sense them as sure as Stan Kalpi smelled oniony stew on the wind. Which was funny, Raoul's being followed on that very day, when he meant to embark on some dogging of his own. First, though, a quick and furtive stop at the dock to check in with Garvin.

Garvin and Raoul had been meeting daily in the narrow gap between the farthest edge of the Customs outpost, and the shed behind the This Way That Way Garage and Body Shop used for storing used oil in need of removal. Some days Garvin's package logs were short, just one or two entries; some days he had none at all. Other days, he might report on half a dozen parcels arriving for Cora, which Dwight Williams eventually scurried off with. Garvin, as thorough as only Raoul himself could have been, provided not only the date, size, weight, and provenance of each package, as ordered, but also personal commentary he hoped might crack the case ("package appeared to have been wrapped in haste"; "address written in green ink—ALL CAPS"), though he didn't fully understand what the case was to start. Lastly, for each arrival he noted the precise time it was handed over to Dwight, the number of minutes or hours it remained in Dwight's care, and the very minute in which Dwight left to deliver it. Sadly, Garvin never managed to spot the contents of a single box, though to be fair, Dwight always carried them off unopened.

After a week of Garvin's updates, Raoul's next step had become clear, hence the dogging he was about to do: Officer Dwight Williams needed tailed.

———

Raoul and Garvin parted ways, the former leaving the latter with praise for a job well done and instructions to carry on. Raoul then set off on foot to find a suitable spot from which to surveil the dockside compound's main street entrance, through which Dwight would likely leave to make his rounds. Raoul passed through the lot of the body shop and crossed the street, where the makeshift sidewalk (that is to say, a worn path in the grass that ran the length of the road) flanked a rocky hillside. He followed the path until he found himself almost opposite the entrance that interested him and ducked behind a hedge. Because Raoul had planned on camouflage to aid in his surveillance efforts, he put on a dark green cap he'd tucked in his back pocket, and a pair of sunglasses with great, dark lenses that reflected the sun, giving him the appearance of one of the flies that lived in his head.

Nearly two hours passed during which Raoul saw no one suspicious exit or enter the Customs area, though his own side of the street was busy with foot traffic, islanders headed to town to do shopping or pay bills, hungry islanders looking to buy a bite for lunch. Some of them saw him and pretended not to, but most, to his annoyance, politely said "Good morning," unaware that his camouflage was meant to render him invisible. At last, as his own stomach bordered on rumbling and he contemplated fish roti from the stand at the roundabout in town, Dwight appeared.

The very sight of him made Raoul scoff in disgust, his swagger and his thick-heeled shoes! He had a sack in hand that surely contained packages, the exact number of which Raoul would learn from Garvin's report the next day. While Dwight made his way along one side of the road, Raoul shadowed him on the other, creeping half-bent between purposeful pedestrians and the odd hedge, or flattening himself against the hillside. When they reached the roundabout, where Raoul expected Dwight to head toward the market and Cora's shop, Dwight did nothing of the sort. He purchased a fish roti and took the road opposite. Now what was the meaning of this?

Dwight's change of direction so intrigued Raoul that his rumbling stomach and the nose on his face paid no mind to the assault of curry and sizzling butter; no sir. Raoul's feet were in charge, and they followed his bug eyes, which followed the fish-eating Dwight. Perhaps he was just making a detour, looking for some rum. Or was he headed to the barbershop for a trim on company time? The nerve! Raoul followed Dwight through the traffic of Port-St. Luke until they'd reached its very heart. There, Dwight stopped at a junction and bought pineapple from a man on a corner. (Or nearly. Though Raoul couldn't hear their words, he could tell the transaction was made on credit.) The traffic light changed just then and a crowd of pedestrians stopped mid-step, blocking Raoul's view of Dwight and the fruit vendor. By the time the light changed once more, and the crowd moved along, Raoul saw the seller again, but there was no sign of Dwight.

From across the road, Raoul scanned the four corners of the junction, sure his suspect had crossed one way or the other with the crowd, but if so, Raoul couldn't spot him. He pulled off his hat, smacked it against his leg and cursed. While the breeze cooled his sweaty head, his stomach got to rumbling again and Raoul crossed the street to buy some fresh pineapple. (He didn't dare ask the seller about Dwight; the men were clearly friends if Dwight had walked off without paying.)

'So now what?' Raoul wondered as he ate up the sweet and sticky slices. He looked out at the junction again, wondering if perhaps Dwight hadn't ducked into a local business, but none of them seemed up Dwight's street: not the Staircase to Beauty Salon (which catered exclusively to women), not the Oh-Tel offices (he was hardly there paying his telephone bill, if he couldn't afford some fresh fruit), not Finton's Furniture, and certainly not the

Parliamentary Museum against which Raoul leaned as he made his deductions and ate his paltry pineapple lunch.

When he finished, he wiped his hands on his trousers and taking one last look around (no Dwight), crossed in the direction of the Customs headquarters. There was no more dogging to be done today and piles of paperwork no doubt awaited on his desk. Raoul crossed one more time and found himself now catty-corner to the pineapple seller in front of the Parliamentary Museum. He was about to turn away, leaving the seller at his back and proceeding away from the junction, when suddenly he spotted Dwight again. There he was, plain as day, exiting the museum.

Odd, that. Why pop in for a bit of history when Cora's deliveries awaited and in the opposite direction, no less?

Odder still, Raoul watched Dwight pass a small rainbow bill to the pineapple vendor, whose demeanor clearly communicated that Dwight's account was paid in full. Why had he made the man wait and not paid him when he first made his purchase?

"Stupidness!" Raoul exclaimed under his breath.

Never mind. His surveillance was on again! Quickly Raoul crossed one street back, making his path again parallel with Dwight's. He followed Dwight through the traffic of Port-St. Luke, only this time they headed away from its heart. Soon they were back at the roundabout with the fish roti stand. Here Raoul expected Dwight, finally, to head toward Cora's, but once more Dwight did nothing of the sort. Instead, he jumped on a bus headed back down the road to the Customs compound at the docks! Raoul watched him flip two shiny coins into the conductor's hands before taking a seat near an open window. Now what was the meaning of *this*?

Raoul stood in the middle of the roundabout, looking round and taking stock. His surveillance had determined that Dwight had left for his usual delivery to Cora's jewelry shop atop the market square. Only instead of stopping at her shop, he had bought fish and pineapple, visited the Parliamentary Museum, and returned to work (presumably) with his sack still in hand. Or had he? Raoul struggled to recall the catty-corner portrait of Dwight Williams, standing on the corner outside the museum, chatting with his fruit-vendor friend and passing him a rainbow bill. Hadn't he clapped the man on the back with the other hand as he did so? What had happened to the sack with Cora's parcels? Had he set it down in the museum and forgotten about it? Tossed it in a rubbish bin, thinking Cora would be none the wiser? The flies were buzzing fast and furious now! Raoul would have to see Garvin, find out exactly what was in the missing sack. Did Raoul have a legal obligation to inform Cora Silverfish of what he'd seen? Could Customs and Excise be liable for costly cardamom or bits of almond?

Raoul shook his head quickly from side to side to silence the spiraling buzz. He put himself in his favorite book and asked, "What would Stan Kalpi do?" He would keep his cool, that's what. He would line up his variables and tally them into something. Turn questions into answers. No sense in rushing to reveal unfounded suspicions—to Cora or to anyone else. Not until he did a bit more digging and dogging. At the very least, he would have to sniff around the Parliamentary Museum. Perhaps Cora's parcels were merely mislaid. He could get on a bus, go back into town, and barge into the museum, badge in hand and demanding to inspect the premises.

Yes. He could do all that...but for the mango fly on his brain that suggested a sweeter tack. Until Raoul knew what Dwight was up to—exactly—more discretion might be in order, it said.

Fair enough. A master of camouflage like Raoul knew his business, and what's more, he knew just how to finagle a discreet look around the museum. He would take Ms. Lila on an outing! Neither of them had been there in years. Raoul, not since his boy days. They would spend a civilized evening—why not that very evening?—at the Parliamentary Museum for the Preservation of Artistic and Historical Sciences, and have a late dinner at the Belly. Ms. Lila would forget her foot troubles, and Raoul would tick off a variable.

Who knew? The pair of them might even learn something.

22

"Right this minute? But I've only just come from work! Why in the world must we see a museum this very evening that we could see any other time? A museum that has *never* interested you in all the years I've known you." Ms. Lila, it appeared, was not at all up for an outing.

"I thought it might be a nice distraction from all this ankle business, that's all. We could take a nice stroll, spend an hour or two at the museum, then have some food at the Belly," Raoul explained.

"A nice stroll? On crutches?" Ms. Lila saw right through Raoul's excuses. "Tell me this minute what's going on," she demanded.

Raoul pouted a moment, weighing his options. He could insist he had Lila's best interests at heart, try his I-only-wanted-to-take-you-out bit a little longer, or admit defeat and tell the truth. He sighed and looked at his wife, who was looking at him crossly. Fine. The truth it would be.

"If you must know, I need to have a look round the museum." Raoul bowed his head sheepishly. "For clues."

"Mm hmm." She cocked her head at an angle that said 'I knew it!'

"Clues to what?" she went on.

"I'm not too sure. That's why I need more clues."

"And by clues you mean 'variables,' don't you?" (Sometimes Ms. Lila was sorry she had ever let that Stan Kalpi book into her library!)

"You could say so."

"And why must I drag myself on crutches tonight to help you hunt for clues you could easily find tomorrow?"

Lordy, Ms. Lila wasn't easy! Raoul explained that a certain Customs official appeared to have misplaced some government property (private goods not yet claimed were the interim property—and responsibility—of the Republic of Oh, and of Customs and Excise in particular), and that he (Raoul) suspected the goods might have been left by mistake at the Parliamentary Museum.

Ms. Lila had no idea what Raoul was talking about. It all sounded rather unlikely. But she knew that Raoul wouldn't give her a moment's peace until she acquiesced. She pouted a moment, weighing her options. She could insist she was tired from her day at the library, try her I-can't-stroll-on-crutches bit a little longer, or admit defeat and agree to go along.

"Fine," she capitulated. The museum it would be.

They set out from their cottage shortly thereafter. Raoul attempted to support his wobbly wife, but she impatiently shrugged him off of her, more easily managing her balance unencumbered. Raoul quickly realized that the "strolling" part of his plan was impractical and at the nearest bus stop, they stopped to wait for a bus.

Buses on Oh were difficult enough to navigate on two firm feet. Passengers pushed and shoved; the buses rocked and jostled; rarely was there room for all the riders aboard at any given time. Factor in a cast and crutches, and the challenge of getting from Point A to Point B turned into an all-out ordeal. Nevertheless, Ms. Lila was eventually situated in a seat, Raoul beside her. To take her mind off the bumpy ride that made her visibly wince, Raoul tried to engage her in conversation. He commented on the weather and complained about the Customs loss to Trevor's Bakery in the very first week of the Pineapple Cup. He griped about Bang's incessant boasting, and about a certain young man he'd seen earlier that day who "bought" a plate of pineapple without bothering to pay.

"The man ate his food and took his time in the museum. Only when he came out did he decide to pay for the food he swallowed before he went in! Stupidness!" Raoul shook his head. Lila stared out the window of the bus, only partly hearing what he had to say. Raoul, though, heard his words echo inside his head, where the midday mango fly had taken up its buzz again. 'The man ate his food and took his time in the museum...only *when he came out* did he decide to pay.'

No! It couldn't be, could it? Was Dwight selling off Cora's gemstones behind her back? Conducting his illicit business in the middle of the day, in the heart of the Parliamentary Museum, the most deserted spot on all of the island? It was as ingenious as it was reprehensible!

"Raoul! Are you listening?" Ms. Lila elbowed him in the ribs. "I said, 'Help me up,' we have to get off. We're in town."

"Yes, dear. Sorry for that." Raoul turned his attention from the mango fly in his head to the wife at his side.

With the help of the bus conductor, he managed to get Lila out of the vehicle and propped on the sidewalk across from the museum. There, he took her arm and took in the building they were about to metaphorically storm. Raoul had never paid proper attention to the changes it had undergone over the years. It was nearly double in size, both horizontally and vertically, though the top level appeared to be offices. He could see above the corner where Dwight's pineapple transaction had taken place a small ledge with tall windows through which curtains billowed.

"How long has it been like this?" Raoul asked Ms. Lila.

Ms. Lila sighed. Why did her husband always assume she knew what bugs and butterflies danced inside his skull. "How long has what been how?"

"The museum. How long as it been so...big? When I was a boy it was half this size, if that."

"What are you talking about? It's been this way for years. You must have walked past this junction a thousand times since they renovated the museum. Decades ago."

To be fair, occupying a corner of the very center of town as it did, the Parliamentary Museum did not stand alone but butted right up against businesses on either side. The entrance, though refurbished, was the original one, owing to the fact that over the years its narrow wooden threshold had been crossed by lesser royals and a one-time president, and as such constituted a part of the museum's permanent collection. (A plaque with an engraved list of these illustrious threshold-crossers hung right on the door.) Thus, as the museum grew over the years, and Port-St. Luke grew up around it, a disinterested eye could still see it as it always was, tucked into the brick and concrete of George Street, an air of speakeasy about it, as if the uninitiated needn't bother knocking.

On the night of the Orleans's outing, the door was flung wide, inviting passers-by to follow in the footsteps of those the plaque immortalized—none of whom had used crutches, Lila hoped, for she found it rather difficult to get her injured self inside. Once she did, and Raoul followed, they found themselves in a somewhat modern (or so it had been at one time) and surprisingly cheerful square room. The walls were white and the flooring dark, the whole of it illuminated from above by more light fixtures than Raoul had ever seen in one place before. In contrast to the clean architectural lines, along the room's perimeter marched a line of glass cases that had long failed to contain the entirety of the museum's holdings. The overflow trickled upward and down, sparing no empty surface. Pelts and papyri were mounted above the cases, rocks and crockery piled below (more lighting had been installed in the cases' underbellies), and against the room's four corners leaned swords and daggers. Only the center of the room was vacant, the nucleus of a bursting cell that had divided itself into a second room much like the first.

Raoul and Ms. Lila looked around and looked at each other. They were lost in time and place. Fossils mingled with silver forks, petrified tree bark with Civil War trumpets. For reasons neither could have explained, they gripped each other tighter as they slowly shuffled thru the second cell of miscellanea. When they finally stumbled into the third room, where Seafus had installed a stage and seating, its relative emptiness hit them both like a fresh island breeze. Ms. Lila collapsed onto one of the chairs and, dazed, whispered to her husband, "What—in the world—was all that?"

All Raoul could do in reply was scratch his head. He tried to replay in his mind the minutes between their entering the museum and their finding themselves where they were. He remembered brightness and relative cheer, a sense of something impressive, a sense that had quickly transformed itself into sensations of wonder, befuddlement, and ultimately dread. The random assemblage of objects was so at odds with itself and its surroundings that it was disorienting, even frightening!

"Raoul, let's go," Ms. Lila said, pulling Raoul from his mental review. "There's something weird about this place."

Although Raoul struggled to disagree, he would not allow himself to be swayed by funny feelings, or his official investigation deterred by ancient worms preserved in jelly. Why, the museum was a tribute to science and history and the arts—if a bit fragmented perhaps. What was there to fear in that? Raoul was undercover. On official Customs business. He wouldn't leave until his business was done!

Not that many clues had jumped out from the confusion of maps and maracas, he had to admit. Did Dwight and some accomplice have a secret hiding spot amongst all that bric-a-brac where the one deposited gemstones and the other left behind cash? If Raoul were to examine every case and corner, he would need a whole team of officials. An undercover sweep was impossible.

"Raoul!" Ms. Lila urged, tugging at his shirt as she struggled to stand up.

"Just one minute, dear," he said. Another fly was hatching. Maybe, just maybe, Dwight didn't bother with drop-offs but met up with his accomplice face-to-face. Raoul hadn't noticed anyone leave the museum behind Dwight that day, but had he really been watching? Perhaps some museum staffer had seen something and could shed some light.

"Hello! Good night!" he suddenly called out at the top of his lungs.

"What are you doing?!" Lila squealed at him. "Have you lost your marbles?"

"Hello! Good night!" he cried out again louder, pacing the length of the room. To Lila he explained: "There must be someone here. I just want to ask a question or two."

"Hello!" he tried again.

"Hello?" An answer from above!

"Hello! Who's there?"

In reply, Raoul and Ms. Lila suddenly saw a pair of legs descending from a dark spiral staircase they would both later swear they hadn't noticed until that very minute. The legs belonged to Seafus Hobb, who had come down planning to shout about all the shouting—until he saw the scene beneath him. He had only a vague impression of Raoul Orlean's appearance, their paths never having officially crossed before, so it took the Curator a minute to place the characters arranged before him. He recognized Ms. Lila before he recognized Raoul. He knew her from the library years before and had taken note since then of how sweet she still looked as she did her shopping in town. Even so, it took him a moment to place her face, there in his Museum at that hour. It was only when he spotted her crutches, and remembered reading something about her fall in the *Morning Crier*, that he made the connection. Her companion was of course Raoul Orlean, the very same Raoul Orlean called to his attention that very day by Dwight. Well, well, well.

"Welcome!" he called out, feigning absolute delight to see them both there. He finished his descent and walked straight over to Lila. "It's been such a long time, my dear! You're as pretty as ever. Such a shame about your injury."

While Raoul tried to work out the When, Where, and How of his wife's last meeting with this man prancing about before him, the man grabbed Raoul's hand in a violent shake and said, "You must be Raoul Orlean. What a treat to meet the man behind the reputation!"

"And you are...?" a stern Raoul inquired cautiously.

"My name is Seafus Hobb, and I am the Curator of this Museum. Have you had a chance to examine our collection?"

"Oh, yes, it's quite remarkable," Ms. Lila chimed, trying to compensate for her husband's caution. He stood studying Seafus, a scowl on his face and a string of flies no doubt buzzing behind his eyeballs.

"I'm glad you enjoyed it. Is there anything you'd like to hear more about? I'd be happy to give you some explanations. There isn't a collection comparable to this one anywhere in the world, you know."

"I don't doubt it," Ms. Lila replied, nervously tugging again at Raoul's shirt. "Raoul, is there anything you'd like to ask Mr. Hobb?"

Raoul's flies scattered and his head cleared. "As a matter of fact there is," he answered. His cover good and blown, and no noticeable clues there to carry off, Raoul decided to conduct his official business officially.

"Mr. Hobb, I am here on Customs business. Nothing to concern you. I would merely like to know if you've witnessed any unusual activity here at the museum, any visitors acting strangely, something along those lines."

"I couldn't honestly say."

"I see. No peculiar visits?"

"None more so than this one, if I may say so."

"What about a man named Dwight Williams? Are you acquainted with him?"

"Should I be?"

"He's an Officer of Customs and Excise."

"I see. A colleague. Well, any colleague of yours is a colleague of mine!"

The more Raoul spoke to Seafus the less he liked him. He seemed to answer questions without giving answers, to help without helping at all. And why did his eyes drift to Lila again and again?

Raoul decided the man was a waste of time. If Dwight Williams were up to something in the Parliamentary Museum or elsewhere, Seafus Hobb would certainly be of no use in catching him. The Curator's thoughts were no doubt as jumbled as his display cases. Raoul would have to figure out for himself what role the museum played, if any, in Dwight's illegal scheme.

"Thank you for your cooperation," Raoul said, writing him off. "I think we'll be going now." Raoul moved toward Ms. Lila to help her to her feet. Before he could take hold of her, Seafus rushed to her assistance, one hand around her shoulders and the other firmly around her arm. Lila's fearful eyes met Raoul's.

"You two really must come back for one of our Cultural Soirées. You could bring a mutual friend of ours, Mr. Orlean. Cora Silverfish."

Both Lila and Raoul stopped dead and looked at Seafus. While Lila tried to work out the When, Where, and How of her husband's friendship with Cora Silverfish, her husband, with a violent twist, freed her from the Curator's grasp.

"*Officer* Orlean," Raoul clarified.

"You really are as pretty as ever," Seafus said to Lila, smiling at her as he let her go. "*Officer* Orlean, you are a lucky man."

"If I need anything more from you, I'll be back," Raoul barked.

The last word got, he turned and ushered Lila toward the door. As they made their hasty departure, her body jerked its way along, in sync with the crutches' footfall. Her blue birthday pendant, which swung to and fro at her chest, slapped hard against her skin, beating her heart every time she propelled herself forward.

23

The island of Oh can be cruel, to be sure. It will rain on your Rainbow Fair, trick you off a cliff, and bury your very last hopes beneath a tree. Sometimes its meanness is muted: it merely tickles your nose with the island breeze or topples your bottle of fresh honey. But when the mood strikes, and the moon is cool, Oh will make amends. It will save your life, build you a house, get you out of jail free. Sometimes the amends are muted, too, and the island simply sends you the things that you need when you need them.

Like a taxi when your wife is on edge and on crutches and needs to eat some dinner. Even better, a *free* taxi, driven by a friend who never makes you pay (never mind that he might be sleeping with your wife). Even better than *that*, a free taxi driven by a *chatty* friend who is so taken with the first week of the annual Pineapple Cup that he talks incessantly about keepers and coaches and penalty kicks, leaving you (and your wife) free *not* to discuss your upsetting visit to the Parliamentary Museum and your encounter with its creepy Curator, who suggested you were friends with a Silverfish witch and that *he* was friends with your wife.

The chatty taxi-driver was Nat of course, and he happily shuttled Raoul and Ms. Lila from the corner of George Street, where he happened to spot them, to the Belly. While Nat nattered on as he drove, Raoul ruminated and Lila sulked.

Ruminated, because he hadn't liked one bit the things he'd learned that evening: Seafus Hobb was an eerie man, running a jumbled lair of a museum from the top of a secret staircase; he knew nothing about Dwight Williams; he was far too familiar with Ms. Lila; and, apparently, it was now commonly believed on the island that Cora and Raoul were well acquainted! How had *that* happened?

Sulked, because *she* hadn't liked what she'd learned that evening either: her husband, apparently, knew Ms. Silverfish so well that everyone—except Ms. Lila—knew it! Could that possibly be?

Had either been privy to the other's puzzlement, they would have agreed it had been a strange evening, a rum outing, one of the rummest they could recall. Which explains why, as soon as they got to the Belly, they both ordered ice-cold rum punch.

———

"You went *where?*" Bang asked incredulously. "What's with you, Raoul, man? First you shop at Cora's and now you're taking your wife to that freaky museum?"

Along with their rum punch and their fish broth with dumplings, Raoul and Ms. Lila were enjoying (to various degrees) the company (and the commentary) of Bang, who took Seafus as seriously as he took his island magic.

Raoul didn't answer, but Ms. Lila, trying to nip Bang's inevitable tirade in the bud, explained that their visit was semi-official.

162

"Oho!" Raoul exclaimed, his focus on slurping his soup. "Now we'll never hear the end of him."

"Me?" Bang joked. "You think I would carry on just because you're investigating a known criminal? I was about to go on stage anyway."

"Wait!" Raoul stopped him. "What do you mean, 'known criminal'?"

"He's a bad man, man! You never heard?"

"Bad? How so?" A variable? A clue?

"Well, no one really knows. That is the thing," Bang elaborated. Raoul's shoulders sunk and he rolled his eyes. If there was one thing he disliked almost as much as island magic, it was island gossip (most especially when so devoid of detail). "Ahh! Go on and play with your marimba mallets."

"I'm serious, man!" Bang insisted.

"Serious about what? Raoul, how's the soup?" Cougar arrived at the table and jumped into the conversation, which he splintered in the process. "How's the leg, Lila?"

"It's there," was her lackluster reply.

"The soup's good," Raoul said.

"We were talking about the Curator," Bang clarified. "Raoul doesn't believe me when I say that he's a criminal."

"I don't 'not believe you'!" Raoul insisted. "You didn't *tell* me anything to believe or not!"

"You mean Seafus Hobb?" Cougar interjected. "Bang's right, Raoul."

Raoul wondered how his friends knew so much about the island's criminal element. A line of thought perhaps better not pursued, he decided. Mind you, he found it very easy to believe that Seafus Hobb was guilty of...something, even many things, but

Raoul was a man of facts. Black and white, plain-as-noses-on-faces facts. Simply saying that Seafus was bad was not enough to make it so.

"Tell me then. What has the man done?" Raoul questioned.

What followed was a fractured tale that limped between Bang and Cougar, who disagreed on as many particulars as they agreed on. The gist, however, was this: Seafus Hobb was once a rising-star cricketer who lost his way. His status on the island bloated his pride and he forced himself on a female, who bloated with child soon thereafter. The baby, who fell out sooner than it should have, never stood a chance. No, that wasn't right. The child survived and Seafus sold it off to the highest bidder. Or was it another man's wife he had seduced, who passed off her Hobb off-spring as her husband's own? (Abigail Davies, the island midwife would know for certain, though she'd probably never tell.) After whatever-it-was-that-happened happened, Seafus fell in with the wrong crowd. His game began to suffer, a result of bad magic for surety, whether stirred by his own bad actions or cooked up from a book at the library, nobody knew. But the whispers turned to grumbles turned to gale force winds—as island rumors are wont to do—that pushed sportsman Seafus off the cricket pitch and the national team, and straight into the seedy bar by the port.

As Raoul listened to the story, in his stomach the dumplings he'd eaten felt as if they'd doubled in size. Why did his Customs cases so often come back to babies? Mysterious babies, secret babies, disappearing babies who never knew where they came from? Raoul had nothing against babies, to be sure, but babies meant midwives, and the only midwife that mattered on Oh was Abigail, who just happened to be Raoul Orlean's sworn enemy. (Their animosity was decades old, ever since Abigail had assisted at the birth of Raoul's granddaughter, Almondine. Suffice it to say that, generally speaking, Abigail kept too many secrets for Raoul's liking, and Raoul managed secrets too poorly for hers.)

"So," Bang concluded, "the Curator's cursed and gets up to all kinds of no good. Criminally speaking, I mean."

"Right," Cougar confirmed.

Their tales cut straight to Lila's heart. She kept replaying what the Curator had said about his and Raoul's common acquaintance, Cora. What if Raoul *was* having an affair with Cora after all and considered the Curator to be competition for her favor? She couldn't bear the thought of even a cheating Raoul squaring off against the criminal Curator. Instinctively she grabbed for the vial of stones around her neck and nervously spun it between her fingers.

"I see you're still wearing that pretty blue noose," Bang observed. "You figure out what it does yet, Lila?"

"Can we *please* talk about something other than island magic?!" Raoul pounded his palm on the table. "How about a couple more rum punches instead of old talk?"

Cougar snapped his fingers at one of the waiters and motioned for refills for Raoul and his wife.

Bang kept at it: "You never did say why you were investigating Seafus."

At this, Lila raised an eyebrow, for she, too, wanted to know. That story of the misplaced government property had made little sense from the start, and where in the world in that mess of a museum would one begin to look for a misplaced anything?

"Who says I'm investigating Seafus? I needed into the museum, is all. To see what it is I'm up against. Now that I've met the man, I know."

The response satisfied neither Bang nor Lila. The one gave up, shrugged, and headed for the stage, while the other gulped rum punch to choke her tears.

"Finally some peace!" Raoul patted Lila on the knee.

Before long Nat came back, done with his taxi-ing for the night, and the talk turned to pineapples and football. Specifically, it turned to the Pineapple Cup match-up between Higgins Hardware, Home and Garden, and Ashbee's Appliances, Tackle and Tools, whose Spin-O-Matic turf war would eventually play out on regulation pineapple-cup turf. They discussed the he-said-he-said of Howlander Higgins and Alexander Ashbee, respectively, and ribbed Raoul for fanning the flames with his fair distribution of washing machines between them. Didn't he know that the islanders don't like a draw? Winners and losers, that's what they want. Victors and spoils! How had Raoul not known better, he with his penchant for black-and-white truths?

Raoul took their kicksing in stride, happy to be discussing anything but...well, you know. Lila only half-listened to what Nat and Cougar were saying. All she could think of was Cora. Cora and her husband. Cora and the Curator. The whole of it wrenched her gut.

Thus the evening went. To the buzz of rum punch, Raoul and his mates cracked wise, Ms. Lila worried at the links of her chain, and as he often did at the Belly, Bang sang. Something haunting, about loves new and loves old—*whoa oh oh oh*—about kindred souls—*oh oh*—and giving-up ghosts.

24

Raoul awoke to a punching headache, but not because he'd consumed massive amounts of rum punch the night before. It was bottles, not cups, that had Raoul troubled. His head pounded with bottleflies, a pair of them, one green and one blue, both relentless in their assault. He had picked them up not at the Belly over punch, but much earlier in the day, after his confab with Garvin behind the body shop shed, and they had lain in wait ever since. That green-bottle and blue- had chosen this particular morning to spar inside Raoul's brain, oh, Nat was to blame for that. Nat and his fancy taxi.

When Raoul and Lila had decided to put an end to the previous evening's outing, Nat had graciously offered to drive them home. It was a kindness that Raoul could hardly refuse, what with Lila's crutches and all, though Nat was the last person Raoul wished to spend another minute with. Lila had been odd and pensive ever since Nat had turned up at the Belly, a fact that had Raoul guessing and second-guessing the reasons behind her behavior. Was she feeling guilty? Torn between her husband and one of his very best friends? Was Raoul being too harsh? Perhaps Lila was simply in shock after their exchange with Seafus Hobb. Or concerned about Raoul's having learned that she and Seafus were acquainted. How *were* they acquainted anyway?

Ahh! Raoul shook his head. One fly—or two—at a time! He would get to Seafus later. First things first: Raoul needed transport, he decided, so that Ms. Lila wasn't forced to resort to Nat every time she needed a ride. And Raoul had the perfect vehicle in mind. A smallish but bulky old pick-up parked at the This Way That Way Garage and Body Shop with a cardboard FOR SALE sign pressed against the windscreen.

He had spotted it as he'd headed out to tail Dwight. It looked mint green at first, then powder blue, then mint green again (hence the sparring bottleflies). Raoul had found its chameleonic pallor appealing. Though faded, it boasted no rust, and the tires looked sturdy. There wasn't a dent or a scratch on it, and not a single lamp was cracked, head or tail. The exterior was clean, and from what Raoul could see of the interior, that was tidy, too. Its previous owner had obviously shown it great care, and why not? It was a truck that commanded attention and respect! A vehicle superbly suited to the Head of Customs and Excise, with plenty of room in the back for hauling variables in the form of evidence or clues. Raoul could see himself in the driver's seat, a siren on top, spinning and wailing. (He would requisition one of those portable ones he saw in movies at the Loyal Cinema, the ones the officers of the law stuck on the roofs of their unmarked cars with one hand, while steering with the other, in mad pursuit of wrongdoers.)

Raoul wondered how quickly he could get himself behind the wheel. He had to first negotiate the selling price with Munroy

Daniels from the body shop, withdraw rainbow bills from the bank to pay, and sort out what paperwork was involved in purchasing a vehicle, something that, like many islanders, Raoul in all his days had never done. Once that was handled, he would learn how to drive—better read up on that at the library, Raoul mentally noted—and then Ms. Lila would have her chauffeur, and the likes of Dwight Williams wouldn't elude Raoul's surveillance by jumping on a bus.

Though his bluebottle and greenbottle had calmed down considerably, a damselfly crept up in their wake. Should Raoul first discuss the matter of his mint-green-powder-blue pick-up with Ms. Lila?

As Raoul walked to town and the sun beat down on his still slightly throbbing head, he felt overwhelmed—hot and bothered, and pulled at from all sides. He needed to talk to Garvin, to his wife, to Munroy, and possibly to Cora Silverfish. Before the day was out he would have to go to Customs, to the library, the body shop, the bank, and, possibly, to Pineapple Jewelry and Gems. Raoul disliked a morning when he woke up with nothing to do, no task at hand to point him in the direction the day should take; it made him ill at ease. He was equally anxious, however, when a morning presented itself with so many commissions to see to that one didn't know where to look first. Lucky for Raoul, all his commissions that morning were in the direction of Port-St. Luke, and so when he left home (having sent Ms. Lila off to work in Nat's taxi, alas), he looked toward town and set off. His path would become clear as he followed it, if only he got himself going.

He had walked but a short piece of road when he realized it only made sense to stop first to see Garvin for their daily tête-à-tête, and since the body shop was right there at the docks, he would then talk truck with Munroy. Once that was all done, Raoul would know what to do next.

————

"You sure?"

"Yeah man! I mean, Yes sir," Garvin confirmed. "The sack had three small parcels inside. Dwight left before lunch to take them to Cora."

Raoul examined the package log that Garvin had compiled the day before. The packages in question had arrived from the corners of the globe: India, Iceland, and one stamped Timbuktu. Why closing-up Cora was still ordering so many supplies, Raoul couldn't fathom, but fact of the matter was, Dwight Williams was selling off her gems! It was the only explanation.

Raoul instructed Garvin to continue his undercover investigation and bid him goodbye until the next morning. A visit to Cora's was most definitely in order now. Raoul's priority had become catching Dwight.

But first, Munroy.

In turns, Raoul and Garvin took their leave from the gap by the shed, so as not to arouse any suspicion that they were cohorts. When it was Raoul's turn, instead of cutting quickly through the body shop's lot to get to the main road, he strolled the lot's perimeter, feigning interest in the work going on and waving a "Good morning" to the men inside the garage. Munroy returned the greeting with a tip of his head and went about his business; he figured Raoul was merely passing through, as he had done just about every day now for a week. Which is why he didn't notice Raoul's nosing around the faded blue-green truck until one of the mechanics called it to his attention.

'Oh, dear,' Munroy thought to himself. It was common island knowledge that where Raoul Orlean poked his nose, trouble soon followed. He picked up a cloth and wiped his hands on it as he made his way out to the pick-up.

"Morning, Raoul. Can I help?"

"Yes, as a matter of fact. Morning! Morning! I am interested in this truck." As Raoul spoke, he walked around the vehicle, his eyes lovingly taking in every inch of it.

"Did it do something wrong? Er, that is, are you investigating it for some reason? It hasn't been off this lot in weeks, you know."

"No, no, nothing like that! I'm interested in purchasing it."

"Purchasing it? Ah! For official Customs hauling? Good idea! She's sturdy."

"I don't doubt it," Raoul agreed. "I expect to use it for Customs business as well."

"As well as what?" Munroy was confused.

"As well as personal transport. I'm interested in purchasing this vehicle myself."

Munroy was even more confused. "But you don't drive, Raoul." Or did he? "Do you?"

"Not to worry. That's a small matter. Easily fixed! How much do you want for the truck?"

Munroy was so surprised at the idea of Raoul buying—and driving!—a vehicle, especially the faded and puffy old pick-up that had sat on the lot for so long, that he was rendered speechless and

RUM FOR THE PINEAPPLE CUP

left completely unable to haggle. By the time the two men finally shook on it, Raoul had brokered himself a real steal.

———————

His tête-à-tête and truck talk done, Raoul should have known which commission to tackle next; such had been his theory.

Only he didn't. Should he go straight to the bank to get Munroy his money? Or to the library to talk it over with his wife? Pineapple Jewelry and Gems was near the bank, so whenever he got there, he should go talk to Cora, too.

Hmm.

Like a small boy about to buy an ice cream or a brand new toy, Raoul lacked the restraint to put off his purchase. The bank would have to be his first stop, and he would pop into Cora's after. Lila would certainly not mind Raoul's buying a truck if it meant he was able to take her wherever she needed to go. A trip to the library was a waste of time. As for a book on driving, Raoul had brokered into the bargain a driving lesson from Munroy. If things went as planned, Raoul would be giving a ride to his bride before the day was out.

He was so giddy as he continued into town, he practically skipped his way there. Wouldn't Ms. Lila be delighted!

25

If whoever Raoul felt had been following him the day before was still at it, they would have noticed, as he climbed the steps to Cora's jewelry store, that the spring in his step had lost some of its bounce. His pockets were heavier, that was true, but they were not to blame. Rather, in his giddiness, Raoul had spilled the beans at the Savings Bank about his new used truck—he regretted it instantly—and all those islander noses in his business had gotten right up his nose. From the teller, to the bank manager, to the locals waiting in line, it was a chorus of "But you don't drive, Raoul...do you?" Raoul had a firm policy of always treating the islanders' opinions with utter disregard, but their rain on his pale blue-green parade had dampened his spirits nonetheless. Judging by the number of cars and trucks and buses he saw on the roadways, driving didn't require some remarkable strain of genius. Was it so far-fetched, then, to assume that Raoul might be just as unremarkable as everyone else who lived on Oh?!

Served him right for not keeping his counsel! Raoul of all people knew that no good ever came of broadcasting one's business all over the island. With his palm he smacked the side of his head in reprimand as he huffed up the stair, cursing audibly under his breath.

Cora, whose door was propped open to capture the island breeze, heard the commotion and looked up from her work. Soon the smacking and huffing and cursing produced Raoul, who poked his nose inside.

"Good morning!" she said, pleased to see him. "I've been waiting for you. Is it Mr. Orlean or Officer Orlean today?"

"It's Officer Orlean." Raoul pushed the nosey islanders out of his mind and turned his focus to the matter at hand. What did she mean she'd been expecting him?

"Good. Have you come about more butterflies?" she teased.

"Uh, no. I came because I have reason to believe that some parcels addressed to you have gone missing at the hands of a corrupt Customs officer."

"Is that so?" Cora let Raoul see that she was intrigued. "Tell me more."

"I came to ask you if, to your knowledge, you are missing any shipments. Small ones. Perhaps as many as three. Have you ordered any supplies that failed to arrive?"

"Oh, I should think so," Cora told him.

"Can you be more specific? What would the street value be of what you're missing?"

"I couldn't begin to guess that. I don't precisely know what it is that I don't have. I also doubt that anyone on any street on Oh would know what to do with my 'supplies,' as you call them. You can't buy your groceries with some bits of moonstone, now can you?"

"Moonstone?" Raoul's eyes opened wide. "You mean pieces of the moon?" Good god, what was the woman capable of?!

Cora chuckled. "No, not from the moon. Mine comes from Madagascar. Do you know where that is?"

Did he know where that is? Of course he did! Raoul was no fool. His day-off Tuesdays at the library he spent reading up on everything from geography to cactus gardens, and re-reading the story of Stan Kalpi—and he told Cora so. (Truth be told, since Bruce's article about Lila's fall, and Lila's trip to Cora's in Nat's arms, Raoul had skipped now two consecutive Tuesdays, telling his wife he had to work instead.)

"Stan who?" Cora asked.

"Never mind that now." Raoul paused to think. He had asked Cora about Dwight Williams before and she had laughed and called Dwight a fool. If he was up to no good with her moonstone, she must not know about it. She knew the Curator, though, didn't she? If she couldn't help him with his Customs case, maybe she could help him with his marital one.

"What about Seafus Hobb?" Raoul asked her.

Cora, who had in the meantime returned to her work, polishing the now-finished larimar moon brooch, stopped and met Raoul's gaze. "What about him?"

"It is possible that the Museum, curated by Mr. Hobb, is connected in some way with your disappearing parcels.

"What way would that be?"

"My investigation is only beginning, and I can't answer that yet. If you could tell me anything about Seafus Hobb, that might be helpful."

"You don't know anything yourself about Mr. Hobb?" Cora asked. "He has quite a reputation on Oh."

"Yes, I know. Then again, island rumors wax and wane with the moon. As Mr. Hobb's friend, I thought you might speak more directly on his behalf," Raoul said.

"His friend? Who told you I was his friend?" Cora's tone, which always struck Raoul as either slightly mocking or slightly annoyed, as if she didn't take any conversation entirely seriously, not even serious ones, without warning turned severe. She was neither poking fun at him nor was she mildly miffed; she was—no doubt about it—*serious* for once. Dead serious. The effect was as disorienting as a visit to the Parliamentary Museum.

Raoul's mouth went dry and he cleared his throat. "*He* did. Seafus did. At the Museum."

"When?"

"I took my wife there last night to have a look around and he said we should come back sometime. With you, our...that is, mine and his," Raoul gulped, "our mutual friend."

Cora's tone was calmer. She had wanted Raoul putting his fingers into the Curator's pies, hadn't she? Best not to scare him away. Less severely, but still subdued she said: "In all the years I've known Seafus Hobb, I have never, not for one single minute, considered myself his friend. Quite the contrary. I'm given to think that Seafus sees things one way in his head, while in truth, they are another way altogether. You see, in fact, that he even went so far as to elevate your commercial transactions here to a personal friendship with me."

That was, in fact, exactly what he had done!

"He did the same with my wife!" Raoul elaborated.

"Oh?" (Did Cora sound...what? *Concerned?*)

"He said how pretty she was and how it had been such a long time since they had seen each other, as if they were the best of friends. I suppose he knows her from town or the market."

"No. The library," she said dryly. "Years ago, before there was a library at the museum, he used the island library frequently."

"A library at the museum? There was no library. Everything plus the kitchen sink, yes, but no library."

"It's upstairs. You and your wife won't have had reason to go there."

Cora could see that Raoul was about to ask how she knew all she knew about Seafus, if the two of them weren't really friends. She held up a hand to silence him before he could.

"I've heard tell," was all she said, and Raoul believed her. A bug in his head said she knew even more than that, but Raoul wouldn't push his luck, not today with so much still to do. He had his answer about Seafus and Lila and the missing parcels (sort of), and confirmation from Cora's tone that the Curator was as bad a man as everyone had told him. He had also learned that the Museum held some secrets, and if that was the case, then its Curator had some, too. Raoul began to suspect that Dwight's illicit dealings were taking place in the heart of the Parliamentary Museum for very good cause.

"Thank you," Raoul said sincerely. "This information will be very useful indeed. Please call the Customs headquarters if you think of anything else."

"Wait! You won't have this brooch before you go? For your wife? I've just finished it." She held up the larimar moon. It was beautiful, Raoul had to admit. Every time he blinked and re-focused his eyes on it, its face seemed to change, to show him something different. Had he been asked to describe it, he would have said it oozed knowledge, though he would not have been able to articulate the effects of its wisdom, which his heart perceived as more affront than reinforcement.

"No, thank you." Raoul declined the precious moon. "I have an appointment. I need to go."

"Does your wife wear the pendant you gave her for her birthday?" Cora asked, before he could turn to leave.

"Yes," Raoul replied. "She's been wearing it every day."

"Good," Cora nodded. "Good."

Raoul looked from the moon to Cora and back, sure there was a link between the two that he was supposed to see and grab hold of. Some golden design that bent the midday sun creeping in past the balcony and held it fast. Raoul's mind had almost seen its solidity, almost sensed its strength, when the loud honk of a horn from the street below burst into the shop and broke his chain of thought.

"Right." His afternoon commission awaited.

———

Making his way past the market and back to the body shop to pay Munroy, Raoul let his head fill with the scents of the vendors' wares. The onions and lemongrass, the guava cheese and tamarind, the curry and cocoa. It smelled like home, and Raoul was happy. In that moment it struck him that if he never found another variable, never caught another clue or solved another case, it didn't matter. Raoul was where he was meant to be, walking past the market in the town of Port-St. Luke, on the island of Oh, in the middle of the sea. He would sleep in his bed that night, in his rose-colored cottage, with his wife Ms. Lila by his side, and wake up to the island sun in the morning. Wasn't that what Stan Kalpi had sought all along? His *place*? Raoul had always believed that variables were the means to an equation, and the equation a means to a solution. What if the variables were just *means*, full stop? Why hadn't Raoul seen it this way before?

"Look, man!" A driver yelled at Raoul through the window of his minibus as he nearly ran Raoul down.

"You go too fast!" Raoul yelled back, but the bus was already past him. So too was his Stan Kalpi wisdom, which had managed to slip away the minute Raoul got distracted, his thoughts lost to the dust and the dirt stirred by the speeding vehicle.

Huh.

Raoul crossed to the other side of the road and kept his course. He watched the This Way That Way Garage and Body Shop sign grow closer with each step he took. This. Way. That. Way. He scanned the sign in his head. He also tried to put his finger on... what? There was still a question on the tip of his tongue, a mystery he'd been contemplating only a short while ago. He tried to grab onto it again before it got away for good.

"Wait," he said out loud and stopped dead in his tracks. Cora. It was coming back into focus. Cora behind her counter with the moon resting between them. Raoul had walked in and Cora had said it. She had said she'd been expecting him. What did she mean by that?

Even Raoul hadn't known his own mind when he left his cottage that morning; he had made his plans en route. Cora Silverfish certainly couldn't have known he was coming, couldn't have known that he had skipped the library and Ms. Lila, in favor of the Savings Bank and Pineapple Jewelry and Gems. So why did she say she'd been expecting him?

What—in the world—did she mean by *that*?

26

Back at the body shop, Raoul set all his flies free, trading questions about Cora and Kalpi maths for schooling on clutches and coolants. The commercial part of his transaction with Munroy had been simple (money paid, receipt signed, truck title turned over). The theoretical part, only somewhat less so (Raoul had a general idea about how vehicles worked, after all, and about the maintenance they required). The practical part of his pact with Munroy is where Raoul ran into difficulty. It was all well and good to explain how one went about shifting gears, second to third to fourth, but Raoul was stalled (literally) at first. When he wasn't stalled, he (or the truck, rather, for it felt to Raoul as though he had little say in the matter) lurched forward angrily. Sometimes it scolded him, too, grinding its gears in reprimand.

After more than an hour of stalling and lurching behind the body shop, Raoul was forced to admit that his bride would get her ride home that evening once again from Nat. Try though Raoul might, he couldn't seem to coordinate his right foot and his left, nor the pair of them with the gear shift at his side. Munroy was a good sport; he agreed to leave the truck on the lot till morning, and to give Raoul another lesson then. In the meantime, Raoul remained a pedestrian—no shame in that—although for the second time that day he didn't know where his feet should carry him.

Leaning against his truck, for which he felt great affection when the engine was off, Raoul weighed his options. He was hungry; his day's runnings had kept him too busy to eat. He could find a snack at a rum shack or at the Belly. His mouth watered at the thought of a hot tuna pie! Then again, the sun was leaning, and the afternoon was winding down. Hot tuna might spoil his dinner. The late hour was justification, too, for deciding against a stop at his office in town. By the time he turned up, all his staff would be gone—if they weren't already. They had learned over the years that if Raoul didn't turn up by lunch, it meant he was working in the field, so to speak (sometimes it meant he was literally in a field looking for clues), and likely wouldn't turn up at all. Which meant they left for lunch and didn't come back.

Maybe Raoul should go to the library after all. If he couldn't drive Ms. Lila home himself, he could at least be there when Nat did. And despite his rocky driving lesson, Raoul couldn't wait to tell Lila about his truck.

———

Poor Raoul! He may have looked into a magic moon and caught a glimpse of truth as he walked past the market square; may have seen his island home of Oh, and his place there, in all its inevitably perfect imperfection; may even have recognized that he was as blessed as the hero of his favorite book; but poor, foolish Raoul, for all his belonging and all his means, would never learn to keep pace with the island tide. It swept in and collected whatever it could, then went again, further out every time, until it came back to sweep some more. A case in point: Raoul's new used green-blue transport.

That Raoul believed he could break the news to his spouse of a deed done hours before, was almost endearing in its artlessness! From the body shop to the bank and beyond, and back again, the tide that had got word of Raoul's truck was swift and all-encompassing. It had washed its way across the island by lunch-time, and by dinnertime not a single toe of a single citizen of Oh wouldn't be wet, least of all Ms. Lila's.

When Raoul reached the library, he found her seated at her desk, drumming her fingers impatiently.

"I've been expecting you," she said. (Why did everyone keep telling him that today?)

"You have?"

"Well, I should hope so, that you might turn up and tell me yourself what everyone else has been telling me all day!" she huffed.

"What would that be, dear?"

"You know very well, Raoul!"

"I don't, I'm afraid." What was she talking about?

"You bought a vehicle? You don't even drive!" (At least not as far as she knew.) "Do you? What was going on in that head of yours?"

Right then, as a matter of fact, two bottleflies were back at it in his head, telling him how stupid he'd been to broadcast his business at the bank. Or maybe the body shop. But how could he not broadcast it there, merely by virtue of making his purchase? Ahh! Once again, he cursed audibly under his breath. (It had turned into that kind of day.)

"What's the problem with owning a vehicle? I can drive you while you're on your crutches. And after that, I can drive you to work when it rains." Raoul began to present his case.

The 'problem,' though Ms. Lila couldn't bring herself to say so, was that her husband was prone to flights of fancy in his incessant search for the variables he needed to solve whatever mystery was at hand. She had known him to chase ghosts (to disprove them, of course), to ponder the holes in doughnuts, and to advertise for clues in the newspaper. Once, before they were married, she had banned him from the library for tearing the pages out of books and for removing his socks and shoes. Back then, Raoul had a habit of wandering the island barefoot, hoping his toes would touch clues in the tide. (After the wedding, Ms. Lila had put a stop to that.) With a vehicle that could carry Raoul to the island's roughest edges, Lila worried about how far he would go, and about what messes he might get his flywheel stuck in, somewhere far out and all alone.

To Raoul all she said was: "You never even thought to talk to me before taking such a big step?"

"I did, you know!" Raoul defended himself. "But the body shop was right there by the docks at Customs and the library was the other direction."

Their marital tiff—at least the first round of it—ended there with the arrival of Nat, who had come to drive Lila home. Both Raoul and Lila heard his vehicle pull right up to the door, and sure enough, his sure footsteps a moment later.

"Halloo," he called out, bouncing in purposefully. "Lila, you ready?" When he saw Raoul he stopped mid-step. "Raoul! Hey, man! What are *you* doing here? It's not Tuesday, is it?"

Raoul took undue offense at Nat's surprise at seeing him; undue, for it really was out of the ordinary for Raoul to be at the library at that hour. Lately even on Tuesdays he'd been a no-show. Worse than Nat's surprise, when Raoul tried to insinuate himself in the proceedings—locking up the library, accompanying Ms. Lila to the van, getting her situated and her foot propped just so— he was unable to. The pair of them, Lila and Nat, had obviously settled into a routine, perfected a daily choreography *à deux*, and Raoul was in the way.

When they were finally headed home, then, the talk turned to Raoul's new vehicle. How could it not? Taxi-men drove in and out of the tide of island gossip the whole day long. Unlike Raoul's other compatriots, however, Nat was less interested in whether or not Raoul knew how to drive, than he was in the vehicle itself. He had gone through dozens of used cars and trucks and vans over the years, shuttling tourists and islanders, too, from one end of the island to the other. Speaking to Raoul's reflection in the rear-view mirror (Raoul had found himself seated behind his wife and Nat), he asked Raoul about the make and model, grilled him about the truck's specifications (engine, transmission, horse-power), and wondered aloud about its payload capacity. Raoul answered as best he could, remembering most of what Munroy had told him, but he was distracted. Distracted by the way Nat's arm shot out to block Lila's upper half every time he stopped short; bothered by the way Nat reached to steady the crutches that leaned against her leg, every time he took a sharp turn; downright angry at the picture of them in the front seat together, like some bloody happy couple, with Raoul playing gooseberry in the backseat!

"You hear what I say, Raoul?" Nat was going on about the air-conditioning feature in his new van, a luxury missing from Raoul's old truck.

"Yeah, yeah, sure, sure," Raoul replied, attaching a head-nod to each syllable and watching out the window.

"I don't find it's so important, since you never had a vehicle before," Nat droned. "Once you have it, you wouldn't want to give it up, but if you never had it at all, you wouldn't know to miss it."

"Say again?" A fly jerked in Raoul's head.

"I say, if you never had it, you wouldn't know to miss it."

Indeed.

"Stop!" Raoul yelled out.

Nat hit the brakes in a panic and nearly got hit from behind. "What is it?! What's wrong?" He turned to look at Raoul behind him.

"Nothing, nothing, sorry. Leave me here," he said, jumping out of the van in the middle of the street. "Take Lila home. Thanks." He slid the door shut and banged twice on the roof with his hand.

"Go!"

27

Raoul ran at top speed (for him) toward the docks. He had jumped from Nat's van as suddenly as he did, because he saw the Customs entryway go past just as Nat mentioned missing things. The combination of Nat's words and Raoul's sighting triggered a split-second plan, one he wished to implement immediately. It would require some even stealthier collaboration on the part of Garvin, whom Raoul hoped to find alone at Customs, lingering to log Cora's packages after hours.

It was so obvious! Why hadn't Raoul thought of it before? One couldn't miss what was missing all along. Cora had said something similar. He had thought her somewhat vague on the matter of her lost parcels, and now he knew why. What sense in spying on Dwight's mysterious package doings, if the packages themselves were a mystery? Garvin would have to find a way to open the packages up, and log their insides, too, before passing them on to Dwight. When Raoul explained as much to Garvin, he was met with a dubious scowl.

"But how?" he argued. "Those boxes come from all over, with different color ink and different wrapping, some tied with string, some taped. How could I open them and put them back the way they were?"

"The only one who knows the way they were is *you*. Be as delicate as you can when you open them, certainly, but if you have to substitute string for Sellotape to shut them back up, so be it! Dwight will never know," Raoul assured him. "Did you log any packages today? Is there something here we can open right now?"

"There was one, but Dwight took it when he left. He was stopping in town on his way home." Anticipating Raoul's curiosity as to his package-less presence there at that hour, Garvin added, "I stayed back to tidy up. With all this secret reporting I have to do, I let my desk become cluttered."

"From where?" Raoul demanded.

"The clutter?" Garvin asked, confused.

"The package!" Raoul barked. "Where was the package from that Dwight took to town? Show me your log entry."

Garvin fished in his desk and pulled out the notebook for Raoul to examine. Raoul's finger followed the entry as he read. It said that Cora's package was medium-sized, a square with ten-inch sides and edges, postal-stamped FRANCE, and addressed in a neat hand. It was tied with string, made no sounds when shaken, and weighed easily over a pound.

"And Garvin went to deliver it this afternoon," Raoul confirmed.

"Yes. He left work early to do so."

Hmph! If Raoul only had his truck now, he could jump into it, drive to town, and maybe catch Dwight going in and out of the museum. (Also, he remembered, he could have been the one to drive Lila home.) He was going to have to solve this driving problem once and for all. "Enough is enough!" he said.

Garvin assumed it was Dwight who had Raoul so fed up, and he nodded in agreement.

To conclude their meeting, Raoul reiterated: "Do as I said and try to find out what's in one of Cora's boxes. I won't come by the shed in the morning. No reason to now. Look for me there day after tomorrow. If anything, call my office." With that, Raoul took his leave.

Garvin finished sorting through a pile of papers on his desk, and then he left, too. Walking home, he thought about Raoul and this latest secret assignment for Customs and Excise. He didn't doubt for a moment Raoul's authority to recruit him for special duty. He did wonder, however, if the investigation had any point. To be sure, home delivery was beyond the scope of Dwight's mandate; but if Cora had received her packages that way for as long as anyone could recall, was it such a terrible bending of the rules? It was only by virtue of all the exceptions to every island rule, that the islanders knew what the rules were meant to be.

At the end of the day, how Cora Silverfish got her dead butterflies or her rocks was of no consequence to Garvin. About his future, though, he cared greatly, and in fact aspired to Raoul's position one day, at the wheel of Customs and Excise. Garvin indulged Raoul's package whims not only because Raoul was his boss, but because an endorsement from Raoul Orlean could fast-track his career. On the other hand, Garvin feared Raoul's investigation might prove a huge waste of time—or worse! Who knew what the truth was behind the Cora Silverfish exception to the Customs rule?—and if so, if Raoul was traveling blind alleys or headed for trouble, then Garvin wanted no truck with either.

———

The workday now good and done, the This Way That Way Garage and Body Shop was empty and locked up tight. On the lot sat Raoul's truck, alone and blue in the dusk. Raoul found its faded beauty daunting; still, he was determined to drive it home to Ms. Lila if it took him all night.

He climbed in and closed the door and sat. Munroy had rushed him earlier in the day! Raoul needed a moment to acclimatize himself to the height and feel of the truck's seat, to the views in the mirrors, the tension of the foot pedals. Without turning the motor on, he gently pushed on the clutch, the accelerator, the brake. He fiddled with all the mirrors until he could see things just as he liked. He found the levers to adjust his seat and perfected his positioning behind the wheel. He cranked open the window and listened to the sounds of the dusk. It was quiet, all the islanders off preparing their supper, and Raoul could hear the slap of the sea against the docks nearby. The tree frogs were just beginning their evening chirp, and the palms rustled, egging them on. How he loved his island when the darkness and the nature blocked out the gossip, and the magic!

A mosquito landed on Raoul's neck; he attended to it with a loud slap that recalled him to his purpose. He exhaled. He felt calm, felt certain he could conquer his new vehicle. It was just a little old truck, after all. He put the key in the ignition and the engine turned over. It had a healthy, rhythmic sputter that he hadn't noticed before. The next step was getting himself some light. In the darkening dusk, Raoul fumbled to find the switch for the headlamps, which Munroy's day-time lesson had omitted. Once that was done, he put his hands on the steering wheel, satisfied and determined.

About this time, Lila was home stewing pork with papaya and stewing over Raoul's rude behavior with Nat. Jumping out of the van like that! When Raoul got home, she would feed him a piece of her mind for dessert!

For Raoul's part, food was the farthest thing from his mind. His stomach knotted every time he tried to play the clutch against the accelerator. He finally got it, though, and managed to creep backward and forward behind the body shop garage, never venturing forward in more than first gear. This wouldn't do, of course, to drive himself home so slowly. He stopped and surveyed the space before him. If his calculations were correct, he should have just enough room to push the truck into second for a short time, without crashing into the fence that delineated the edge of the Customs outpost next door.

By now Lila's pot was bubbling, as impatient for dumplings as Lila was for her dinner.

Raoul had calculated correctly. The strip of empty lot behind the garage was more than sufficient for taking the truck into second gear—assuming one knew how to do so. Overly eager to get to second, he rushed through first and stalled. Frazzled by the stalling, his shifting took a hit and he grinded the gears. When at last he got to second, he panicked in the face of the fence that drew nearer, and forgot how to slow down and stop. Instinctively he hit the brakes hard, and stalled himself out again.

"Ahh!" he spat out loud. He got out of the truck to stretch his legs and dust himself off (every stall was as if he had fallen down and dirtied himself). It was the noise that was disturbing his concentration! The incessant chirp of the treefrogs and the infernal moan of a far-off motorbike! He stomped his feet and collected himself and got back on the proverbial horse. One last go and then he would have to admit defeat, a prospect that galled every bone in his body and every fly in his head.

It was getting late, and at home Lila was galled, too. She got angrier with every pork bone she sucked on as she dined all alone. Not only had Raoul abandoned her rudely to Nat, but he had also missed their evening meal!

Having mastered first gear and stopping and starting, Raoul's stomach had unknotted and was hungry. He wondered what Ms. Lila had cooked for dinner. Maybe chicken legs, stuffed with peppers and thyme. Or perhaps some spicy lamb with cinnamon? Warm rice and callaloo on the side? Or cold cabbage salad and baked yams. He hoped she wouldn't be upset at his arriving home late, but he would tell her he was learning to drive his truck. Which—hold up!—is exactly what he was doing! He *was* driving his truck! Somewhere between the chicken legs and the cabbage, he had found his way to second gear and back again, without knocking over a single fence. When he realized what he'd accomplished, he patted the steering wheel with glee.

Raoul was grinning from ear to ear and drenched in sweat. He had done it! He was the spanking new driver of an old blue-green truck, and he was tickled pink about it! Even so, Raoul knew better than to push his luck. It was time to head home, and second gear would have to do. (He was too spanking new to realize that the shift from second to third to fourth and back was exponentially much less difficult.) He edged his way onto the main road that loosely hugged the shoreline, and slowly and steadily made his way. The other vehicles he encountered passed him by or honked in anger, but Raoul didn't care. He and his truck were having too nice of a time together. That is, until he reached the gap that should have carried him to his cottage. There, his truck did a dangerous jerky dance, stalling and rolling in turn, that nearly pitched Raoul into the sea.

The gap was sloped inland and upward, and though its degree of incline was negligible, Raoul had neglected to practice shifting up and down hills. Indeed, it hadn't occurred to him that he ought to. His oversight angered him—he had been around enough to know that hills sometimes posed problems—but he was too hot and hungry and tired to do anything about it right then. He pulled his truck to the edge of the road, and left it to spend the night there, ensuring its windows were all up and its doors were locked. He would walk the rest of the way home and surprise Lila with his truck in the morning.

Resigned but a tad disappointed still, Raoul made the easy climb up the gap on foot, while in his mind he revisited the evening's events. Sometimes when things didn't go according to plan—when the island threw salt, pepper, and vinegar into the stew—they went way better in the end, didn't they? The islanders called this island magic, but Raoul didn't call it anything. Hills were hills and sometimes they were hard to climb. And, sometimes, climbing them by day just made more sense. A morning climb meant showing his wife his new used truck in the flattering warmth of the sunlight, where the truck's soft, shifting colors would melt her heart, and this just sweetened Raoul's pot.

Speaking of pots, the cottage was growing closer and Raoul's stomach kicked. He couldn't wait to eat the leftover dinner his wife must have wrapped up and left him on the stove. He only hoped that Ms. Lila hadn't prepared jerk chicken. She was always a bit heavy-handed when she did, and Raoul wasn't in the mood for much more pepper.

Harvest Tournament Week One Done
Auto Mart Out and Bakery In

The first round of the annual Pineapple Cup is halfway finished, with one week done and one more to go. Three matches were played in the past week, about which this paper reported individually, but a recap follows for those readers who missed the results: Ashbee's Appliances, Tackle and Tools tackled Garrison's Auto Mart 5-2; Higgins Hardware, Home and Garden raked the Island Post 4-3; and Trevor's Bakery taxed Customs and Excise 6-0. There is however more to these scores than just the numbers. The win by Trevor's Bakers, with an average age of forty-plus among them, over the hearty young Excisemen is commendable. It remains to be seen whether the over-40s will make it through the next round. The respective victories of Ashbee's Appliances and Higgins Hardware means the pair will face each other in Round Two, a grudge match owing to their continued battle for dominance in the washing-machine arena. Islanders will be treated tomorrow to the first match-up of the second week of Round One of the Cup, at 5 o'clock at the playing field in Port-St. Luke. The Parliamentary Museum will battle Piper's All-Stars, sponsored and equipped by their local Member of Parliament Gerald Piper, in a legislative face-off, MP v. PM. On Friday, same time and place, Belmont Stationery hopes to write off Campbell's Drug & Sundry (another reputed grudge match, owing to their respective goalkeepers' continued battle for dominance in the dating arena, specifically as concerns a young woman from Port-St. Anne); and on Saturday at 5 o'clock in town, the Savings Bank will seek to withdraw the Island Police from next week's Round Two. Although the government authorities lost out last week with the defeat of Customs and Excise and the Island Post, they remain in the running for the prized Cup, with the two parliamentary teams and the Police still in play. As always, the pineapple-inspired cup in question, commissioned by the Ministry of Sports and Culture, will be created by Cora Silverfish of Pineapple Jewelry and Gems, where closing-doors discounts continue.

28

"There you are!" Raoul set down the morning paper when he saw Lila come into the kitchen. "I put on the kettle. Do you want some tea?"

"I'll do it," she said, dragging herself to the kitchen counter. She had fallen asleep before Raoul reached home the night before, and the anger she had planned to unleash when he did, was only somewhat abated. "You reached late," she stated.

"Sorry for that." Ms. Lila's demeanor told Raoul it was best to wait until after she'd had her tea to spring his surprise.

"You missed dinner."

"I ate it all when I got here. Delicious."

"You were rude to Nat."

"I was?"

"You jumped out of his van in the middle of the street! For no reason at all!"

"I had a very good reason!" Nat, Nat, Nat, Raoul thought to himself. Always Nat. He smirked thinking of his truck and Nat's soon-to-be diminished role in Lila's life.

"You think it's funny?" Ms. Lila caught him out.

"No, no, no. Sit. Sit. Have your tea." Raoul got up and helped her to a chair.

By way of ice-breaker, Raoul opened his mouth to ask Lila if she fancied watching the football match the next evening in town, only just as he started to speak, he remembered it was the Museum team playing, and thought better of putting his wife in the Curator's path again. Ms. Lila, who had been watching Raoul read his paper as she decided how angry (or not) she still was at him, realized that he swallowed the words on the tip of his tongue.

"What?" she asked, almost eager to start a fight. "What is it?"

"Mm? Nothing."

"What were you going to say?" (Her tone told Raoul that 'Nothing' would be an insufficient answer.)

"I was just reading about the Pineapple Cup cup. Cora Silverfish is making it, like always. I have to see her today. Her name in the paper reminded me, is all."

"Why do you have to see Cora Silverfish?" Lila snapped.

Odd, that, Raoul noted. Why should Lila be bothered if he went to speak with Cora?

"The property I was looking for at the Museum the other night belonged to her," Raoul explained.

"But you said it was government property," Lila objected.

"Technically, it was, but only in a custodial sense. Customs is liable for property in its possession."

"Raoul, what are you talking about? What property?"

"Packages! Packages addressed to Cora that went missing at the Museum."

"We didn't see any packages at the Museum!"

"I know. It's a complicated case. I haven't figured it all out yet, which is why I have to talk to Cora. Don't trouble yourself about it." He put the paper down. "I have a surprise for you."

Lila was indeed troubled. It seemed as though Raoul were making things up, silly reasons to go see Cora Silverfish.

"Did you hear?" Raoul insisted. "I said I have a surprise."

"Oh?" Lila had been married to Raoul long enough to know that his idea of a surprise was sometimes surprising in the wrong sort of way.

"Wait here!" he said, and ran out. She could see how excited he was, which only increased her apprehension.

Lila picked up the paper and perused the article about the football tournament. Raoul's Customs team had been knocked out, so why wasn't Raoul more bothered? She knew in her heart the reason why. He was preoccupied with Cora. Tears were beginning to prick at her eyes when she heard a sudden and terrible sound. "What in the world?" she said out loud.

The sound came from outside, from the road. It was a painful, strained buzz, or maybe a growl, that slid up an octave and came back down. Up and down. Up and down. Up and down it buzzed and growled until her curiosity got the better of her. She pulled herself up and plunked to the door with her crutches. Lordy!

Nothing could have prepared her for the sight before her eyes.

The growl she'd heard appeared to be coming from a beat-up old truck so faded that she couldn't tell if it was green or blue. Its motor idled frantically as the truck tried to clamber up the gap in front of her cottage, and then slowed pitifully as the truck slid back a piece for every two pieces it made its way forward. What was the driver doing? He seemed at odds with his vehicle, she couldn't help but notice. She squinted in the sun to make out the face of the odd driver, and nearly fell over and fractured her other ankle when she realized it was Raoul.

"Raoul!" she shouted at the top of her lungs. "Stop that this instant!" She was mortified. What would the neighbors think?

Such was the fury in her voice that it jarred Raoul into overcoming his difficulty with the clutch. He managed finally to propel the truck up the incline and stopped it in front of the house.

"Are you mad?" she asked him when he joined her by the door.

"I just need some practice. Don't worry. Isn't it something?"

"*This* is the new vehicle I've been hearing so much about? What year is it from?"

"What difference does it make? It runs fine. Now I can drive you wherever you need to go."

In her mind, Lila juxtaposed an image of herself in Nat's air-conditioned champagne-colored van with one of herself bouncing up and down in the old faded pick-up that Raoul could barely control. She bowed her head in defeat. What was she to do? Break her husband's heart? Raoul's excitement was undeniable.

Unless he was a *cheating* husband, and then what did she care about his heart? Hearts aside, what about her foot? Would it hurt her ankle to jostle it about in Raoul's old truck? She was certain the ride wouldn't be as smooth as in Nat's taxi. Nat would be there any minute; would she simply send him away? He had been so kind to her, chauffeuring her day after day to work and home again at night.

Sigh.

She might not avoid driving with Raoul at some point, but there was no need to rush.

"Raoul," she told him, somewhat more kindly than she felt toward him right then, "you will not drive me anywhere until you've learned how to operate that thing safely. Do you want me to break my other ankle, too?"

In light of his tortured climb up the gap, Raoul had no good comeback. His displeasure at her dismissal was so obvious and so great that, Silverfish aside, Lila felt for him. She gave him a peck on the cheek that went far in soothing his bruised ego, and returned inside to finish her tea before Nat arrived. Reluctantly Raoul followed her. He noticed as he sat opposite that she was wearing her birthday pendant. (It had become such a habit to put it on, that even in her anger that morning, she hadn't thought to leave it off, to punish her rude and tardy husband.)

"You look sweet," he couldn't help saying, even as miffed as he was that Nat would be coming to collect her any minute. A damselfly in Raoul's head told him he would get Ms. Lila in his truck eventually; all he needed was a little practice. In the meantime, and in spite of himself, he still went gooey when he looked at her. Raoul loved Ms. Lila no matter what and always would. There was no point in fighting, because she would always win, and he didn't need a fly to tell him so. He shrugged, then he picked up the *Morning Crier* and returned to his breakfast, as if the tension between them had never been.

Odd, that, thought Lila. Why was he so cheerful all of a sudden?

"Cora asked me if you wore it," he said from behind his paper. "She seemed pleased when I told her you did."

"What?" Cora, Cora, Cora, Lila thought to herself. Always Cora. "Wore what?"

"Your pendant. What else?"

"When did you talk to Cora? I thought you had to see her today."

"I do. Yesterday I saw her, too. I told you it's a complicated case." He reached across the table and gave her hand a squeeze. "Hurry, now, or you'll be late."

Yesterday, too? Lila hadn't thought to leave off her pendant to punish her husband for being rude, but had Raoul been equally kind? Had he bandied about Cora's name in rebuke for her refusing a ride? Was that why he was smiling? Why his mood had turned like the island tide? Because he had had the last vengeful word? Or did the mere mention of Cora's name, the idea of her, fill his heart and his eyes with such contentment and love? Lila was positive it was love that she'd seen when Raoul looked at her with her pendant and said how sweet she looked. Gooey, no-matter-what love that had lightened his mood!

Bang was right. The necklace was a noose. A gift from her husband that Lila wore, out of love, to appease him, and instead it made him think of its maker and smile.

29

Cora Silverfish lived on a hill overlooking Port-St. Luke, in the village of Monfruie. She walked to town most days, not only because she preferred the breezy solitude of her thoughts to the hot, crowded buses, but also because she liked the view from the road that wound its way out of Monfruie and into the eastern edge of Port-St. Luke. True, on an island like Oh, a less-than-breathtaking view was hard to come by. Still, Cora preferred this one especially, for its exhaustive display of island flora. She could leave her little villa at 8 am, and by the time she reached her shop at 8:45, she had more jewelry ideas than she knew what to do with. From the pineapple patches that burst from the ground near her house, to the giant buttercup at the cemetery just above town, Cora's commute spared her no fruit or flower. The apples and berries and petals mingled with coral and pearl and turquoise as she passed them by; almond trees and mango called opal and amber to mind; coco palms and aloe vera, ivory and jade.

This particular morning she was up and about earlier than was her usual, hoping her walk might send her into work with a pineapple problem solved. The Pineapple Cup final was just over three weeks away, and it was time to design the Cup. Traditionally the cup was not so much a cup, as a statue, a trophy in the form of (what else?) a pineapple. She had her materials—copper for the body and pineapple jasper for the leaves—but in order to transform the flat, square pieces of metal and the blunt, lumpy stones into a round and prickly exemplum that looked good enough to eat, she needed the kind of inspiration that only the island could provide.

Once on the road, Cora paid special attention to the patches close to home. She gently paced their edges, letting the perfume of dirt and leaf fill her nose. She closed her eyes and said a prayer of thank you for the magic that had cooked up so much of the island's favorite fruit. Gingerly she stepped between the pineapple plants on the ground; they proffered their green and golden offspring, as if the latter were a gift held out to her alone. Cora stooped and ran her hand over one of the pineapples, let her finger trace the mathematical perfection of its skin. Not yet ripe for picking, it was both gentle in its greenness and rigid in its design. As she continued to touch it, she felt it turn to copper; in her mind's eye she saw the points and grooves and indentations that her hammer would have to inflict. The leaves on the pineapple's top, they would be cut from copper, too, she saw, only with yellow-green ones of jasper set in between them. With another prayer of thank you for the magic that had cooked up the cup in her head, Cora stood and smiled.

She returned to her journey on the Monfruie road, where, as if to congratulate her for her problem solved, the sugar apples and coffee berries that usually inspired *her*, bowed low to the ground as she passed. The trees shook their leaves in applause. Even the aloe spikes, who admired her ability to cut island beauties from copper, stood a little straighter when Cora walked by. She nodded graciously to them in response, as impressed by the island's vegetation as it was of her. Cora recalled an old island adage that said 'if you plant a stick—any stick—anywhere on Oh, it will grow.' The soil was as magic as Oh's winds.

As Cora approached her shop from the road above it, she was forced to trade the rustle of cheering leaves for the shouts and chatter of the market square. Given the early hour, vendors were just beginning to unlock their stalls, or to brush off their tables and stock them with tubers and tamarind balls. Vehicles filled with breadfruit and green banana were stopped here and there outside the square, blocking the roads until all their wares were unloaded. Drivers, vendors, and passers-by all shouted to one another—greetings, information, gossip, complaints—and horns honked good-mornings, get-out-of-my-ways, and worse.

From the balcony of her shop, Cora watched it all, as enamored of the bustle and color of the quaint Market Square atop Market Square Hill, as she was of the shimmy and scent of the frangipani or the crack of green coconut against machete (required to reach the fresh water and jelly inside). What a fine morning it was turning out to be!

Climbing up Market Square Hill, or trying to, a truck in the distance caught Cora's eye. It was faded green (or was it faded blue?), and it screeched and stalled and grinded its way painfully up the inclined street, after nearly sliding back down it a number of times first. Cora chuckled. Who on the island had gotten behind the wheel of a truck they didn't know how to drive?

'Oh, dear,' she thought with a grin. Raoul Orlean. She had heard talk of his buying a beat-up old truck and surely the truck now flanking the market square had to be his. To be fair, the truck was old, but not beat-up, and when Raoul was on the flat pieces of road, judging by what Cora observed from her balcony, he managed to keep the truck from stalling out. Too bad for Raoul that, apart from the Sea Road along the island's coast, most of Oh was hilly.

Cora watched Raoul's truck skirt the market and stop in front of the building that housed her store. Officer Orlean two days in a row? A fine morning indeed!

It would take Raoul some time to get his truck parked properly and to get himself to Cora's door. While she waited, she went back inside to do some work. She wanted to sketch the copper and jasper pineapple cup, so that from the sketch she could make a clay mock-up, to guide her cutting, bending, soldering, sanding, and hammering into shape of the final product. She sat on a stool behind the display case closest to the door, pad and pencil in hand, and began to draw. She outlined the body of the pineapple first, a plump oval, narrower at the top than the bottom, which was flattened, so that the cup would stand up on its own. Then she drew the crisscrossed diagonals, up to the right and up to the left. Her sketchpad constrained her, but her three-dimensional model, she noted in the margins, would contain thirteen spirals in one direction and twenty-one in the other. The leaves would be a column of stacked, vertical starbursts, one copper, one pineapple jasper, each one springing from the one before, the jasper lending its yellow-green hue to the pineapple cup's upper half.

Lost in her drawing, Cora didn't hear Raoul come in. How long he stood looking at her before finally she lifted her head and said 'hello,' she couldn't say. Raoul, on the other hand, perceived the depth of her concentration from the moment he entered the store and felt awkward disrupting her. Once their conversation got going, though, it moved at quite a clip, each party sincerely interested for once in what the other had to say.

"Nice vehicle, Officer Orlean. I saw you coming from the balcony."

It *was* a nice vehicle, wasn't it! Imagine, that it should take Cora Silverfish of all people to pay Raoul a long-awaited compliment on his new purchase. A purchase he was not only more satisfied with every day, but one that an impatient motorist had that morning forced him to push into third gear, his favorite by far up to now. Hills were still a challenge, but he had made it up to the market without crashing into any*body* or any*thing* (and blissfully oblivious to the finger-pointing and laughter that his efforts evoked).

"Thank you," Raoul replied to Cora. "I think so, too."

"Tell me, Officer, what have you come for today?"

"I came to discuss further the matter of your missing property, specifically a package from France that arrived yesterday."

"France?" Cora got up and disappeared into the back of her shop. When she returned she was holding a square box with ten-inch sides and edges, postal-stamped FRANCE, and addressed in a neat hand, just like the one Garvin had described. "You mean this one?"

Raoul's eyes went wide and he fumbled for his words. "What? Where? How did you get that?"

"Dwight delivered it. Yesterday afternoon."

"Dwight?" So then he wasn't selling off Cora's packages after all? Or was he? "But that's the only delivery you've received in the last two days, correct?" Raoul asked.

"Mmm," Cora nodded.

"May I see the contents, please," Raoul ordered her.

"Aren't you all supposed to keep track of that at Customs?" Cora rebutted. "It was already cut open when Dwight brought it by." (It was true that Customs opened every parcel, but only ever in the presence of the addressee.)

"You're sure?" Raoul couldn't tolerate such gross oversight in the lower ranks of his organization!

"Yes."

Again Raoul asked to see the contents. Cora dumped out of the box a rectangle of soft cloth wrapping that had clearly been undone and redone a number of times. As she unrolled the cloth, each successive fold revealed a long piece of rock, a dozen of them in all, like giant, irregular fingers. They were pale green, like the flesh of green lemon. When Raoul tilted his head, he saw they hid a hint of yellow.

"What are they? Are they valuable?"

Cora tilted her head left to right, formulating her answer. "Pineapple jasper. Not so expensive, no, although it's rare to find such large samples as these."

"Won't you just chop them up, to make them into smaller pieces of jewelry?"

"Not these. These are for the tournament cup." She showed him her sketchpad.

Raoul studied it but didn't understand where the jasper fit.

"It's for the leaves at the top."

Still, Raoul was confused about the jasper. Not about where it fit on the cup but about where it had come from. Was Dwight opening Cora's parcels, determining their value, and then deciding whether to sell them or not? Was he delivering one every so often so that Cora would be none the wiser? Four packages in two days and only one delivered. Raoul remembered the Black Diamond butterfly and supposed that Dwight would have sold that one, too, had Raoul not intercepted it.

"What?" Cora could see in Raoul's eyes the reflections of the buzzing flies that posed questions in his head.

"I don't understand why some of your parcels get through and some of them don't," he confessed. (A tsetse deep in his brain marveled at Raoul's comfortable conversing with Cora; perhaps their kindred appreciation for his pick-up had loosened his lips.)

"Have you determined where they get tied up? The ones that don't get through?"

Raoul was reluctant to mention Dwight, since he knew Cora considered Dwight a fool. There was more to him than she realized, Raoul feared. "As near as I can tell, they're being sold off, possibly under cover of the Parliamentary Museum."

"I see." Cora kept a straight face, but behind her eyes she thanked the island once more for the fruits of the very fine morning it had turned out to be.

"So Seafus Hobb is the...sticking point? Shall we say?"

"I doubt that he would have a hand in such petty thievery. I rather suspect a petty functionary of Customs and Excise."

"Not Dwight?" Cora objected, her tone disgusted. "The man is an idiot. He couldn't orchestrate any of this! You underestimate the Curator's baser instincts, I'm afraid."

"I'm afraid *you* underestimate Dwight Williams!" Raoul retorted.

Cora sighed. Caught between an empty-headed man and one whose head was full of flies, there was no sense in arguing. Dwight would lead Raoul to Seafus eventually. "If you say so," she conceded. "What do you mean to do about it? About Dwight, that is."

Raoul told her not to worry. His investigation was well under way. He would go to the ends of the island—he swore—and to the ends of his authority, to ensure no funny business was conducted at Customs and Excise. All he needed was a stick to plant, to grow himself some clues. If all went as it should, he assured her, his plant at Customs would have a stick for him the very next day.

30

Raoul hadn't been to his office at the Customs headquarters in town for three days, so when he left Pineapple Jewelry and Gems, he thought it best to head there. He ran a tight ship and his staff carried on well without him, at least until noon on any given day, but he needed to ensure that nothing urgent was left sitting on his desk. Since he passed the Savings Bank on the way, he would make a stop there, too. (He liked to check on his balance now and again, to ensure that it hadn't fallen.) Thanks to Raoul's new pick-up, the entire island was at his doorstep. He could get to wherever he wanted in a (third-gear) flash.

Perhaps after the bank and the office, he would head to the library. It was a Tuesday, and officially his day off, which meant a day he could spend perusing the new acquisitions. Over the course of his long Customs career, Raoul had sacrificed many a Tuesday to the tasks at hand, to be sure, and the swindling Dwight Williams was tasking him indeed. But Raoul had skipped two library Tuesdays now due to his sulking over Lila and Nat, and he wasn't sure he could bear missing a third. He missed touching both the books and their keeper. Although Raoul still went gooey where Lila was concerned, it didn't mean he was no longer sulky about Lila and Nat; nevertheless, to Raoul's mind his new truck had somewhat leveled the playing field, especially now that he knew how to drive it.

Balance. Urgent Matters. Lila. Thus he laid out the day before him as he shifted his way to the bank. (In truth, the bank was so close to Cora's shop that he could have more easily walked there.) Maneuvering his way through the pedestrians that were descending on the opening market, Raoul reached the Savings Bank and only had to circle the block twice to find a place to park his truck. He really must requisition that siren, he reminded himself; with that on his dash or his roof, he could park wherever he pleased.

The bank was as busy inside as the market square was out, and Raoul resigned himself to a long wait in line. He examined the backs of the heads in front of him, nodding to the ones who felt his gaze and turned around. Near the front of the line, Raoul noticed a customer who was carrying a cloth sack. The outline of the contents pressed against the fabric, chunky and square. Raoul couldn't stop staring. What was it about the man and the sack in his hand that were so compelling? Raoul furrowed his brow and squinted to get a better look. Wait. No! Was it? It was! The man was Seafus Hobb, and the sack (Raoul would bet on it!) was the very same that Dwight had carried *into* the Parliamentary Museum the day Raoul had followed him, but had never carried back out!

The contents of the sack could only be the three missing parcels that Dwight had logged and Raoul had never found! It all made sense! Dwight was selling Cora's property to Seafus Hobb, hence the museum venue for his crimes. No, that didn't make sense at all. What did the Curator want with Cora's moonrock and

210

her lapsus lorelai? As she herself had suggested, there was little chance of passing them off as currency on Oh.

Raoul watched as Seafus told the teller to call over the bank's manager. He watched them whisper, manager and curator, and then the latter opened up his sack and the former peeked in. With an agreeable nod, the manager motioned for Seafus to follow him, and the pair disappeared into the bowels of the bank. There could be only one explanation: Seafus was storing Cora's property in a safe deposit box. But what was the explanation for *that*?

The line slowly shuffled forward as Raoul waited for the Curator to emerge. After a handful of minutes there he was, the now-empty sack in one hand, and the other shaking that of the bank's manager. Seafus had a polite smile on his face that cracked almost imperceptibly—but crack it did, Raoul saw it!—when he turned to leave and caught Raoul's eyes watching him. He composed himself as quickly as his dimples had, and greeted Raoul as if neither of them were there transacting any unusual business.

"Mr. Orlean! Good morning!" He jovially grabbed for Raoul's hesitant hand and shook it. "Or is it Officer Orlean today?" he teased. "You aren't here in your official capacity, I hope, waiting in the queue like a common citizen!" He clapped Raoul on the back and, laughing heartily at his own observation, made a hasty exit.

When it was Raoul's turn at the window, he didn't bother with his balance, but instead pulled out his badge. "I need to see the manager," he instructed the teller.

She left her post and returned with the same man who had escorted Seafus Hobb from the bank's main lobby some minutes before. He looked at Raoul's badge, nodded agreeably again, and turned for Raoul to follow him. They ended up in the manager's office, where they introduced themselves more properly.

"Please sit down," the manager invited. "I'm Victor Forteneau. I run the Savings Bank."

"Officer Raoul Orlean," Raoul replied. "Head of Customs and Excise."

"Yes, I know! That is, we've never met, but I know you by reputation." Raoul wasn't sure if the remark was a compliment or not, but he decided to take it as one.

"I am here on a sensitive and urgent matter involving one of your customers. Seafus Hobb."

"Mr. Hobb was just here."

"Yes. As part of my investigation, I need to examine the items that Mr. Hobb put in his safe deposit box."

"There must be some mistake. Mr. Hobb doesn't have a safe deposit box."

"Mr. Forteneau, I know what I saw. Seafus Hobb walked in here with a sack full of...of...items, and he walked out without them. Please do not hinder the activities of the Island government by refusing to assist me."

"Mr. Hobb did come with a sack, but the 'items' inside were blocks of money. He made a cash deposit, is all."

"Blocks?" Raoul didn't understand. "Of money?"

"Yes, blocks. Piles, stacks—call it what you will—of bills. Rainbow-colored legal island tender."

Raoul didn't buy Mr. Forteneau's story. The size and thickness of the "stacks" that Raoul had discerned through the cloth of the sack indicated far too much money to contemplate.

"May I see the record of the deposit, please?" Raoul requested.

"Absolutely." The bank manager fanned out a series of carbon-copy receipts that must have documented the most recent of the bank's customer transactions, and plucked out the one signed

212

Seafus Hobb. He handed it to Raoul, who blinked when he saw the number of zeros marching behind the figure in the boxed marked AMOUNT. Amount, indeed!

"Mmm," nodded the manager, as if to assure Raoul that he was counting the zeros correctly. "I was surprised at first, too."

"What do you mean, 'at first'?" Raoul asked.

"I assumed this post a few years ago and at that time Mr. Hobb's large deposits used to shock me. Now I'd be shocked if they stopped."

"Stopped?"

"He's here every couple of weeks," Mr. Forteneau explained. "Always with blocks of cash to deposit. Usually even more than what you saw today. A savvy investor, that one! Not that he ever has any financial advice to share, take it from *me*. I've tried."

"Investor?"

"You know, global markets, bonds, stocks, foreign currency. How else could he possibly get his hands on so much money?"

How else?

How else? How else? How else?

That's precisely what a robber fly inside Raoul's head demanded to know.

———

The Island Police, their sirens flashing and wailing, followed Raoul and his truck through the center of Port-St. Luke. Cora was right! Dwight was a petty thief and a fool, a small fish in a small island pond. Seafus Hobb, he was the shark, and Raoul wouldn't stop until he figured out what Hobb was up to. There was more to it than the swiping of parcels, and Raoul feared that Seafus's crimes might overstep the bounds of Customs and Excise. Raoul didn't know about global markets and bonds and stocks, but he was fairly certain that if one dabbled in any of them, they did so the way it was done in the movies. With stockbrokers and telephone calls and stealthy wire transfers, not with blocks of cash money, and most definitely not with blocks of cash money in the form of rainbow bills good only on Oh.

Raoul tried to sort through the flies popping up in his brain. Now, supposing Dwight had delivered a parcel to Seafus containing something of Cora's of unusual value; and supposing Seafus, who was known to frequent a certain island element, found a way to sell off that something; and supposing the 'something' was a priceless gemstone; supposing all that, Seafus might in fact raise enough cash to make a deposit of the sort he had made. 'But the bank manager said that Seafus had been making such deposits, even bigger ones, every two weeks for years,' a stonefly objected, which implied more than just a priceless one-off 'something.' 'And if such priceless somethings went missing every fortnight,' another stonefly interjected, 'wouldn't Cora Silverfish have contacted Customs or even the Police?'

"True. Very true," Raoul answered the flies aloud. The Police. He saw their lights in his rearview mirror. It was all he could do to keep pace with them. He feared they might run into him or run him off the road before they all got to where they were going. How was a man to focus on shifting gears and shifty curators with all that blasted flashing and wailing in the air?

What was this now? Raoul saw in the mirror that one of the policemen had stuck his head out the widow of his vehicle and was shouting into a megaphone. "Surrender!" he was saying. "Surrender now!" Raoul looked about but couldn't see either the

Curator or any other known suspects anywhere near his vehicle or those of the Police. In fact, with all the racket they were making, the traffic had parted and the pedestrians had stopped crossing, so as to cut a clear path forward. What were the bloody Police up to?

Raoul had no idea, but he was glad when he spotted a small carpark where he could pull off the road and get himself out of the policemen's way. He turned off the engine and sat collecting himself for a minute. "They could have gotten me killed!" he complained to the truck. "Racing us through town like that! What were they thinking?"

"Stop the truck and surrender now!"

What the—? Raoul looked in his side mirror and saw that the Police had followed him into the carpark. Who in the world were they after? He sat in the driver's seat watching, and waiting to see what would happen.

"Stop the truck and surrender now!" a policeman insisted via megaphone. "Stop the truck! Stop! The! Truck!"

It was only when Raoul saw four officers jump out of two cars and rush his vehicle—which had been stopped since he pulled it off the road—that he realized they were coming for *him*!

"Are you mad?" he shouted at the officer who pushed his face through the driver's side window and demanded that Raoul raise his hands.

When the police offer recognized Raoul, for everyone on Oh had an idea of who he was, the young man was torn between carrying out his duty and offending a governmental official.

"I'm sorry, sir," he explained, "but this vehicle has been reported stolen."

"Stolen?! *I* am the owner of this vehicle. Who the hell reported it stolen?"

"Munroy Daniels, proprietor of the This Why That Way Garage and Body Shop. He said it was taken last night right off his lot."

"Yes, *I* took it. It's my vehicle, only it was parked on his lot. Here!" Raoul dug under his seat for an envelope from which he fished the car's title, clearly transferred from Munroy Daniels to Raoul Orlean.

The policeman examined it and said, "Must be a mix-up. Did Mr. Daniels know you had taken the vehicle, sir?"

"Well, evidently not, if he reported it stolen!" Raoul appreciated that Munroy had acted so quickly when he saw Raoul's truck missing that morning, but good grief! What a ruckus!

"Stand down! All clear!" the police officer shouted to his colleagues through the megaphone. "Sorry again, Officer Orlean," he apologized.

Raoul got out of the truck to stretch his legs and shake off his nerves. "No harm done," he said, and he gave the policeman's hand a shake.

The scene that a passer-by would have witnessed, passing by just then as the two men shook hands, might have looked like the prelude to a sting, a Customs and Excise collaboration with the Island Police, complete with convoy, megaphone, and flashing lights. At least that's how it appeared to Seafus Hobb, who happened to walk past the carpark on his way from the bank to the Parliamentary Museum, which, it so happened, was located not far away.

Seafus felt a twitch as he caught sight of Raoul Orlean for the second time in the space of a morning. It wasn't fear that he felt, for he had nothing to hide at the museum. If that's where they were headed, they could sting to their hearts' content. No, what made Seafus twitch when he saw Raoul was something else. Seafus was a sportsman born, remember, despite the path his life had taken (or been pushed down, Seafus would have said). What stirred him was an urge he had never been able to describe, not even at the height of his athletic success. It was uncertainty and certainty, the prospect of facing an unknowable rival and the conviction that one would win out. It was dread and excitement, the wait to see what one's challenger was made of and the challenge of breaking him down. It was a killer instinct less confident than it sounded, for only real and true danger could set it off. It was all of those things, which Seafus hadn't felt stirring in a very long time.

But fear?

Nah.

It wasn't that.

31

Raoul's visit to the bank had been useful, though not in the way he'd imagined; he forgot all about his Balance, having been thrown by the sight of Seafus and his sack. Now, back at his office to clear up any Urgent Matters that awaited, he wondered what he would find. It turned out that he hadn't missed much during the three days he'd been working in the field, only some routine forms that wanted his signature. Despite the fact that his staff sneaked out early when Raoul was away, they had managed to keep the Customs headquarters running just fine without him. Even so, they were glad when he walked through the door that day at last, for the phones had been ringing off the hook the whole of the morning. A man from the Garage and Body Shop had been calling every five minutes, they told him; in between, there were calls about a crisis at the port that 'only the Head of Customs and Excise himself' could resolve.

Munroy and Garvin.

Raoul signed the forms in want of signing, then he picked up the phone. He called Garvin and told him to be in the gap by the oil shed in twenty minutes. ("But—" Garvin had objected. "No 'buts.' Meet me there," Raoul said, cutting him off.) After that, Raoul announced he was going out but would return again soon. He grabbed his keys, dashed out to his truck, and sped to the Body Shop as fast as his third gear would take him. What a luxury to have a vehicle he could jump into any time he needed! He was quite certain the truck had been his smartest purchase ever.

When Munroy saw Raoul pull up in the pick-up, his shoulders collapsed with relief.

"Raoul! Thank goodness!" Munroy rushed over to the truck before Raoul could get out of it. "Where did they find it?" he asked through the open window.

"Where? I'll tell you!" Raoul got out and slammed the door. "They chased me through town like a thief!"

"What? Who?"

"The Police. *I* took the vehicle, last night. I was driving it through town just now and they tried to arrest me."

"You?" Munroy was stunned. He was also amused: "They chased you? Through town?" He started to laugh, and Raoul did, too.

"Yeah, man! They thought I stole my own truck."

"Well, I thought *someone* stole the truck when I didn't find it here this morning. I didn't know, man. Sorry." He turned to go back inside the garage and then stopped. "Wait. When did you learn to drive it so well?"

"Last night. I came back and practiced."

"Okay, okay." Huh! Munroy wouldn't have believed it, if he hadn't seen Raoul drive up with his very own eyes.

Raoul gave him a wave and headed for the gap at the back of the property. "I'm just cutting through," he said.

"Sure," Munroy said. "Sorry again."

"No problem," Raoul reassured him. "Nothing came of it."
To which Munroy tapped his cap, and returned to his work.

———————

Garvin was already there waiting when Raoul got to the gap by the shed. He had apparently taken Raoul's last package orders to heart, for he had carried with him a small wooden box, a tiny crate it was, that appeared to have some weight. Raoul knew even before he asked that the box belonged to Cora.

"What are you doing here with that?!" Raoul scolded him. "I told you to document the contents, not tote Cora's parcels about! What if someone sees you? Or if Dwight gets suspicious?"

"I tried to tell you on the phone. Dwight didn't come today. He said he was sick, but if you ask me, he drank too much rum last night."

"Then why are we sneaking around here?" Raoul scolded further. "I could have come to see you in the sorting office."

"I tried to tell you that, too."

"Never mind that now," Raoul dismissed him. "Let's get on with it. What's in there?" Raoul pointed his chin at the box.

"I don't know. I haven't opened it yet."

"Did you bring a pry bar?"

"No."

Raoul sighed. He and Garvin were simply not on the same page today, were they?

"In here!" Raoul suggested, motioning to the shed where Munroy kept the used oil to be disposed of. It was surely stored up in barrels, with lids that needed prying off. Probably, a pry bar was somewhere close to hand inside.

It was a wooden shed, and dark. Raoul found a hinged panel that served as a window. He pushed it outward and propped it open. The early afternoon sun was bright and filled up the space in the shed.

"There!" Garvin said, motioning with his eyes to a bar hanging on a peg on the wall.

"Good," Raoul answered, grabbing it. "Set the box on one of the barrels."

Just as Raoul was about to say "any barrel but that one"—'that one' being a barrel whose lid was dented and on which a puddle of dirty oil had collected—Garvin set the box down in the greasy goo.

"Youths!" Raoul muttered under his breath.

Raoul looked more closely at the box before prying it open. The addresses—both sender's and sendee's—were half-written in characters that Raoul assumed to be Chinese, aided in his assumption by a large handwritten "CHINA" that he spotted amidst some other semi-English scribblings. Raoul lifted the box and put it back down again, testing its heft. Hmm. Heavy, yes, but not excessively so. He and Garvin exchanged anxious glances and Raoul set into the box with the pry bar. He carefully jimmied the lid, raising up one side, then the next and the next. Garvin grabbed onto the nearly freed box top and held it as Raoul detached the fourth edge from the crate beneath it. After Garvin put the lid on the ground, where it leaned up against the side of the barrel, he and Raoul looked inside the box. All they saw was rudimentary packaging: strips of newsprint, chips of wood, empty shells from nuts unknown to Oh.

The pair of them stood staring at it, as if they expected the packaging to part of its own accord and reveal a treasure, or a horror. After a few seconds Raoul came to his senses and slowly pawed at the strips and chippings. As his hand neared the box's center, his fingernail hit something hard. Soon the other hand followed the first, until they had wrapped themselves around what felt like a grainy ball of thick ceramic. If this was one of Cora's gemstones, thought Raoul, it was the size of a small football! Gently he edged the object from the box, careful that none of the packaging should fall to the floor, so that he and Garvin could re-pack the crate as if it had never been opened.

At first glance, Garvin was unable to discern the object that emerged. Cradled in Raoul's dark brown hands, it mingled with his color and lost itself. Once Garvin's eyes had adjusted for the camouflaging, and picked out the outline of what Raoul held, his jaw fell. He couldn't believe what he was seeing! In his mind he registered only fear. He had put his future in Raoul's hands, a future, he now saw, that was destined to get as lost there as the cracked, brown teapot Raoul held onto. A teapot! How had Garvin been so stupid as to get involved in one of Raoul's crack-pot schemes? Defiling property and flouting procedure! Secret logbooks and clandestine meet-ups in oily sheds! All for a teapot! His Customs career was cooked!

Garvin covered his face with his hands in dismay. Through his fingers, he watched to see what Raoul would do next. To Garvin, Raoul didn't seem at all dismayed by their seemingly insignificant discovery. On the contrary! Raoul's brow was furrowed and he was studying the pot. He turned it in the light, rubbed its sandy texture. Had it had a lid, Garvin might have thought that Raoul was waiting for a genie to escape from it. If one *had*, Raoul would have been no less surprised.

"It can't be!" Raoul muttered, mesmerized by the pot. When he first laid eyes on it, it seemed to him a simple teapot of *terra cotta.* Raoul had read about *terra cotta* at the library one Tuesday long ago. But the texture was wrong, the color too dark. Where had Raoul seen a pot like this before? It was rounded, and just imperfect enough to be perfectly, authentically, handmade. Into the dark clay were etched leaves and vines that climbed up the side of pot and disappeared inside. Only they didn't disappear inside! The inner wall of the pot was etched as well, and from the bottom of the teapot—inside it!—blossomed the flower that the leaves had foreshadowed. Raoul recalled a book he read at the library on Chinese pottery, with pages of color photos that he had thumbed through and admired. Had he seen the pot in there?

"Look at the top of the box. See if you can make out any other English writing," he ordered Garvin.

Garvin bent down and stared at the markings. After a bit of squinting and tilting his head he declared, "I see some letters, but no words that make any sense. "

"Tell me. What words?"

Garvin squinted some more. "This one says Y-I-X-I-N-G. Yixing." (He pronounced it to rhyme with 'kicksing.')

"Let me see that!" Raoul set the pot in the box and bent to grab the box top. "It can't be!" he said again.

"What's 'yixing'?" Garvin asked, unimpressed.

"Not 'yixing.' It's pronounced *yee-sing.*"

"Ye sing?" Garvin had heard a 'sing ye' at the Pentecostal church before, but never a 'ye sing.' "What's 'ye sing'?"

"Not 'what.' *Where.* It's a place in China famous for its clay. If this pot is authentic, and as old as I suspect, it's worth a fortune."

"A fortune? It's old and cracked!' Garvin objected. "And there's no lid!"

But Raoul wasn't listening. He was pushing the pot back inside the crate, ensuring it was well cushioned on all sides by the wood-chips and nutshells and newsprint. In his head, a flower fly made its presence known, whirring in doubt: What was Cora doing importing priceless Chinese pots? Dare Raoul relinquish the pot to Dwight? What end would it meet? Would Dwight realize the treasure he had? Did Cora know it herself?

Then Raoul remembered the cash that the Curator had deposited. Was he swindling the dim-witted Dwight? Paying cut-rate for Cora's possessions and selling them off at market value? But who on Oh could afford to buy an ancient Yixing teapot, and why would they want to?

'Whoa!' whirred the flower fly. It reminded Raoul that the pot was not Seafus's (to sell or to do otherwise). The pot was, *seemingly*, the property of Cora Silverfish...wasn't it?...wasn't that right?

'Yes,' Raoul asserted in his head. 'Yes, it was. The pot was the property of Cora Silverfish.'

To which the fly pitched, and returned to its whir.

32

What a day-off Tuesday Raoul was a having! First Cora with her jasper, then Seafus at the bank and the policemen in town, topped-off by Garvin and his teapot in the shed. Raoul rued the day he had ever forgotten Ms. Lila's birthday, for although he couldn't recall how, he was sure that his purchase from Pineapple Jewelry and Gems was what had gotten him mixed-up in...in whatever it was he was mixed-up in. How he dreamed of a quiet afternoon at the library, re-reading his favorite book about Mr. Stan! Soontime, he told himself. But not today. Mentally he crossed Lila off his afternoon agenda as he drove from the Body Shop back to town.

Despite the value of the property that Garvin had intercepted, Raoul decided to send him back to Customs with Cora's crate. Raoul had sought a stick to plant, hadn't he? To harvest for clues? Well, the teapot was it. He and Garvin had hammered the crate shut with the heels of their shoes, and Garvin had carried it back to where it came from, to hand off to Dwight like always. Once in Dwight's possession, the crate would either end up at Cora's

227

shop, as the pineapple jasper did, or—and this was the part of the hypothesis that Raoul had yet to polish—it wouldn't.

If it didn't, that meant that Dwight took it somewhere else. Could Raoul assume, based on his one day of dogging Dwight, that he would take the crate to the Museum? And what would it mean if he did? 'That Seafus Hobb would be making another large deposit soon, that's what,' Raoul suggested aloud. Maybe Dwight was in cahoots with the Curator, not swindled by him but employed. Did Dwight decide which parcels to deliver to Cora and which ones to Seafus? Or did he take them all to the Museum for the Curator to examine? Why Cora's parcels and hers alone?

Ahh! As usual when Raoul threw himself into a case on Oh, there were always more questions than answers. Thankfully this particular case lacked two things Raoul was rarely spared: a cloud of island magic fogging things up and islander old talk (gossip that spun colorful truths before Raoul could pluck out the thread of the real black-and-white ones). No, indeed, *this* case had nothing magical about it, and for that Raoul was glad. What's more, it was a private government investigation—*Raoul's* investigation—and so one that Bruce couldn't possibly get wind of or plaster on the front page of the *Morning Crier.* Despite the fact that the case required Raoul's visiting Cora over and over, it might just be one of his favorites yet, since solving it would also mean cleansing Customs and Excise of the dishonest and thieving Dwight. Raoul took his office and his Office seriously, and a worm in the Customs apple bothered him almost as much as Nat's worming his way into Lila's heart (assuming he had—this was another hypothesis in need of polishing).

Raoul (evermore adeptly) made the climb up Market Square Hill, thinking as he went. When he reached the top, he parked in front of Pineapple Jewelry and Gems and climbed up the stairs, anxious to tell Cora of the stick he had already planted (and curious to know how and why she had ancient teapots shipped to her). Little did he expect to find her planting a stick of her own—literally. Just as Raoul walked through the door, he saw Cora standing over her jewelry counter, forcefully ramming a long stick into what looked like a ball of clay the size of a small coconut.

"Mmph!" She grunted as she pushed the stick in farther, until she felt it touch the piece of wood on which the ball-and-stick project sat. When she was satisfied with the stick's position, she looked up and acknowledged Raoul.

"Hello! Good afternoon," she said cheerfully.

"Hello," Raoul said, his attention drawn to the stick. It was over a foot tall, half in the clay, and half protruding. "What is that?"

"For the Pineapple Cup," she said cryptically. As she spoke, from a bucket perched on a stool at her side, she fished out fistfuls of clay that she pressed onto the part of the stick that stuck out.

"You're making the cup out of dried mud?" Raoul knew little of trophies, but he was quite certain the best ones were made of metal.

"Don't be silly." Cora continued pressing and patting chunks of clay up the length of the coconut's axis. "This is just a dummy to work from. The cup will be made of copper."

"With jasper leaves," Raoul added, eager to show Cora that he wasn't a complete idiot.

"Exactly."

Cora's hands were mesmerizing. They rubbed and smoothed and massaged and, Raoul had to admit, the clay coconut with its protruding stick had begun to take on the form of a pineapple.

Minus the leaves and the detail on the skin, but a pineapple none the less. The stick was no longer visible and Cora was gradually fattening up the fruit, padding it with more and more clay.

"I've come about another package." Raoul forced his mind to focus on his work.

"Oh?" Cora replied, distracted. *Her* mind was focused on *her* work.

"Not just any package," Raoul pressed.

"Mmm?" Cora pressed her clay.

"One from China."

"China?" Cora did indeed receive parcels from China now and then, with jade, and sometimes synthetic gemstones. She didn't make a habit of using fakes in her work, but every so often, it was the only way to accommodate a customer's pocketbook. "I'm not expecting anything from China at the moment."

"No, this wouldn't be for your shop," Raoul said. "At least... that is...I don't think it would be." Raoul remembered the Black Diamond butterfly and wondered if the flower inside the teapot or the leaves on its sides might serve as models for Cora's pieces. "Maybe it is," he concluded.

Cora looked up from her work, impatient. "Raoul." (She had had enough of Officer and Mister. Raoul was becoming an everyday— nay, twice-a-day—event.) "What are you talking about?"

"I'm talking about a Chinese teapot worth a fortune, which I had no choice but to hand off to Dwight Williams. If I can follow the trail of the teapot, then maybe I can figure out what's going on with your packages. Unless the teapot ends up here, in which case, I'm back at square one and will have to find a new stick."

"Raoul," Cora repeated, "what...are...you...talking...about? Begin at the beginning!"

"I'm talking about your Yixing teapot! Which, by the by, has nothing to do with your shop and should not be subject to concessions! You're cheating Customs and Excise out of a sizable duty payment, you know!" Raoul pounded his fist on the glass.

"If I have to ask you *one* more time...," Cora threatened. "I don't know about any Yixing teapot, from China or anywhere else. *What* is going on?"

Cora's anger told Raoul she was telling the truth (as did the flower fly's 'I told you so' in his head). He fumbled for what to say next, his brain divided between the tasks of bringing Cora up to speed and determining what really was going on. Eventually he put his mind to the former and explained to Cora about Garvin's log and the intercepted crate from China, with the Yixing teapot inside. He told her Dwight had the crate and would either deliver it to her or not. If not, they had only to follow the trail of the teapot, which would lead them right to the thief. Raoul went on to explain that he believed Dwight might be in Seafus's employ, that he swiped Cora's valuables and delivered them to Seafus, who sold them off and gave Dwight a cut for his troubles. Seafus was in the habit of depositing large sums of cash at the Savings Bank, Raoul confirmed, and why hadn't Cora ever reported losing such valuable property?

Lord have mercy! Cora didn't know where to begin. If ever a man needed a pocketful of pyrite to clear his head it was Raoul Orlean!

"The trail of the teapot?" she asked sarcastically. "How are you going to follow a damn teapot?"

She raised a good point, Raoul confessed to himself. Perhaps in hindsight, he should have acted on the unpolished hypothesis that the pot would end up at the Museum and not at Cora's shop.

Perhaps he should have driven to George Street to stake out his stick; to wait for Dwight to arrive and carry the crate inside the Museum; to watch him come back out without the pot. Perhaps if he hurried, he could still get there, to do all of that and more.

"Raoul!" Cora saw that he was thinking and put a stop to it immediately. "Has it ever occurred to you that *perhaps* the reason some of my packages are delivered and others aren't is because some of them are, indeed, *mine*, while others of them are, in fact, *not?*"

"They all arrive at Customs with your name on them!" Raoul insisted.

"Do they now?" Cora, still sarcastic: "Well, fancy that!"

"You mean...?" Raoul began.

Cora watched as the pieces fell in line in his head, like gemstones in a tumbler.

"Then you didn't...?" he continued.

She shook her head.

"And the Curator...?"

She shrugged suggestively.

"But why would he...?"

Only Raoul already knew the reason. He had seen Seafus Hobb with a sack full of them...that morning...in line at the bank.

33

Atop the spiral stair that climbed to his office, which sat atop
the Parliamentary Museum, Seafus Hobb sat taking stock.
Both literally and figuratively, he examined his position, assets vs.
liabilities.

In the assets column, he listed the following:

No. 1 – a phone call from Dwight describing a certain crate from
China. It appeared the Yixing teapot had arrived. 'A proper treasure
for my collection!' he marveled. (For an even more proper sum!)

No. 2 – no visit from the Island Police, and the day nearly done.
Despite their suspicious presence, together with Raoul Orlean, a
few steps from the Museum that morning, they had conducted no
raid or sting. This meant one of two things:

   a) that Seafus was merely being paranoid; or
   b) that Raoul and the Island Police were merely rethinking
     what to do as far as Seafus was concerned. (Which made 2*b*
     a potential liability, he noted.)

No. 3 – not one reason Seafus could think of to suppose the Police were on to him. No hitch in any plans, no snitch of which he was aware. It was Business As Usual, his pieces arriving for Cora by boat or by plane, and intercepted by Customs Officer Dwight. How serendipitous, his granting her that scholarship all those years ago, just to shut her up and ship her off! He relished the delicious irony that saw her return to open her shop, an enterprise that, like his own, got in shipments from the far corners of the globe.

Seafus then offset his assets thusly:

No. 1 – That witch Cora Silverfish was still intent on closing up her shop; Oh's idiot newspaperman mentioned her closing sale every chance he could, in articles on everything from washing machines to football. Cora was the gem in Seafus's crime ring. Losing her would call undue attention to what was left behind. Customs duty calculations on costly museum treasures, Seafus knew, would have the Excise officers wondering where all the money he paid out came from.

No. 2 – See, 2*b* above. If the Island Police, together with Raoul Orlean, had something else up their sleeves, some offense Seafus couldn't put his thumb on, then how could he plan his defense? What weakness could he exploit to keep his enemy in check? 'Enemy,' in the singular, for Seafus was sure that Raoul was the real liability, merely dragging the Police along for the ride. Raoul had visited the Museum only two days before, the first time in... well, ever. And just that morning Seafus had bumped into Raoul at the bank:

a) coincidence?

b) surveillance? (Another problematic 2*b*, Seafus sighed.)

No. 3 – the Black Diamond butterfly that Raoul Orlean had delivered to Cora ten days before. There had in fact been that one hitch, and Cora had suggested at the March Past that Raoul, as a result, might go sniffing to see what he could find. Hence the Savings Bank surveillance and Raoul's visit to the Museum with his pretty little wife? Banking transactions were innocent enough. So, too, were museums housing priceless treasures. What else should they harbor? As for butterflies, Raoul won't have known the value of the Black Diamond, nor the fact that Seafus was the one for whom it was meant. Not unless Dwight had betrayed him, which Seafus doubted, for he paid him too well for that.

Still, as Seafus studied the accounting before him, the *b*'s and the butterfly weighed on his mind. The sportsman in him contemplated his opponent, Raoul Orlean, and again Seafus asked himself where his enemy was most weak. If Seafus Hobb had dominated the cricket pitch (and Cora Silverfish after that), it was because he had learned to play to the fears and the injuries of those against whom he faced off. Breaks and bruises were his stock-in-trade. A battered spirit, sore back, tired knees; he took advantage of them all.

That was it!

Seafus leaned back in his desk chair and let out a loud and hearty laugh.

Ha! He clapped his hands together. That was most definitely it!

He spun his chair and smiled at the bright blue sky of Oh outside his window, pleased that his killer instinct had not let him down. There was but one way to play the *b*'s and the butterfly that bothered him, Seafus realized, and that was with a partridge. A pretty little partridge, who had a damaged foot.

Ms. *Lila* Partridge the librarian—aka *Mrs.* Raoul Orlean.

———

While Seafus balanced his accounts, and Raoul's thoughts tumbled at the jewelry store, the antique Yixing teapot began its journey from the docks at Customs. Cumbersome as the pot was in its wooden crate (and dirty, having been set down by Garvin on top of the greasy barrel), Dwight decided to deliver it to town by taxi. He took it straight to the Museum, as he always did with Cora's packages, where the Curator would have a look inside and either send Dwight off empty-handed (of packages, that is) or with instructions to take the packages back to Cora's. Either way, Dwight left with his pockets stuffed full.

When Dwight arrived with the crate from Yixing, he carried it up the Curator's spiral stair. Although Dwight was permitted access to Seafus's private office, he was typically paid and sent back downstairs to await the verdict on the package in question: remanded (to Cora) or not. Not today. As soon as Seafus saw the crate and the markings on it, he knew it was the teapot and didn't bother asking Dwight to wait downstairs while he examined it. He handed Dwight a fistful of new rainbow bills and told him he could go home.

On Oh, when men like Dwight find their workday finished (or near enough) and their pockets bursting at the seams with rainbow bills, home is the last place they want to be. A rum shop will do in a pinch, if time is short or rain is coming, but a Bar and Lounge like the Belly, with its live music and lively waitresses, is better by far. Given that Dwight had nowhere to be, and seeing as how the sky was bright in spite of the setting sun, to the Belly was where Dwight headed.

Raoul was headed there, too, for a beer with his mates before dinner. He would have preferred to go to the library, to chauffeur home Ms. Lila, but he didn't dare. If he did say so himself, his driving skills had improved remarkably after just one day behind the wheel—what with all his trips up and down Market Square Hill to reach Cora's, and holding his own in a police chase through town—but he knew that Lila would see things differently. So while Nat was off fetching his wife, Raoul would unwind for an hour with Cougar and Bang. Barely had Raoul pulled into the Belly's carpark, in fact, when the pair of them rushed out to check out his vehicle.

The truck was too faded and too old to turn Cougar's head, but he was genuinely glad for his friend's purchase and the freedom it implied, and, accordingly, he faked his admiration. Bang, on the other hand, not only turned his head at every angle, to inspect and compliment the truck's every feature, but his body ran circles around it as well, as thrilled by it as if it were his very own. He complimented the color (or lack thereof), and the condition of the body and tires, the interior, the sound of the horn. Only after completing his inspection did it dawn on him to remark, "So you drive then, Raoul, do you? Since when?"

"Since never mind that!" Raoul snapped. He walked purposefully toward the entrance to the Belly, Cougar and Bang behind him snickering and poking fun.

"What other hidden talents you have?" Bang called after him. Raoul didn't pay him any mind.

Inside the three of them took up at a table close to the bar, and Cougar gestured to a waitress to bring three beers.

"Seriously, man," Bang said as he sat down, "nice vehicle, in truth."

"Thanks," Raoul muttered. Bang's was an apology of sorts, but Raoul hardly noticed. His attention rather was drawn to a corner table where a noisy crowd had gathered, drinking (of course), clinking glasses, making old talk. At the center of the scrum a loud game of dominoes was under way. Raoul could hear the slaps of the tiles against the table top, each one followed by a round of cheers and commentary.

"What's going on there?" Raoul asked Cougar, tilting his head toward the rowdy crowd.

"Big spender," Cougar replied. "Came in a short while ago buying drinks for all his friends."

"Mm," Raoul replied with a nod of his chin.

The waitress arrived with their beers, and as she passed them round the table, Cougar continued. "He's one of yours, you know." Beer in hand he added, "Cheers."

"Cheers." (Bang and Raoul in unison.) They all raised their bottles and drank.

"Who?" Raoul asked with disinterest, after swallowing a cold, tasty gulp. "Who's one of mine?"

"The big spender," Bang interjected. "He was wearing a Customs uniform."

"Eh?" Raoul looked more intently into the animated corner, but from where he sat he could see no one in uniform, big spender or otherwise. He shrugged and went back to his beer.

"You come from the office?" Bang asked him.

"Nah," Raoul said. "Fieldwork."

Bang and Cougar shared a furtive glance and the hint of a smile. They knew that "fieldwork" could mean anything from climbing an almond tree to visiting the Chief of Police.

"Yeah?" Cougar asked. "Far?"

"Nah," Raoul said. "Town." He took another drink of beer and without thinking, he elaborated: "Cora's pineapple jewelry shop."

Raoul's mention of Cora's name was met with hoots and jeers from both Bang and Cougar. Though investigatory encounters with her had now become second nature to Raoul, it was quite a shock for his friends to hear him mention the reputed island witch so casually. Normally when Raoul spoke of such matters, he was spitting flies or curses.

"Cora's?!" Bang was delighted. "Oho! So you *are* hiding something. Raoul Orlean cavorting with a magic-maker. I never thought I'd see the day."

"There's no cavorting, and there's no magic-making," Raoul calmly explained. (Almost *too* calmly. If one didn't know better, one might have thought Cora had slipped him a chip of falcon's eye to curb his convictions.) "She's involved in a case I'm working on, is all."

"What kind of case?" Bang wanted to know.

"Can't discuss it. Confidential Customs business," Raoul told him.

"And Cora Silverfish is involved?" Bang pushed.

"I just said she was. Can we talk about something else, please? I can't discuss the case."

"Did she give you any magic stones?" (Bang.)

"I don't need magic stones." (Raoul.)

"You might solve the case faster if you had one." (Bang, again.)

Cougar agreed. "Why don't you have her make you a bracelet or something," he suggested. "Look here." He put his hand in Raoul's face.

"What am I looking at?"

"My ring! What else? Cora Silverfish made this for me years ago."

Raoul looked at the cloudy green gemstone set in silver. "What is it?"

"Nephrite," he said. "To protect me from love spells."

"Love spells? Who wants to put a love spell on *you*?"

"No one, thanks to this!" Cougar wagged his hand, and Raoul rolled his eyes in reply.

"It's true, Raoul!" Bang defended Cougar's position. "It's thanks to this ring"—Bang grabbed Cougar's hand and held it up—"that Cougar Zanne is still a carefree, single man without a wife to stress him."

Raoul could have countered with any number of arguments (Cougar was single and carefree because he treated women carelessly; Bang was single, too, and had never owned a ring in his life, of nephrite or anything else), and might have done, had Nat not arrived just then, clearly upset about something.

"I need some rum," he said, and sat down. Cougar got up himself to go get it from the bar.

"What is it?" Raoul asked him anxiously. "Is it Lila? Where is she? Is she okay?"

"She's fine, man. Relax yourself. I just dropped her home." Nat's snippy tone indicated to Raoul and to Bang that he was not so much upset as angry.

"What happened?" Bang asked.

"Here." Cougar returned and handed him a glass with rum in it, extra dark.

All three of them watched as he drank from it, waiting to hear what misfortune had befallen.

"It's the van."

"Was there an accident?" (Raoul.)

"You okay?" (Bang.)

"More rum?" (Cougar.)

"Nah, man. Nothing like that. Some fool dirtied the van. I just spent half an hour trying to clean it."

"Is that all?" Cougar said. "I thought you killed someone with it."

"What do you mean, 'dirtied the van'?" Bang asked.

"A guy got in with a big box and I took him to town. Then I went to the library to get Lila, and when I put her in the van, I saw the backseat black with grease."

Poor Nat! Grease on the seat of his new champagne-colored minivan taxi!

"He was one of yours, you know, Raoul," Nat added.

"One of mine *what?*"

"He was a Customs guy. I picked him up at the docks."

"How is it that I am personally responsible for every rowdy, dirty Customs employee in the country? I'm the Head of Customs and Excise, not a bloody babysitter! Take your van to Munroy at the garage. He'll get the grease stain—" Raoul stopped midthought. Wait just a minute. Grease?

"What kind of box was it?" Raoul changed tack.

"I don't know. A wood box. A crate. Like so." With his hands Nat traced the dimensions of an invisible box in the air.

"What did the Customs officer look like?"

Nat proceeded to describe what could only be Officer Dwight Williams, complete with garish belt-buckle and thick-heeled shoes.

"You know who it is, Raoul?" Bang asked.

"Yeah. Dwight Williams. Where'd you take him?"

"The Parliamentary Museum. Why are all you Customs guys suddenly so interested in the Artistic and Historical Sciences?"

"You saw him go inside the Museum? With the box? You didn't just leave him out front?"

"Nah. I mean, yeah. I saw him go in as I was pulling away."

"I see." So the trail of the teapot went from Customs at the docks to the Parliamentary Museum! At least that much Raoul now knew for sure.

"Hey, Raoul," Bang called out, interrupting Raoul's thoughts, "you know where to find this Dwight Williams?"

Before Raoul could answer, Dwight himself appeared. He had been walking from his private corner party to the bar or to the exit—maybe to the toilets?—and he had overheard his name.

"Someone looking for me?" He was too tipsy to be threatening, or Bang might have replied with more reserve.

"Yeah, man!" Bang shouted. He motioned toward Nat and said, "You dirtied the man's van with your greasy box!"

Dwight looked from Bang to Nat and back, trying to work out in his rum-drunk head his connection to the words Bang had said. "Ahh!" A smile lit up his face as he figured it out. He pointed a finger at Nat. "Taxi-man! Sorry for that, man." He reached in his pocket and pulled out enough rainbow bills for Nat to get his vehicle detailed, inside and out, twice over. "Here," Dwight said, holding out the money for Nat to take. "Clean your van."

Nat and Bang looked at each other, incredulous. Raoul and Cougar did the same.

"Take it now, man!" Bang insisted.

Nat reached out and did as Bang said. "Thanks," he said feebly to Dwight.

Dwight put up a hand and smiled, and kept on walking to wherever it was he was going.

Raoul, Cougar, Bang, and Nat didn't immediately say a word to one another. There was no need. Each was thinking the very same thing and all of them knew it. That a near stranger should hand over such a sum so readily, was nothing short of island magic. Drunk men in bars on Oh threw punches or drinks or dominoes, not rainbow bills. *Never* rainbow bills. (They rarely had them to spare, and if they did, they didn't give them away.) For Raoul's part, he was thinking even more than all that: namely, that Dwight's generosity wasn't magical, but rather the result of his absolute certainty of more rainbow bills to come. As long as Dwight kept intercepting packages addressed to Cora Silverfish, Seafus Hobb would be standing by with generous tips. (Raoul was also thinking how shameful it was that Dwight was drunk in uniform, so drunk that he had failed even to recognize Raoul, but mostly Raoul thought about the business thing with Seafus.)

Eventually one of them broke the silence.

Then Bang told Nat about Raoul's top-secret Customs affair with Cora the jeweler, and Nat joined in on their ribbing. He assured Raoul that if Cora was keeping him busy, no worries, for Lila was in good hands. As a matter of fact, Nat said, Raoul should take his sweet time learning to drive, as Nat was reluctant to relinquish sweet Lila. Once Nat mentioned *that*, Bang went on about Raoul's driving—Did Nat know that Raoul drove? Did Cougar? When had any of them ever seen Raoul behind the wheel? When and where had he learned what to do?—and about Raoul's truck—the color, the condition, the interior, the horn. Wasn't the pick-up a peach! Nat wholeheartedly agreed. He had seen it parked outside Raoul's cottage that morning and had taken note straightaway.

They talked over beer, over rum, and over the noise of the Belly that was slowly getting full. Raoul hardly listened to what they said. He had no time for talk of pick-ups or peaches, or even of Ms. Lila. His mind was mulling pots and rainbows instead. *Tea*pots (well, one teapot in particular) and all those rainbow bills that Dwight had pulled from his pocket and handed to Nat. Yes, one very old teapot and some new rainbow bills are what monopolized Raoul's thoughts as he sipped his beer at the Belly and let his friends chatter on. The pot and the bills. And—oh, yes—Cora Silverfish as well.

34

The only thing better than a perfect day on Oh, with its true blue skies and its rampant greenery, is a perfect night. In that hour or so as the sun sets and the town quiets, the stars begin to show themselves, and the breeze, though gentler by a degree or two, remains hot with promise. All the more so when the perfect night falls on a Saturday. The evening soundtrack—hidden crickets, shrieking frogs, the thump of dancehall bass from a distant speaker—suggests the excitement the night might hold. Perfumed and primped, the islanders make their way to town, to the rum shacks and roti stands that line the road hugging the curves of Port-St. Luke's crescent lagoon, and there they make their plans. Some will get drunk, some lucky at love. For some, the lime will be the planning itself, the killing of time and the sipping from plastic cups, while waiting on rides or rendezvous or proverbial partners in crime. Add to a promise-filled, perfect Oh Saturday night a tournament football match, with pineapple fritters and rum-pineapple-punch on the sidelines, and you'll think you've died and gone to Paradise.

Although every match of the Pineapple Cup drew a decent crowd, the main events were the Saturday matches. Scheduled for five o'clock, they rarely began before seven, which meant they were played under the playing field lights, whose brightness (and shadow) lent extra drama to the athletic (and otherwise) goings-on.

The second and last week of the tournament's first round had just about come to an end, with both Seafus's Museum team and Campbell's Drug & Sundry advancing to Round Two. The Saturday night match that remained would determine whether the last second-round spot would fall to the Savings Bank or the Island Police. The latter had taken the Cup the year before, which made their every game this year especially captivating. What's more, Raoul had promised the two cops who had stopped him, after chasing him through Port-St. Luke, that he would come to see them play, and so he and Ms. Lila took the truck and went to town. It was a dry run for the week to follow, since Raoul had nearly five days of practice under his belt, and he wanted to show Ms. Lila that he was now quite capable of driving her wherever she needed to go. Because Lila didn't have to work the next day (the Pritchard T. Lullo Public Library was open only one Sunday in two, for patrons whose church was poetry or the Planters' Almanac), she had agreed to let Raoul take her out.

At the playing field, they sat in the section that supported the Police, along with Bang, Cougar, and Nat, who had no loyalty one way or the other, but had arrived together after Lila and Raoul, and so had joined them. On the side of the Savings Bank, Raoul spotted Seafus. Dwight was on the Bank side, too, though nowhere near Seafus. The only key figure missing, as far as Raoul was concerned, was Cora Silverfish. He wondered if she would show.

Soon the coin was tossed, the ball kicked, and the clock began ticking off the minutes of the first half. As the players scattered across the grass to smatterings of handclaps and cheers from the stands, the *real* action began *off* the official field of play. Not that *on* the field didn't matter—it did—points and penalties, yellow cards and red, goals stopped and goals stolen; all the same, most every spectator at any given island match-up had turned out for more than just football.

Take Johnson Campbell of Campbell's Drug & Sundry. His team had conquered Belmont Stationery, its romantic rival, and Johnson was eager to see what team his players would play next. If the Police won the night, it would mean Campbell's team had a shot at beating them in Round Two, thus unseating the current champs—the reputational value of which was far greater than that of beating the Bank. Reputational value always translated into greater drugstore sales, so Johnson was, in fact, at the field on sundry business.

Cougar Zanne, proprietor of the Buddha's Belly Bar and Lounge was also at the match on official mission. Cougar still had to come up with his signature tournament cocktail, which he planned to serve in cups made of pineapple husks. As soon as the whistle blew, he left his seat and went to scout amongst the pineapple vendors, for someone to supply him the fruit (and husks) he needed at a decent price.

Taxi-man Nat, from his seat near Raoul and Ms. Lila, was scouting the crowd in search of mechanic Munroy Daniels. Thanks to Munroy and his crew, Nat's grease stain was gone and his taxi good as new, and Nat wished to thank him. (Monroy wasn't at the body shop when Nat picked up his van.)

Bang actually did have his mind on football, only he was mainly interested in the team from the Parliamentary Museum, which he and the Bakery boys would be playing in just a few days' time. Bang paced round the field and lurked at the drink stands, waiting to spy the Museum team players, to size up their average age and size. When they finally arrived, as the match was ending, Bang found them to be a mean and strapping bunch, bulky and rude. They might just have the upper hand against the Bakery's over-40s (and over-50s), Bang was sorry to admit.

Garvin Charles spent the evening with one eye on football and one eye on Raoul. Ever since Garvin had intercepted the old teapot, Raoul had been a real pest. He had spent the remainder of the week hounding Garvin for information he didn't have. Cora hadn't received a single parcel and as a result Dwight had made no suspicious movements. He had taken away the teapot on Tuesday, as expected, ostensibly to deliver it to Cora, and that was all Garvin had to report all week. He was sick to death of silly secret meetings behind the oil shed and wasn't about to talk Customs with Raoul behind the bleachers, too.

Seafus Hobb was of course in attendance, his team having already secured a spot on the second-round roster, but he had little interest in either the Bank or the Police (as far as football went at least). He was however very interested in Raoul, whom he studied from the opposite side of the field. Raoul had been surveilling the museum for three days and Seafus was getting sick of him. (Raoul had failed to recognize how recognizable his light-blue-green truck was.) Seafus studied Lila, too, her foot still in a cast, her crutches close by and indispensable to her movement. Good. Very good. If Raoul wanted to persist in investigating whatever crime he believed Seafus guilty of, then Seafus would stop at nothing to stop him. That reminded him, where was Cora? He looked around but didn't see her and wondered if she'd show.

Cora, it seems, was on everyone's mind. Raoul and Seafus both watched for her, and Lila did, too. Lila wanted Cora there so that she could study Raoul's reaction to Cora's presence. Ms. Lila couldn't care less whether the Savings Bank won or the Island Police. *She* was there to determine just how in love her husband was with another woman.

What about Raoul? What flies buzzed in Raoul Orlean's head that night as the coppers and bankers clashed on the playing field? Was his brain as plagued with midges as were the players' knees and ankles in the grass? There must have a been a midge that wondered where Cora was. Another that wondered if she was coming at all. A few more for Seafus: one to keep an eye on him, one trying to decide Raoul's next official move. Days of surveillance had failed to reveal any teapot-related transaction at the Museum; no one out-of-the-ordinary had been there, and no teapot-sized bundle had ever come out. Was Seafus struggling to find a buyer for so precious a good? There *was* one midge Raoul had silenced the day before, when he figured out that the Curator's appropriation of Cora's address was nothing more than a ploy to avoid Customs duty on the items he got in to sell. Seafus Hobb was stealing her concessions, and Dwight Williams was his accomplice. Together they were cheating the Republic, only did Raoul have the evidence to prove it? The midges listed Garvin's log and Seafus's deposits, the fact that Dwight delivered boxes to Cora himself, and did so via the Museum. But apart from the bank receipts, which Raoul could get copies of, he had no photos, no bills of sale, no proof that Seafus had purchased anything under Cora's name. On the contrary, a flurry of midges warned him, Seafus could deny everything and say that the parcels belonged to Cora, that he had no idea who Dwight Williams was (hadn't he as much as done so already?), and that his cash deposits had come from private investment. Worse, if Raoul brought his suspicions to light, he might incriminate poor Cora. She could be charged with defrauding Customs and Excise, accused of abuse of concessions and forced to pay for Seafus's crime.

All the midges together made up a fuzzy, wobbly cloud that told Raoul the problem was bigger than the sum of its parts. It didn't make sense, such foofaraw to save a few island dollars on duty. Surely Seafus wasn't importing priceless teapots every week. And what of all those deposits at the bank? Raoul wasn't buying that Seafus was finding buyers to turn teapots into cash for his account.

The only way to sort through the confusion in his head was with some tried and true Stan Kalpi maths. It was, to be sure, what Raoul *always* did when his cases grew more cloudy instead of clearing up—lined up all his variables to solve the equation, or at least to determine the solution's next logical step. Sometimes his variables were clues he had stuffed in his pockets, and other times they were far more abstract. Usually they fell somewhere in the middle, a few of the one kind and a few of the other. As Raoul mentally shuffled and reshuffled the variables he'd collected this time around (concessions, Dwight Williams, special deliveries, the Black Diamond butterfly, the Museum, the larimar moon, parcels of almandine and pineapple jasper, the teapot, the cash deposits), he noticed they fell into two distinct columns, one he could head Cora Silverfish and one he could head Seafus Hobb. Like entries in an account book the variables offset each other, leaving Raoul in doubt as to whom the balance favored. But the sums were what mattered, like the midges had said, not the parts that made them up.

That was it! He could see it all very clearly now! He was wasting his time meeting Garvin in the gap and dogging Dwight Williams in town. The devil lay not in the detail at all, but in the names at the tops of the columns: with Cora and Seafus themselves, at the Museum and at the jewelry store, and first thing Monday morning Raoul would head straight for both. Seafus was up to more than it appeared, and Cora knew more than she was saying, Raoul was sure of it. His Stan Kalpi maths never failed him!

In his head the wobbly cloud of midges broke and the crowd broke out in cheers. Raoul smiled from ear to ear, eager for Monday to come. After a minute of sustained applause he realized that the cheering wasn't for him or his midges, but for the Island Police, who had shut out the Savings Bank three-nil. Raoul basked in the celebration all the same. It wasn't professional pride that he felt, solidarity with his law-enforcing colleagues, no. Rather he felt a warm and sudden kinship with the winning team, these still-undefeated champions who were one step closer to settling their Final score.

Savings Bank Knocked Out
in Last Round-One Knock-out
Island Police Head to Round Two

Saturday evening at the playing field in Port-St. Luke the Island Police clinched the final second-round spot in the annual Pineapple Cup tournament, defeating the Savings Bank 3-0. The initial twelve teams have now been whittled to six:

1) Ashbee's Appliances, Tackle and Tools
2) Higgins Hardware, Home and Garden
3) Trevor's Bakery
4) The Parliamentary Museum
5) Campbell's Drug & Sundry
6) The Island Police

The Bank-Police match was well-attended by spectators and vendors alike, who offered such delicacies as pineapple puffs, pineapple fritters, pineapple juice, frozen pineapple snow-ice, and pineapple-rum-punch. The island itself turned out, too, supplying a picture-perfect evening for the last Round-One match. The only sour note in an otherwise sweet event was a brief altercation that broke out, just as the match ended, among the players of the Parliamentary Museum team for reasons unknown (though likely having to do with too much rum). Police did not intervene, as they were mid-match when the fight occurred, but a number of civilians managed to diffuse the tension. In a fine show of island sportsmanship, players from all participating tournament teams were spotted observing the match, though notably absent was Cora Silverfish, whose pineapple-cup trophy is the prize for which all teams are vying. (We remind our readership that Pineapple Jewelry and Gems will soon be closing its doors and encourage loyal patrons to take advantage of closing-doors sales before time runs out.) The three Round-Two tournament matches will take place this week in Port-St. Luke. Wednesday afternoon at 5 o'clock, Spin-o-Matic rivals Ashbee and Higgins will meet up on the playing field. Friday at 5 o'clock, the Museum will take on the Bakery. Saturday, Campbell's Drug & Sundry will attempt to unseat the reigning Police champions, who will in turn defend their title, also at 5 o'clock island time. Three teams will advance to the third and Semi-Final round, along with a wildcard fourth team to be randomly selected by the Ministry of Sports and Culture. The two teams to survive the Semi-Finals will play each other in the Final, three weeks from today at 3 o'clock in town. The day's events will start with a pre-game show at 1 o'clock comprising the unveiling of the Pineapple Cup trophy and a third-place match between the two losing semi-finalists. Vendors are invited to present themselves at noon to set up their stalls and stands.

35

Raoul was up early on Monday, keen to start his day, and Ms. Lila's. When she emerged from her toilette, she found breakfast made and Raoul's already consumed. As soon as he saw her enter the kitchen, he jumped up to serve her tea, toast, and cheese, and told her he'd take her to work as soon as she was ready.

Ms. Lila sighed with nostalgia for Nat's champagne van, but resigned herself to Raoul's rum pick-up. At the football match on Saturday night she had been unable, when asked, to think of any good reason why Raoul shouldn't tell Nat that his taxi services were no longer needed. She longed for the day when her foot was freed of its cumbersome plaster and she could walk to work at her leisure. 'Three more weeks!' she told herself—'just three more weeks'—mustering the will to withstand the first of the next twenty-one days of bumpy commutes with Raoul.

"You're up early today," she remarked to him.

"Lots to do. I feel a break coming in a case."

"Oh?"

Raoul didn't hear her. He had sat himself back down and was busy reading the newspaper, tsking with his tongue as he did.

"Hear this," he said to her. "Now Bruce reports what happens, and what *doesn't* happen, too!"

"Oh?"

Raoul read aloud from the *Morning Crier*: "Players from all participating tournament teams were spotted observing the match—he means on Saturday night—though notably absent was Cora Silverfish." He tsked again and put the paper on the table.

"Why would he single out Cora?" Lila asked. (More importantly, why did Raoul take note of it?)

"Because she's making the cup, I guess."

Lila took a stab in the dark. "Have you seen it?"

Raoul shook his head. "Just the start of a model and some stones for the leaves."

Good heavens! Lila never dreamed her stab would hit the mark! She swallowed her tea the wrong way and began to cough. While her chest convulsed, her mind stuck on what her husband had said. The Curator was right! Raoul and Cora *were* friends, if he was privy even to her private designs.

"Are you alright?" Raoul was suddenly behind her, patting her forcefully between the shoulders.

"Yes," she finally spat out. "I'm fine, I'm fine." She shrugged her shoulders free of his touch.

"Are you ready to go then?" Raoul pressed her. "I need to get to town."

Lila nodded and stood, still coughing under her breath.

"Cora's?" Lila stabbed again.

"Mm," Raoul confirmed casually, as he tidied up the table, clearly anxious to make a move. "And the Museum. Nothing for you to trouble yourself about." He pecked her on the cheek and grabbed his keys from the peg he had hammered into the wall near the doorframe. "I'll pull the truck a bit closer."

"No!" Lila objected, more forcefully than she meant to. She suddenly couldn't stomach the idea of letting him out of her sight. "I mean...let's go together. Take my purse for me."

Raoul picked up her bag and led the way out to the yard. Lila watched him spring ahead, saw him unlock the doors of the truck and open hers for her. She had always thought of Raoul as a lovable bumbler who needed her—if only she knew how much he truly did!—but that morning as he fussed by the pick-up, putting her handbag on the seat just so, she realized that, in spite of the bumbling, *she* needed *him*. Not only now that she was on crutches, but when she was sure-footed, too.

'What's *for* you, won't pass you,' the islanders said, but Lila wondered if the adage held true—especially when 'what's *for* you' was at the wheel of a new old truck.

On his way back to work from the library, Raoul thought about the solution's next logical step. He had to do some snooping at the Museum, and he needed to get some information out of Cora. But which to do first? The Museum, he decided, since whatever he might find there could be used to break the ice with Cora after.

He drove to George Street and parked his pick-up in front of the Museum. (The Police all recognized his truck and would never ticket it.) Inside, he found a young woman, Seafus's assistant Joanie Daniel, seated near the entrance. She told Raoul that Seafus was out for the morning, but that Raoul should feel free to have a look around the exhibits.

"We have an exciting new addition," she boasted. "Just arrived. A very ancient teapot. In the second showroom." Raoul hardly let her finish before he took off. He rushed through the first room, seeing nothing of what it contained, and entered the second to find the center no longer vacant, but occupied by a tall glass case that housed the Yixing pot. In truth, Raoul had gone to the Museum unsure of what he was seeking, but the teapot was surely his clue. He walked around the clear case, examining the pot from all sides as his brain performed more Stan Kalpi maths. Raoul knew that Seafus was sneaking in high-priced goods, and using Cora's name so as to avoid his civic duty, namely the payment of Customs duty. Seafus then sold off the goods for cash, which he took to the bank.

No! That wasn't right, for the priceless teapot had not been sold off at all but was a featured display. Perhaps this one costly good was simply too good to sell off? Yes, that must be it, Raoul told himself.

And yet.

He continued to circle the Yixing pot. Something about the equation in his head was not adding up. How had Seafus afforded the teapot in the first place? Could his bank account be as big as all that? (Raoul would stop by the bank to find out for sure.) Without realizing, Raoul gradually widened his circular path around the teapot as he reasoned, and he found himself spiraling slowly toward the display cases that lined up against the walls of the room. His eyes no longer looked toward the room's center but toward its edges, where his Kalpi calculations continued. What had seemed a mere jumble of junk when he was at the Museum with Lila, now added up in Raoul's estimate to a not-so-small fortune. Amidst the mummies and petrified tree bark (neither of which could be cheap), he noticed glints of gold and silver that he hadn't seen the week before, a scepter with pearls, a ruby. The chipped and painted pots on the floor! If they were as old as the teapot, then they were even more priceless. Nothing Seafus could possibly sell would bring in the kind of money required to purchase the Museum's holdings.

Raoul inventoried his way around the second room and soon he was back to the first. He began to estimate its value as well, when an enormous glass shadowbox on the wall drew his attention. It was full of the most spectacular butterflies Raoul had ever seen outside the library, *The Wingèd Wonders of the World* lined up and come to life! Raoul interrupted his tallying-up. A butterfly fluttered inside his head and his equation fell in line. The variables— the teapots, the Black Diamonds—weren't gotten in to sell off, they were gotten in to *show* off, at the Parliamentary Museum.

Raoul was almost disappointed. He had hoped to expose Seafus as the kingpin in a ring of black-market dealers who traded in smuggled goods. Instead, he would have to content himself with the much less glamourous charges of Customs fraud and tampering with the post. Raoul sighed. Just as well, he thought. Better that Oh shouldn't have a black market to expose. Still, he needed clues before he could accuse Seafus of anything. If he could find the crate from Yixing with Cora's name on it, that would be a start. She could deny knowledge of the pot and the Police would see it was in Seafus's possession.

Raoul glanced at Seafus's assistant, who seemed distracted with her work or her own affairs, and began poking around the showrooms. He didn't expect to find the crate there; the only empty space was dead center in the first room and one could hardly camouflage a wooden crate in thin air. Raoul eventually ended up in the Museum's third room, the small auditorium of sorts, and he saw no crate there either. He walked onto the stage and examined the areas offstage and backstage, too. Nothing. He stomped hard on the stage itself and could tell it was hollow, but he could find no trap door that led to the space underneath it.

And the space above it? What about that? Raoul remembered the Curator appearing as if from nowhere via a strange spiral stair. Once Raoul thought to look for it, he saw it immediately. Straining first to see that Joanie Daniel, at the opposite end of the Museum, was still amply distracted, he tiptoed up. As he emerged into the rooms at the top, he felt he had stepped into a drawing, a *chiaroscuro* such as he had read about at the library. Tall windows allowed the Oh sunlight to pour in and pour over the ubiquitous dark wood of Seafus Hobb's private office. Without wasting any time, Raoul looked around for the crate and saw at once that it wasn't there. Hoping for any kind of clue he could use, he tried Seafus's desk, but that too proved useless. There was nothing on its surface and all its drawers were locked.

Raoul hurried across the room, where a partly open door revealed a library, just as Cora had said. Raoul went in and, despite his investigatory haste, couldn't help stopping to admire it. A great table filled the center of the room, while books lined the shelving built into three of the room's four walls. Many of the volumes were leather, their titles painted in gold. Raoul ran his fingers across the spines. Reference books they were, for the most part, encyclopedias, anthologies, histories, compendiums, on archeology, anthropology, genealogy, letters, the arts, the sciences, and war. Why, it put the Pritchard T. Lullo Public Library to shame!

Collecting himself, Raoul turned to complete his search of the room and saw that on the fourth wall hung a huge map of Oh. Was it? Raoul both recognized it and didn't. The shape was Oh's, only the black lines and arrows on the map didn't correspond to the island's roadways or the boundaries of each parish. The X's that marked it didn't match up with Oh's biggest towns or its landmarks, its waterfalls and Crater Lake. And yet Raoul could readily discern the points the map wanted to make. They connected to form a ring around the island that touched the airport outside Port-St. Luke, the seaport, and what could only be the site of the seedy port bar some distance away down the coast. After that the X's led off to the country, where Raoul could picture nothing of particular interest—a few small villages, some planted land, a mangrove swamp—before looping back to town, where the ring cut through the heart of the Ministerial Complex, the Savings Bank, and something nearby marked "PJG" (and circled) in red. It seemed to be the capstone of whatever the ring of X's, with the various lines and arrows that traversed it, was meant to signify. If Raoul had to guess, he would say its location corresponded more or less to Cora's shop. Cora's shop. Pineapple Jewelry and Gems. PJG!

The site of Cora's shop on the Curator's map gave Raoul such a jolt that he suddenly remembered where he was and what he was up to. He quickly left the library and as he did, under the table in the middle of the room he spotted the crate from Yixing. There was no mistaking it. Raoul scrambled down the spiral stair as swiftly as he could. Had he seen the crate before he saw the map, he might have seized it as Evidence and carried it out of the Museum, right past Joanie Daniel, in the name of the Law. But the sight of the sinister map had distracted him. Sinister in what way, Raoul wasn't sure, but in the dark of the library, the culmination of all those mysterious X's in a blood-red PJG had sent a shiver up (and down) his spine. He had barely the time to wonder what Cora was hiding from him, what her true involvement with the Curator was, when he sniffed a hint of peril, not complicity.

Though Raoul couldn't leave the Museum fast enough, he maintained an appearance of leisure (to the best of his ability), as he walked back through the showrooms to get to the door. Joanie asked if she should leave word with Seafus of Raoul's visit, but he bid her 'Good morning,' and told her there was no need.

Raoul couldn't recall getting into his truck after that, or driving the length of George Street, but somehow he had reached Market Square Hill and was half the way to Cora's. He hadn't a clue what he would do when he got there. Interrogate her? Warn her? Could he even begin to convey to her the whiff of peril he had caught? In spite of himself, he wondered if perhaps she had a gemstone to help him—not that he would ever dare ask.

Lucky for Raoul, Cora already knew of the danger he sensed. She had foreseen it on her own well before, and she had given him not *one* gemstone to help, but *four*: Lapis lazuli, Iolite, Lazulite, and Azurite, to ward off, together, whatever dark spirit the Library might hold.

36

When he finally arrived, he sat outside the door for a moment, reviewing in his head the words he wanted to say. He must be firm and unyielding—keep the conversation in hand—but kindly, even flatteringly, so; flies required honey, not vinegar, at least to start. No barging in and demanding of information, but instead, he would cultivate their...what? "Friendship" was too grand a word. "Rapport" suggested a mutual and spontaneous understanding that didn't quite define their past interactions. Association? Collaboration? Cooperation? Their involvement was basically a business one, a professional courtesy born of each trying best to do his (or her) job. He would play off of that then, her sense of duty. He was her customer, after all.

Once he had settled on his line of attack, he stood up, opened the door, and peered inside. Seeing that no other patrons were present, he called out as he went in, cheerily and a bit too loud, "Halloo! Good morning."

"Good morning," she replied, taken aback. Good grief. What was *he* doing here?

He walked to where she sat working and greeted her again. "Mrs. Orlean! It's nice to see you again so soon. How are you?"

"Mr. Hobb," she said hesitantly. "I'm afraid I'm still not very quick on my feet at the moment"—she indicated her nearby crutches with a tilt of her head—"but otherwise I'm well. Thank you."

He watched her and smiled.

"Can I...can I help you with something?" she asked.

"I'm sure that you can. I came here to check something out."

"Yes?"

"Do you have any books on Chinese pottery?"

A book on Chinese pottery? Well, *that* was all he wanted! "Oh, yes!" she answered cheerily, a bit too much so. "We have a very nice volume with pages of color photos. My husband read it and found it quite informative." She began to pull herself up and before she knew it, Seafus was right behind her, his hands around her waist.

"How *is* your husband?" Seafus asked, as if his presence so close to her body was perfectly natural and warranted no pause in their conversation. "Has he had any luck with his case?"

"His case?" she muttered, supporting herself on her crutches and wrenching free of his touch.

"Last week. At the Museum. He said he was investigating unusual activity."

"I'm not too sure," Lila replied, as she made her slow way across the floor to the pottery shelf. "I think he said a break in the case was coming." Why was she telling this man Raoul's business? She knew that she shouldn't, but words were all she had to put between herself and the Curator, who stuck too close to her side.

"Excellent! What kind of break? There's been no trouble to speak of at the Museum."

She propelled herself as fast as she could toward the Chinese volume. "I don't know," she panted. "I think the Museum is where he was going today. And to Cora's," she added suggestively, easing her pace a bit. Might Seafus say something more about Raoul and Cora?

Apparently not: "Cora's?" was all he said. And "very interesting."

By then they had reached the section with the pottery book, which Seafus took from the shelf. He stood thumbing through it while Lila, winded from her trek, took her time getting back to her desk. She had hardly sat herself down again when Seafus reappeared, thanking her for her time and trouble.

"So fast?" she asked him. "You found what you were looking for?"

"Oh, yes," he told her, "for now. I'll be back to do more another time." His eyes bore into her chest as he spoke, and she shifted uncomfortably in her seat.

"Is there anything else?" she asked him, wishing he would turn and leave.

"Your pendant," he said. "I couldn't help notice it."

She began rolling the vial of blue stones nervously between her fingers. "A birthday gift from my husband."

He cocked his head. "And from Cora, too, I see."

She looked down at it. "He got it from her shop, but it's not exactly—" Lila looked up from the pendant, about to finish her thought, but Seafus Hobb had disappeared. She looked around and thought that perhaps she saw the library door closing behind him. Or perhaps not. She felt a funny shiver and, in a lonely whisper, she finished her thought all the same.

"—a gift from Cora."

———————

While Raoul spied in the Curator's private library, and Seafus checked out Ms. Lila in the island's Public one, Cora Silverfish was up to her elbows in pineapple and clay. She was working on the model for her tournament cup, etching into it the details that would make it complete. It was delicate work, marking out the articulated and uniform spirals that wrapped around the pineapple's body, each one stacked on the one before and dissecting those that crossed them. When she was finished, every spiral would be ridged and pocked to mathematical perfection, a string of puffy diamonds full of slender stars.

As Cora was scraping the clay with calm and precision, loud footsteps suddenly pounded her stair and Raoul charged in like a bull in a jewelry shop. He still hadn't worked out what he wanted to say, so once inside, he stood in confusion, his thoughts outpaced by his body.

"What is it?" Cora asked him, looking up from her work only long enough to see what bull was before her.

"I've come from the Museum." He announced it as though it was all he needed to say.

"And?" Neither her hands nor her eyes abandoned the stars or diamonds.

And...and...*and*, indeed! Where to start? Once he did, though, he couldn't stop.

"He's not selling anything off. I had that part wrong. He's importing showpieces for his museum, *priceless* showpieces, that he has sent to *you* because you don't pay Customs duty, which saves him a bloody fortune. Dwight intercepts the packages and Seafus has him deliver to you what's yours, and the rest goes on display. I saw the teapot. It's right in the middle of the Museum. There was a wall of butterflies, too. I didn't notice it last time, but I'm sure that's where the Black Diamond was supposed to go. It was Seafus's all along, not yours. Why didn't you say so?" Raoul stopped to catch his breath.

"Would you have believed me if I had...?" she asked, still more interested in her model than in Raoul. She was bent over the pineapple, her face inches away from the lines and grooves she was tracing into it. She went on, "...if you hadn't first discovered for yourself that Seafus was somehow involved? It had *my* name on it, didn't it?"

Though she was right, Raoul didn't say so, but continued with his story.

"I went up to the library, and I saw—"

Cora dropped her etching needle. "You went *where*?" she interrupted. "How?"

"Seafus wasn't there, and his assistant was distracted, so I went up the spiral stair."

Cora watched him and listened intently now, which made Raoul feel—for once—not belittled by the mere presence of her. He stood a bit taller and carried on.

"I went up to look for the teapot crate from China, to prove that Seafus had imported goods under false pretenses, namely by using your name, Cora Silverfish, and that he had thereby defrauded Customs and Excise of duty on said teapot."

"For Oh's sake, Raoul, would you *please* leave the teapot!" she shouted at him. "Don't you see there is more to this than that?"

"You mean the map," he suggested.

"What map?"

"The one in the library."

"Seafus's library or Lila's library?"

"Lila? We're talking about Seafus, not Lila. Seafus's library!"

"There's a map? What map?"

Raoul tried to explain that it was a map of Oh and not. More of an outline it was, scribbled all over and marked up with X's (the airport, the seaport, the seedy port bar), X's and a PJG.

"PJG?"

"PJG! Pineapple Jewelry and Gems. All those X's dead-ended into *you*. P. J. G."

Cora, momentarily defeated, let her weight fall onto a tall stool behind her.

"What does it mean?" Raoul asked.

"I'm not sure what it means exactly. But I know that his library is the headquarters for all that Seafus does—Museum and otherwise, that is."

"Otherwise? So if the outline of Oh is all marked up, then his...activities...are island-wide?"

"I should think so."

"But what does the rest of the island have to do with the Museum in town?"

"Absolutely nothing!" Cora stood and shook her finger at him. "That's why I tell you 'leave the teapot'!"

"Leave it for what?" Raoul raised his voice, exasperated. "Tell me what you know, Cora. What is going on?"

"Look at this." She motioned for him to come closer to her clay model. "This pineapple? It's Seafus Hobb."

Huh? Had the woman lost her mind?

"It's you, too, and me, and all of us." She paused, as if waiting for Raoul to catch up, but he couldn't.

"I don't understand," he said.

"You see these diamond shapes that mark up the pineapple?"

He nodded.

"They were berries first and flowers before that. You've seen a pineapple plant. You know what I'm talking about."

Of course he had seen one. You could hardly step past your front door on Oh without tripping over one. Pineapples began as a cone of flowers, hundreds of them. The flowers turned into tiny fruits, berries, as Cora said, and all the berries turned inward. They grabbed onto each other and onto the central stalk, until they fused into one giant pineapple.

Cora saw that he understood. "All that remains of each flower," she continued, "is the diamond on the outside. You can't say if the flower was purple or pink or white. You don't know if it had scent. It's gone now. But without it, the pineapple couldn't be as it is."

That was all well and good, thought Raoul, but what did it have to do with Seafus Hobb?

"I'll tell you," she said, reading him. "The diamond marks mark out the pineapple's past, all the bits of its history that stuck together to form the fruit. Don't you see? Seafus Hobb is cut from the diamonds of *his* past. Like all of us are."

"But I still—"

"Wait. Let me finish." As she spoke she put her hands on the clay pineapple. "To appreciate what Seafus is capable of, you have to consider the diamonds that make him up." She traced one of the rhomboid shapes with her finger. "He was a cricketer. Strong, strategic, proud." And another. "His pride grew. He became boastful and entitled. Mean." And another. "He sinned. Fell from grace. Humiliated. Forgotten. A champion transformed into island gossip. Imagine." She met Raoul's eyes and moved her finger back to the first diamond. "But ever a sportsman. Determined to win at all costs. Resilient. Of great endurance." She looked at him again. "Every choice, every dream, every mistake. They're all right here." She patted the pineapple admiringly. "They line up to geometric perfection. None can ever be left out or taken away. Ever. Or there is no fruit."

Raoul sat silent, processing all that Cora had said. Almost immediately, two flies hatched in his head. The first one told him that the pineapple was a fruit Stan Kalpi would have adored. The second said that Cora was correct in saying there was more to this—whatever this was—than a teapot. A Seafus Hobb built of diamonds didn't need to scrimp on Customs duty or sell off old pots for cash.

"He's not selling anything off," Raoul mumbled, repeating his earlier words and counting more flies. Then more loudly and forcefully: "He's not selling anything off!"

"And?" Cora coaxed him.

"He's not selling anything off and yet he makes massive cash deposits every other week. So where does the money come from?"

"Contraband of some sort," Cora said plainly. "Drugs...guns. Girls."

Raoul looked to the pineapple, to Cora, and back. He couldn't believe that a fruit so perfect could communicate such ugliness, or that Oh could disguise such evil. He swallowed, and feebly put to her, "Drug-running? Guns? Trafficking? Are you sure?"

Cora raised her eyebrows and shrugged.

Raoul stood before her and didn't say anything more.

She could see that he was overwhelmed, and so she reached into her pocket and pulled out a chip of pineapple jasper the size of a pea.

"Take this," she told him, "and carry it with you. It broke off of one of the jasper sticks for the pineapple cup."

"What's it for?" Raoul asked reluctantly.

"It will give you clarity and perspective. The ability to see things clearly."

Raoul looked at her, skeptical. It seemed to him that all Cora's gems did the very same thing. Hadn't she said something similar about the larimar moon?

He took the chip from her hand and examined it. Normally his own pineapple diamonds would have precluded his pocketing of charms, but this Seafus affair was starting to outsize Raoul's flies.

"Thanks," he said. "I better go. Figure out the next logical step."

She raised her hand in a wordless goodbye and he turned toward the door. Cora debated calling him back, asking (or not) the question that weighed heavy on her mind. She was dying to know if Lila's library appeared on Seafus's map.

Of course it didn't when Raoul saw it, or he would have said. But by the time Cora died to ask, it decidedly did.

37

The jasper chip in his pocket did little for Raoul that afternoon. By the time he left his office and set off in his truck to pick up Lila from work, he had yet to recognize what the solution's next logical step ought to be. He hoped a peaceful evening at home would help to clear his head, and that the morning would bring the clarity the case required. Lila, for her part, had planned for war, not peace, that evening. She thought Seafus's visit to the library might make Raoul jealous, and despite her discomfiture in Seafus's regard, she intended to talk him up. No sooner had Raoul got her settled into the truck, and the truck turned toward their cottage, than Lila laid her bait.

"How was your day, dear?" she inquired innocently. "Did you get the break in the case?"

"No," Raoul said in reply, distracted by the confusion of flies in his head. "How was *your* day? Everything okay at the Library?" (Now why had he asked her that? he wondered to himself.)

"Yes, and I had an interesting day. A *very* interesting day."

"Mm? That's nice." Raoul kept his eyes on the road, and so perhaps didn't notice the bait Lila dangled.

"I said I had a very interesting day," she repeated. "You hear?"

"I hear, I hear. You had a very good day."

"Not *good*," she insisted. "*Interesting.*"

"That's nice," he repeated, patting her on the knee.

Either Lila was a poor fisherman, or Raoul was the sort of fish that needed a hammer to the head, rather than a worm on a hook.

"Seafus Hobb came to see me," she announced.

"What?" Raoul slammed on the brakes, neglecting the clutch and stopping the truck with a start. Lila put her hands on the dash to brace herself.

"Seafus Hobb was at the Library?" Raoul asked her. "What did he want?"

"You remember the Chinese pottery book you liked so well?"

"He wanted that?"

"Well, he said so, but he hardly spent a minute looking at it."

"What did he say about it?" Raoul slowly put the truck in motion again, Lila's hammer having knocked his head clear of flies.

"About the book? He said he would be back to look at it more. And he said it was nice to see me again so soon."

Two flies crept back into Raoul's head. He should have heeded the first above all, bothered as it was that Seafus Hobb was more interested in the librarian than in her books. Instead, it was second one that Raoul indulged.

"Why should Seafus Hobb use the Public Library?" he asked his wife.

"Why shouldn't he? It's public. That's the idea."

"Because he has a library of his own, that's why."

"What do you mean, he has a library of his own?"

"At the Museum," Raoul explained, "on the top floor, Seafus Hobb has a private library. Well-stocked it is, too. I've seen it with my own eyes."

"When?"

"Today. I went to the Museum. Seafus was out, so I went upstairs and found the library, just like Cora said."

"What does Cora Silverfish have to do with everything?" Lila complained.

"She's the one who told me he had his own library."

"Of course she did," Lila remarked. She turned her gaze out the window so Raoul wouldn't see the tears that had begun to form in her eyes.

For the rest of the drive, neither of them said a word. Lila watched the island go by and marveled that Raoul wasn't bothered by Seafus's dropping in at the library, at least not in the way she had hoped. His every thought and deed seemed to revolve around Cora! It hadn't escaped the tide of island talk that Raoul Orlean spent more time at the local lady jeweler's than he did in his office at Customs Headquarters. Lila tried to ignore the gossip, but more and more it appeared that the tide was right.

By the time they reached home, Lila, who saw how unfit for battle she was, devised a new plan: some hot tea and biscuits, a cool bath, and an early surrender to bed with a brand-new library book. Raoul, too, had taken a decision: he would spend the next day, his day-off Tuesday, at the Library, like he used to before the birthday debacle, just in case Seafus turned up. If Raoul could discover what Seafus came in to research, it might shed some light on his island-wide map of crime. When Raoul told Ms. Lila what he had decided to do (without telling her the reason why), she mistook his solution's next logical step for husbandly love after all—and jealousy, yes, indeed!—and she devised a second new plan to replace the first: some hot soup and dumplings, a cool mango cocktail, and an early surrender to bed with her loving husband.

If Lila couldn't have her war, then Raoul would get no peace.

———

In spite of the auspicious night that preceded it, the next day didn't offer Raoul much. He took his wife to work at the library, and stayed with her there from open to close. Though he enjoyed himself, back between the covers of the library's many books, it felt like a lazy luxury, one he couldn't permit himself while the case of the crooked Curator remained unsolved. Seafus hadn't shown up all day; thus Raoul had collected no additional variable or clue. Even Ms. Lila, who seemed only too eager to have Raoul close by when the day began, was testy with him by the time they finished their lunch. Raoul would have considered the day a total waste had it not been for the idea that came to him as he and Lila ate cheese and chutney sandwiches at her desk.

"I think I'd like to read about gemstones," he declared out of nowhere.

Normally, no request of her husband's at the library ever gave Lila pause, for he had proven his tastes to be far-ranging over the years. His sudden interest in gems, though, had Cora's name written all over it, and on this of all days, when his love for Lila had forced him to join her at work! Lila, fed-up, pointed to the shelf he wanted and said, "Over there." She said little else to him after that, until it was time to go home.

Raoul didn't know himself what he hoped to find as his fingers moved across the spines of the books on rocks and gems. The ones on geology didn't intrigue him, nor did those on gemstones in jewelry and art. Perhaps it wasn't a topic he wanted to read up on after all. He had nearly made up his mind to go reread his favorite book about Mr. Stan Kalpi instead, when a title caught his eye: *The Incidental Properties of Precious Gems*, by Heinrich Kopt. Heinrich Kopt. The named oozed authority, Raoul thought, and he took the book to his table in the corner. It was a scientific treatise to start, one that explained about the formation and mining of stones, then ranked them in charts according to how hard or dense they were, where they could be found and how easily, and whether they cleaved or fractured. Next, it devoted a page to each mineral (gemstones were minerals, Raoul had learned), complete with color photo. Unlike the book's beginning, which described the stones' physical properties, the single pages discussed their incidental ones, which Mr. Kopt defined as characteristics considered secondary by geologists, but still, in his scientific opinion, worthy of note. They were mostly medicinal, though for many stones Kopt also listed the ways in which a given stone could be of psychological or even magical benefit (or detriment).

Raoul made no bones about his black-and-white, plain-as-noses-on-faces philosophical bent. If he could see something with his own eyes, prove it to mathematical or geometric certainty, or read about it in black and white at the library, then—and only then—it must be true. Hence his disdain for island magic, which was little more than words tossed about and embraced by Oh's inhabitants, whose philosophies were wanting. Now Mr. Kopt was putting Raoul in a pickle, presenting himself (and irrefutably so, it seemed to Raoul) as a man of science, who purported the magical powers of malachite and pearl. Raoul didn't know what to make of him, though Kopt seemed to confirm everything Cora had ever said about corundum or almandine or iolite. Still, Raoul was a man of Kalpi principles, of tangibles and tangents that one could measure and quantify. Kopt himself had called his findings "anecdotal." Wasn't that just a fancy way of saying "old talk"? Then again, Mr. Kopt's methods, as he described them, were scientific, logical and methodic, nearly Kalpi-esque.

Raoul wasn't sure how long he sat contemplating his Kalpi-Kopt dilemma, trying to reconcile maths and magic, but at some point an angry scrape of Lila's deskchair told him it was time to go. He closed up Mr. Kopt and his Properties and returned him to his home on the shelf with the other rocky volumes, then Raoul helped his wife turn off the lights and lock up. Lost in thought, he hadn't even noticed how quiet she was, which irked her more than magic irked Raoul.

Once outside, in the late sun of early evening, Raoul managed to clear his head for a moment of Kopt and Kalpi both and asked Ms. Lila what she fancied for supper. She answered him, but only because she was hungry. Oxtail. With carrots and pepper. She planned to go home, she told him, and stew.

38

L ike Raoul's Tuesday visit to the library, the remainder of the week brought no new clues. Although Raoul traced the Curator's crime ring around the island in his green-blue truck, none of the X's he could recall revealed anything out of the ordinary: nothing amiss at the airport or the docks; the seedy port bar was as seedy as always, but no more so; and the X's far in the country were all deserted when Raoul stopped to check them out. Raoul continued his daily meetings with Garvin, too, though Cora had just about convinced him that the packages per se didn't matter. Three days and nothing to show for his surveillance, his meetings, and his sniffing around. All he knew for sure about the Curator was that his large bank deposits continued—weekly now—and that his Museum team was on to the semi-finals, having beaten Bang and the rest of Trevor's bakery team the night before 4-2. (A respectable showing by the bakery "boys," Bang maintained, given their ages and the Museum's aggressive play.)

There was nothing like an early morning to shake the flies from one's head, though, and renew one's conviction. Raoul had a good feeling he was in for a windfall. Saturday was the day.

He took Ms. Lila to work and headed to Cora's shop. He didn't know what else to do or where else to go. Only to Cora he could report on his efforts, however fruitless. If she didn't have any ideas about the solution's next logical step—he planned to ask her outright—all he could do was to re-trace the steps he'd already taken, revisit the X's, only this time on foot, so his toes could feel around in the dirt and the muck, and make sure he hadn't missed any clues. It was the technique he had learned from Stan Kalpi, certainly, who had employed it to great success, but one that Raoul resorted to less and less over the years. It bothered Ms. Lila terribly when he did, for inevitably someone saw his tiptoeing about and word would spread that he was mad. Raoul had no doubts about his sanity, and didn't mind what the islanders thought of him, but it pained him to worry or embarrass his wife, so he tried to behave as best he could. That he was even contemplating removing his shoes was a sign of how desperate he was.

At the jewelry shop Raoul found Cora engaged in some odd behavior of her own. She appeared to be fitting her clay pineapple for a garment of some sort, wrapping every inch of it (except the bottom) in stiff sailcloth and pinning the edges.

"What are you doing?" he said to her by way of greeting.

"Oh, hello," she replied. "I didn't see you come in." Humming happily, she continued her wrapping and pinning.

"What is that?" Raoul asked again about the strange sight.

"It's nothing yet. It will *be* a pattern."

"A pattern for what?"

"For the cup, what else?"

"I thought the clay pineapple was the model."

"It is. The model for the pattern for the cup."

Because Raoul didn't know what to say to that, he didn't answer.

Cora elaborated: "I'm making a pattern to follow when I cut the copper sheets. If the pattern fits the mold perfectly, then the copper I cut will, in the end, look exactly like the model does. You see?"

"Copper sheets?" Raoul wasn't certain but he supposed he had imagined a big block of copper out of which Cora would chisel a giant pineapple.

"The model is three-dimensional, but the copper sheets are flat. If I wrap the cloth around the model and trim it so it fits snugly, then trace that onto the copper and cut it out, when I solder the ends of the copper sheets together, they will duplicate the model's shape. Just like making a dress."

"And the copper one will look exactly like the clay one after you solder it together?"

"Not at first. I can't hammer much of the detail into the flat copper sheets beforehand. The real finishing work will happen after it's soldered and upright. The details hidden under the cloth now will still be hidden inside the copper. I'll have to hammer and poke them out. I'll copy them from the clay model. You understand?"

He nodded, but Cora wasn't satisfied. She bore into him with her eyes.

"Sometimes there isn't a model, Raoul. Sometimes you have no idea of the detail hidden inside the metal. You simply have to hammer and poke and hammer and poke until you fall in, lose yourself in the very heart of it. Only then do you see what it was hiding. Hammer and poke, Raoul. Hammer. And. Poke."

The shop had grown completely silent. Not a voice or a vehicle engine or a birdcall filtered in through the open balcony doors that overlooked the bustle of Market Square. The din that usually filled the space was such a part of it, that only in its absence did Raoul take note of it at all. Odd, that.

Cora returned to her cutting and fitting then, and asked Raoul the reason for his visit.

He told her about his trip around the island, told her that he had found nothing suspicious, and that, unless she could suggest something better, he was left no choice but simply to pound the same pavement once more. (He omitted the fact that he would do so barefoot, although on some other occasion he would quite like to discuss both Mr. Kalpi and Mr. Kopt with Cora.)

Her movements belied any special enthusiasm for Raoul's next logical re-step, but Cora's words, directed more at the sailcloth than at him, renewed Raoul's hopes that he might yet land himself where he was meant to be.

"I couldn't have suggested anything better myself," she said.

———

Although one could debate the magical properties of Oh (that "one" being Raoul Orlean, since no other islander would put them into question), little doubt could be cast on what the island thought of the Annual Harvest Football Tournament. To date, not a single Pineapple Cup match had been rained on, and Saturday night's match-up was proving no different. Oh had lined up another perfect island evening, and the islanders were lining up to take buses into town. It was the last night of the Second Round, with

Campbell's Drug & Sundry playing the Island Police for a spot in the Semi-Final.

Because the next day was a Sunday on which the Library opened, and because Ms. Lila was still sulking about Raoul and Cora, Lila had declined Raoul's invitation to go out to the playing field with him that night. Raoul considered going alone, sure to run into Bang or Cougar or Nat (for whom he harbored no more rancor, since Nat no longer drove Lila around), but he decided instead to spend the evening at work. With most of the island at the football match, it was a perfect opportunity to snoop around without getting snooped-on himself, or gossiped about. He could wear (or not) what he wanted and act as strangely as the circumstances required. Although the sunlight would leave him before he finished his trek, he could wear the headlamp that he typically strapped to his forehead when pursuing clues on foot. The darkness would provide him cover, and his investigation might be all the better for that.

Telling his wife he was off to town, Raoul set out in his truck for the country. He had packed his headlamp, binoculars, and magnifying glass, along with a flashlight and toolbox. He had a sack for putting clues inside and a notepad for sketching them. He also took along some old beach towels, cold tamarind juice in a cooler, and a piece of leftover fish wrapped up between two slices of bread. He had decided to head to the country first, since the distance from town and the remoteness of the X's there made them more suited for eluding the eyes of the authorities. Raoul knew the airport and seaport like the backs of his hands, and found it unlikely that the bulk of any criminal activity could be conducted in either location. There was the seedy port bar to take into account, right in town nearby, but surely even a criminal element needed to relax at night, Raoul reasoned. He doubted they would mix too much business with their hard rum and their easy women.

On the seat beside Raoul in the truck lay the map he had drawn from memory of Seafus's hotspots, the map he had used when he checked out the X's the first time. Raoul decided to drive to the first X, park his vehicle, and then walk around, looking for variables in the dirt and the grass, and listening for clues on the wind. Oh's so-called "country" was mostly up in thick, lush hills. The wind at those elevations would be loud and strong. After securing each X, Raoul would continue by truck to the next one.

He started at the mangrove swamp. As a life rule, Raoul believed one should always attack the most daunting aspect of any given job first. If he was to feel for clues all night with his feet, the swamp would be the worst place to do so; thus he best get it over with, and while he still had some sun at his back. He stopped his truck a good distance from the swamp's edge, lest he contaminate any evidence in its immediate vicinity, and got out. With his trousers pushed up to his knees and his shoes abandoned to the floor of the truck, Raoul began to walk about. He approached the swamp, finding nothing out of order along the way. Once he reached the border, he stepped in, but just barely, and slowly dredged the swamp's perimeter with his toes. Stan Kalpi or no, Raoul wasn't prepared to cross through the middle of it, where the salty water would easily climb as high as his chest.

As Raoul circled the swamp by light of the setting sun, his eyes scanned both the water and the sandy brush beyond for signs of Seafus's doings. Raoul was nearly halfway around the brackish body—thankfully, it wasn't very big—when he decided he was wasting his time. The swamp would have gobbled up any evidence

Seafus might have left behind, and there were other X's in need of dredging. The only way back, though, was to follow the swamp's perimeter, so Raoul decided he might as well return via the other side.

When he had covered as near-perfect a half-circle as he could, given the swamp's imperfect outline, he took one last look around. The sun was nearing the horizon and throwing shade on everything in its path. Raoul covered his brow with his hand and squinted. Nothing about the water caught his eye, so he turned his back to it, and looked across the ground that stretched out past the swamp. There, he noticed the light falling into tiny indentations in the sand, a regular and geometric pattern that was vaguely familiar. Raoul climbed out of the swamp and walked through the tangle of roots and branches toward the markings, which at close range he recognized as tire tracks. Tire tracks from the kind of oversized vehicle that could drive across sand without getting stuck. Hmm. 'Why should any such vehicle have business at the mangrove swamp?' he wondered.

Raoul pulled a notepad and pencil from his pocket and sketched the scene, the border of the swamp, the position of the tracks. He followed them as best he could in the dusk. He hadn't thought to strap his headlamp onto his head, seeing there was so much sun when he entered the swamp. As near as he could tell, the tracks went all the way to the secondary road that led deeper into the country, the road Raoul himself would take to get to the next X on Seafus's map. Keen to keep going, Raoul quickly made his way from the tracks back into the swamp, and then around its other side. The second side was as bereft of clues as the first, which led Raoul to note below his drawing that the mangrove swamp per se was likely of little importance. Rather, it must be a meeting spot, or perhaps a drop-off, but for what, Raoul had yet to determine.

He dried his legs, put his shoes back on, and began to drive off in his truck. He stopped when he heard a strange humming sound, suspecting some problem with the motor, but realized the hum came from far off, some swarm of insects—was it?—or some whistle of wind through leafy branches. Nothing to concern himself with, he concluded. In the country one could always hear the sounds of the island more clearly.

Soon Raoul was back on the main road. It circled the mangrove swamp and then picked up the secondary road, onto which Raoul veered. Made of cement, the secondary road boasted no tracks of its own, but no matter. Raoul had found one clue already, and in his experience, clues gathered like flies once one turned up. Before long he'd be tripping over variables, if he just stayed the course.

Next stop: Halfway Hill.

39

Halfway Hill, so designated for the halfway view it afforded halfway up its southern side, was a thin, wedge-shaped mound, a gigantic sliver of rocky cake frosted in tall, green grass. Midway up the hill, on the pointy part of the sliver, there jutted a ledge that granted a breathtaking and panoramic 180-plus-degree view of Oh and the sea beyond. Throughout the island's centuries of history, Halfway Hill and its look-out had served both conquerors and conquered alike, who could easily see from its vantage point what their enemies were doing. Raoul recalled school trips to the hill in his boy days, and how its strategic significance had been impressed upon him and his classmates.

On this Saturday night of the football match, Raoul, his boy days long past him, drove up the hill in his pick-up truck, the twisting, narrow road barely wide enough for two vehicles to pass each other. The sun had dipped too low to be useful by the time he reached the look-out and parked, but the moon was full and taking over, bathing the island in silvery light. All the same, Raoul fixed his headlamp to his forehead before removing his shoes and stepping gingerly across the road and onto the path toward the ledge.

When he got there he stopped to admire what lay below. How spectacular his island appeared from on high! Raoul was always inclined to contemplate its beauty when he found himself in the hills, far from the noise and the talk and the magic. Shrunken by the distance, Oh's flaws seemed to vanish. Or perhaps they melded together and corrected each other, transformed themselves into tiny parts of a bigger, unflawed thing.

The ledge was shaped like half a moon, so Raoul began at one side and walked to the other. He saw the seaport in town and Port-St. Luke's crescent-shaped lagoon, his office, the Market Square, the buildings nearby where the bank and the jewelry store were housed. He picked out the library, his cottage, the airport. His eyes followed the Sea Road along the coast and as they did, his feet walked the length of the ledge. His glance retraced his journey inland as well, to the mangrove swamp he had just examined. Neither eye nor foot had fallen on a clue so far, and Raoul had nearly finished looking. He sighed in resignation, about to turn back, when his foot caught on a clue that his eyes had overlooked, throwing Raoul to the ground.

His headlamp flew from his head and went out, but thankfully the moon provided plenty of light. Raoul crawled to the spot where he had tumbled, and saw that the culprit clue was the leg of a tripod pushed as deeply into the grass as it could go. The third of its legs pressed right into the hillside. On top of the tripod, a telescope. Raoul stood up and without moving the telescope, which was positioned not up toward the stars but downward, he looked into the eyepiece. The spyglass was spying on something specific, that much was certain, for a blurry blob was centered perfectly in its sights. Raoul felt for a knob or some other movable piece that would help him put things into focus. Aha! A building. At first

Raoul didn't make out which one. It was a big structure, and old; long and low, made of wood and topped with sheets of galvanized steel. It sat not far off the road, but a backroad, with almost no lighting. A single streetlamp illuminated its farthest end. Raoul was quite sure it was a place that he knew, and yet he couldn't place it.

He sat on the ground and pulled his notepad from his pocket. He had slung his clue-carrying sack around his body, and from there he pulled out a flashlight. He set it on the ground and switched it on, using it to illuminate the page where he began to draw the building. Despite the island breeze so high up—with its incessant hum of leaf or bug, which had followed him from the swamp to Halfway Hill—Raoul was hot and thirsty. He looked forward to the cold tamarind juice that awaited in the cooler in his truck.

Tamarind juice! A fly pitched in his head. Tamarind juice! Raoul remembered now what the building was! It was the Old Market at Morne Vert, where his class trips to Halfway Hill always ended, with cold tamarind juice or mango snow-ice. The Old Market was known as such because it had shut its doors decades earlier. With the proliferation of vehicles and vans on the island over the years, even country villagers could take a bus to town, where market offerings were far more vast. What had been a bustling hangar of wares and bargains when Raoul was a youth, now was old and deserted. So why would anyone spy on it?

Raoul stood up and looked through the telescope again. He could see nothing out of the ordinary, though much of the Old Market was in shadow, owing to the evening hour. Perhaps in tucking the telescope up against the hillside, whoever had left it behind—Who *had* left it behind? And *why?*—had aimed it inadvertently and haphazardly at Morne Vert. No, Raoul argued with himself. He couldn't believe that. The Old Market was centered perfectly in the scope's sight. Someone had been studying it. Could Morne Vert be the next X on the Curator's map, he wondered? It didn't show up on Raoul's drawing, but he had drawn the map from memory, and a doubt began to niggle. Had he forgotten Morne Vert, or overlooked it when he spied at the Museum? Mistaken it for the village next door instead? He gathered up his things and made his way to the pick-up to double-check.

The cold juice from the cooler sweated and dripped on the map as Raoul studied it. Raoul had made an X of Prickly Ridge, the next village over. He had found nothing there on his first trip around Seafus's crime ring, and now he knew why. Prickly Ridge wasn't an X at all, but Morne Vert—or more specifically the Old Market—must be. Catching clues made Raoul hungry, so he leaned on the tailgate of his truck and ate the fish sandwich he'd brought. He washed it down with the last of the tamarind juice and then made his way to the market.

The farther inland Raoul got, the louder the country hum became. It was a windy night, that was true, but Raoul had never heard the wind buzz in such a way. He wondered if a storm was coming, if maybe some clever insects were trying to let the island know, by making as much noise as they could. All Raoul knew for sure was that, between the buzzing hum outside and the flies in his head, he would have a headache before the night was done.

The Old Market was only a few kilometers away, but on the narrow backroads, the going was slow. Each side of the road dropped off sharply into a deep ditch that would hold a vehicle hostage. No sooner had Raoul congratulated himself on his brilliant idea to work during the football match, when the roads would be free of traffic, than a van full of rowdy young men came speeding toward him. He heard it before he saw it, the laughter and music and shouting. Apparently the van, too, expected the roads to be deserted due to the football match. The driver was as startled as Raoul when each caught sight of the other. Raoul slammed his breaks, stalling the truck, and the van stopped, too, barely a few feet from Raoul's vehicle. Though Raoul was agitated and shouting at the men as he re-started his truck, the van driver quickly composed himself. He put the van in reverse and backed up a considerable distance, until he found a spot in the road where the ditch was more shallow and the road a bit wider. There he waited so Raoul could pass. The man's passengers, meanwhile, didn't skip a beat, still laughing and shouting and listening to the loud music, as if nothing had happened. Slowly Raoul made his way forward and around the van. He passed literally within an inch of it. The bottom of his side mirror even grazed the top of the side mirror of the van, which was lower to the ground than Raoul's pick up. Raoul was so intent on pulling his truck to safety that he couldn't pay much attention to the van and its occupants, or give them a piece of his mind, as he would have liked.

"Bloody youths!" he shouted, when he had safely gotten by and the van had continued, unfazed, on its way.

Never mind that. Raoul was very near the Old Market now, and perhaps a few new clues awaited. He had better things to think about than rowdy young men. Or did he? Barreling toward him was another van full of them, laughing, shouting, music blaring. Exactly like the first!

The same scene repeated itself: slammed breaks, stalled truck, reverse maneuver, Raoul squeaking by, and the men unbothered. This time Raoul tried to get a look at the men inside. He didn't know them, not exactly. And yet he was sure somehow he did. As his heartbeat slowed to less excited rhythms, Raoul mulled over the faces he had spotted (while remaining alert to more vans with screaming radios and shouting men). Although his heart pounded, he realized his eardrums did not. Silence at last! The loud music was too far off now for him to hear it, and the incessant hum of the island bugs had suddenly stopped. The night was completely silent. Not a mysterious rustle of leaf or a strange buzz of insect filtered in through the open windows of the truck.

Huh.

The din that had accompanied Raoul for most of the evening had become such a part of it, that in its absence, Raoul couldn't help but feel something must be wrong. Odd that.

He also had the distinct feeling, as he pulled his truck into the yard of the Old Market building, that the sound itself had led him to that very spot. He looked around and wondered if the buzz had somehow come from there. Mr. Stan Kalpi made a practice of catching clues on the wind—both scents and sounds, which, Raoul knew, hid there in plain sight. But at first glance, nothing near the market indicated whether his hunch was right. Raoul would have to investigate further.

His headlamp had gone out in his fall on Halfway Hill, but he still had a flashlight. Between that, the light of the moon, and the lone streetlamp near enough to illuminate one of the rectangular building's shorter sides, he hoped to see what clues lay hidden. A barefoot walk around the building's outside proved fruitless, however. There may have been some footprints—Raoul couldn't be sure—but if so they were jumbled and overlapped, and who knew how old. A few food wrappers and empty bottles lay scattered around, too, but those only suggested loitering and inconsiderate youths, of the type Raoul had passed in his truck a short while before. No, if he was to learn anything from the Old Market, he was going to have to get inside. But how? He had noticed that the main door, on the short end of the building far from the streetlamp, was chained and padlocked. The other sides of the building were dotted with windows, all closed, and all high off the ground.

Raoul got an idea. If he backed his truck up against the side of the building bathed in the light of the streetlamp, he could climb from the bed of the truck to the roof of the truck, and just possibly be high enough up to break in through one of the windows. He positioned the pick-up and put his sack around his shoulder, with, inside it, the flashlight, hammer, and notepad. The window Raoul had parked below, like all the others, was a typical rudimentary island model, a panel of galvanized steel fastened with hinges over a hole in the wood structure. It might swing outward or inward, or both, with a latch at the bottom.

Standing on the roof of the pick-up, Raoul poked at the metal. He could feel it give, but it was definitely latched shut. Hammer in hand, he set to it, beating on the lower edge until he heard the latch break. He tried to push the steel panel inside but the latch hadn't broken cleanly and still a part of it blocked the window from opening. With his fist, Raoul punched and poked at the upper part of the window, and alternately hammered at the bottom. He poked and hammered, hammered and poked, until finally the metal gave up its secrets. But it did so so abruptly, that it caught Raoul off-guard. His body lurched inward, and he might even have stopped it, had a wild gust of island wind not lifted just then, causing Raoul to fall into the building.

As luck or island magic would have it, Raoul fell onto a pile of cardboard cartons, stuffed full and softened by the tropical humidity, otherwise he'd surely be dead. As it was, his head had knocked against his own hammer in the fall and Raoul could taste blood trickling from the injury. In the dark and on his back atop the precarious pile, it took him a moment to collect himself, to remember what he was up to, and to sort out that he had made it inside the Old Market. He reached into his sack and pulled out the flashlight, which he held between his thighs as he sat up and dabbed his head with the tail of his shirt. He tried to gauge by the blood how badly hurt he was, and decided the cut wasn't so deep that he couldn't carry on.

He turned the flashlight on his surroundings and saw that he was perched on a pile of boxes that contained old tarpaulins from the days of the market's operations. No doubt the roof was leaky, and when it rained the vendors would have used the tarps to protect their products. Sometimes, too, the sellers were too numerous to fit inside, Raoul recalled, and the tarps must have served a double function as makeshift umbrellas to protect outdoor vendors from the sun. Looking at the construction beneath him, he imagined someone had built it there precisely for the purpose of reaching the window to open and close it. The rest of the market, one large open room, just as he remembered it from his youth, was full of old wooden tables (more market remnants), and what appeared to be some sort of machinery. Was someone squatting in the old building? Using it as some sort of warehouse?

Carefully Raoul climbed down from the window. His flashlight was bright, but it only illuminated one part of the building at a time, so Raoul walked around, putting together in his head the various pictures the light fell on. There were tables lined up along one wall of the place that showed clear signs of recent attendance:

more food wrappers and balls of tinfoil, empty bottles, just like outside. The other wall was lined with more tables, and two machines. The tables were piled high with cans and jugs of different sizes and colors, and mixing trays. Paint? Raoul didn't see any brushes or any sign of renovations under way. The two machines were also mysterious. They had an almost homemade appearance, rigged with sheer island ingenuity. If Raoul didn't know better, he'd say one of them was meant to be a printing press. It resembled presses he'd read about at the library, and it was not unlike the machines that Bruce employed to produce the *Morning Crier*. The other machine looked like it belonged on a factory assembly line. It had conveyor belts and blades. Raoul touched the machine and felt it was warm. Not because it was on Oh, where every thing and every body was hot all the time, but because it has been turned on and functioning only a short while ago! Both machines were great and cumbersome. Could they have been the source of the buzzy hum that had bothered Raoul the whole night? If so, what were they printing and conveying and cutting up? Who was working them?

Raoul forgot for a moment that the Old Market was an X. Whatever was going on there, the Curator was behind it. Raoul walked back to the pile of boxes and found one to sit down on. He needed a rest. His head hurt from thinking and from knocking it with his hammer. His upper body ached from poking and hammering at the metal of the window. His lower body ached from dredging the swamp and tumbling over the telescope at Halfway Hill. He could feel blood trickling from his forehead and felt around for something to blot it. His shirttail was saturated, so it was no good. Maybe he'd find a rag or a piece of old market tablecloth stuffed in with the abandoned tarps.

With his head tilted backward to stem the stream of blood, Raoul's hand explored the contents of the box nearest his reach. He touched folds of plastic (another tarpaulin), and then course cloth. A blanket? He grabbed the edge of it with his fingers, but it was too heavy to pull out. He wrestled his hand underneath it, to liberate it from the weight of the tarp on top of it, and as he did, he felt sheaves of paper. He thumbed them to be sure. Yes, pages and pages of paper. Was he seated on a box of books?

The idea excited him even more than a Stan Kalpi clue, for nothing got his black-and-white, plain-as-noses-on-faces philosophical juices flowing like a dusty old volume that, forgotten and hidden away, or found and sold off for pennies, might reveal a wealth of history or science. He yanked on the paper, hoping to dislodge one of the books and remove it, but instead he pulled out a handful of its pages. 'A pity!' he thought to himself and lowered his head to examine the pages by flashlight. They weren't pages at all but bills, rainbow bills, brand new legal tender as colorful as the island itself, and stamped "Republic of Oh."

Incredulous, Raoul studied them. He turned them over and over in his fist, while blood dripped onto the images of Oh's palm trees and Crater Lake. He jumped up and shined his light inside the box from which they'd come. It was full of bills, lined up and hidden beneath blankets and dusty tarps. Raoul grabbed a fistful of them and stuffed them into his sack. He rearranged the box's contents so that no disruption to them was immediately evident and, boosted by his excitement and the cheer of flies in his head, he scrambled up the cardboard mountain, out the window, and onto his truck. There, in the light of the streetlamp and with the aid of his grazed side mirror, he wiped his head with one of the beach towels he'd brought along and wrapped it in another.

He secured the towel to his head by means of the strap on the busted headlamp.

Although he had yet to revisit the rest of Seafus's X's, Raoul decided to call it a night. It was getting late and the match would be over soon, the islanders flooding the roads out of town. He had collected some significant clues nonetheless, some remarkable variables in need of defining, and he needed to go home and line them up, discuss them with Cora as soon as he could—once he got a good rest. On the way to his cottage, he replayed in his head all that had happened, and what it all meant. He was so preoccupied that he forgot having told his wife he planned to spend the evening watching football in town. Imagine Ms. Lila's surprise when she saw him walk in, his head in a beach-towel turban and spent headlamp, his shirttail hard and bloody, the sack on his shoulder brimming with bills.

"What's happened to you?!" she exclaimed.

Raoul shrugged. He told her he was just tired. He hammered and poked, he said, until the wind felled him, and now he would have to re-paint the mirror of his truck.

Pineapple Cup Full-Up
Island Police Advance,
Customs and Excise Snags Wildcard Slot

Yesterday evening the still undefeated Island Police team beat Campbell's Drug & Sundry 2-1, securing a place in the Semi-Final of the Annual Harvest Football Tournament, alongside the Parliamentary Museum and Higgins Hardware, Home and Garden. The Police will defend their title from the Museum team (which reached late yesterday and missed most of the match) on Friday evening. Higgins Hardware will play on Saturday against the wildcard team, Customs and Excise, drawn from a hat last night by Sports and Culture Minister Tristan Torrus. The hat was knitted by Evangeline Thomson of Port-St. George, head of the Women's Artisan Council. Though the Head of Customs and Excise, Raoul Orlean, was not in attendance, the team's goalkeeper, Bertram Marcus, spoke on behalf of the club, which celebrated its second chance at the Cup with rum and pineapple juice. "We drink to this opportunity and will not disappoint our superiors," Marcus said. "I can promise that Customs and Excise will take the cup." It should be noted that the captain of the Police team, Police Captain Reginald Dawson, said more or less the same thing: "The Island Police will ensure that Customs and Excise leave the cup with us." Speculation continues as to the cup's design. Cora Silverfish, proprietor of Pineapple Jewelry and Gems, and the cup's creator every year, was in attendance for the Police-Campbell's match up, but would say no more about the trophy other than that it would be pineapple-shaped, as tournament history demands, and life-like, as are all of her designs, which are currently on discount, due to the upcoming closing down of her shop. Also in attendance were the previously eliminated teams, including Trevor's Bakery and Ashbee's Appliances, Tackle and Tools, knocked out earlier in the week by the Museum and Higgins teams, respectively. Both semi-final matches will take place at 5 o'clock island time on the playing field in Port-St. Luke, where local delicacies, primarily pineapple-themed, will be on offer.

40

"That's who they were! Good old Bruce!" Raoul slammed the *Morning Crier* on the table in excitement, startling Ms. Lila, who sat eating porridge and papaya.

"That's who *who* were?" she asked. "It's not like you to spare a compliment for Bruce Kandele."

"Nothing for you to worry about, love." He pecked her on the cheek. "You ready to go?"

Raoul was keen to get Lila to work, so that he could get himself to Cora's and tell her of the clues he'd collected in the country.

"Why are you in such a hurry? I've hardly had my breakfast!" Lila protested.

"Sorry. Sorry. Big case, is all. I finally have some clues, and I need to go put them together."

"Pfft." Lila didn't need Raoul to tell her he had clues. She could see as much from the shape he was in when he'd returned home the night before, cut and bloodied, full of money. There was no sense pressing him for details. What few he'd reveal would make little sense to her. She sighed. He was playing at Stan Kalpi again.

"Fine," she said. She swallowed one last mouthful and slowly eased herself up and onto her crutches. "Let's go."

Raoul left her at the library, promising to collect her a few hours later, and drove to town. At Cora's he parked his truck and ran up the steps two at a time. He couldn't wait to see her. He put his hand on the door handle and with the inertia of his energetic climb, he propelled himself through the doorway. Sadly for Raoul, the door was locked, and so he merely propelled himself *into* the door, knocking his head for the second time in two days. Thankfully, this time it was bandaged in advance. Raoul pressed his nose against the glass and shaded the view with his hands.

Empty. Cora must have taken the day off. Silly of her, Raoul thought, what with Sunday church traffic, and Bruce having given her free advertising that very morning in the paper. Raoul bolted back down the stairs and got in his truck. He'd look for Cora in Monfruie. He didn't know where she lived, not exactly, but everyone on Oh knew where everyone else lived more-or-less. He was sure once he got to the village, he'd find someone to point him toward her house.

As he drove, he thought of the variables he had lined up, including the one that Bruce had furnished with his football report: the Museum team reached late. The Museum team reached late and Raoul knew why. As he read the article it struck him that the faces he'd seen laughing and shouting to too-loud music in back-to-back vans on the secondary road to Morne Vert, the faces he knew but didn't, were none other than those of the Museum team footballers. What's more, he was quite sure they had come from the Old Market, where they had been doing the Curator's bidding. Ah! How Raoul loved it when the variables fell in line and added up!

Soon he was in the vicinity of Monfruie, suppressing a giggle, so filled with glee was he at the prospect of delivering his news to Cora. He looked to the sides of the road for a neighbor of whom he might inquire about Cora's address, when a strange sight distracted him. He slowed his truck and put his head out the window, trying to make sense of what he saw. It was a creature, an alarming creature, with a head of partly rusted metal that glinted in the sun. Part alien, part knight, its big eyes were only just visible through a small glass window on the front of its head. Its hands were gloved and its feet wore boots, which protruded from underneath an old skirt. An old skirt? Raoul did a double-take. He wrinkled his brow, unsure, and blinked. Was it? No! It couldn't be. Could it?

Though well disguised, Raoul was quite certain that underneath the strange ensemble he discerned the physique of Cora Silverfish. He sat in his truck and watched her. In one hand she held a canister that spit out a thin, blue flame, which her other hand regulated. On the grass before her he could make out two pieces of copper, a round one, and one that looked something like a thick half-moon. She turned off the flame and set the canister on the ground. On her hands and knees, then, she began pounding on the half-moon of copper with a hammer. Raoul shifted to get a better look at what she was doing and accidentally honked his horn.

At the noise, the creature looked up from its hammering and lifted up the front of its helmet. Cora it was, and when she saw Raoul watching her, she motioned for him to approach. He pulled his truck into the gap that led to what he now knew must be her home—a clean and pretty cottage it was, surrounded by every flower Oh knew how to produce—and joined her in the yard behind it.

"Hello, good morning," he called out.

Cora stood up from her work and looked at him. "What's wrong with your head?"

Raoul instinctively touched the bandage on his forehead. Cora's tone was harsh, almost ridiculing, even, but he sensed underneath it a hint of concern.

"A small thing." He shrugged it off.

Cora got back down on the grass and with her hammer continued putting marks in the copper.

"Congratulations," she said to him as she worked.

Raoul was shocked. How did she know that he had figured out the Curator's crimes? He had yet to tell her of a single clue!

Cora read the surprise on his face. "The Pineapple Cup? Customs and Excise in the Semi-Final?"

"Oh, that! Thanks. Thanks." Raoul had rushed to Cora's home with plans to tell her all about his country outing, and yet in her presence, he felt awkward, *lesser*, and didn't know where to start. He refused to believe for a moment that she was truly an island witch, but even he had to admit that—.

"I'm glad you're here," she said, interrupting his thoughts.

"You are?"

"I need an extra pair of hands. Here." She took off her gloves and helmet and gave them to Raoul. "Put these on."

Raoul looked at her. Was she joking? It appeared she wasn't, so he obeyed. Cora meanwhile disappeared inside, returning with a second pair of gloves that she put on herself, and a pair of protective goggles that covered half her face.

"What are we doing?" Raoul asked.

"Can't you see?" Cora replied.

They were both kneeling in the yard now, their eyes locked despite the protective equipment they donned, and for the most fleeting of seconds, Raoul *did* see. He saw the odd, flat copper shape laying in the sun and knew it to be the copper cut-out of the sailcloth pattern he'd seen Cora working on in the shop. He saw it rolled over onto itself and attached to the copper disc that lay next to it. He saw it upright and pocked to perfection, an exact replica of the clay mold Cora had scraped at. He even saw the copper leaves interspersed with others of pineapple jasper, though there was no jasper anywhere in sight right then. He saw the cup in its completion, and he saw it in Cora's eyes, or her mind, or maybe in his own mind. He didn't know which it was, and the image was gone before he could try to explain it away.

Raoul drew his gaze from Cora's. For the next few minutes—it might have been an hour or more, Raoul had lost his bearings—he and she together built up the pineapple cup. Or rather, she built it up with his help. As he held together the two edges of the copper moon, she soldered them together, one fingertip's width at a time, ensuring the seal was neat and smooth, barely detectable. When that was done, he held the hollow, pineapple-shaped tube in place on the heavy copper base, while Cora attached the one to the other with solder as well. It was a hot day on Oh, as all of them are, and Raoul sweat inside his helmet as Cora toyed with the fire, inches from his face and hers.

The pineapple cup had no leaves, and the body's detail was still incomplete, but Cora turned off the flame and announced they were finished. She slid the goggles to the top of her head and removed her gloves.

"Thank you," she said to him. "I'll finish the rest in my workroom at the shop."

Raoul removed his gloves, too, and flipped up the front part of the helmet. Still on the ground, still inches from Cora, he blurted in a wild whisper: "He's making money, you know!"

"Who is?"

"Seafus Hobb!"

"Well, of course he is," Cora said plainly. "That's generally the reason why criminals do crimes."

"Shh!" Raoul hushed her. "No, I mean he's *making* money! Look." His bag of clues hung across his body, where he had put it before leaving his house that morning, and from it, he pulled out a handful of bills. Cora for once was silent. She examined the bills, turning them over and over in the sun. When she saw that some were covered in blood, her gaze moved to Raoul's bandage, but she said nothing. Raoul, who kneeled across from her, dropped to his hands and crawled even closer, as close as his flipped-up facemask would allow. He told her about the tracks at the mangrove swamp, the tripod on Halfway Hill, the telescope, the inks (he knew now they were inks, not paints) and machines at the Old Market, and the boxes of money. He told her about the country buzz and the vans of men who turned up just as the buzzing stopped. He told her how Bruce's article had made Raoul see it all very clearly: Seafus's football team was working for Seafus, printing up fresh island bills by the bundle.

"What are you going to do?" Cora asked him.

"Tell the Police! What else?"

"Tell them what? That you passed some vans in the night and found some boxes of money? That won't stop Seafus! Do you have one bit of proof that he's involved in all of this?"

Raoul hesitated. Seafus was involved, both he and Cora knew it. But *did* he have any proof? "What about his cash deposits?"

"Maybe." Cora wasn't convinced.

"His footballers! We'll get them to testify," Raoul suggested.

"How will you do that? Why would they ever? You don't think Seafus is handing off some of that money to them? They're probably stealing half of it from under his nose besides."

"The Museum then! Seafus couldn't afford all those artifacts if he wasn't printing the money to buy them."

"Yes, but you have to prove it, Raoul. Hammering and poking is fine to start," Cora said, her hand on the start of the pineapple cup, "but the finishing takes time. It requires planning, precision, the proper tools. You can't just go banging about or you'll make a big mess."

Raoul and Cora reasoned for a few more minutes after that, but Raoul didn't hear much else of what she said. All he would recall of their goodbye, when he tried to remember it later, was two promises he had made her: to keep her up to speed on what he got up to, and not to do anything rash. But while the end of their conversation was fuzzy in his head, the part that came before it was clear as crystal: 'planning, precision, the proper tools.' These were the words—Cora's words—that buzzed and ricocheted inside Raoul's brain like so many flies. Scorpionflies, to be precise. Scorpionflies that told Raoul to plan a sting.

41

Raoul left Cora's so quickly, eager to roll up his sleeves and get to work, that he was halfway to town on foot when he realized he'd forgotten his truck in Monfruie. Judging by the position of the sun, he determined it was after lunchtime (although it sure felt much hotter), and his stomach agreed. Raoul was hungry, and Ms. Lila would be anxious to lock up the library—when she opened on a Sunday, she only opened for half a day—so Raoul turned and headed back up the road to the gap where he had parked his pick-up. There was no sign of Cora when he got there; she must have been inside, having lunch herself. Just as well, he thought. The heat was unbearable and he couldn't wait to get home and have a cool shower. He almost regretted that his petty jealousy and his pride had driven him to take on Nat's chauffeuring duties. It had made little difference to Lila. He'd noticed no change in her behavior, or Nat's, no suffering because he'd pulled them apart. Perhaps Lila was a tad more moody than usual of late, but Raoul attributed that to the discomfort of her injury. Now, instead of heading home for a shower and a cold beer, Raoul was headed all the way to the library to collect her.

He opened the windows wide and drove as fast he could, filling the truck with cooling gusts of island air. As he pulled up to the library, he could see Ms. Lila outside, waiting. From a distance she looked vexed, and he braced himself for a reproof. Instead, once he got close enough for her to see him, her face went funny. Raoul couldn't tell if it was shock or concern or resignation that crossed her brow. He watched as she climbed into the truck, hoping for a sign.

"Raoul, what are you doing?" she said to him sharply. (If this was a sign, he couldn't make it out.)

"What do you mean, love? I'm taking you home. Hot today, uh?" He started to pull away from the library, but she stopped him.

"Wait!"

"What is it?" (Raoul's nostalgia for Nat was growing with every trickle of sweat he felt run down his back.)

She sighed. "Why are you wearing that ridiculous thing?" She pointed to his head.

Raoul was losing his patience. She knew very well he had cut himself. She had helped him dress the cut herself. He reached up to check the bandage and his knuckles knocked into the metal helmet that Cora had given him to wear.

"Ah!" he cried, pulling it off with relief and a chuckle. "That explains why I was feeling so hot." (It also explained why he had received such odd looks as he walked halfway to town and back from Monfruie, but he decided not to tell his wife about that.)

"What's the matter with you?" she persisted.

"Nothing. I was soldering."

"Soldering." She looked at him sternly. "Soldering what?"

"The Pineapple Cup cup, believe it or not. Cora let me help."

"You went to the jewelry store again today?"

"No. Well, yes. Cora wasn't there, so I went to her house."

"Her house? You went to Cora's house?"

"I had to tell her some things about the case, and she was working on the cup and wanted my help."

"I'm getting tired of this, Raoul. Why do you suddenly have to discuss every case with Cora Silverfish seven days a week? A month ago, you could barely mention the woman's name!"

Good grief! Why was Lila so agitated? It was for *her* birthday that he had ever walked into Cora's shop in the first place! Raoul had been married long enough, however, to know that this thought was best kept to himself. "Not every case, dear. Just this one. The Museum one. Cora knows about Seafus Hobb."

"What about him?"

Raoul's failure to answer this question could, he knew, have serious consequences for his hot lunch and cool shower, and yet he wasn't sure what to say. Cora, he realized, had been pointing him in the right direction at every turn, but how much had she really told him about the Curator? That he had a library; and how he'd met Ms. Lila; that Cora didn't consider him her friend. Other than that, Cora's was more insight than information. One of Raoul's scorpionflies suggested he give that more thought later. Another recommended a simpler answer to Lila's question, and for that Raoul was grateful.

"Customs fraud," he told her. "Seafus is involved in Customs fraud, and Cora knows something about it."

Lila wasn't sure he was telling her the whole story, but she wanted to believe him.

"After this case is done, you won't have to see her every day?" she asked with hope in her voice.

"No," he replied simply, which was the simple truth.

Lila smiled weakly and they finished their trip home in comfortable-enough silence, each caught up in his or her suspicions and thoughts.

The thought of not seeing Cora so often, now *that* made a tiny stonefly flutter inside Raoul's chest. Which was strange, indeed, because Raoul couldn't recall ever having flies there before. Generally they kept to his skull. Unnerved, Raoul patted at the fly to quiet it, tentative fingers on sweaty chest, until he felt nothing at all. Just the weight of his hand, pressing down on his heart.

Raoul liked a good sting as much as the next guy, and he had set up more than one during his lengthy Customs career. Cora had been correct when she spoke of precision, planning, and proper tools, for these were the touchstones of a successful operation. Not even on Oh could one rush skimble-skamble into a take-down and think the tide and wind would pick up the slack. Then, too, one couldn't take *too* long to strike, either; fermented plans were sour plans, the islanders liked to say. What Raoul had to do was find the sweet spot.

To start, he made an island map of his own. While Ms. Lila tidied the kitchen after their late Sunday lunch, Raoul re-created Oh in the sitting room. The Old Market at Morne Vert was the corner bookshelf, the endpoint of the line segment Raoul had to draw between the Curator and himself. Working backward, he made Halfway Hill a tall wooden chair, which he positioned so that it offered a clear view of the shelf. Next was the mangrove swamp, or Ms. Lila's knotted rug, which Raoul lined up with the empty chair. But what came after that? The Savings Bank? The Museum? The Headquarters of the Island Police?

While Raoul stood thinking in the knotty swamp, with a lamp in hand that he couldn't decide where to place, Ms. Lila hobbled into the room on her crutches. She saw the chair pushed close to the bookshelf and the rug in the wrong spot on the floor. She didn't bother to ask Raoul what he was doing; she knew. Well, he better do it without disturbing her furniture!

"Raoul, stop your playing around!" she scolded him. "Put this room in order this minute!" She continued her hobble toward the bedroom, shouting back over her shoulder, "Why don't you go to the Belly for a while?"

Lost in his thoughts and his re-creation, Raoul only half heard Lila's words. When she slammed the bedroom door shut behind her, he jumped—and decided he ought to try and piece them together, before he made her even angrier.

Now what was it she said? He replayed her voice in his head as he surveyed the sitting room.

'Why don't you go...,' she said.

'...in order...,' she said that, too.

Why don't you go in order.

'Stop...,' she said.

And '...around...'

Stop around what?

She said 'playing...,' didn't she? The playing field?

Stop around the playing field.

That was it! If Raoul was to go in order, the next point on the line was the playing field! The Museum football team was moon-lighting as Seafus's moneymakers after all. Moonlighting, yes, for

Raoul had seen the men off the field, too, here and there, around town, working jobs, if not well-paid ones. Which is why, Raoul reasoned further, they must gather on Saturday evenings to do what they did inside the Old Market. It made perfect sense. On Saturday nights the islanders all went to town to party, whether there was football or not. Who would take note of a buzz in the country that meant someone was printing notes?

If Raoul was right, then—and he must be! Hadn't the Museum team arrived late the Saturday before, as well, when Bang waited almost the entire match to get a good look at them?—if Raoul was right, then he had a week to organize his sting for the following weekend. Was that time enough, he wondered? Could he cope on such short notice? Then he heard Ms. Lila's scrambled words again.

'Put...,' she said.

And '...your...' and '...belly...'

Put your belly. "Belly" meant courage on Oh.

If Raoul put his courage behind his plans, there was no reason to think that he couldn't get done what needed doing by Saturday next. The key was to stay courageous, and to get started at once.

'...this minute,' in fact.

Just like Lila said.

42

First thing Monday morning, after taking his wife to work, Raoul went straight to the jewelry store. The plans for his Saturday-night sting were well under way, but he wanted to run them by Cora, as he had promised. He also had some questions to ask her. Throughout the previous evening, as he thought through his sting, two worries had niggled like gnats, and Raoul hoped Cora could shoo them; it didn't take Stan Kalpi to know that building plans on a wobbly and worried foundation was a bad idea.

The first thing he asked her, was *why* Seafus was printing phony money.

"For that collection of nonsense he calls a museum, that's why!" Cora insisted.

Raoul pointed out that an ancient Yixing teapot was hardly nonsense, nor was a rare and well-preserved Black Diamond butterfly (though the latter, thanks to Raoul, now hung in Cora's backroom instead of at the Museum). But he did concede her point. Piled atop each other the way they were, displayed with no rhyme or reason, the artifacts in Seafus's collection gave more the impression of broom-closet than showroom—which made it all the more strange that he went to such lengths to acquire more and more of them.

When Raoul said as much to Cora, she replied with a snort, "You obviously don't know Seafus Hobb."

No, he didn't. Cora did, though, and this was Raoul's second worry, raised as he discussed the case with Lila in his truck the day before. What more did Cora know about the Curator that she hadn't told Raoul?

Cora seemed reluctant to answer, and Raoul could tell she weighed her words before saying them, measured the information meted out.

"I've told you before," she said, "that Seafus Hobb is a man of pride. The kind of pride that makes a man so obsessed with himself and his importance, that he will stop at nothing to have the fame and glory he feels he deserves. He thought as a cricketer he would put Oh on the map. But he didn't want a championship trophy so he could hold it high in the air, you see. No!" Cora wiggled her finger in Raoul's face.

"Seafus Hobb's ego was much too big for that," she continued. "He wanted the trophy so all of Oh would raise *him* high on their shoulders. He wanted attention for the *island*, so that every islander would worship him. So that every corner of the island would believe itself Seafus's cause, and every soul on Oh believe him its redeemer."

Raoul crinkled his brow. "What does all that have to do with the Museum and counterfeit money?"

"When Seafus's dreams fell apart, he channeled his desires into the only thing he had."

"The Museum."

"Yes, the Museum. Seafus still sees himself as a soldier, a savior who must fight to raise up his island, bring it recognition and stature—as if we were as bad off as all that!—so that his island in turn can raise *him* up. Worship him."

"Nah," Raoul objected, turning away from Cora in disbelief. "You're telling me Seafus thinks he can do all that with his ragbag museum? That's madness!"

"Precisely! The first time Seafus met failure, it ran so contrary to what he thought of himself, that his mind couldn't take it. It warped, laid blame, twisted Seafus's perspective until he no longer *saw* his failures, only his aims—and it bloated those out of all sense of proportion, too. That 'ragbag Museum,' as you call it? For Seafus it is his calling, his lifeblood."

"Pfft," Raoul puffed. It simply couldn't be. It was absurd.

"You think I'm wrong?" Cora went on. "Ask yourself why he's printing money. For no other reason than to deposit it in the bank by the bundle, that's why. To cover purchases to fill up the Museum. You've found nothing to suggest he's using it for anything else." Raoul nodded. That was true.

Cora wasn't done: "Ask yourself why he has a library to put Lila's to shame. Why he researches the rarest and most priceless of pieces and goes out of his way to get them." That was true, too. Garvin's package log, which he and Raoul still met to discuss daily in the gap behind the oil shed, consisted of the odd shipment of rocks for Cora, plus costly curios that never made it to her shop.

"Never mind that he has no room for them, or more than a class of schoolchildren that bothers to visit the Museum!" Cora was worked up. Her fervor lent a ring of truth to her words that Raoul couldn't ignore.

"Say you're right," he began. "Why not print up the money, pay off whoever he gets these...these...*things* from, and carry his ancient pots and platters home in a sack? Why bother with Dwight and deliveries and all that business at the Customs docks?"

"How else is he supposed to get his hands on ancient pots and platters? At the Sunday market? He has to ship them in by boat or fly them in by plane."

"So why not ship them to the Museum? If he's printing all that money, he could afford to pay the duty even on a Black Diamond."

"Yes. But if he started paying a fortune in duty every day, some nosey Customs officer might start to wonder how a tiny island museum paid for such goods. He might call the matter to the attention of someone who would go sniffing around and make trouble."

"True," Raoul admitted. "That doesn't explain why he chose to involve Pineapple Jewelry and Gems. He must have dozens of connections, back-alley and otherwise. On that map in his library, the whole of the Ministerial Complex was one big X. *Why*," Raoul leaned in close to her, "of all his possible options, does he have his pots and platters shipped to *you*?" His tone was more suspicious than he intended it.

Cora shrugged. "I told you his warped mind laid blame. He can't accept that he might be responsible for his own undoing. He has decided that responsibility is mine."

"But *why*?"

"I already said. His perspective is twisted." Before Raoul could pursue the matter further, Cora shifted the discourse. "In any case," she said, "a Saturday sting won't work."

"Why not? It's time enough to get ready."

316

"The Pineapple Cup. You made the Semi-Final, remember? Your team has to play on Saturday."

Raoul answered without thinking twice. "The keeper runs the team. It won't matter if I'm not there."

"You sure?" Cora raised an eyebrow.

"I'm sure," Raoul said.

"Well," she cocked her head, "then I guess we both better get to work." Raoul nodded in agreement, as Cora turned toward the workroom at the back of her shop.

"Trophies don't make themselves," she said.

43

While Cora spent the next few days working on the Pineapple Cup cup, tapping diamond details into its body and, with a hand torch, attaching copper leaves (and copper prongs for leaves of jasper) to its top, Raoul readied himself to raid the Old Market on Saturday. So busy was he with his variables and his flies and his planning, that he asked Nat to resume driving Lila back and forth to work. Nat was happy to oblige, and though Lila feared Raoul was trying to ditch her to spend more time with Cora, Lila so preferred the comfort of Nat's new van to the jarring of Raoul's old truck, that she didn't object. Her wounded pride would happily take a back seat to her wounded ankle, at least until her cast came off. Two more weeks! How she longed for life to return to normal, for her foot to bend the way it was supposed to when her brain ordered it, for Raoul to be done with his Cora-Curator case—surely that would be over by then, too, if not sooner. The plan was for Lila's cast to be removed the day before the Pineapple Cup final. What a thrill it would be to celebrate the tournament's finale with a liberated ankle and—who knew?—maybe even a Customs team victory!

Raoul's readying, in the meantime, entailed first and foremost a painstaking review of the clues he had gathered. When he looked them over collectively, they painted a far more detailed picture than he had expected. Take the tracks at the mangrove swamp, for instance. In light of what else he'd learned, Raoul saw that they were a perfect match for a vehicle like Seafus's big black one. And the telescope that spied the Old Market from Halfway Hill surely sought a sign, a signal that a delivery was en route. Once Seafus saw money was coming, he would head from the Hill to the swamp to get it. Thus, the illustrious Curator never set foot in the counterfeiting factory, nor anywhere close. It was a crime with a built-in out.

If Raoul was going to incriminate Seafus, he would have to line up his variables for the Island Police: the cash deposits, the pricy pieces at the Museum, the money-making machines at Morne Vert, the boxes of bills, and the scheme to piggy-back on Cora's concessions. Garvin's log would be key, especially the entries for days when he managed to open packages, and seal them back up without Dwight's noticing. Dwight Williams, he was a variable, too. Raoul himself had watched Dwight enter the Museum with a sack of packages that never came back out. Cora could testify that her packages had long been delivered by Dwight, and were already opened when they arrived.

Variables wouldn't be enough to arrest Seafus Hobb, though. Just like he never set foot in Morne Vert, he never once touched or tampered with a package at Customs and Excise. He had managed to keep himself distanced by degrees from the site of any criminal activity, a cunning and sacrificial geometry that Raoul hoped to disprove. He would use his Stan Kalpi maths, plus some islander assistance. By 'assistance' he meant the knowledge of the footballer-counterfeiters, whom Raoul hoped to scare into snitching. They were savvy men, and enterprising; he could tell by the bills they designed and printed and packaged so well. Their consort with Seafus Hobb had turned them blustery and rude, that was true, but Raoul suspected they would have as readily devoted their talents to more licit ends, had the island put any in front of them. (Sadly, island winds sometimes don't carry the savvy or enterprising too far.)

If Raoul could make the men see sense, convince them to rat on Seafus Hobb *en masse*, their combined accusations would close the distance between Seafus and themselves. One man alone, even two, Seafus and his seedy port dominoes could knock down; but a whole *team* of repentant footballer-counterfeiters would be too bizarre for even the Island courts to refute. Not to mention, Raoul would point out, their islander assistance might keep them out of prison.

Having reviewed his clues and performed his calculations, and reviewed his clues and performed his calculations again, Raoul decided to run through the country crime ring once more before taking his case to the Police. He had no intention of wading through the swamp or hiking barefoot up Halfway Hill, and certainly no wish to hammer and poke his way to another windfall. But he did want to make sure that in the daylight his evening impressions remained unchanged.

He made the drive on Wednesday, about ten o'clock, when the morning traffic was over and the lunchtime traffic not yet begun. At the swamp, the tracks were still there, and still appeared to be Seafus's, as near as Raoul could tell. At Halfway Hill, he found the telescope still hidden and in position. And although at Morne Vert the Old Market was still locked up, in the sunlight, all the clues outside it were clearer. There were footprints, yes, overlapping and muddled, but Raoul could see now they were fresh. They stopped suddenly beside a neat set of tire tracks, as if the swarm of excited stompers had jumped on a bus. Raoul looked for evidence of a second bus, too, and sure enough, there it was. The two minivans had parked back-to-front, it appeared, and a second set of excited footprints ended at a second set of tracks.

Raoul circled the building. The windows were too high for him to see in, but some were partly open, and he thought a higher vantage point might afford him a peek inside, however obstructed. He couldn't park beneath a window and climb atop his truck like the last time, not mid-morning, but he wondered if with the telescope, he might not be able to zoom in on the Market's interior. It was worth a try, he decided, and so he backtracked to Halfway Hill.

He parked his truck as close to the look-out as the road permitted and made his way on foot to the crescent-shaped ledge. He had gotten nearly halfway round it, halfway to where the telescope was hidden, when he saw that someone else was already there, already peeking through it. Raoul could see the peeker's back, partly; he—it was definitely a he—was veiled somewhat by branches and leaves, but Raoul knew in his heart it was Seafus. He must have parked his vehicle on the opposite side of the look-out, for Raoul hadn't seen it when he drove up.

Raoul did a quick tally of his options as he stood and watched Seafus, who was far enough away that he hadn't heard Raoul approach. Raoul could confront him, though a face-to-face confrontation on a deserted ledge midway up a mountain seemed unwise. Raoul wasn't certain he'd make it back down the way he came up. He could retreat, but that seemed a waste. He was there now; shouldn't he watch and see what Seafus got up to? Add another clue to his sack? The only problem was that the look-out offered little in the line of a hiding place. If Seafus bothered to turn around for any reason at all, he would spot Raoul for certain.

Hmm.

In the end Raoul chose a combination of tactics. He would retreat to his truck, then circle around to the other end of the look-out and see if he could spy Seafus or Seafus's vehicle from there. Maybe Raoul could get an incriminating snapshot of the one or the other. (He had brought along his camera this time, but left it in the pick-up, or else he'd have taken a shot of Seafus's alleged back-side.) Raoul only wished he had a disguise, in case Seafus spotted him. Back at the truck, he looked through what tools and accoutrements he had, but there was nothing that served such purpose. He did notice that in the sun on the hillside his pick-up appeared more light green than blue, and this was reassuring, as he might hope to camouflage it amidst the mountain foliage. He got inside it, turned it around, and drove off.

When Raoul drew near the place where he expected to see Seafus's vehicle, it wasn't there. Seafus must have driven right up to the look-out, instead of parking, as signage advised, and going on foot. It would be impossible for Raoul to do the same without being seen. Instead, he retreated again, just a bit farther down the road, where he camouflaged his truck as best he could in the brush. There he would sit, camera at the ready, and when Seafus drove past, which he would have to do to get down the hill, Raoul would snap his picture. To be safe, Raoul put on the welding helmet that he had forgotten to return to Cora. He found it sitting on the front seat next to his camera, and it seemed a sure disguise.

Alas, little is less stealthy than a man in a metal helmet holding a camera to his face, seated in the front seat of a truck parked halfway in a ditch on a country road. Seafus saw Raoul a mile away, so to speak, and decided to speak to him. There was nothing suspicious about Seafus's presence at Halfway Hill, was there, late on a Wednesday morning? Why should he hide from Raoul Orlean?

"Officer Orlean? Is that you?" Seafus pulled up alongside Raoul's truck and shouted into the window.

Raoul lifted the front of his helmet, startled. "Uh, uh, can I help you?" he said to Seafus, feigning authority, barely.

"I was about to ask you the same thing. Are you in some sort of difficulty?"

"Of course I'm not," he spat, regaining his composure. "This is official Customs business. Please continue on your way."

"Customs business? Up here all alone?"

"Yes. And you are disrupting my investigation."

"Investigation of what?"

"I am not at liberty to discuss that with you."

"That's a pity," Seafus said. "I know these parts well. I might have been able to help." With a smirk, he then asked Raoul, "Is that a welder's helmet you're wearing?"

"Never mind what I'm wearing. What business do you have up here?"

"None whatsoever. I just enjoy the view," he said. "I like to look out." Seafus gunned the engine of his oversized vehicle. "You should look out, too, Mr. Orlean," he added before taking off. "You should look out, too."

44

"He threatened you?"

"I think so."

"You told him you were investigating a Customs case?"

"Yeah."

"You don't think he knows *he* is the case?"

"I'm not too sure."

"Did you go back to the telescope after he left? See if there was some sign for him to make a pick up?"

"Nah."

"You mean you followed him to the swamp. To see if he went to get the money."

"I wanted to, but after he saw me at Halfway Hill, I couldn't risk it."

"No."

Cora sighed. Raoul had rushed back to Port-St. Luke, fuming, to tell her about his morning (How dare Seafus Hobb issue a direct threat to the Head of Customs and Excise?!) and about his week so far. He planned on taking his case to the Police the very next day.

His variables were in line and his Seafus sighting had cemented his suspicions. While the rest of the island watched football on Saturday evening, Raoul and the Island Police would be making a bust at the Old Market. By the time the match was done, Raoul hoped to have a dozen or more witnesses to testify against the Curator.

"You're still going through with this on Saturday?" Cora was surprised.

"Why not?"

"After Seafus saw you up there today? He's not stupid, Raoul. He will know that you were spying on *him*. If he thinks you know about the telescope pointed at his print shop, you don't think he'll shut it down and lay low for a time?"

Cora might be right. On the other hand, Garvin's log of Packages Received told of yet more and more valuable Museum miscellany (verified by Raoul behind the oil shed—an ancient Roman lamp, a medieval tapestry from France), and suggested that Seafus need print as much money as he could. Although...he could hardly do so if his men got arrested. If Seafus knew Raoul was onto them, he might furlough them until further notice.

Cora read his worries and reiterated what she'd said before: "Your place is with your team on Saturday."

"But—" Raoul tried to object.

"Seafus hasn't missed a match, and if he sees you aren't there to cheer your own men to the Final, it will make him suspicious. *More* suspicious than I suspect he is already. I wouldn't be surprised if he shut down his operations for a month or more."

"A month?! I can't wait that long to break the case! He could clear out the Old Market altogether in that amount of time. Then I might never have the chance to prove what he's doing."

"From what you say, it would take all of Seafus's men a week of night shifts to clear everything out and—trust me—as long as they are still in the tournament, they'll be too excited for that. I can hardly believe Seafus manages to wrangle them on Saturday nights to work. You see how riled up they are when they finally get to the playing field, acting rude and starting fights. I guess he pays them a good sum. A fake one or a real one, now that's anyone's guess."

"Fine," Raoul sighed. "No sting on Saturday. I'll take Lila to watch the Semi-Final. But the Museum team plays on Friday, and if they get knocked out, then what?"

"Then they'll be so vexed, that Seafus will have to give them at least a week to cool their heads. Don't you worry."

"And if they win...."

"If they win, they might still be drunk on Saturday night from celebrating—that is, if Seafus wants them working at all, after he caught you sniffing around."

While Raoul appreciated the importance of perfect timing, and knew firsthand what happened when a plan's precision was put in jeopardy, he was disappointed at having to postpone his raid at Morne Vert. He was anxious to wrap up the case of the counterfeiting Curator, mostly because a carrotfly inside Raoul's head had been dangling a doubt. Though Raoul tried to grasp it, he couldn't quite; all he knew was that he *had* to get Seafus Hobb behind bars, and he hoped a delay in doing so wouldn't cause collateral damage.

"Wait here," Cora said, interrupting his worries. She went to her workroom and came back with the trophy for the Pineapple Cup. She still had to carve the leaves of pineapple jasper, and fasten them in place, but the body of the fruit was finished, as were the leaves of copper. When Raoul saw it, his mouth fell open. He could hardly recognize in this masterpiece the copper pieces he had helped Cora put together in her yard. Though made of metal, Raoul would have bet his life that, inside it, the pineapple hid the sweetest and most juicy pulp his tongue had ever tasted. He reached out and touched the diamond shapes that Cora had finished hammering into the copper. The copper felt stiffer and thicker than it had when he helped her roll it up and solder the ends in place. It rose strong and majestic from the heavy base it sat on, as if it were bursting mightily from the very earth of Oh. The leaves, though copper-colored, appeared more true than any green ones Raoul had ever seen on a real pineapple

"It's...it's...." Raoul didn't know what to say.

"Good, eh?" Cora said, proud of her work, which she stroked lovingly. I'm working on the jasper leaves now and just have to attach them.

"Ahh!" Raoul cried out. "That reminds me. I have your helmet in my truck." He bolted out of the shop to go get it, so abruptly that Cora didn't have a second to tell him she was in no hurry to get it back. So abruptly, too, that Raoul nearly knocked over Dwight Williams, who just then was reaching the top of Cora's stair, with a package in hand. Dwight Williams? Raoul continued his bolt without stopping, but as he ran to his vehicle, a second doubt now dangled: *was* Dwight Williams reaching the top of Cora's stair just then? Or had he been there, outside the door, lurking and listening the entire time Raoul and Cora talked? The door was propped open, to allow in the breezy afternoon. Had Dwight heard mention of the Curator and remained outside it, eavesdropping, to gather facts to take back to his boss?

Raoul got Cora's helmet out of the pick-up and lingered there, watching for Dwight to descend the jewelry-store stair. Once he had, Raoul waited as Dwight disappeared down Market Square Hill.

Raoul bolted back up to Cora. Their eyes met and in one look, their mutual fears were shared and confirmed, their common questions posed, and left unanswered.

Cora sighed a sigh that left Raoul cold. A sigh that said *she* had dangling doubts, too. Normally she kept them hidden, and in her casual indifference to most of what he said, Raoul took an odd comfort, as if he understood her lack of enthusiasm to signal lack of concern. But now she was worried, and that worried Raoul in turn.

"You definitely can't make a move on Saturday now. Not without being sure of what Dwight heard, or didn't."

"What was he doing here?" Raoul asked.

"This." Cora held up a package. "Opened and resealed," she commented, as she set the package down and cut into it. On a piece of velvet that sat on the jewelry counter, she spilled out the contents, a single stone that looked like a small cloudy ice cube, somewhat irregular in its shape.

"What is it?" Raoul asked. "It's not too pretty."

"No?" Cora shrugged. "Rock crystal. It was, it *is*, for an important piece I have to put together." She shook her head with an annoyed little chuckle. "Imagine Dwight bringing it just now."

Raoul raised his brows in an expectant look that told her to explain herself.

"Rock crystal has a unique and very special power." She paused, as if reluctant to tell him what she had to. "It predicts time," she finally said.

"What does that mean?" Raoul asked.

"It means," she sighed, "that whoever carries it will find himself in exactly the right place at *exactly* the right time."

45

Though Raoul should have spent his Thursday at the Head-quarters of the Island Police, and his Friday hammering and poking out the details of the joint Police-Customs sting, he spent both days instead doing business as usual, killing time until the football on Friday night. He still had Nat chauffeuring Ms. Lila, so Raoul began each morning with a quick tête-à-tête with Garvin in the gap by the garage, then he went to the Headquarters of Custom and Excise, where he stamped and signed forms distractedly, and thought about Seafus Hobb. If Cora's rock crystal had worked its magic, and Cora seemed sure that it had, then Raoul must assume Dwight Williams knew everything, which meant that Seafus did, too. Raoul despaired of ever getting to raid the Old Market now. He hoped Cora was right about Seafus's men, and that in a week (or two? three?) the authorities would still be in time to act.

Thursday after work Raoul went for a drink at the Belly. He hadn't been for a while, but that didn't matter to Bang, Cougar, or Nat. When Raoul had a tricky Customs case, they often went weeks without seeing him there, as if his life were a book, and they, left out of some chapters. Eventually Raoul turned up to drink with them again, and every time he did, they found that their friendship had withstood the omissions.

Together, the four of them attended the Semi-Final match on Friday between the Parliamentary Museum and the Island Police. The Police were strong, and defending a title, so Raoul felt sure they would win. As it turned out, the Parliamentary men were stronger and meaner, and won 3-2. Every last one of them had adopted Seafus's swagger, which the policemen had matched, in attitude and well-aimed shin-kicks if not in goals. Should Raoul's Customs and Excise boys beat Higgins the next evening, Museum and Customs would face off at the Final, and Raoul shuddered to think of the battering his boys would take.

Cora was at the match, too, and though she gave Raoul a perfunctory 'Hello' when she walked by him, she sat some distance downfield, with newspaperman Bruce, but still among the Police team's supporters. (Bang had insisted they back the Police—since the Museum team beat the Bakerymen in the previous round—which was, of course, fine by Raoul.) Seafus had paced the sidelines for the entire match, shouting angrily at his players when he wasn't staring down Raoul or Cora. His gaze went from him to her to the field of play and back. Seafus was letting Raoul know that he knew of the confidences between the two of them, between Raoul and Cora Silverfish, and that he knew what Raoul was scheming. The steadfast way he locked eyes on Raoul said something more, too; namely, that Seafus would never allow Raoul's schemes to ever play out.

So vicious was the Curator's stare that when the match ended, Cora managed to pull Raoul aside and discreetly put a rough-edged rock the color of green peas in his hand. She wrapped his fingers around it and told him not to let go, not until he was safely home.

She answered him before he could ask: "Serpentine. To ward off demonic forces," she whispered.

He lifted his gaze from the rock on his palm, to object, but Cora was gone.

'My word,' he marveled, dumbfounded. What his life had come to! The island witch a kindred soul, slipping him serpent-stones to keep away a devil.

———————

At last, Saturday night. Sadly for Raoul, only the bees would be stinging, but he still hoped to pick up a clue or two before the evening was done. For one thing, it was a perfect opportunity to keep watch, on Seafus, on his men. If they arrived late, like they did every Saturday, it would mean that Seafus hadn't suspended operations at the Old Market after all. Besides keeping watch, then, Raoul planned to *look*. Yes, *look*, at Seafus, for the duration of the match. Stare him down the way Seafus had stared *him* down the night before. Grateful though Raoul had been (and still was) for Cora and her serpentine—even adherents of the plain-as-noses-on-faces philosophical school hedge their bets against a devil—once home, he had felt only anger. Seafus's stare was nothing less than a threat, albeit a silent one, and that made two threats in three days. Raoul was a government official. He wouldn't sit by idly as he was looked at and told to 'look out.' It was high time Raoul looked back!

When he and Lila got to the match, Raoul left his wife in the charge of Bang, Cougar, and Nat, and went to take a seat on the bench where the Customs men were gathered. They all nodded to him politely as they laced their boots and tucked their shirts.

Bruce was there, too, soliciting quotes for the newspaper. He asked Raoul what the spectators could expect from Customs and Excise, but Raoul just shrugged and barked, "Football, what else?" Bruce paid Raoul's cheek no mind. He didn't need Raoul to give him a story; he could find one of those on his own.

With the Final one week away, the usual Saturday excitement was ratcheted up. Vendors showed off their finest offerings (cakes, candies, pies, and puffs, sweaty juices they tried to keep cool), hoping that Semi-Final customers would come back for seconds the week after. The organizers had hired a DJ to entertain the crowd before the sports began, and loud speakers vibrated with reggae and soca. They lent a party atmosphere to the athletic goings-on, a hint of what the Final would hold.

Raoul saw Cora arrive. She took a seat on the same side of the field as he, halfway between himself and Lila. He tried to catch her eye but couldn't. Seafus was there, too, sitting directly across the field from Raoul, with a bird's-eye view of Raoul and his team. This suited Raoul just fine, as it afforded him a bird's-eye view of Seafus in return—of Seafus's face, in particular, which he planned to bore into with his pupils. The Museum team was nowhere to be seen, not yet. If previous Saturday matches were an indication, they would turn up some time in the middle of the second half, their pockets full of money, no doubt. Or so Raoul was hoping.

In the end, the evening proved a mixed bag of boons and delusions. The Museum team did reach late, which was reassuring, though Raoul couldn't tell if they had come from Morne Vert. They were as boisterous and rude as usual, a good sign, but though they bought their usual drinks, they didn't appear to be throwing money around as if they had an endless supply. As far as Seafus, he did get an eyeful of Raoul's eyes, but he met the stares in stride (indeed he seemed to enjoy Raoul's quiet counter-attack), which left Raoul even angrier than he was the night before. The football went well for Customs and Excise, although the spectators found it rather dull, pineapple puffs and soca music notwithstanding. Neither team scored in the first half, which would have been impressive, had both teams boasted an impenetrable defense; rather, the strikers from Higgins and Customs alike were equally off their games and off the mark. Finally, as the second half neared its end, a lucky Customs kick hit home. Whether the resultant cheers were for the victors or for a break in the boredom, who knew?

In spite of himself, Raoul found his fingers toying with the lump of serpentine in his pocket for the whole of the night. Cora stopped to congratulate him after the match, and made a point of asking if he'd brought it along. She seemed relieved when he said 'yes.' He pulled it from his pocket to show her, and gently bounced it on his palm. Lila saw the scene from afar, Cora speaking to her husband and her husband playing with what must have been one of Cora's gemstones. Lila stood up on her crutches and made her way to where the two of them were talking, so as to remind them both that she, Mrs. Raoul Orlean, existed.

Although over the course of the preceding weeks Raoul had forgotten all about his jealousy and his suspicions where Nat and Lila were concerned (having grown so engrossed in his case, and having soothed his pride about driving Ms. Lila), Lila, meanwhile, had become more concerned than ever by all the time her husband spent with Cora, case-related or not. And here he was flaunting a gift from Cora right in the middle of the playing field! Lila paused for a moment to watch their easy interaction and her hand went automatically to the blue birthday pendant she now wore every day. It seemed to please Raoul when she had it on, so she never took it off. It hadn't done her any harm (not since her slip and her fall); still, she feared it had powers, and she feared what they might mean.

Alas, poor limping Lila's fears were not allayed when she got to where Raoul and Cora conversed. Cora greeted her warmly, then said how happy she was to see Lila wearing the pendant Cora had made specially, just for her. She took Lila's wrist and gave it a squeeze.

"You must promise me never to take it off," Cora said. She said it with a fearful smile—not one that frightened, but one that said Cora herself was afraid. Afraid of what? What did Lila's pendant have to do with Cora's fear? Lila felt a shiver begin where Cora gripped her skin, a dread that traveled up her arm, through her heart and down her spine, where it lodged itself. There, it would stay—twisting, looping, pushing her belly—until, eight days later, it tied her body in so many knots that she nearly couldn't breathe.

Pineapple Cup Upset
Police Out, Customs In—
Wildcard to Battle Museum

At last the Final of the Annual Harvest Football Tournament, the so-called Pineapple Cup, draws near. Still in the running for the Cup are the teams representing the Parliamentary Museum for the Preservation of Artistic and Historical Sciences, and the Office of Customs and Excise. On Friday evening the Museum team took on the Island Police in a semi-final match of unusually aggressive play on both sides, though ultimately the Museum defeated the reigning champion Police 3-2. On Saturday evening, in a semi-final match of unusually clumsy play on both sides, the Customs team lucked into a 1-0 victory over Higgins Hardware, Home and Garden with five minutes left on the clock. Though the Higgins-Customs rivalry should have dominated the night, due to the Spin-O-Matic washer controversy reported-on in this paper over one month ago, tensions between the two clubs on Saturday was lukewarm and soggy. The real rivalry shaping up appears to be that between the Parliamentary Museum (curated by Seafus Hobb) and Customs and Excise (headed by Officer Raoul Orlean), who will fight for the first-place trophy in the Final next week. Hobb and Orlean spent the entire Higgins-Customs match staring across the field at one another defiantly. As to his team's strategy moving forward, Orlean, when interviewed, would not elaborate, though he suggested something else besides "football" could possibly be involved. "What else" is not for this reporter to speculate, though Orlean's team will undoubtedly need more than soft strikers to take on the hardline Parliamentarians. This year's Tournament will come to a close on Sunday. Festivities, including music and vending, will run officially from noon to moonrise. At 1 o'clock, Cora Silverfish and the Minister of Sports and Culture will unveil the official Pineapple Cup cup, after which the Island Police and Higgins Hardware, Home and Garden will play for third place. At 3 o'clock, the Final match will take place, between Customs and Excise and the Parliamentary Museum. Immediately following the match, the cup will be presented to the winners, signaling the official start of the Pineapple Lime, sponsored by Cougar Zanne of the Buddha's Belly Bar and Lounge. In addition to rum-and-pineapple punch, piña coladas, and pineapple wine, a signature tournament beverage will be sold, as is tradition. On tap this year: rum straight up (spiced, blended with ice, and served inside a pineapple).

46

Normally an article like Bruce's recap of the Pineapple Cup Semi-Final would drive Raoul to distraction. He would be so angered by Bruce's presumption, his splashing of Raoul's personal business across the front page, that he would be completely unable to think. He would go to the offices of the *Crier*, bang on the door, reprimand Bruce, and that would make Raoul feel a teensy bit better. Then he would carry on as best he could with whatever case Bruce had butted into, pretending not to notice the glances, or hear the whispers, of the other islanders as he passed them in town.

Normally. And perhaps it went that way this time, too. If you asked Raoul, though, he wouldn't know what to tell you. His recollection of what happened during the week leading up to the Cup's final Sunday would be as fuzzy as mold on fruit.

He wouldn't remember, not exactly, his dust-up with Bruce.

He wouldn't recollect that all the week through, at home, Lila could talk only of getting her cast removed on the Saturday to come. Or that, away from home, no one else could talk of anything but the rivalry Bruce had manufactured between Raoul and Seafus

Hobb. (To be sure, rivalry there was; it just had little to do with the football.)

He wouldn't remember Bang at the Belly, going on about the Final, about how rough Seafus's men were, how unfairly they played, how tough they would be for Customs to beat; or Nat and Cougar, pooh-poohing Bang, patting Raoul on the back, and predicting a wildcard win.

He *might* recall that the flies in his head those days buzzed only about busting Seafus; that, to the backdrop of football-feud 'old talk,' Raoul pressed ahead with his plans to sting. Seafus's stares at the semi-final had worried Raoul that time was running out, that Seafus had a Plan *b* up his sleeve. If Raoul didn't move quickly, Seafus might move his men and their printing machines out of the Market.

Cora, of course, kept Raoul grounded, made him see sense.

"You can't sting just yet," she explained. "The place is too hot." By 'hot,' she meant 'revved up,' meant that too many eyes were on Raoul and on Seafus, too many tongues spoke their names. Neither could conduct his business as secretively as he ought.

"Now, too, with a football Final put in the mix?" she questioned rhetorically. "Pfft! Seafus's players will think about playing and nothing else." She insisted not one bill more would be printed until the Pineapple Cup had wrapped up, and so Raoul should wait one more week before taking the Police to storm Morne Vert.

In her shop, as Raoul and Cora reasoned, she showed him the copper trophy, complete with its green jasper leaves that, even indoors, seemed to mirror the sun.

Raoul wouldn't remember that either.

If Raoul's recollection of the week before Pineapple Sunday was moldy, it's because the memory of Sunday itself, fresh as a new pineapple flower, so filled his mind. Like a movie on a continuous bloody loop, it replayed, pressing against his brain until his jaw throbbed. Until his stomach smarted. Until it squeezed out even the flies.

The day began well enough. Raoul had breakfast with Lila while he read the *Morning Crier.* Bruce had printed a story a day about the drama the Cup Final would promise, and this day was no different.

'Thank heavens this silly tournament is almost done,' Raoul thought to himself. He had work to do—real work—and all anyone cared about was football and pineapples. A counterfeiter was making a mockery of Oh's rainbow bills and had to be stopped!

Lila was dressed and headed to work soon, with Nat. It was an every-other-Sunday when the library was scheduled to open, though Raoul begged her not to bother, seeing how the whole town would be liming at the playing field all day long. Even stores usually open on Sunday were closed. Lila knew he was right, of course—and she would join him at the playing field later, for the big Customs match—but first she went to work, to spend some time alone. She might even have a little cry behind her big desk in the library's heart. Lila was sad, and frustrated, because she had gone to the hospital the day before, to have her cast cut off, and had been sent home still plastered. Procedure demanded that an X-ray verify she was ready to walk on her own, but the hospital's only X-ray machine was broken. They told her to come back on Monday.

Raoul kissed her goodbye at the cottage door, waved a good morning to Nat in the van, and then returned to his porridge and paper. After he finished his food and cleaned up the dishes, he took a ride in his truck. He intended to spend the day at the playing field, as Seafus surely would; but since nothing would get under way there till noon, Raoul spent the morning driving the length of the counterfeit crime ring. Raoul had done so a number of times that week already, but never had he found a sign to confirm whether Seafus had moved operations from the Old Market or not. Maybe today would be different.

It turned out not to be, as far as Raoul knew, though for Seafus it was a stand-out day indeed. He had spotted Raoul, you see, peeking through the telescope on Halfway Hill, and had decided enough was enough. Seafus had warned Raoul to look out, had made clear with his stares that no challenge would be unmet, and yet Raoul persisted. He left Seafus no choice. It was time to enact the partridge plan and scare off Raoul Orlean for good. Time to teach him what happened when one impeded the desires of Seafus Hobb.

Raoul reached town about noon and went to the jewelry shop to pick up Cora. He had agreed to drive her and the cup to the tournament. When he entered and asked if she was ready to go, she told him, "Not just yet." She put her fingers to her lips to keep him quiet, then, ensuring that the door to the shop was closed and locked, she pulled him by the arm to the glass display case. On top of it, on one of her velvet mats, she set down a small clay pot that she pulled from her apron. The pot was about the size of Raoul's thumb, and was stoppered with a piece of cork.

"What's this?" he asked her.

"Just something I thought you might need today. You have the serpentine I gave you?"

He did, and pulled it out to show her.

"Good. Have this, too."

"What is it?" he asked her again.

With a small pair of pliers she removed the cork from the pot and gently spilled out its contents. There were three small, cut stones. One, Raoul recognized. It was the time-predicting, not-too-pretty rock crystal. The second was dull green, not pea-green like the serpentine, but green like the water of the mangrove swamp, with streaks of rusty red-brown. The third was black and looked like gravel. None shone or sparkled, but Raoul was drawn to them. He couldn't stop himself from reaching out to touch them with his fingertips, something he had never dared to do before to any of Cora's gems. '*Were* they gems?' he wondered? They looked like common rocks.

Cora answered, reading his thoughts the way she often did.

"All three are gemstones. Rock crystal is to get you where you need to be, in time. The green is unakite. Unakite brings objectives nearer; the bearer of it can't fail in his aims. The black, that's meteorite. Meteorite is a volatile rock, violent and unpredictable. But with much force. It will give you an edge over your enemy."

Raoul wasn't sure what to make of what Cora was saying. Was this a good luck charm for the football?

"This is much more serious than football, Raoul," she said ominously. "Carry it with you to the Pineapple Cup." She picked up the stones one by one and dropped them back inside the tiny pot. "Rock crystal. Unakite. Meteorite." RUM.

"Timing...success...strength," she whispered, pushing hard on the cork to secure the pot's top. "Every man has his rum, we say on Oh. Well, this is yours." Cora seemed pleased with herself: "Now, we can go."

She removed her apron and Raoul saw that underneath, pinned to her collar was the larimar moon brooch. Whenever he'd seen it previously, it seemed to taunt him, to confuse, to flaunt its wisdom. Today, as he paused to take it in, he felt only the strength that Cora once told him it had. It made him feel safe to see her wearing it, though he couldn't say why (and wouldn't have dared if he could).

Raoul pocketed the pot of RUM and shook his head. He thought to himself, for the second time that morning, 'Thank heavens this silly tournament is almost done.'

———

The Pineapple Cup Final started much like the Semi-Final a week before. There was music pumping out of giant speakers, and tables and carts covered with any incarnation of pineapple that one could imagine: tarts and tartlets, jams and juices, pastry and pilau, even soaps and lotions to clean and soothe the islanders' skin. Cougar had commandeered the entire end of the field behind one of the goals, and there he had set up a line of open-ended tents from which to dispense drinks and snacks. In one he stocked rum, blenders, barrels of ice, and crates of whole pineapples. In another he had coolers of fish that he grilled on gas grills (and dressed with pineapple chutney). Yet a third boasted pineapple spears on sticks, and pineapple cake by the piece. A fourth housed a fully-stocked bar. Behind the tents Cougar put propane tanks and portable generators, and in the front of them, makeshift tills to fill with money. Every member of his staff— bartender, waitress, dishwasher, cook—had been called in to lend a (paid) hand.

When Raoul and Cora reached the pasture, it was nearly one o'clock. Beyond the touchlines, eating and drinking were in full swing; inside them, the Minister of Sports and Culture paced the field, examining its condition and consulting with referees, bestowing an air of authority to the matches about to take place. When he saw Cora with the covered-up cup in her hands, he motioned for her to come closer, and signaled for the music to cut. An assistant appeared with a portable mic and amplifier, and from center-field, the Minister inaugurated the event. It was a remarkable display of island promptness, one that prompted Raoul to double-check his watch and to pat the pot of rock crystal in his pocket.

The Minister welcomed the islanders to the Final of yet another Annual Harvest Football Tournament—wasn't their little island blessed?—then he passed the mic to his assistant and held the trophy for Cora as she slowly uncovered it. The crowd ooh'd and aah'd admiringly, and broke into applause and whistles. Cora smiled at them. With a wave, she took back the cup and retired to the sidelines. The Minister, mic in hand again, asked everyone to stay safe, not to drink too much, not to fight too much if they did, and, finally, wished them all a pleasant day. "Let the action begin!" he ordered.

So it did, with the Island Police, bitter over the loss of the title, crushing Higgins Hardware four-nil to grab third-place. Raoul hardly watched the game. Instead, he watched for Seafus, who at the start of the Police-Higgins match still hadn't showed. Odd that. Raoul might have panicked, had he not seen Seafus's men suited-up and in attendance, harassing the Customs team and drinking beer though they still had to play. If Seafus's team was accounted for, there wasn't much trouble Seafus could be getting up to alone.

During the break between the third-place match and the final, Cora rushed to speak with Raoul. *She* had taken note of *two* conspicuous absences, not just one, and she was worried. Seafus wasn't there, which was curious, yes, what with his men about to challenge Raoul's. But curiouser yet, where was Lila?

"Lila?" Raoul repeated. "She's over there somewhere." He motioned in the general vicinity of Cougar's tents, where he expected she was sitting with Bang and Nat.

"Where, Raoul? Show me," Cora insisted. Before Raoul could respond, the referee called him for the start of the match—my, wasn't everything running on schedule today!—and Cora was cornered by Bruce, who wanted her photo for the paper, with the pineapple trophy (which she was still holding onto).

Once the play had begun, and Bruce had got his picture, Raoul and Cora, respectively, looked around for Lila. Raoul saw Cougar catering to customers at one of the tents. He saw Bang drinking rum out of one of Cougar's signature pineapples. Not far away, Nat sat on the edge of a bleacher, juggling juice and a slice of cake all by himself. Huh. Where *was* Lila? If Cora was worried, though, Raoul wasn't, not quite yet. Lila could be anywhere, getting a bite to eat, or some water. She was slow on her crutches and would surely turn up soontime. Whatever could happen to her on Oh, after all?

Seafus Hobb had arrived in the meantime, and Raoul was more focused on him. When they weren't playing at staring each other down—was it Raoul's imagination, or were Seafus's looks even more vicious today?—they were shouting at their men, telling them what to do and how to win. Cora watched them watching each other, and though Seafus tried to act cool and collected, she could see there was something wrong. Something more than the fact that Raoul's Customs boys had managed to keep up 1-1 at the end of the first half.

During the half-time pause, Cora went to speak with Raoul once more.

"Raoul, *please* go and see where your wife is," she pleaded. "I'll wait for you right here." She put the cup on the bench of the Customs team and sat herself down beside it. Raoul, who still hadn't cottoned on to her worry, shrugged, and obeyed to appease her.

He walked around the field, passing Cougar's tents, where he took some ice-cold juice, and continued toward where Nat was sitting. En route, he found Bang, tickled that the score was tied and only too happy to eat his words about the Customs team taking a beating.

"How come Lila didn't come to watch?" he asked Raoul.

"Of course she came!" Raoul was getting touchy now, everyone discussing his wife's whereabouts as if he couldn't keep track of her.

Raoul quickened his pace, with Bang on his heels. "Nat! You got Lila from work?" Raoul shouted, as soon as he thought Nat was in earshot.

"Nah," Nat shouted back. "She wasn't there."

Suddenly, Raoul's mouth felt like cotton. Cora's worry was nothing compared to the cataract of fear that Raoul felt slamming onto his head and pouring over him. He ran the last few feet to where Nat was sitting.

"Where's Lila?" he asked, his breath catching and his heart beating fast.

"How should I know?" Nat answered. "*You* picked her up... didn't you?"

"*You* were supposed to get her!" Raoul rebutted.

"I tried! The library was all locked up. She wasn't there. I thought you must have got her."

"Calm down, calm down," Bang interjected, sensing the fears that were crashing around and splashing out of control. "She must be home. Nat, let's go get her. Raoul, you worry about your game. The second half is about to start."

Bang didn't give either of them a chance to object. He pushed Raoul onto the field and grabbed Nat's cake. Though he faked his signature lightheartedness, his heart was heavy and he sensed there was no time to waste.

Raoul got back to the bench, and to Cora, just in time for the kick-off. He told her what he knew and looked at her with a hint of tears in his eyes.

"Hold this," she said angrily, handing him the trophy. "I'm going to talk to Seafus."

"Seafus? Why?" Raoul demanded.

But Cora was already gone, on her way around the field. Raoul watched her, confused and incredulous. Why was she bothering with Seafus now, when Lila was maybe missing? Then the cataract crashed down around Raoul again and he did his Stan Kalpi maths. Cora believed Seafus had something to do with Lila's disappearance!

Raoul didn't know what it felt like to lose one's mind. Over the years, the islanders had called him mad on many occasions, but he always ignored them, quite certain of his sanity. In those minutes, though, when he watched Cora walk the length of the field, and saw her yell at Seafus, her finger wagging in Seafus's face—those minutes when he feared he might never see his Lila again—Raoul came as close to a break with reality as he ever wished to come. He felt dazed, didn't know where he was. He saw the players move in slow motion and the colors of their jerseys trail behind them, like smoke behind a plane. He didn't know Cora anymore, didn't know why he watched her so intently, or why *he* was holding this giant metal fruit that belonged to her and not him. How long would he have to guard it? What if she never came back to relieve him of this copper burden? What if he never learned why her finger was wagging? He felt faint, and sweaty. He was going to die, he was sure of it, and if he did, who would guard the giant pineapple?

Then Cora's finger stopped wagging. She turned her head and looked at Raoul. Her eyes drilled into his from across the field, where she and Seafus stood. She was inside Raoul's head now, and telling him to snap out of it! He tried to pull away his gaze but couldn't, and gradually, as he peered into Cora, or she into him, he felt his senses return. He knew he was in the playing field, at the Final, holding the trophy for Cora, while she tried to find out from Seafus what had happened to Lila. It all took but minutes, though in Raoul's mind it seemed like hours.

Raoul watched Cora as she made her way back. He felt his breathing return to normal and decided he was being silly. Losing his mind on a sunny day on Oh! His fears, and Cora's, were unfounded. Raoul was at the Pineapple Cup and Customs might just win. Men were drinking spicy rum and children were eating pineapple cake. Lila was fine, probably tired from work and resting at home. Why had Raoul let Cora get him riled up? With her worry and her RUM stones and her devil talk? Why, Stan Kalpi would be ashamed!

Cora was a few steps away from him, and Raoul was about to give her a piece of his newly sound mind, when her face stopped him dead. Although Seafus had admitted to nothing, and had laughed at Cora's threats, he did, unwitting, hand Cora a clue, a terrible clue, that Raoul read on Cora's face.

"What?" he asked, in a half-whisper.

Cora was out of breath. She had sat down, huffing, and told Raoul she had seen a bruise on Seafus's forearm.

"A bruise? What does that mean?"

"It caught my eye because it was a strange shape. It was perfectly symmetric, a shape that I recognized."

"What shape?" Raoul was frantic.

"Raoul!" Bang and Nat ran up just then. "Lila's not at home," Bang announced. "What should we do?"

Raoul looked at Cora. He was sure his heart would stop at any second. "Raoul," she said, "the bruise was the shape of the pendant I made for Lila's birthday. He must have grabbed her, or wrapped his arm around her, or...or carried her off. I don't know. The pendant left a mark."

Bang and Nat looked at Cora, at Raoul, at each other. "What's going on?" Nat asked.

Raoul didn't answer. Still holding onto the pineapple trophy, he let out a horrible yell from deep in his belly, and charged onto the field. He pushed aside the players in his path, who were at first too shocked to react, and ran straight for Seafus. He raised the cup high in the air and tried to bring it down on Seafus's head, but Seafus, who still had an athlete's reflexes, saw the blow coming and blocked it. The cup fell, and rolled away. When the Museum team players saw what Raoul had done, they ran to Seafus's aid and would have beaten Raoul to death, had the Customs team not come to *his* aid. Soon the playing field was a scrum of men, punching, kicking, cursing. Bang and Nat joined the brawl and even Cora ran closer to see what she might do. Spectators, too, who by that time had drunk too much rum, ran onto the field and began striking blows for no reason.

The referee blew his whistle to call for help. The Island Police team was in the stands, and though the officers were tipsy, and out of uniform, they ran onto the field. They threw themselves into the ruckus, but this only added to it, instead of busting it up. The Minister of Sports and Culture found the Chief of Police and asked him to radio for reinforcements. In the meantime, the Minister ordered the fireworks to be readied. They should have served as a celebratory display, to close out the tournament later that night, but maybe the noise would shut the brawlers up and distract them. Long enough, at least, for a few extra officers to get the crowd in line.

The tussle continued for a good twenty minutes, a free-for-all of swift kicks and fisticuffs. From the sidelines the islanders not engaged in the skirmish looked on in disbelief, shaking their heads and clicking their tongues. When the fireworks were set up, the Minister gave the green light. His hunch, it turned out, was correct, and the thundering starbursts that lit up the dusk distracted the fighters, who turned their eyes to the sky. Police reinforcements had arrived by that time, and found it easy to escort the men off the field while they were looking heavenward. Because so many of them were involved, the police didn't arrest the layers of men they pulled from the scuffle; they simply told them to cool their heads—with water, not spicy rum.

As the fight broke up, at its heart Raoul and Seafus kept at it, each too single-minded to stop for pyrotechnics. Both men were bruised, though Raoul could have been a lot worse off, had Bang and Nat not tried for the duration to keep themselves between him and Seafus. Eventually the Police came to pull even Bang and Nat away, though they stopped at separating Seafus and Raoul out of respect for Raoul, who shouted for them not to.

Raoul was glad to fight his own fight. Seafus was stronger but Raoul had years of punches he had kept in his pockets and now he knew why. He was storing them all up for this day. He lashed out at Seafus with a violence he didn't know he had inside himself, an instinctive and unpredictable reckoning for every ill that had ever been done him. Every insult, every joke, every heartbreak and betrayal. Although Seafus still managed to land a blow for Raoul's every two, Raoul felt no pain. He heard only the thunder of the fireworks overhead. When his forces were almost spent, he drew his arm backward and threw what he hoped was a final punch on Seafus's jaw. Alas, Seafus, who hadn't the benefit of Raoul's pent-up energy, did have an edge in strength and resistance. He stumbled backward only a step and then popped Raoul on the mouth, knocking out a tooth. Raoul fell, stunned, and Seafus kicked him in the stomach.

Nat and Bang watched helpless, held back by the Police. Nat turned away. He couldn't bear to see Raoul beat up. His eyes happened to meet Cora's, and then to fall on her larimar brooch. He stared into it and it told him what to do. *He couldn't bear to see Raoul beat up.* In a flash he broke away from the policeman's hold and grabbed the Pineapple Cup cup, which Cora had retrieved and set next to her on the ground. With all the force Nat had left in him, for he had spent his energies fighting, too, he clobbered Seafus on the head with the trophy.

The pineapple knocked him out cold.

47

Raoul sped to the Museum in his pick-up, Cora at his side, her hand on her heart and the larimar moon.

"Ahh!" he swore, getting tied up in traffic and pounding on the steering wheel. If only he had requisitioned that siren for the top of his truck!

The Police would be coming, too, but first they had to sort through the mess at the playing field. Assess the damages to the field and to innocent bystanders. Tend to Seafus, then get him locked up until Raoul could explain. In the meantime, it was enough that Lila was missing, and that Cora had pointed out the pendant-shaped bruise on Seafus's arm.

Raoul swore out loud as he drove. Seafus could have hidden Lila anywhere, alive or dead. Raoul would comb every inch of Seafus's crime ring until he found her!

"Raoul, slow down!" Cora yelled. "We will find her. Believe me. She's alive."

"How can you be so sure?" he cried.

"Seafus isn't a murderer. He's—" Cora stopped herself.

"He's what?"

"Listen to me. There's something I forgot to tell you about Lila's pendant. Do you remember the top stone?"

"What?" Raoul snapped. "The top stone? No! Tell me about Seafus."

"Listen to me first," she said, in a quiet tone meant to calm him. "Lapis lazuli was the top stone."

Wait. Raoul did remember reading about lapis lazuli in the book by Mr. Kopt.

"What about it?" he asked.

"Lapis lazuli is ruled by Venus."

"Eh?" (Cora was calming him in spite of himself.)

"Of those stones I gave you for Lila—which will ward off the spirits of darkness, the Seafuses of the world—of those stones, the most important one is governed by the planet of love. If you love her truly, that stone will keep her safe."

They continued in silence, Raoul somewhat more calmly panicked, a state of being he would not have imagined possible. He thought of Seafus and called to mind what Cougar and Bang had said about him at the Belly, about Seafus forcing himself on a girl. Not...?

"Seafus...," he said gently to Cora. "The girl. That was you." It was part question, part statement.

"Me," Cora replied quietly.

"There was a baby?"

"Too early. Abigail—"

"Abigail Davies," he finished. "Island midwife and manager of secrets." (As Raoul knew all too well.)

"Abby never told a soul, nor did I. But this is Oh," Cora began to explain, her story ripe. "The bushes have ears, the walls have eyes. Whether island whispers or island magic, or maybe his own conscience made it happen, Seafus tumbled from fortune. He blamed me, I told you that. I stayed away from him, you can imagine! Then a few years later, at the library, your wife found a scholarship that the Museum sponsored. I needed the money to study metal-working on Esterina, and so I went to see him and demanded he award me the grant. He only did it to get rid of me, I knew that. I banked on it, in fact. But when I came back and opened my shop, he exacted his payment." Cora had looked straight ahead as she spoke, never once at Raoul.

"His payment?"

"My concessions, deliveries through Dwight, my packages pawed at before I ever receive them."

"But you could have gone to the Police."

"Could I?" She turned to him. "Seafus's seedy port crowd has tentacles everywhere. Who would have believed me? I was a girl then, my shop just opened. My name was on everything that arrived. And I knew there was more to it. I didn't know about counterfeiting. I thought he was smuggling. Drugs, or worse. Whatever it was, or still is, with my name so attached to it, how could I call it to the attention of the authorities?"

"That's blackmail."

"Hardly the worst thing he's done to me," she snorted. "I let him conduct his business, and he let me conduct mine, never stole any of my stones, or supplies."

"Because he wanted your shop up and running," Raoul concluded, "to use you as a front."

Cora nodded. She hadn't told her secret to anyone ever, except Abigail. It felt good to confide in a friend, in Raoul.

"We're here!" he hollered. Raoul stopped the truck at the door of the Museum, and he and Cora jumped out. Raoul would drive right into the building if he had to. Thanks to Seafus's ego, which wouldn't let him update the Museum's original entrance, that wouldn't be necessary, for two young men Raoul found loitering nearby were eager to help him knock down the old door.

"Lila!" Raoul ran in and shouted her name at the top of his lungs. He didn't hear anything at first, but a light was on in the back of the Museum. He ran toward it, and as he crossed through the set of showrooms, he tripped over Lila's crutches.

"She was here!" he called out to Cora. "Her crutches. They're here!"

"She is *still* here," Cora said. With determination Cora walked to the small auditorium at the back of the Museum. "There." She pointed to the stage. "Under it. There's a room." They began knocking and pounding on the front of the stage and sure enough, a faint scrape on the wood answered them.

"Lila!" Raoul called to her. "Don't worry, we'll get you out!" To Cora he said, "How do we get inside?"

This, Cora didn't know, so Raoul improvised. He ran through the showrooms looking for something he could use to chop his way into the stage. He found an Inuit axe, with a sharp stone head. He began as far as he could from where they had heard the scrape, so as not to injure Lila. While he chopped at the wood, the Police arrived, with clubs and flashlights, and soon, enough of the stage was destroyed that they could see Lila inside it. Her mouth was bound, and her torso was tied to a chair so tightly with rope that she struggled to breathe. Two of the officers crawled in and carried her out on the chair. Quickly they all set to freeing her of the ropes and the gag.

She couldn't stand up without her crutches, and she was sobbing, but she seemed to be okay.

"Did he hurt you?" Raoul asked, bending to her and hugging her as tightly as he could.

She shook her head 'no.' When Raoul finally let go of her, she put out her arms to hug Cora. "Thank you," she sobbed into Cora's shoulder, as they embraced. "Thank you." Lila now knew the powers of the blue birthday pendant; she was certain it had spared her a fate worse than the one she'd endured.

Raoul tried to carry Lila to the truck, but she insisted she could get there on her own, if someone reunited her with her crutches. She, Raoul, and Cora left the Museum to the Police, who stayed behind to take photos and search the premises. Raoul settled Lila in the pick-up and closed the door. Through the window, she took a good look at him, standing next to Cora (who would take a bus home, not to worry!), and she asked him, "What happened to *you*?"

Raoul looked down at himself, covered in grass and dirt. He remembered the fight then, and as he did, he suddenly remembered his pain as well. His gut hurt, and his tongue sought the ache in his mouth where a tooth he used to have no longer resided.

Raoul shrugged. He told her he was just tired. He punched and kicked, he said, until Seafus Hobb felled him, and then Nat saved his life with a cup.

48

The Customs and Excise team was named the winner of the Annual Harvest Football Tournament, despite the fact that the score was 1-1 when play was interrupted. The Minister of Sports and Culture decided no re-match was called for, since he couldn't award the Pineapple Cup cup to a kidnapper-counterfeiter in any case. If Customs earned bragging rights, however, they didn't get to keep the trophy, which went to the Police as evidence.

Bruce explained everything in the *Morning Crier*, with his usual eye for detail. He devoted an entire week of newspapers to what he called the OH Reports (for Orlean-Hobb). He reported on the events at the odd Final match (**Too Much Rum for the Pineapple Cup**); on the discovery and the dismantling of Seafus's counterfeit print shop (**Old Market a Front for New Money**); Seafus's subsequent arrest for Customs fraud, blackmail, counterfeiting, and kidnapping (**Cricketer, Curator, Criminal**); and the temporary closing of the Museum (**Parliamentary Salmagundi Temporarily Shut**). Just when he thought he had exhausted all his Orlean-Hobb headlines, he learned that Lila's continued incapacity on the day she was kidnapped was due to hospital negligence; thus he wrapped up the OH Reports with a scathing exposé (**Faulty X-Ray Paves Way for Kidnapper**).

Somehow Cora managed to keep herself (and her past) out of the news. With the ghost of the curator gone from her business, she attacked her designs with new zeal. A big shipment of citrine had arrived—for which she received due notification from Customs, and which she picked up in person—that was the perfect shade of pineapple gold. She had a special citrine vitrine planned for the display case nearest the balcony sunlight.

Though Raoul would no longer see Cora every day, he would think of her whenever he perused the volume by Mr. Kopt on his Tuesdays off at the library. Cora remained the only islander ever to succeed at putting a chink in Raoul's philosophical armor, as witnessed by the fact that he never left home without the pot of RUM in his pocket. (The serpentine he kept in his pick-up.) From time to time, he made a Customs exception and delivered Cora's goods to her himself, for old times' sake. (Dwight had been stripped of his Customs stripes and jailed, the only of Seafus's accomplices hard evidence incriminated.)

It took a full week before the X-ray machine was repaired at the hospital. (Bruce credited his investigation with getting the matter resolved.) Lila at last got her cast off and would soon walk on her own again. When she did, her first visit would be to the jewelry shop for more magic gewgaws. Until then, her blue birthday pendant would never come off. This gave Bang much pleasure any time they were all together at the Belly, for it opened the door to 'magic talk' that Raoul would have otherwise forbidden. It also led, inevitably, to good-natured ribbing about Raoul's wild and unexpected attack on Seafus at the Pineapple Final. When

Bang would credit Nat with saving Raoul, neither Raoul or Nat had much to say. Raoul had once saved Nat, too, years before, and Nat was a friend returning a favor.

As island life returned to normal—Bang ribbing, Lila walking, Raoul going to his office every day—Raoul's head returned to normal, too. It cleared out clues no longer needed and this made room for flies. Mainly gnats they were, really, and Raoul planned not to pursue them. But they were there. One of them wanted to know how Cora Silverfish knew of Seafus Hobb's secret room beneath the stage, or his library up above. Raoul refused to entertain the notion that she and Seafus were ever in cahoots. He preferred to believe, as a mango fly hinted, that Cora must have spied on Seafus over the years, must have tried to find a way out from under his thumb. It wasn't until Raoul came along that she succeeded. Another gnat, though, wondered about *that*. Perhaps it was dumb island luck that took Raoul to Cora's the first time, to buy Lila's birthday gift, but what about the time after? Had Lila never fallen, would Raoul have gone back? Would Cora's Customs business have caught his eye at the docks? Had Cora manufactured a fractured foot to rid herself of Seafus? The mango fly objected: now, now, was it not Lila's pendant that protected her from Seafus's attack?

One gnat niggled more than the others. It worried about Oh's rainbow bills. Because Seafus had printed so many false banknotes, and laundered them through Oh's only bank for so long, could anyone on Oh really know anymore which bills were good and which weren't? Not that an islander blessed to hold legal tender would question its validity, mind you, but Raoul's gnat wondered whether somebody should.

Raoul sighed, caught between gnats and a mango fly.

Every rope has two ends. Isn't that what the islanders said? It wasn't easy, always, deciding which end to hold close, and today Raoul Orlean wasn't up to trying.

He had more immediate tasks to tackle.

First, to the office, to requisition one of those sirens he saw at the cinema. Then, to the body shop, to see Munroy Daniels. The mirror of Raoul's pick-up needed painting, and he had to work out if it was green, or blue, in truth.

Acknowledgments

Like a pineapple built from flowers falling in line, this novel owes its shape to all the islands and islanders who have crisscrossed my path. To the Coras and the Curators alike I am indebted, for the former inspired and encouraged, while the latter taught. Every one of them was—and is—a precious, inevitable diamond. Brightest among them, "tantie" Dee LeRoy, and my mother, MaryAnn Siciarz.

No pineapple is without its crown. For mine, Andrew C Bly (cover design) and Patti Schermerhorn (cover art), I thank you.

About the Author

Stephanie Siciarz was born in the US and is a graduate of Georgetown University and The Johns Hopkins University. She is a writer and translator and has worked for high-ranking officials in international, government, and academic institutions in the US and Europe. She currently resides in Ohio, where she is on the faculty at Kent State University. Her debut novel, *Left at the Mango Tree*, was named to *Kirkus Reviews'* Best Books of 2013.

Made in the USA
Las Vegas, NV
14 May 2021